1: Of Taste and Flavor

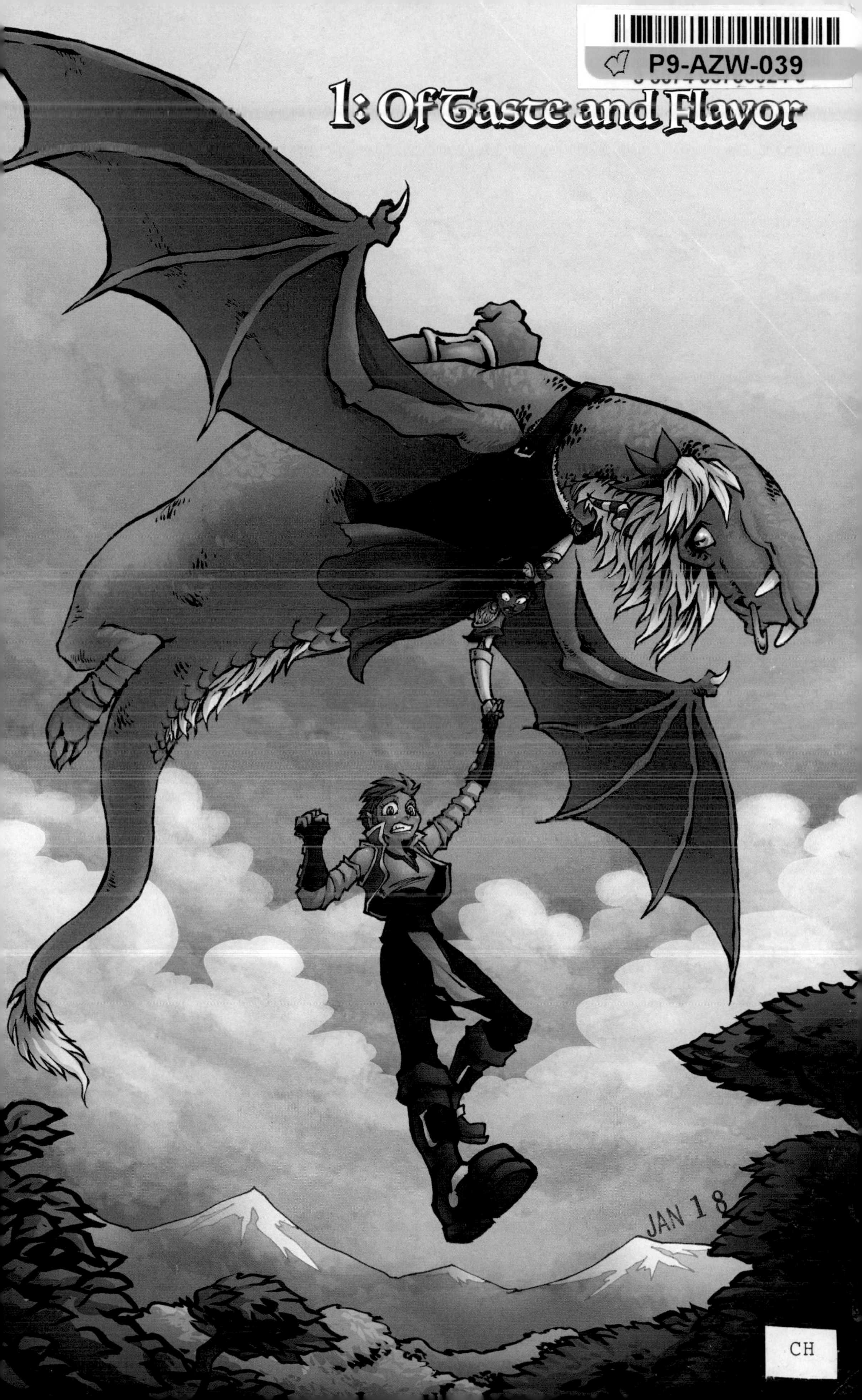

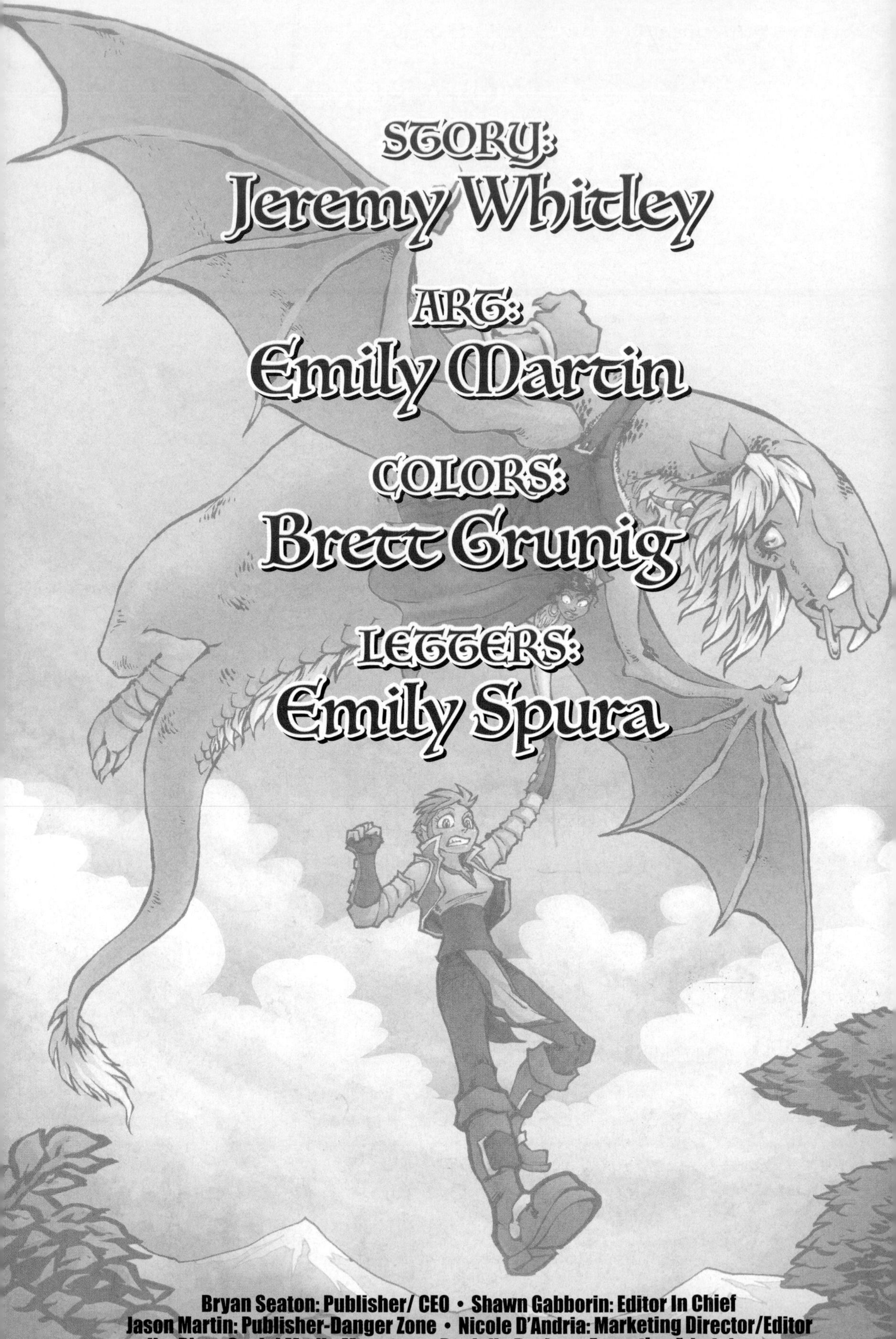

STORY:
Jeremy Whitley

ART:
Emily Martin

COLORS:
Brett Grunig

LETTERS:
Emily Spura

Bryan Seaton: Publisher/ CEO • Shawn Gabborin: Editor In Chief
Jason Martin: Publisher-Danger Zone • Nicole D'Andria: Marketing Director/Editor
Jim Dietz: Social Media Manager • Danielle Davison: Executive Administrator
Chad Cicconi: Still Waiting For His Princess • Shawn Pryor: President of Creator Relations

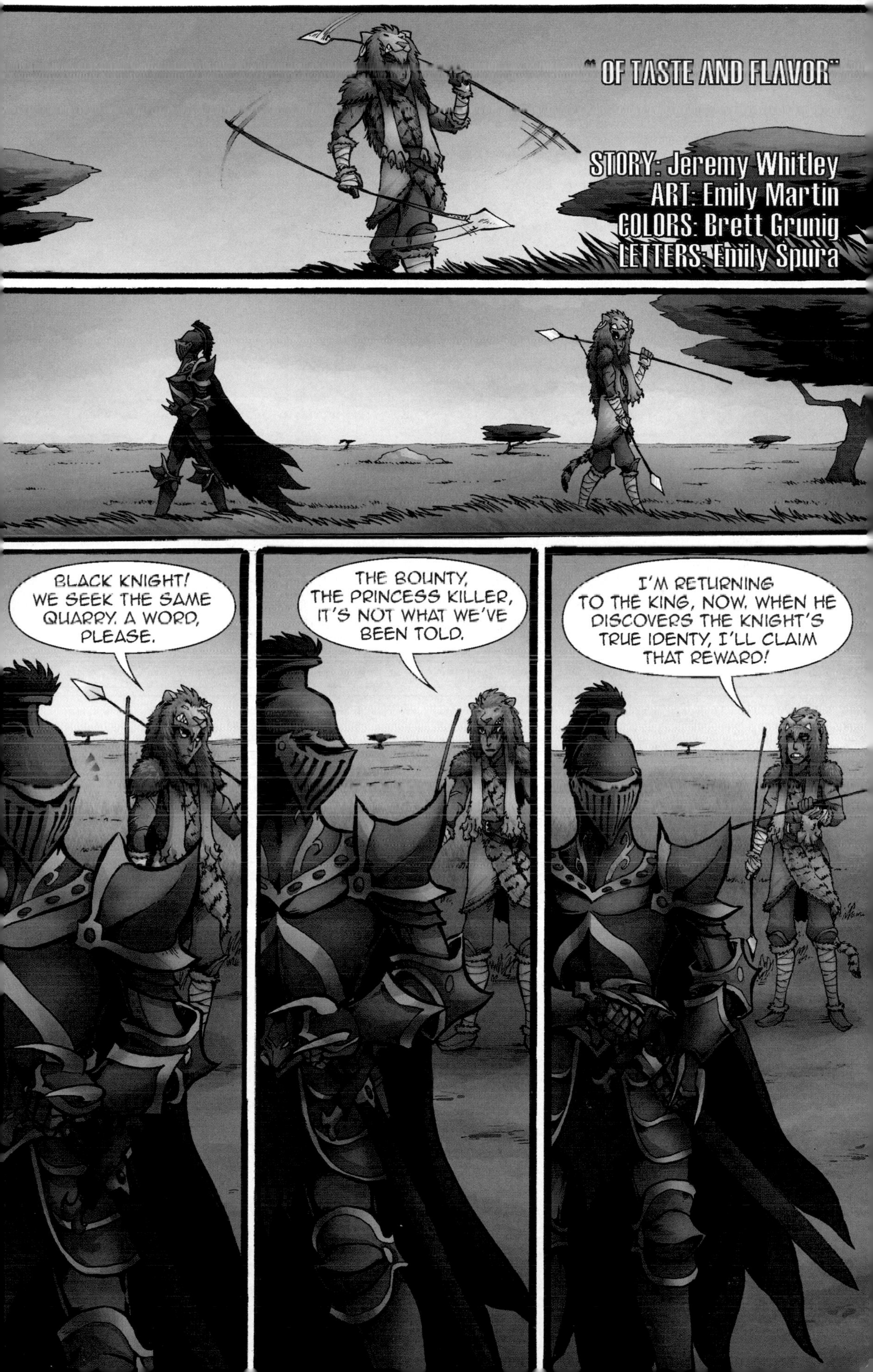
"OF TASTE AND FLAVOR"
STORY: Jeremy Whitley
ART: Emily Martin
COLORS: Brett Grunig
LETTERS: Emily Spura
BLACK KNIGHT! WE SEEK THE SAME QUARRY. A WORD, PLEASE.
THE BOUNTY, THE PRINCESS KILLER, IT'S NOT WHAT WE'VE BEEN TOLD.
I'M RETURNING TO THE KING, NOW. WHEN HE DISCOVERS THE KNIGHT'S TRUE IDENTY, I'LL CLAIM THAT REWARD!

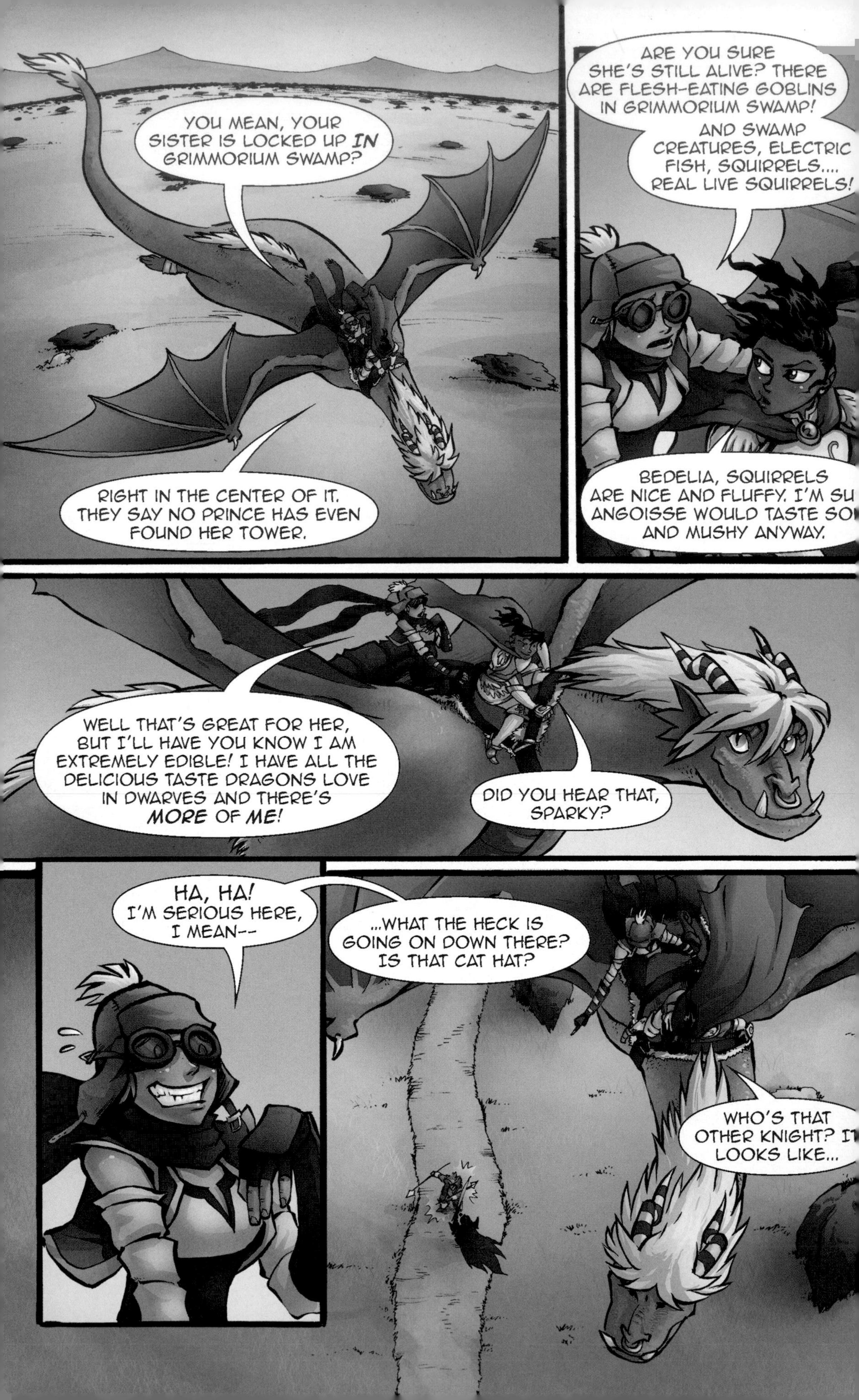

YOU MEAN, YOUR SISTER IS LOCKED UP *IN* GRIMMORIUM SWAMP?
RIGHT IN THE CENTER OF IT. THEY SAY NO PRINCE HAS EVEN FOUND HER TOWER.
ARE YOU SURE SHE'S STILL ALIVE? THERE ARE FLESH-EATING GOBLINS IN GRIMMORIUM SWAMP!
AND SWAMP CREATURES, ELECTRIC FISH, SQUIRRELS.... REAL LIVE SQUIRRELS!
BEDELIA, SQUIRRELS ARE NICE AND FLUFFY. I'M SU
ANGOISSE WOULD TASTE SO
AND MUSHY ANYWAY.
WELL THAT'S GREAT FOR HER, BUT I'LL HAVE YOU KNOW I AM EXTREMELY EDIBLE! I HAVE ALL THE DELICIOUS TASTE DRAGONS LOVE IN DWARVES AND THERE'S *MORE* OF *ME*!
DID YOU HEAR THAT, SPARKY?
HA, HA! I'M SERIOUS HERE, I MEAN--
...WHAT THE HECK IS GOING ON DOWN THERE? IS THAT CAT HAT?
WHO'S THAT OTHER KNIGHT? I
LOOKS LIKE...

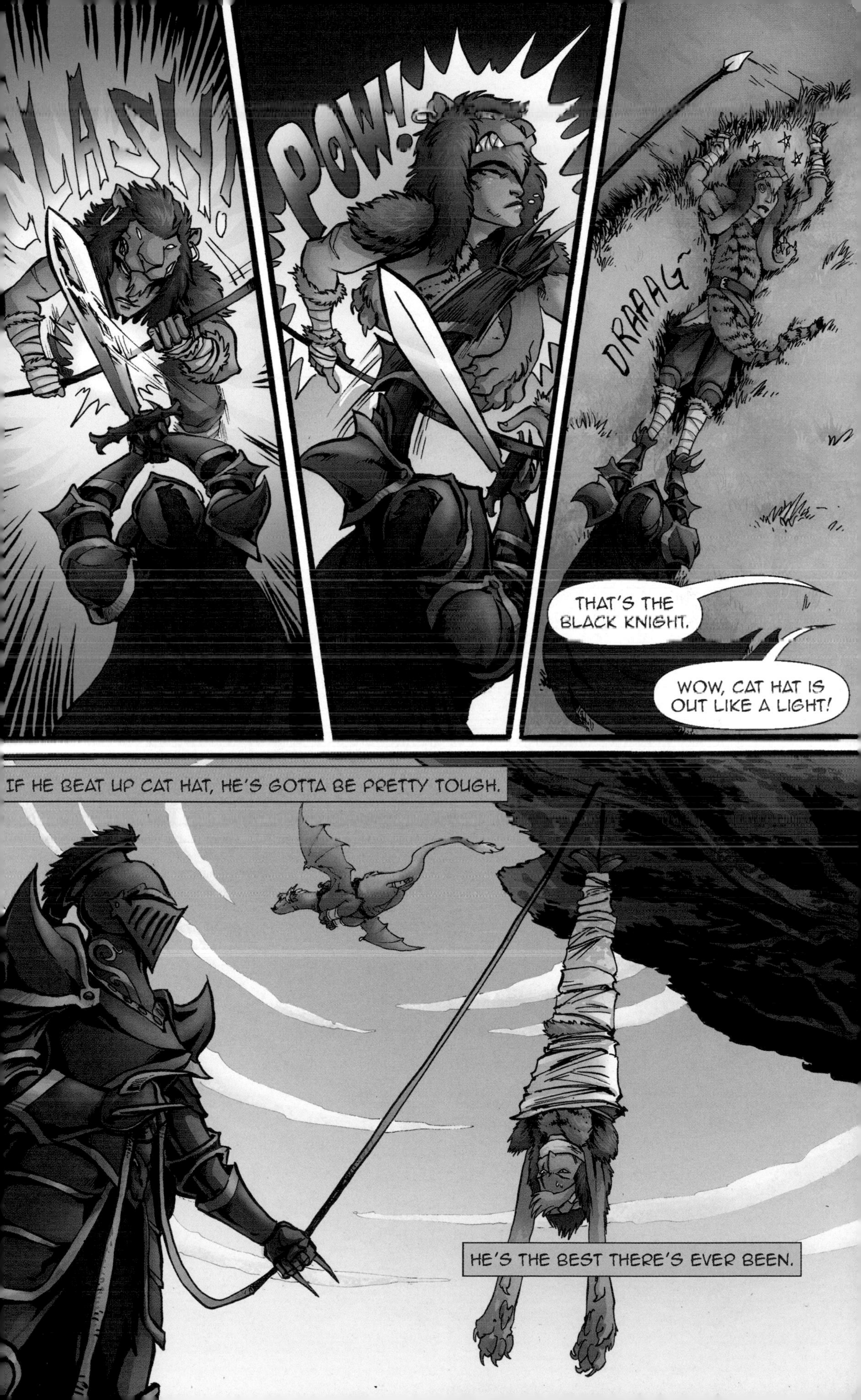
CLASH!
POW!
DRAAAG
THAT'S THE BLACK KNIGHT.
WOW, CAT HAT IS OUT LIKE A LIGHT!
IF HE BEAT UP CAT HAT, HE'S GOTTA BE PRETTY TOUGH.
HE'S THE BEST THERE'S EVER BEEN.

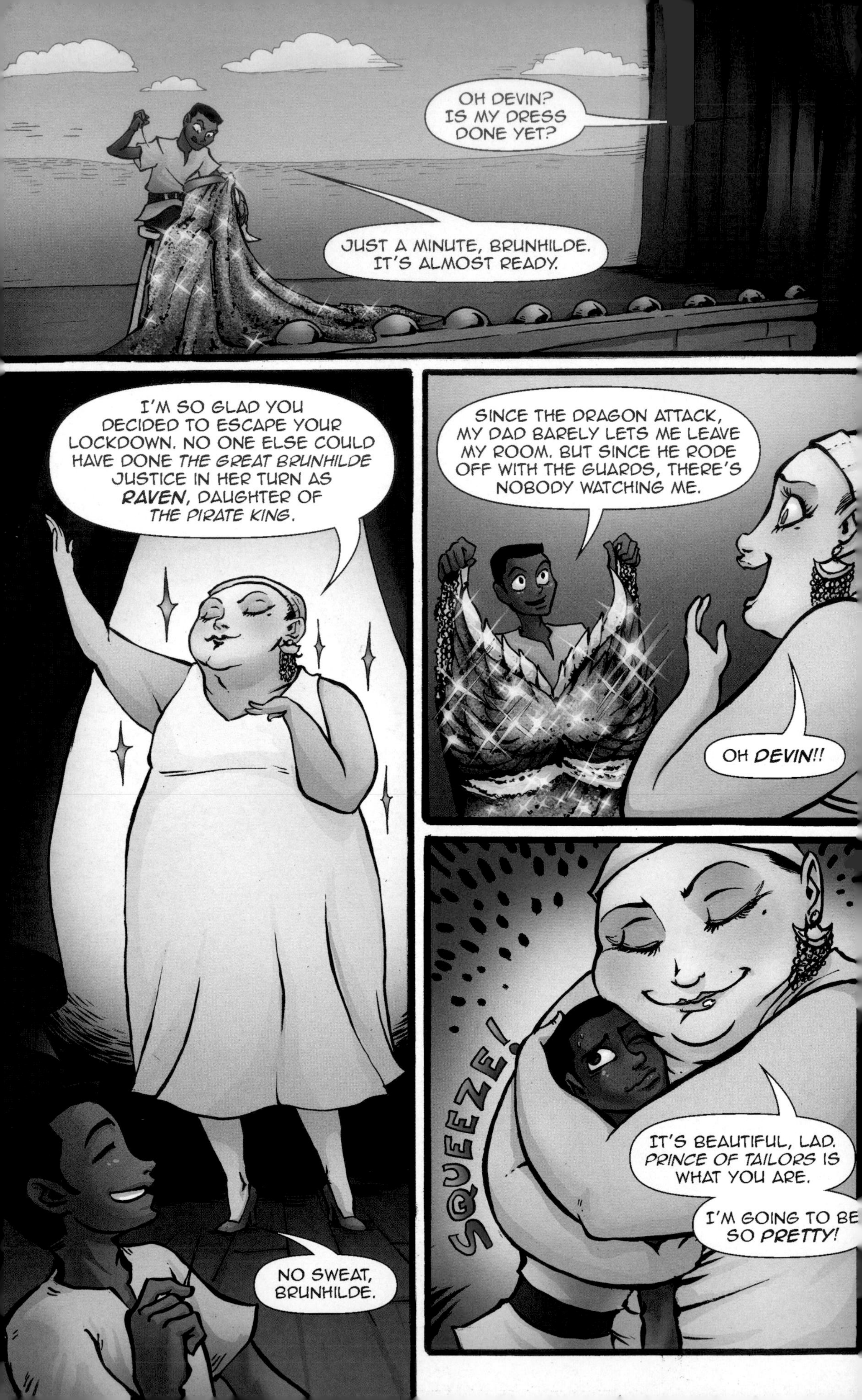
OH DEVIN? IS MY DRESS DONE YET?
JUST A MINUTE, BRUNHILDE. IT'S ALMOST READY.
I'M SO GLAD YOU DECIDED TO ESCAPE YOUR LOCKDOWN. NO ONE ELSE COULD HAVE DONE *THE GREAT BRUNHILDE* JUSTICE IN HER TURN AS ***RAVEN***, DAUGHTER OF *THE PIRATE KING*.
NO SWEAT, BRUNHILDE.
SINCE THE DRAGON ATTACK, MY DAD BARELY LETS ME LEAVE MY ROOM. BUT SINCE HE RODE OFF WITH THE GUARDS, THERE'S NOBODY WATCHING ME.
OH ***DEVIN!!***
SQUEEZE!
IT'S BEAUTIFUL, LAD. *PRINCE OF TAILORS* IS WHAT YOU ARE.
I'M GOING TO BE SO ***PRETTY!***

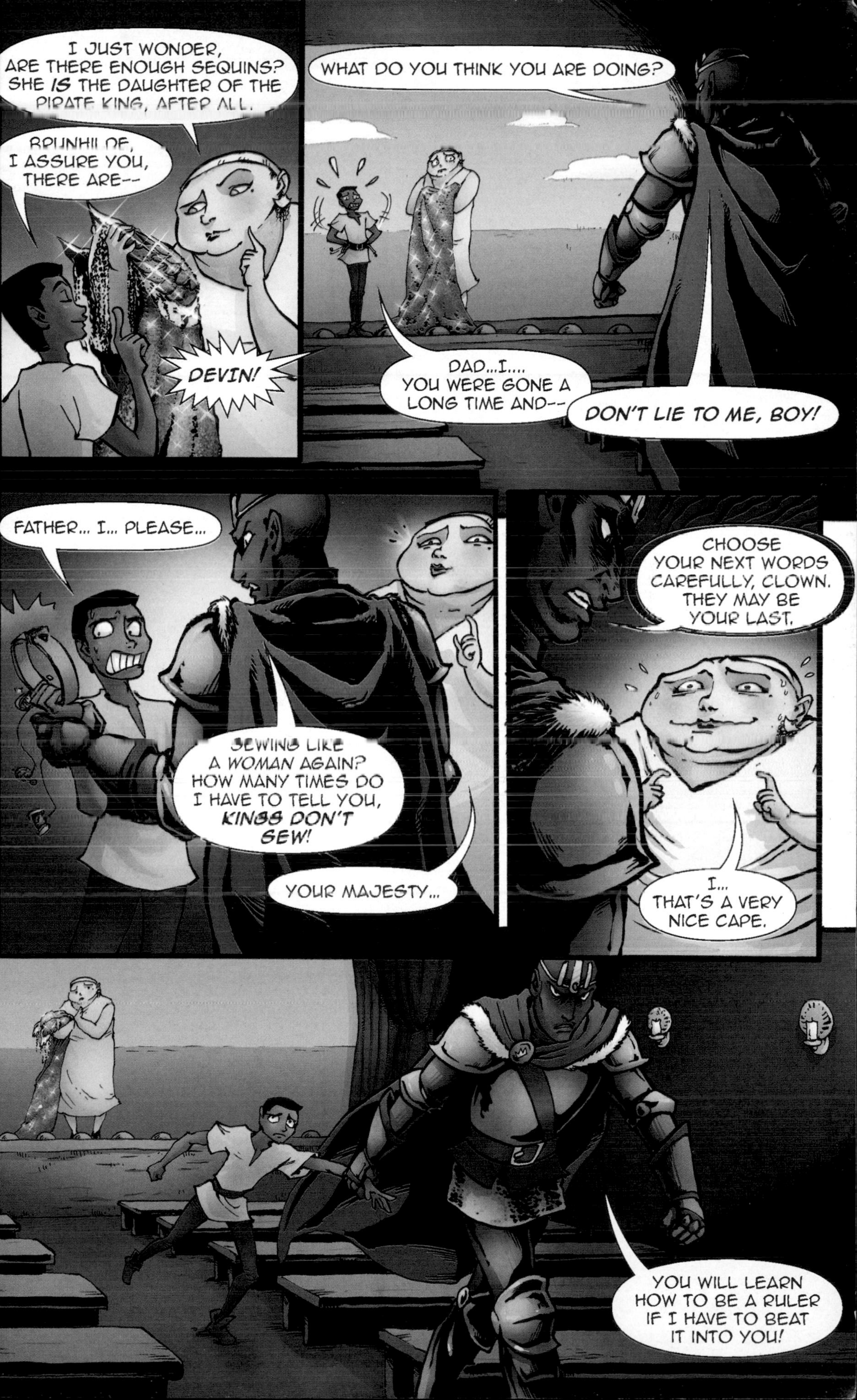
I JUST WONDER, ARE THERE ENOUGH SEQUINS? SHE *IS* THE DAUGHTER OF THE PIRATE KING, AFTER ALL.
BRUNHILDE, I ASSURE YOU, THERE ARE--
DEVIN!
WHAT DO YOU THINK YOU ARE DOING?
DAD...I.... YOU WERE GONE A LONG TIME AND--
DON'T LIE TO ME, BOY!
FATHER... I... PLEASE...
SEWING LIKE A *WOMAN* AGAIN? HOW MANY TIMES DO I HAVE TO TELL YOU, *KINGS DON'T SEW!*
YOUR MAJESTY...
CHOOSE YOUR NEXT WORDS CAREFULLY, CLOWN. THEY MAY BE YOUR LAST.
I... THAT'S A VERY NICE CAPE.
YOU WILL LEARN HOW TO BE A RULER IF I HAVE TO BEAT IT INTO YOU!

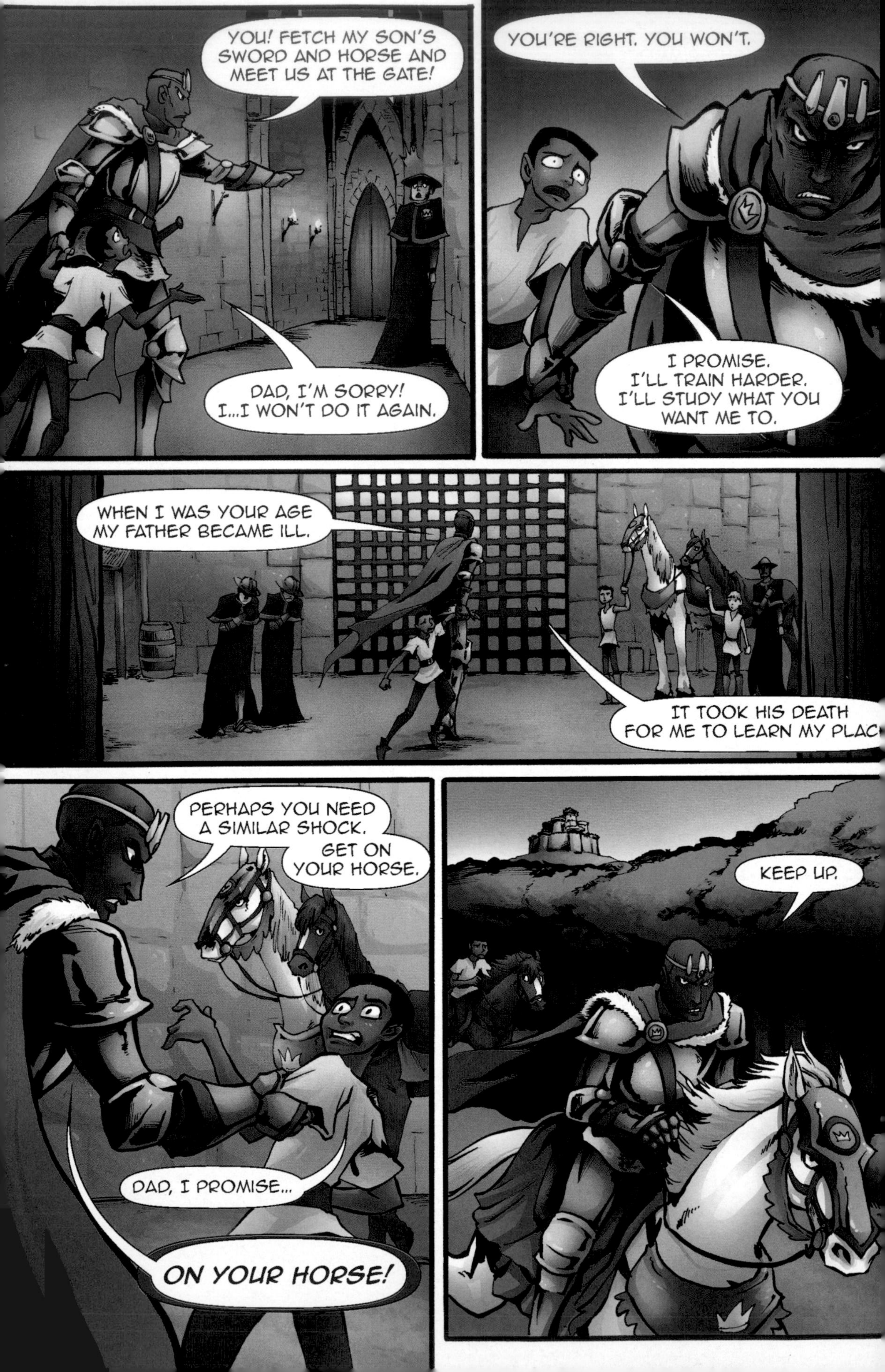
YOU! FETCH MY SON'S SWORD AND HORSE AND MEET US AT THE GATE!
DAD, I'M SORRY! I...I WON'T DO IT AGAIN.
YOU'RE RIGHT. YOU WON'T.
I PROMISE. I'LL TRAIN HARDER. I'LL STUDY WHAT YOU WANT ME TO.
WHEN I WAS YOUR AGE MY FATHER BECAME ILL.
IT TOOK HIS DEATH FOR ME TO LEARN MY PLAC
PERHAPS YOU NEED A SIMILAR SHOCK.
GET ON YOUR HORSE.
DAD, I PROMISE...
ON YOUR HORSE!
KEEP UP.

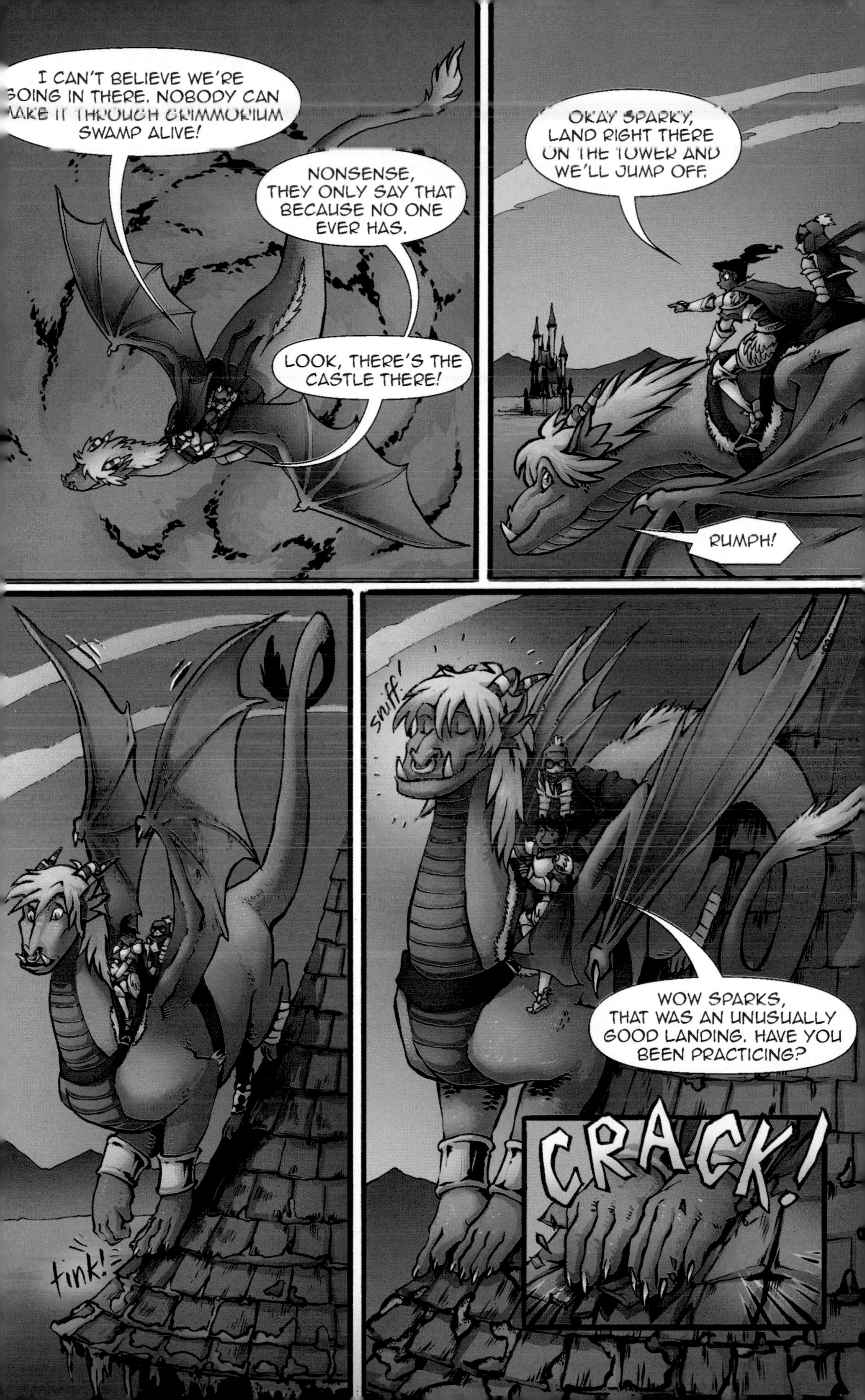
I CAN'T BELIEVE WE'RE GOING IN THERE. NOBODY CAN MAKE IT THROUGH GRIMMORIUM SWAMP ALIVE!
NONSENSE, THEY ONLY SAY THAT BECAUSE NO ONE EVER HAS.
LOOK, THERE'S THE CASTLE THERE!
OKAY SPARKY, LAND RIGHT THERE ON THE TOWER AND WE'LL JUMP OFF.
RUMPH!
tink!
sniff!
WOW SPARKS, THAT WAS AN UNUSUALLY GOOD LANDING. HAVE YOU BEEN PRACTICING?
CRACK!

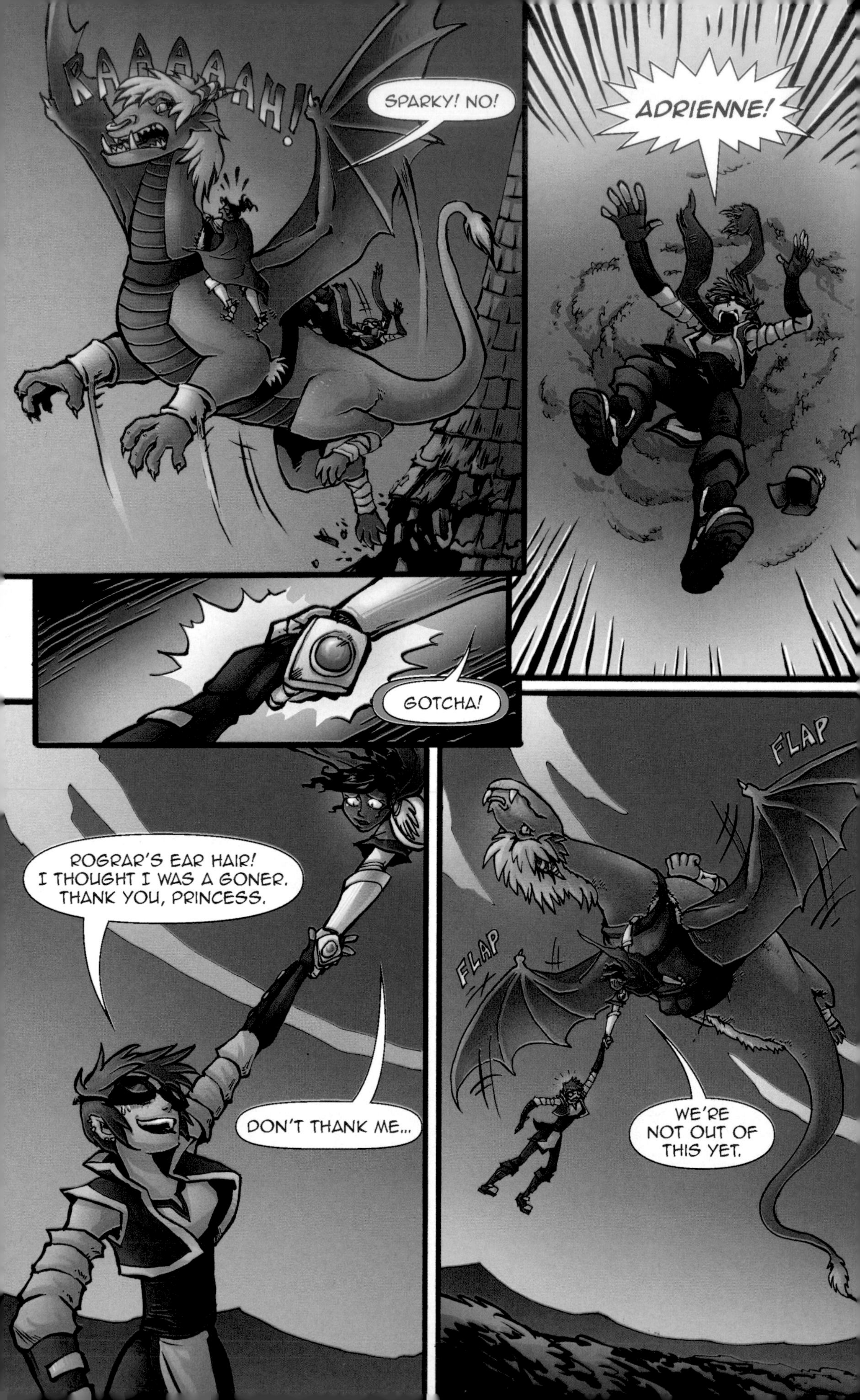
RAAAAAAH!
SPARKY! NO!
ADRIENNE!
GOTCHA!
ROGRAR'S EAR HAIR! I THOUGHT I WAS A GONER. THANK YOU, PRINCESS.
DON'T THANK ME...
FLAP
FLAP
WE'RE NOT OUT OF THIS YET.

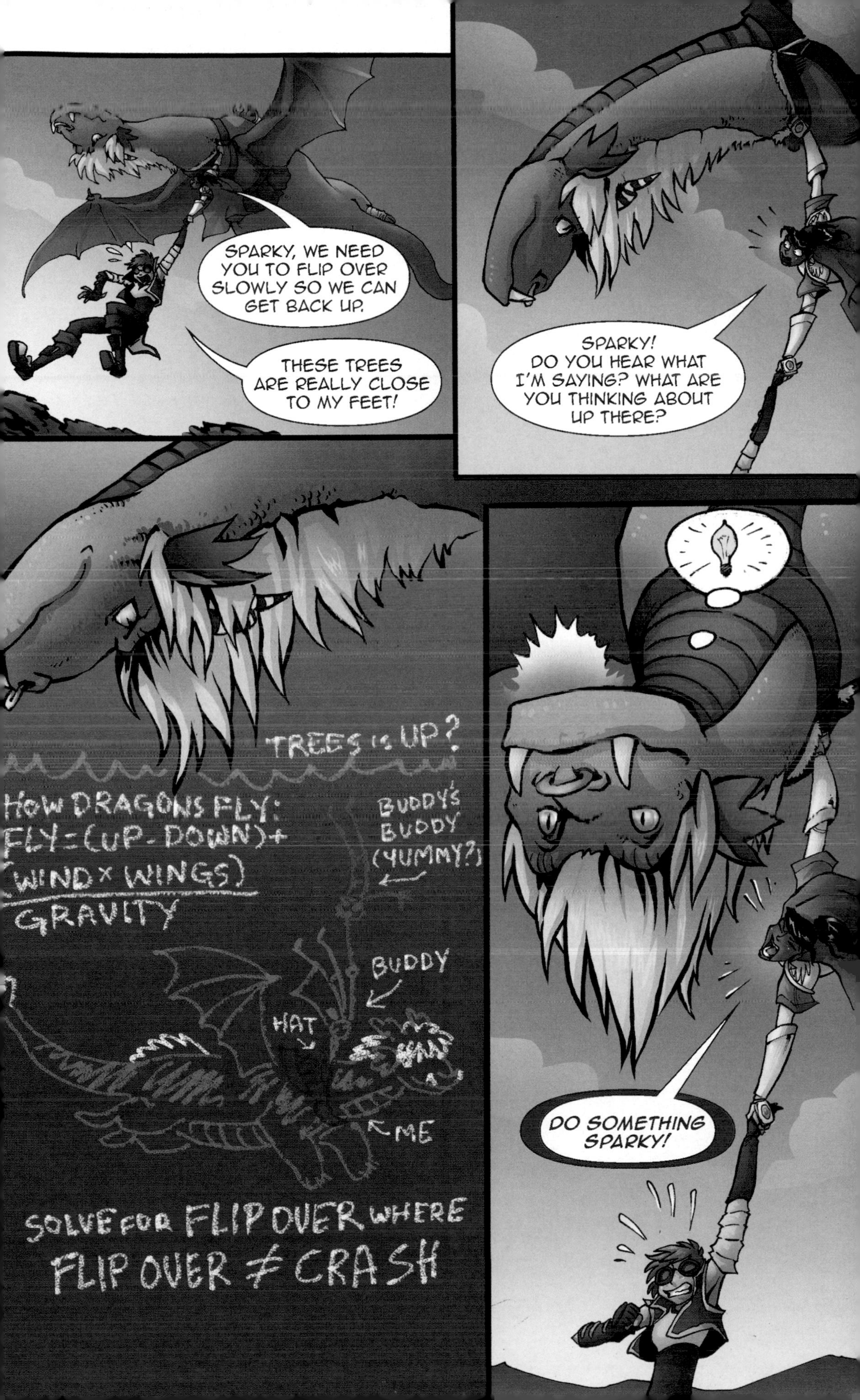
SPARKY, WE NEED YOU TO FLIP OVER SLOWLY SO WE CAN GET BACK UP.
THESE TREES ARE REALLY CLOSE TO MY FEET!
SPARKY! DO YOU HEAR WHAT I'M SAYING? WHAT ARE YOU THINKING ABOUT UP THERE?
TREES is UP?
HOW DRAGONS FLY:
FLY=(UP-DOWN)+(WIND × WINGS)
GRAVITY
BUDDY'S BUDDY (YUMMY?)
BUDDY
HAT
ME
SOLVE FOR FLIP OVER WHERE
FLIP OVER ≠ CRASH
DO SOMETHING SPARKY!

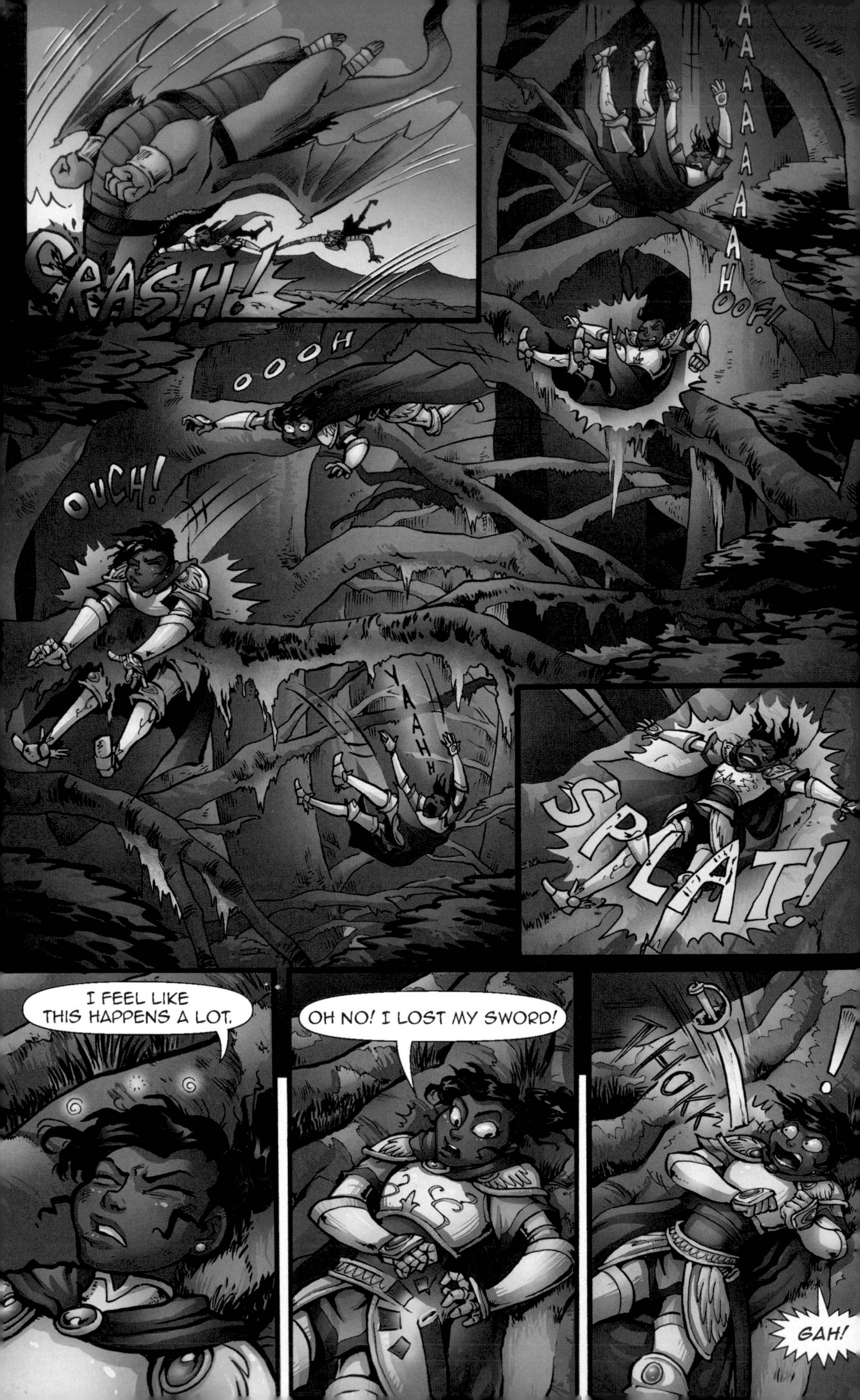
CRASH!
AAAAAAAAAH
OOF!
OOOOH
OUCH!
YAAHH
SPLAT!
I FEEL LIKE THIS HAPPENS A LOT.
OH NO! I LOST MY SWORD!
THOKK
!
GAH!

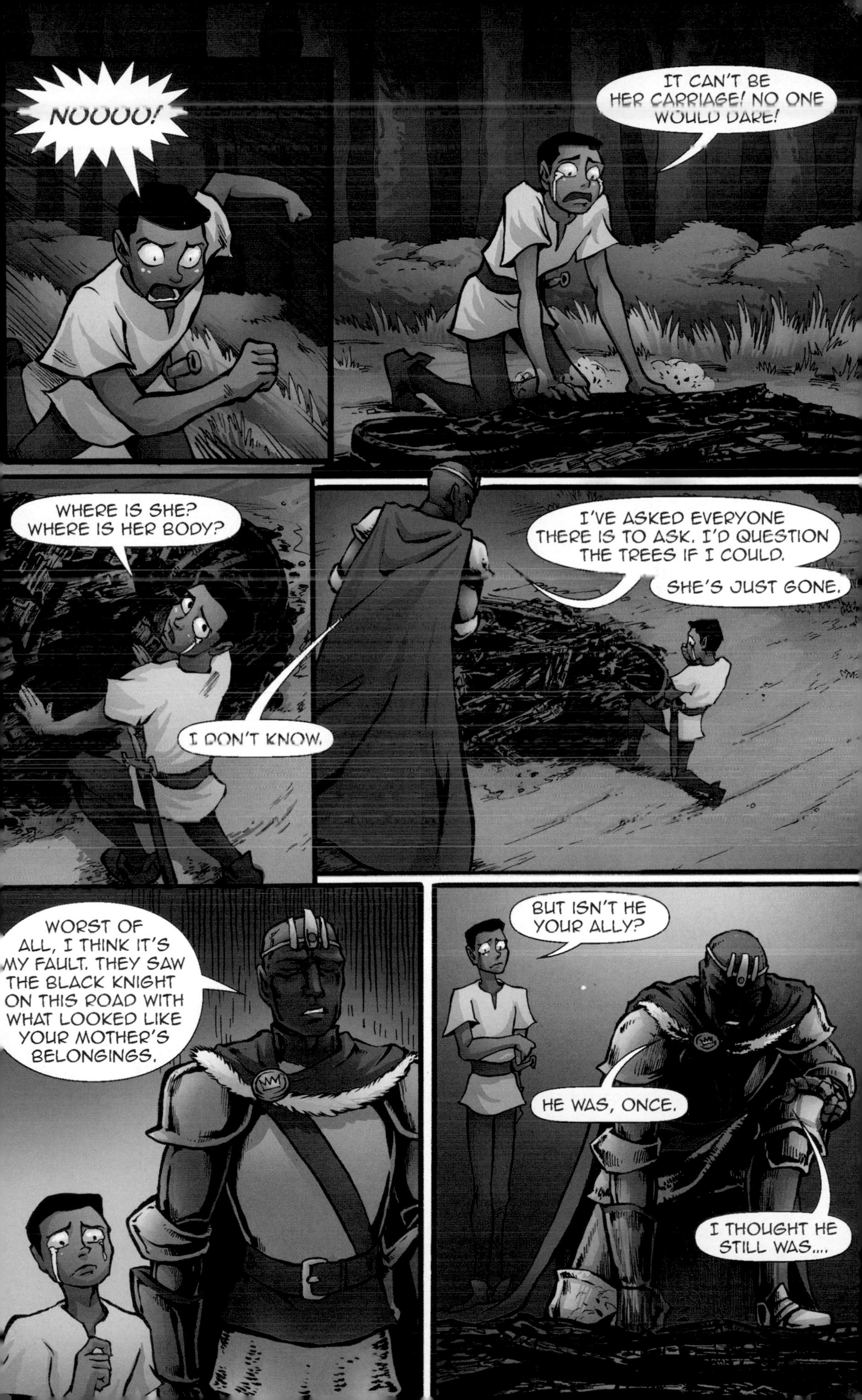
NOOOO!
IT CAN'T BE HER CARRIAGE! NO ONE WOULD DARE!
WHERE IS SHE? WHERE IS HER BODY?
I DON'T KNOW.
I'VE ASKED EVERYONE THERE IS TO ASK. I'D QUESTION THE TREES IF I COULD.
SHE'S JUST GONE.
WORST OF ALL, I THINK IT'S MY FAULT. THEY SAW THE BLACK KNIGHT ON THIS ROAD WITH WHAT LOOKED LIKE YOUR MOTHER'S BELONGINGS.
BUT ISN'T HE YOUR ALLY?
HE WAS, ONCE.
I THOUGHT HE STILL WAS....

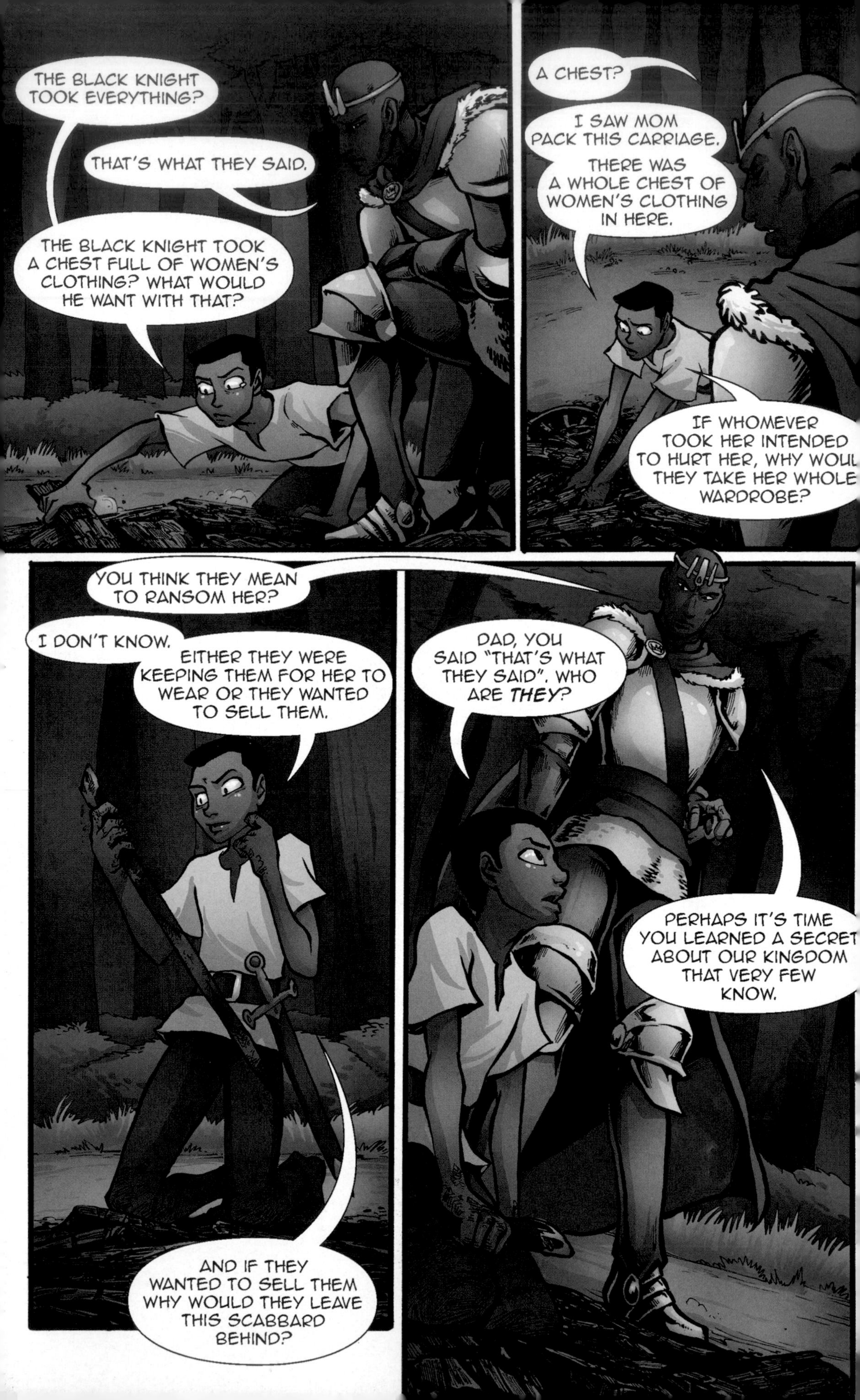
THE BLACK KNIGHT TOOK EVERYTHING?
THAT'S WHAT THEY SAID.
THE BLACK KNIGHT TOOK A CHEST FULL OF WOMEN'S CLOTHING? WHAT WOULD HE WANT WITH THAT?
A CHEST?
I SAW MOM PACK THIS CARRIAGE.
THERE WAS A WHOLE CHEST OF WOMEN'S CLOTHING IN HERE.
IF WHOMEVER TOOK HER INTENDED TO HURT HER, WHY WOUL THEY TAKE HER WHOLE WARDROBE?
YOU THINK THEY MEAN TO RANSOM HER?
I DON'T KNOW.
EITHER THEY WERE KEEPING THEM FOR HER TO WEAR OR THEY WANTED TO SELL THEM.
AND IF THEY WANTED TO SELL THEM WHY WOULD THEY LEAVE THIS SCABBARD BEHIND?
DAD, YOU SAID "THAT'S WHAT THEY SAID". WHO ARE *THEY*?
PERHAPS IT'S TIME YOU LEARNED A SECRET ABOUT OUR KINGDOM THAT VERY FEW KNOW.

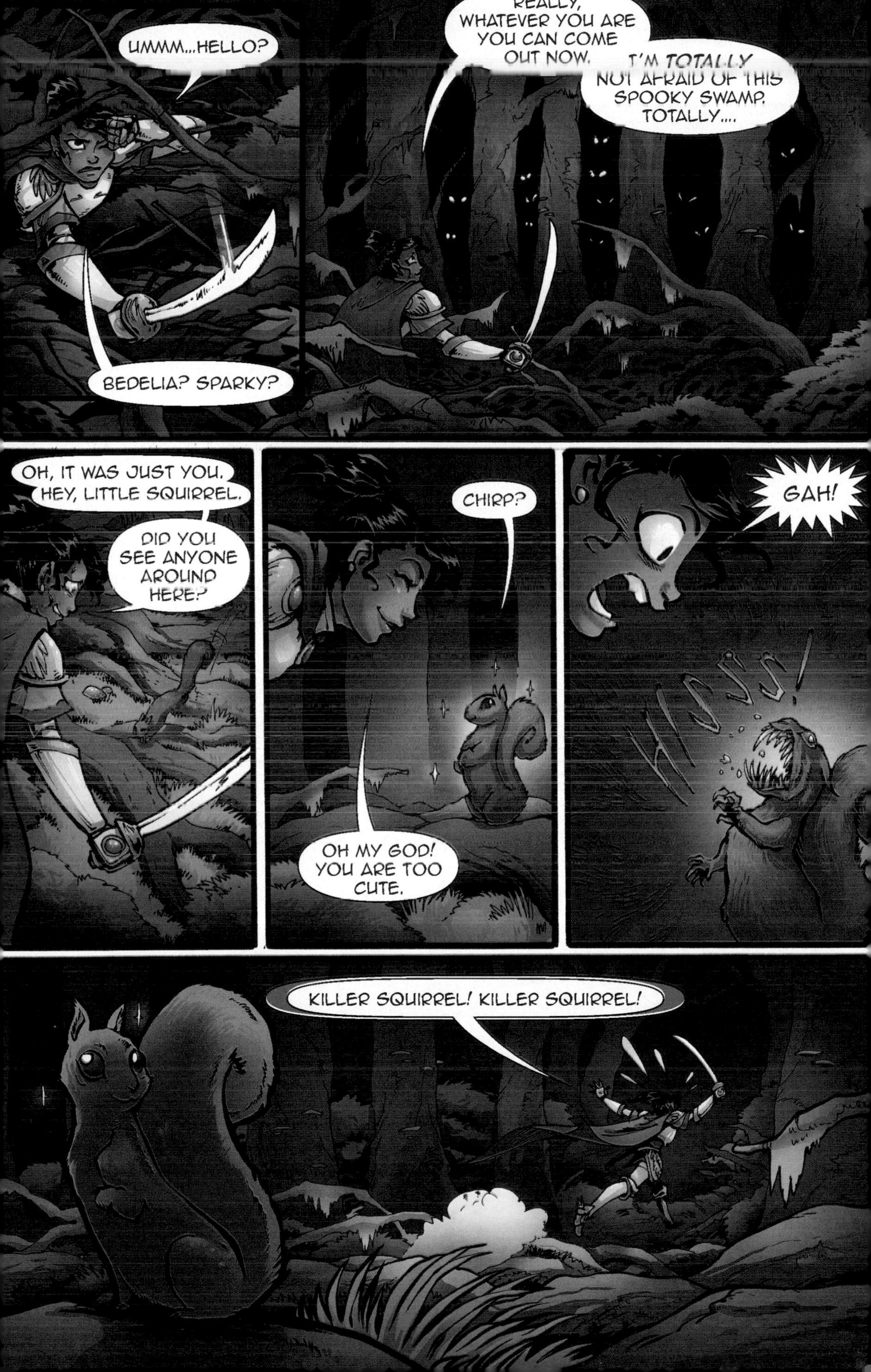
UMMM...HELLO?
BEDELIA? SPARKY?
REALLY, WHATEVER YOU ARE YOU CAN COME OUT NOW.
I'M TOTALLY NOT AFRAID OF THIS SPOOKY SWAMP. TOTALLY....
OH, IT WAS JUST YOU. HEY, LITTLE SQUIRREL.
DID YOU SEE ANYONE AROUND HERE?
CHIRP?
OH MY GOD! YOU ARE TOO CUTE.
GAH!
HISSS!
KILLER SQUIRREL! KILLER SQUIRREL!

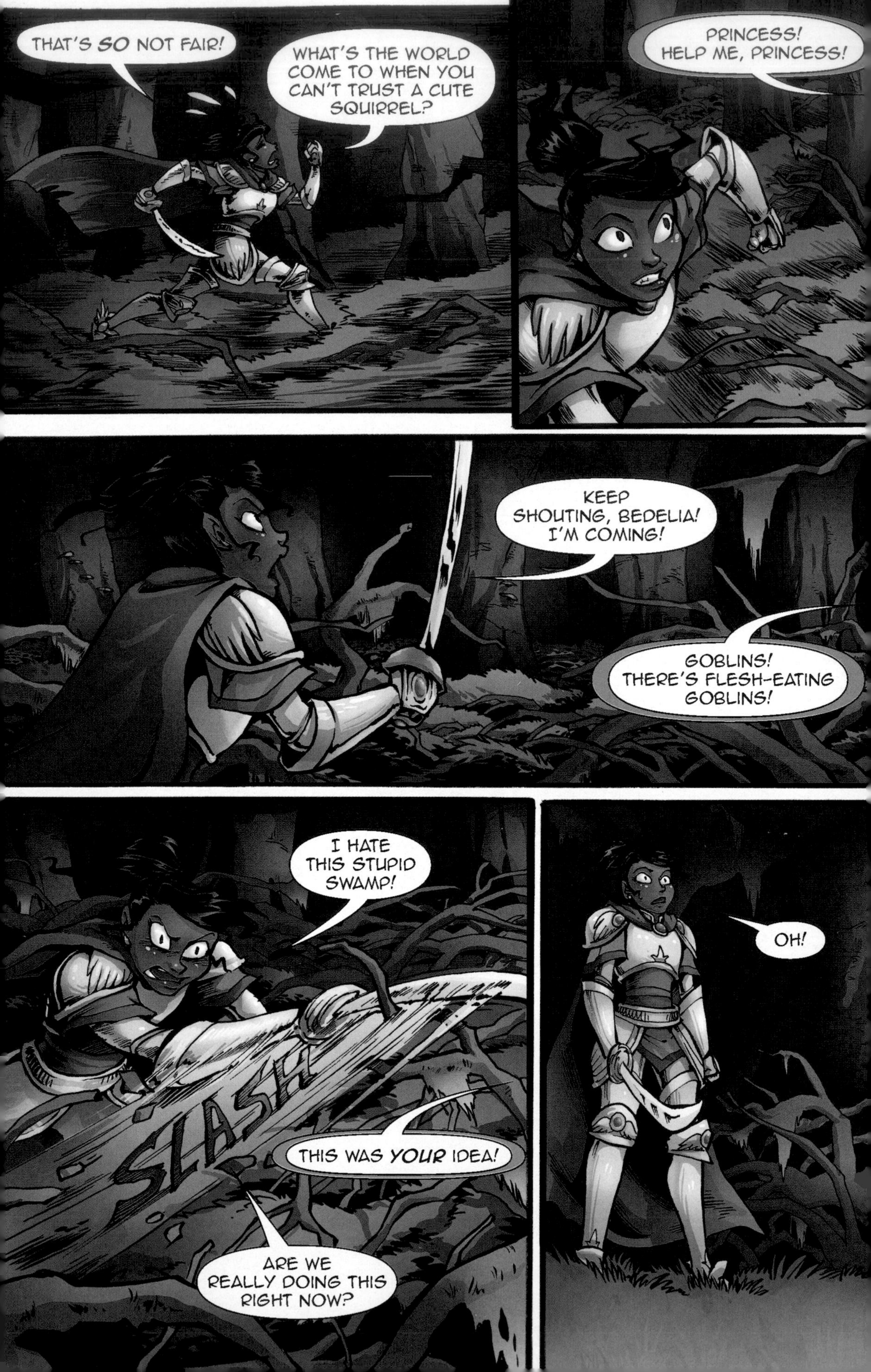
THAT'S SO NOT FAIR!
WHAT'S THE WORLD COME TO WHEN YOU CAN'T TRUST A CUTE SQUIRREL?
PRINCESS! HELP ME, PRINCESS!
KEEP SHOUTING, BEDELIA! I'M COMING!
GOBLINS! THERE'S FLESH-EATING GOBLINS!
I HATE THIS STUPID SWAMP!
SLASH
THIS WAS YOUR IDEA!
ARE WE REALLY DOING THIS RIGHT NOW?
OH!

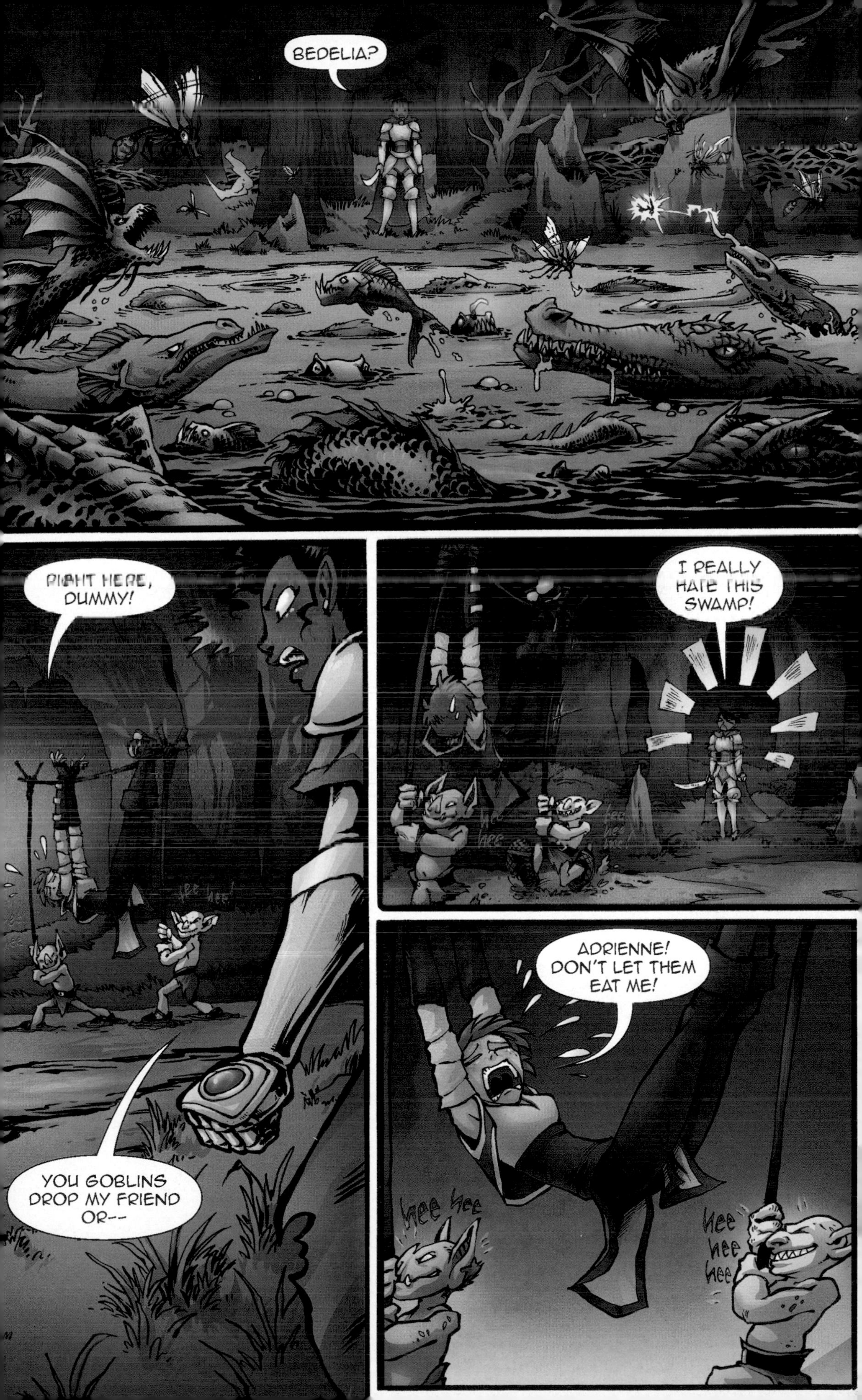
BEDELIA?
RIGHT HERE, DUMMY!
YOU GOBLINS DROP MY FRIEND OR--
I REALLY HATE THIS SWAMP!
ADRIENNE! DON'T LET THEM EAT ME!
hee hee
hee hee hee

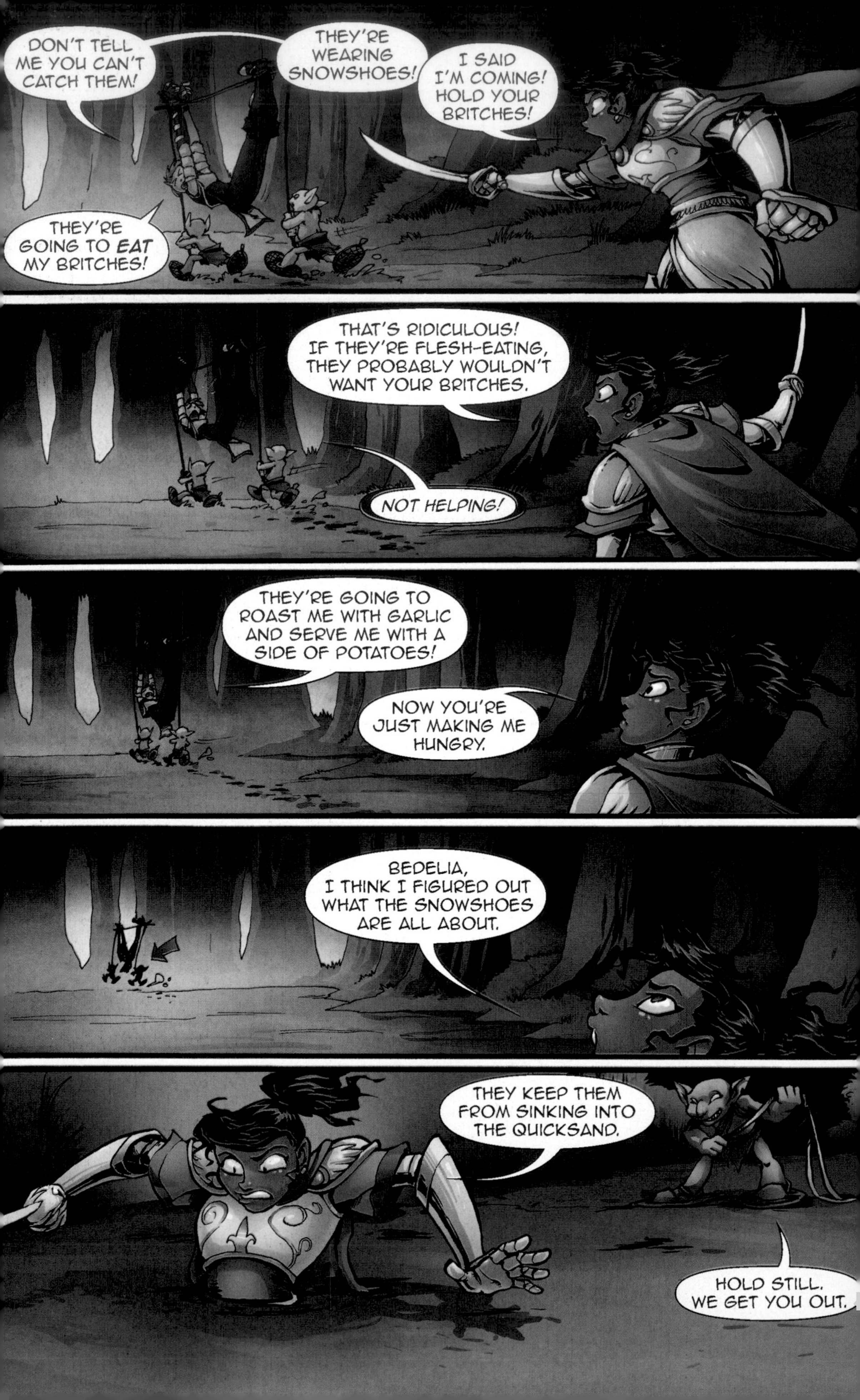
DON'T TELL ME YOU CAN'T CATCH THEM!
THEY'RE WEARING SNOWSHOES!
I SAID I'M COMING! HOLD YOUR BRITCHES!
THEY'RE GOING TO *EAT* MY BRITCHES!
THAT'S RIDICULOUS! IF THEY'RE FLESH-EATING, THEY PROBABLY WOULDN'T WANT YOUR BRITCHES.
NOT HELPING!
THEY'RE GOING TO ROAST ME WITH GARLIC AND SERVE ME WITH A SIDE OF POTATOES!
NOW YOU'RE JUST MAKING ME HUNGRY.
BEDELIA, I THINK I FIGURED OUT WHAT THE SNOWSHOES ARE ALL ABOUT.
THEY KEEP THEM FROM SINKING INTO THE QUICKSAND.
HOLD STILL. WE GET YOU OUT.

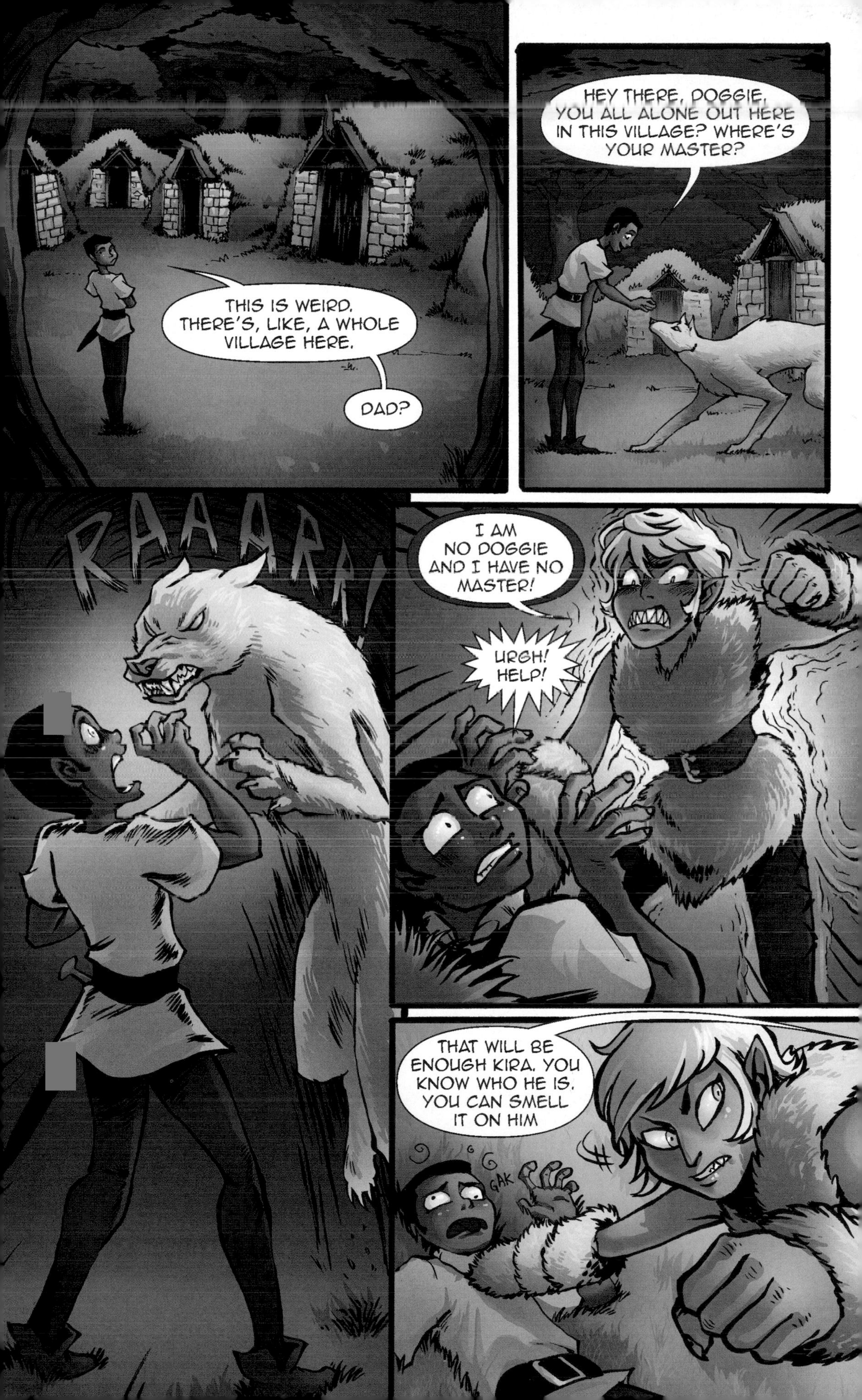
THIS IS WEIRD. THERE'S, LIKE, A WHOLE VILLAGE HERE.
DAD?
HEY THERE, DOGGIE, YOU ALL ALONE OUT HERE IN THIS VILLAGE? WHERE'S YOUR MASTER?
RAAARR!
I AM NO DOGGIE AND I HAVE NO MASTER!
URGH! HELP!
THAT WILL BE ENOUGH KIRA. YOU KNOW WHO HE IS. YOU CAN SMELL IT ON HIM
GAK

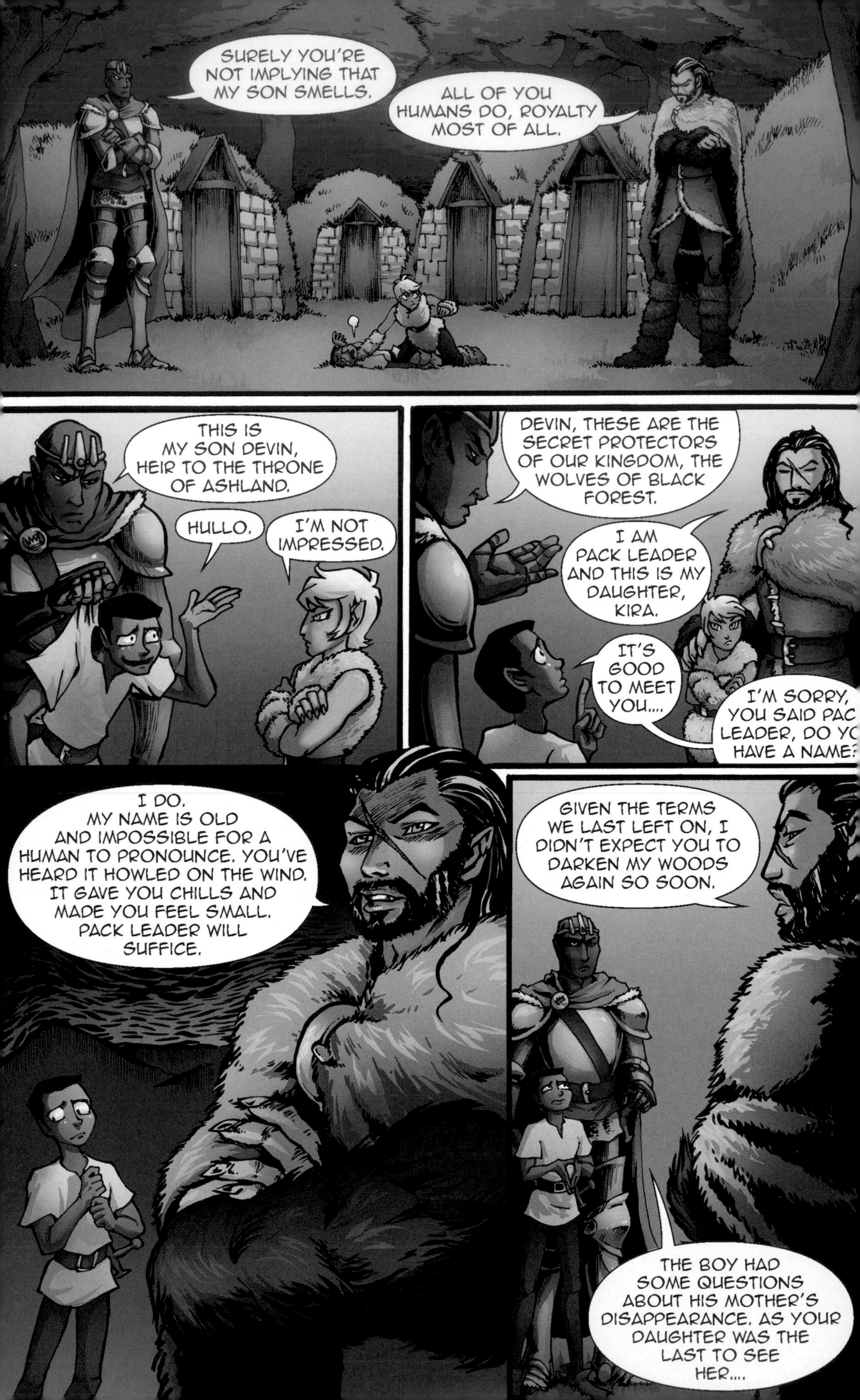
SURELY YOU'RE NOT IMPLYING THAT MY SON SMELLS.
ALL OF YOU HUMANS DO, ROYALTY MOST OF ALL.
THIS IS MY SON DEVIN, HEIR TO THE THRONE OF ASHLAND.
HULLO.
I'M NOT IMPRESSED.
DEVIN, THESE ARE THE SECRET PROTECTORS OF OUR KINGDOM, THE WOLVES OF BLACK FOREST.
I AM PACK LEADER AND THIS IS MY DAUGHTER, KIRA.
IT'S GOOD TO MEET YOU....
I'M SORRY, YOU SAID PAC LEADER, DO YO HAVE A NAME?
I DO. MY NAME IS OLD AND IMPOSSIBLE FOR A HUMAN TO PRONOUNCE. YOU'VE HEARD IT HOWLED ON THE WIND. IT GAVE YOU CHILLS AND MADE YOU FEEL SMALL. PACK LEADER WILL SUFFICE.
GIVEN THE TERMS WE LAST LEFT ON, I DIDN'T EXPECT YOU TO DARKEN MY WOODS AGAIN SO SOON.
THE BOY HAD SOME QUESTIONS ABOUT HIS MOTHER'S DISAPPEARANCE. AS YOUR DAUGHTER WAS THE LAST TO SEE HER....

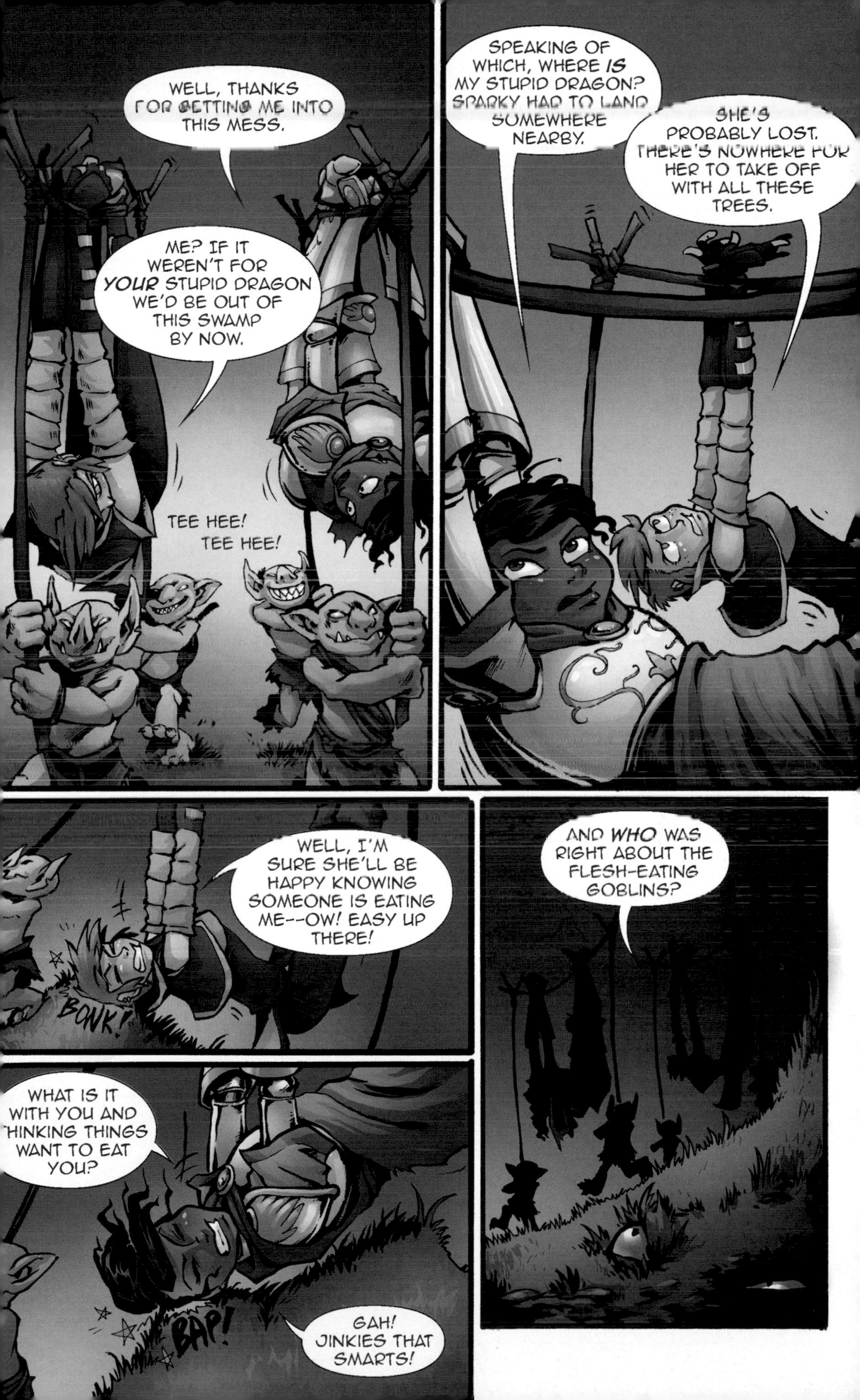
WELL, THANKS FOR GETTING ME INTO THIS MESS.
ME? IF IT WEREN'T FOR *YOUR* STUPID DRAGON WE'D BE OUT OF THIS SWAMP BY NOW.
TEE HEE! TEE HEE!
SPEAKING OF WHICH, WHERE *IS* MY STUPID DRAGON? SPARKY HAD TO LAND SOMEWHERE NEARBY.
SHE'S PROBABLY LOST. THERE'S NOWHERE FOR HER TO TAKE OFF WITH ALL THESE TREES.
WELL, I'M SURE SHE'LL BE HAPPY KNOWING SOMEONE IS EATING ME--OW! EASY UP THERE!
BONK!
AND *WHO* WAS RIGHT ABOUT THE FLESH-EATING GOBLINS?
WHAT IS IT WITH YOU AND HINKING THINGS WANT TO EAT YOU?
BAP!
GAH! JINKIES THAT SMARTS!

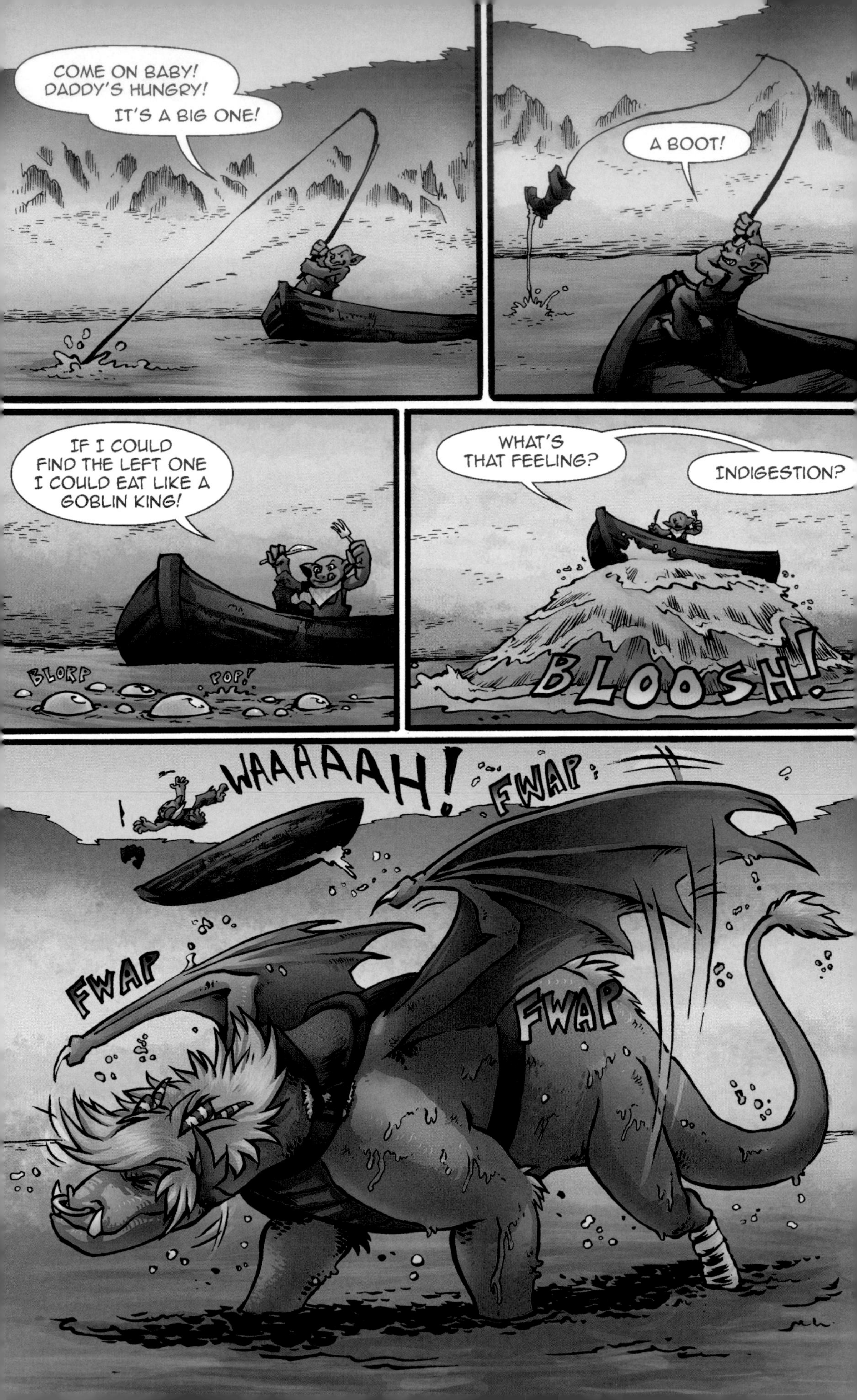
COME ON BABY! DADDY'S HUNGRY!
IT'S A BIG ONE!
A BOOT!
IF I COULD FIND THE LEFT ONE I COULD EAT LIKE A GOBLIN KING!
BLORP
POP!
WHAT'S THAT FEELING?
INDIGESTION?
BLOOSH!
WAAAAAH!
FWAP
FWAP
FWAP

KIRA, YOU ARE THE LEADER OF THE WATCH. YOU WERE THERE WHEN MY MOTHER DISAPPEARED?

YES.

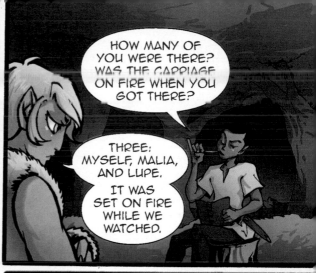

HOW MANY OF YOU WERE THERE? WAS THE CARRIAGE ON FIRE WHEN YOU GOT THERE?

THREE: MYSELF, MALIA, AND LUPE. IT WAS SET ON FIRE WHILE WE WATCHED.

BY THE BLACK KNIGHT, YES? THEN WHAT?

YES. HE CARRIED A LARGE BUNDLE AND PUT IT ON THE BACK OF ONE OF THE HORSES.

THE BUNDLE, COULD YOU TELL WHAT WAS IN IT?

IT LOOKED LIKE DRESSES. BUT I SWEAR I HEARD A WOMAN'S VOICE IN THE CARRIAGE TOO. I THINK THE WOMAN WAS TIED UP IN THE BUNDLE.

WHEN HE LEFT, WHICH WAY DID HE GO?

tap tap

EAST, I THINK. BUT WE BELIEVED THE WOMAN WAS STILL IN THE CARRIAGE. WE TRIED TO SAVE HER. BUT THERE WAS NOTHING THERE BUT AN EMPTY SCABBARD AND AN OLD CHEST.

A CHEST? WHERE IS THIS CHEST?

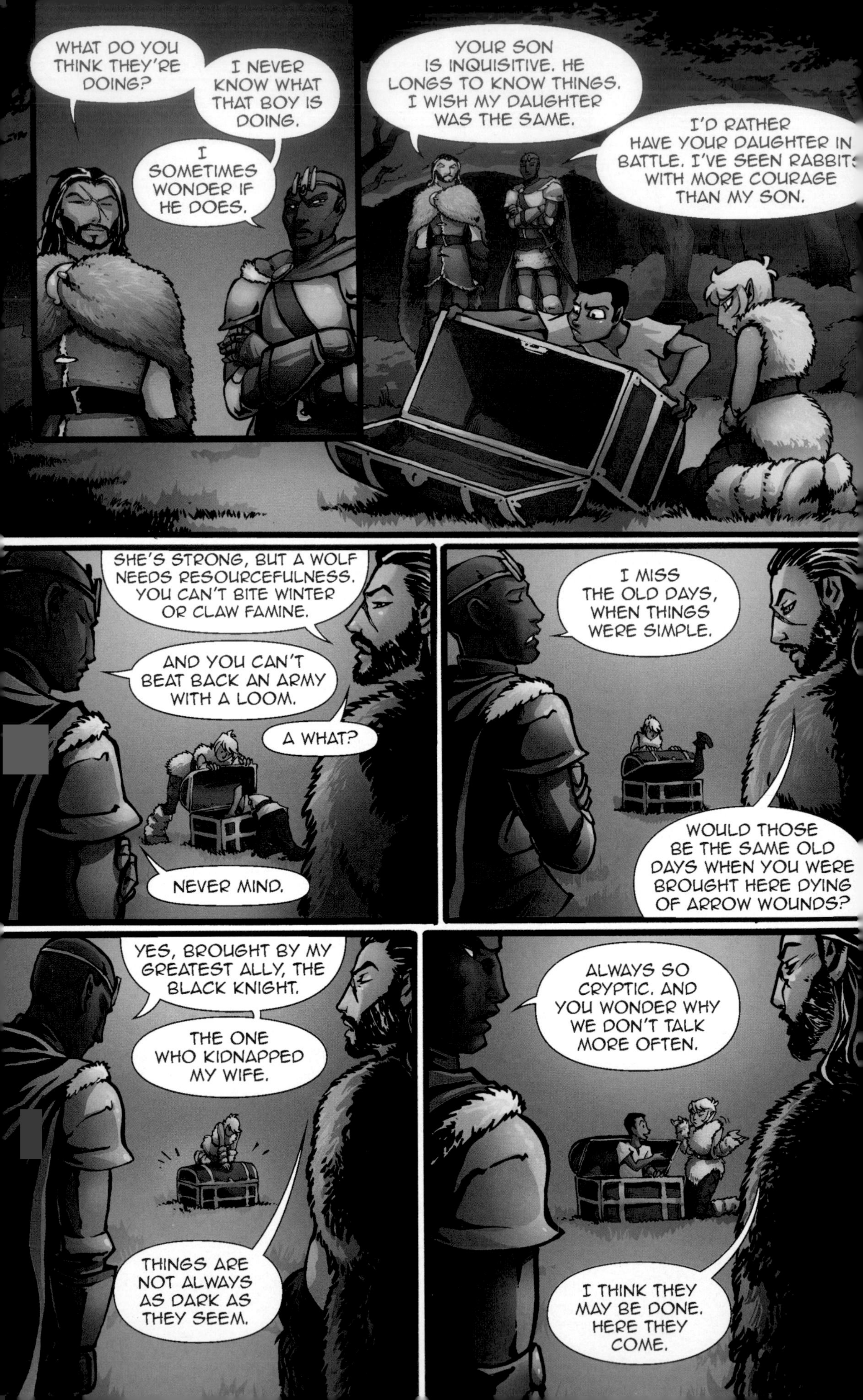
WHAT DO YOU THINK THEY'RE DOING?
I NEVER KNOW WHAT THAT BOY IS DOING.
I SOMETIMES WONDER IF HE DOES.
YOUR SON IS INQUISITIVE. HE LONGS TO KNOW THINGS. I WISH MY DAUGHTER WAS THE SAME.
I'D RATHER HAVE YOUR DAUGHTER IN BATTLE. I'VE SEEN RABBIT WITH MORE COURAGE THAN MY SON.
SHE'S STRONG, BUT A WOLF NEEDS RESOURCEFULNESS. YOU CAN'T BITE WINTER OR CLAW FAMINE.
AND YOU CAN'T BEAT BACK AN ARMY WITH A LOOM.
A WHAT?
NEVER MIND.
I MISS THE OLD DAYS, WHEN THINGS WERE SIMPLE.
WOULD THOSE BE THE SAME OLD DAYS WHEN YOU WERE BROUGHT HERE DYING OF ARROW WOUNDS?
YES, BROUGHT BY MY GREATEST ALLY, THE BLACK KNIGHT.
THE ONE WHO KIDNAPPED MY WIFE.
THINGS ARE NOT ALWAYS AS DARK AS THEY SEEM.
ALWAYS SO CRYPTIC. AND YOU WONDER WHY WE DON'T TALK MORE OFTEN.
I THINK THEY MAY BE DONE. HERE THEY COME.

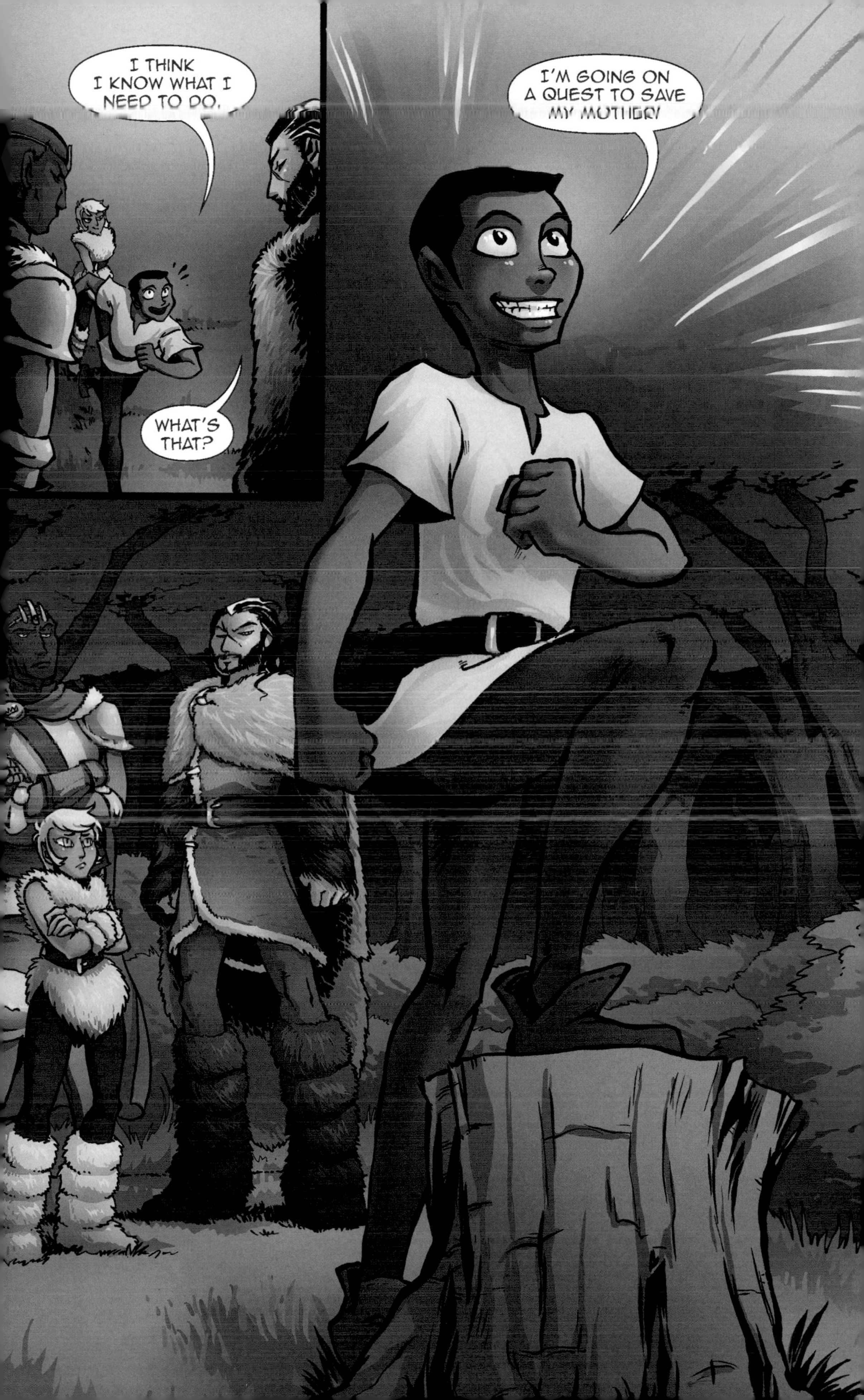
I THINK I KNOW WHAT I NEED TO DO.
WHAT'S THAT?
I'M GOING ON A QUEST TO SAVE MY MOTHER!

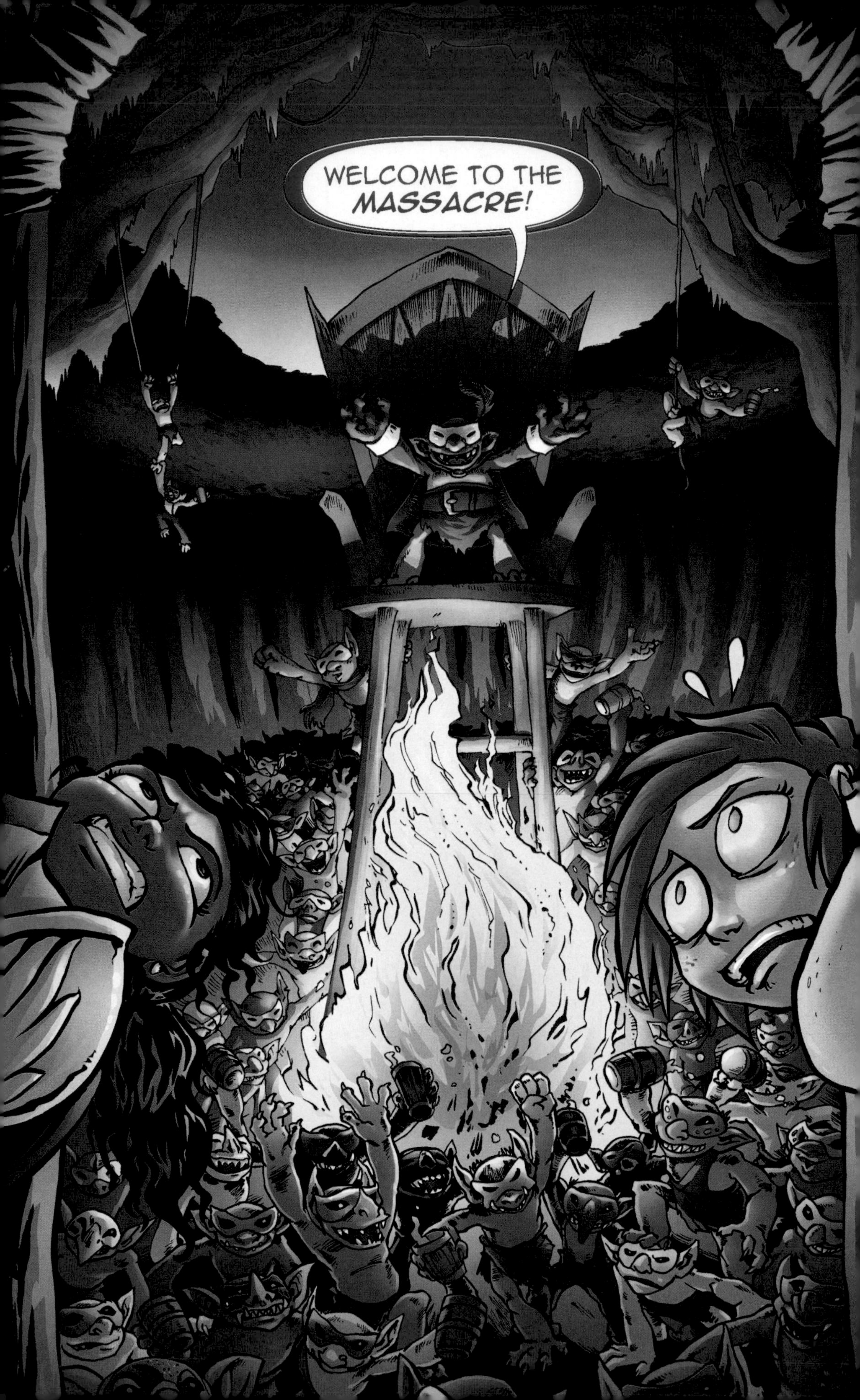
WELCOME TO THE *MASSACRE!*

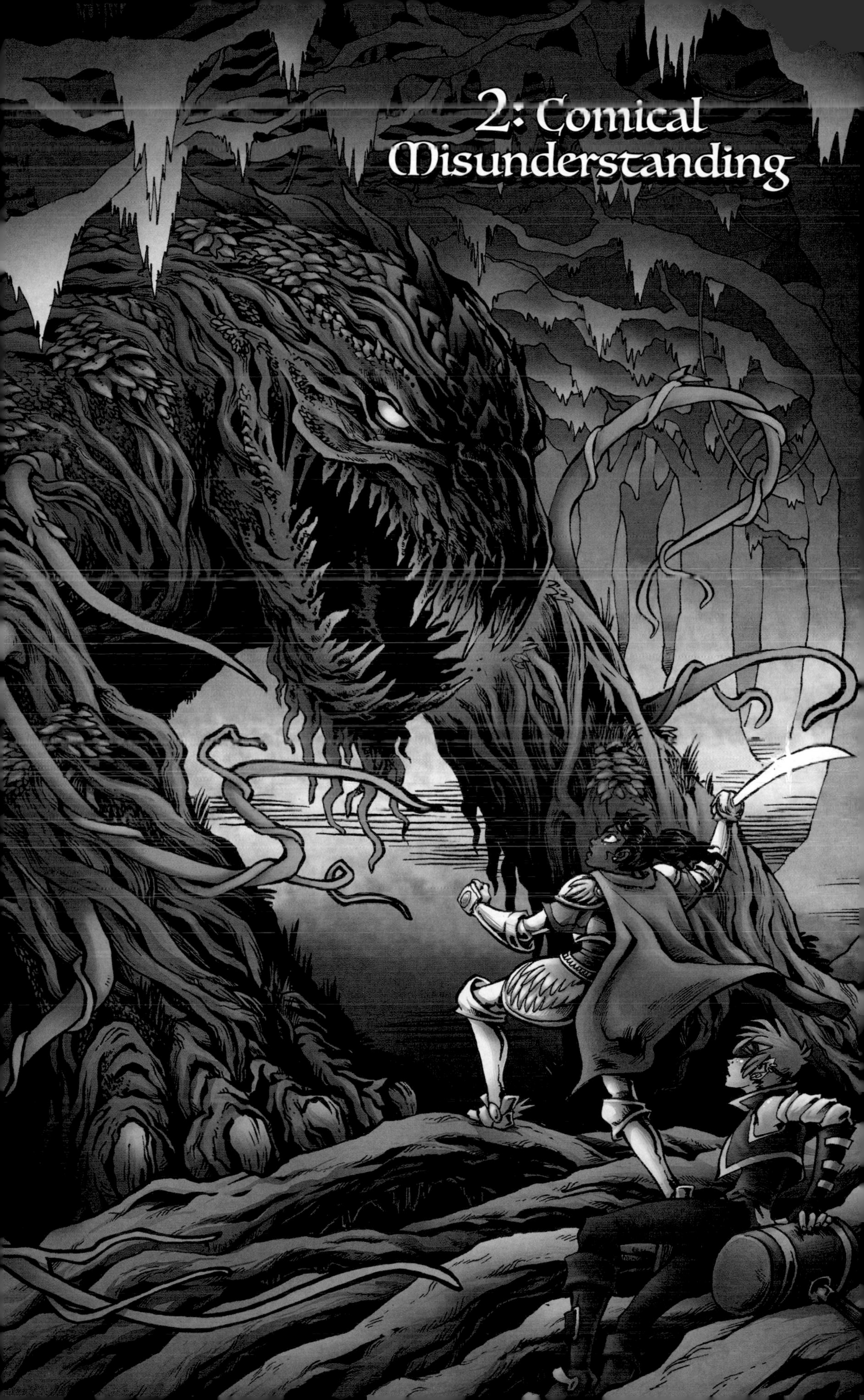
2: Comical
Misunderstanding

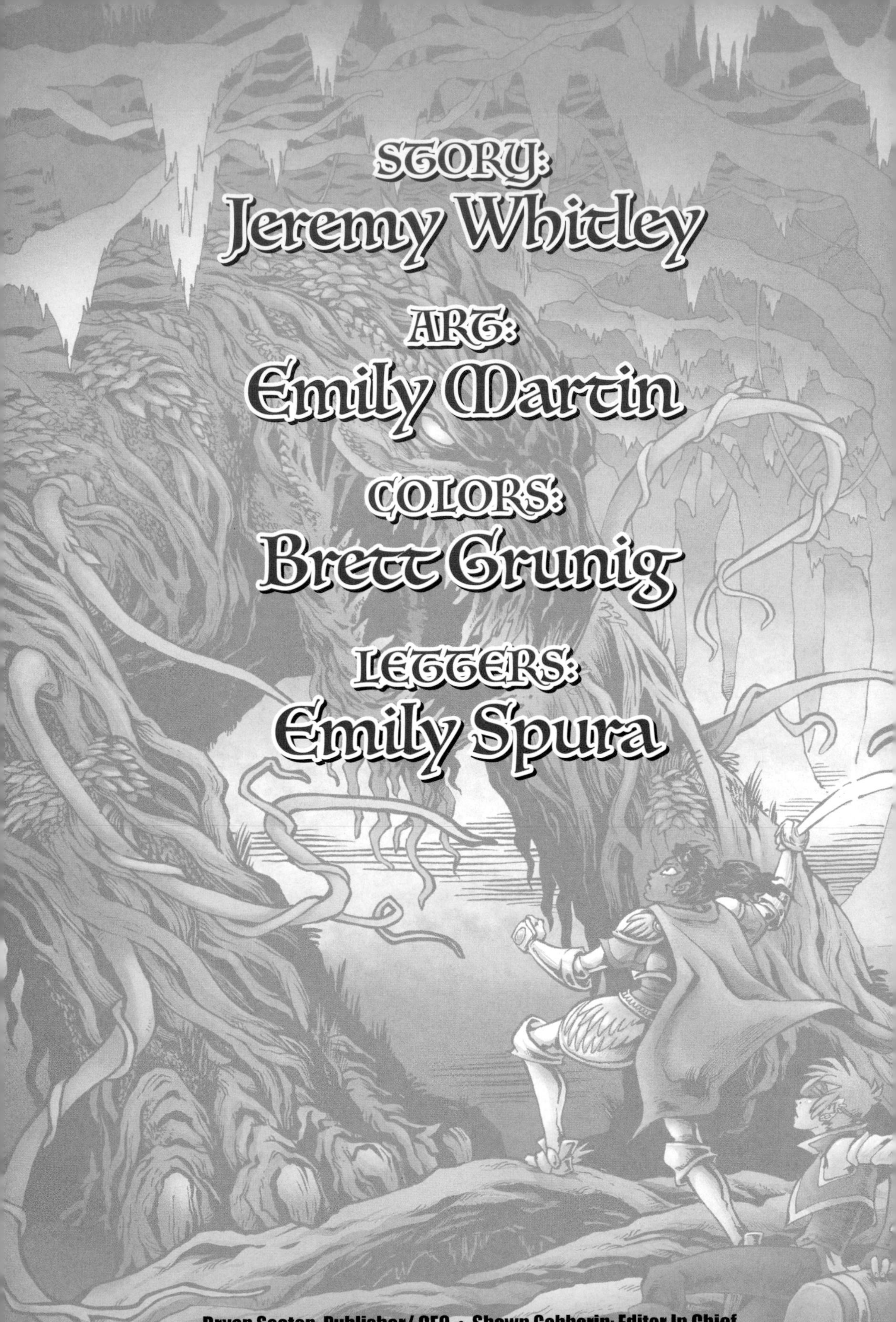

STORY:
Jeremy Whitley

ART:
Emily Martin

COLORS:
Brett Grunig

LETTERS:
Emily Spura

Bryan Seaton: Publisher/ CEO • Shawn Gabborin: Editor In Chief
Jason Martin: Publisher-Danger Zone • Nicole D'Andria: Marketing Director/Editor
Jim Dietz: Social Media Manager • Danielle Davison: Executive Administrator
Chad Cicconi: Still Waiting For His Princess • Shawn Pryor: President of Creator Relations

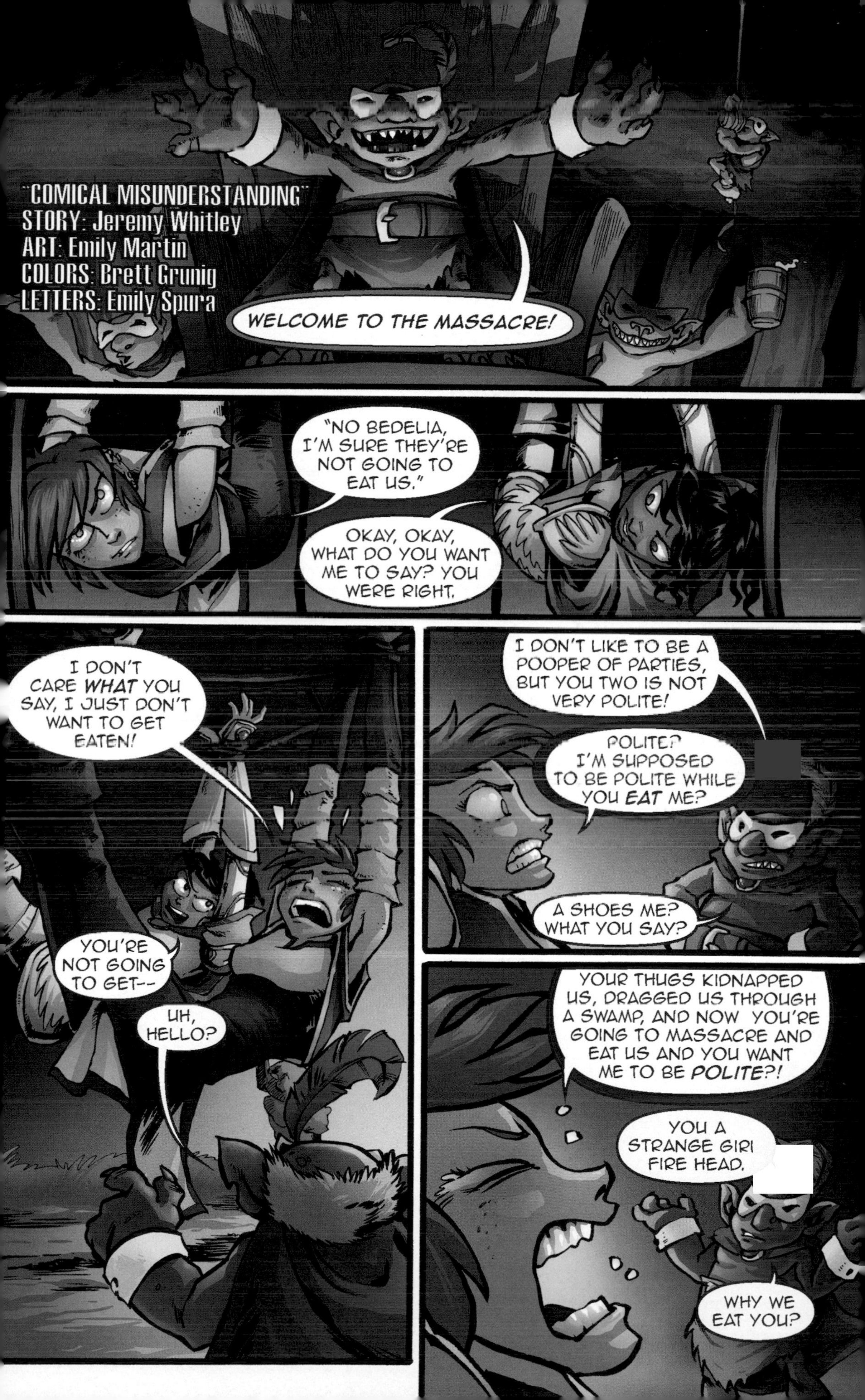
"COMICAL MISUNDERSTANDING"
STORY: Jeremy Whitley
ART: Emily Martin
COLORS: Brett Grunig
LETTERS: Emily Spura
WELCOME TO THE MASSACRE!
"NO BEDELIA, I'M SURE THEY'RE NOT GOING TO EAT US."
OKAY, OKAY, WHAT DO YOU WANT ME TO SAY? YOU WERE RIGHT.
I DON'T CARE WHAT YOU SAY, I JUST DON'T WANT TO GET EATEN!
YOU'RE NOT GOING TO GET--
UH, HELLO?
I DON'T LIKE TO BE A POOPER OF PARTIES, BUT YOU TWO IS NOT VERY POLITE!
POLITE? I'M SUPPOSED TO BE POLITE WHILE YOU EAT ME?
A SHOES ME? WHAT YOU SAY?
YOUR THUGS KIDNAPPED US, DRAGGED US THROUGH A SWAMP, AND NOW YOU'RE GOING TO MASSACRE AND EAT US AND YOU WANT ME TO BE POLITE?!
YOU A STRANGE GIRL FIRE HEAD.
WHY WE EAT YOU?

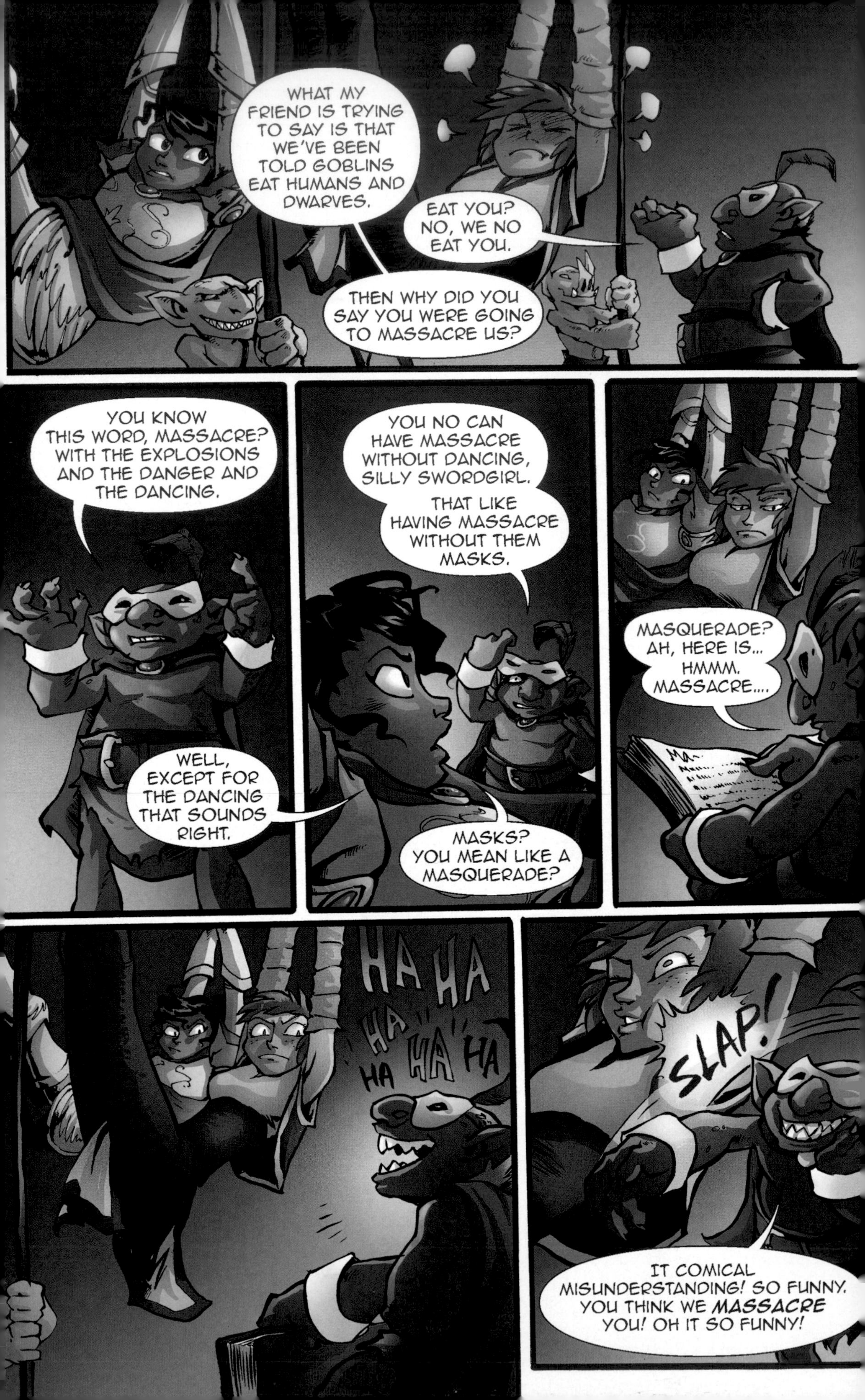
WHAT MY FRIEND IS TRYING TO SAY IS THAT WE'VE BEEN TOLD GOBLINS EAT HUMANS AND DWARVES.
EAT YOU? NO, WE NO EAT YOU.
THEN WHY DID YOU SAY YOU WERE GOING TO MASSACRE US?
YOU KNOW THIS WORD, MASSACRE? WITH THE EXPLOSIONS AND THE DANGER AND THE DANCING.
WELL, EXCEPT FOR THE DANCING THAT SOUNDS RIGHT.
YOU NO CAN HAVE MASSACRE WITHOUT DANCING, SILLY SWORDGIRL.
THAT LIKE HAVING MASSACRE WITHOUT THEM MASKS.
MASKS? YOU MEAN LIKE A MASQUERADE?
MASQUERADE? AH, HERE IS... HMMM. MASSACRE....
HA HA HA HA HA HA HA
SLAP!
IT COMICAL MISUNDERSTANDING! SO FUNNY. YOU THINK WE *MASSACRE* YOU! OH IT SO FUNNY!

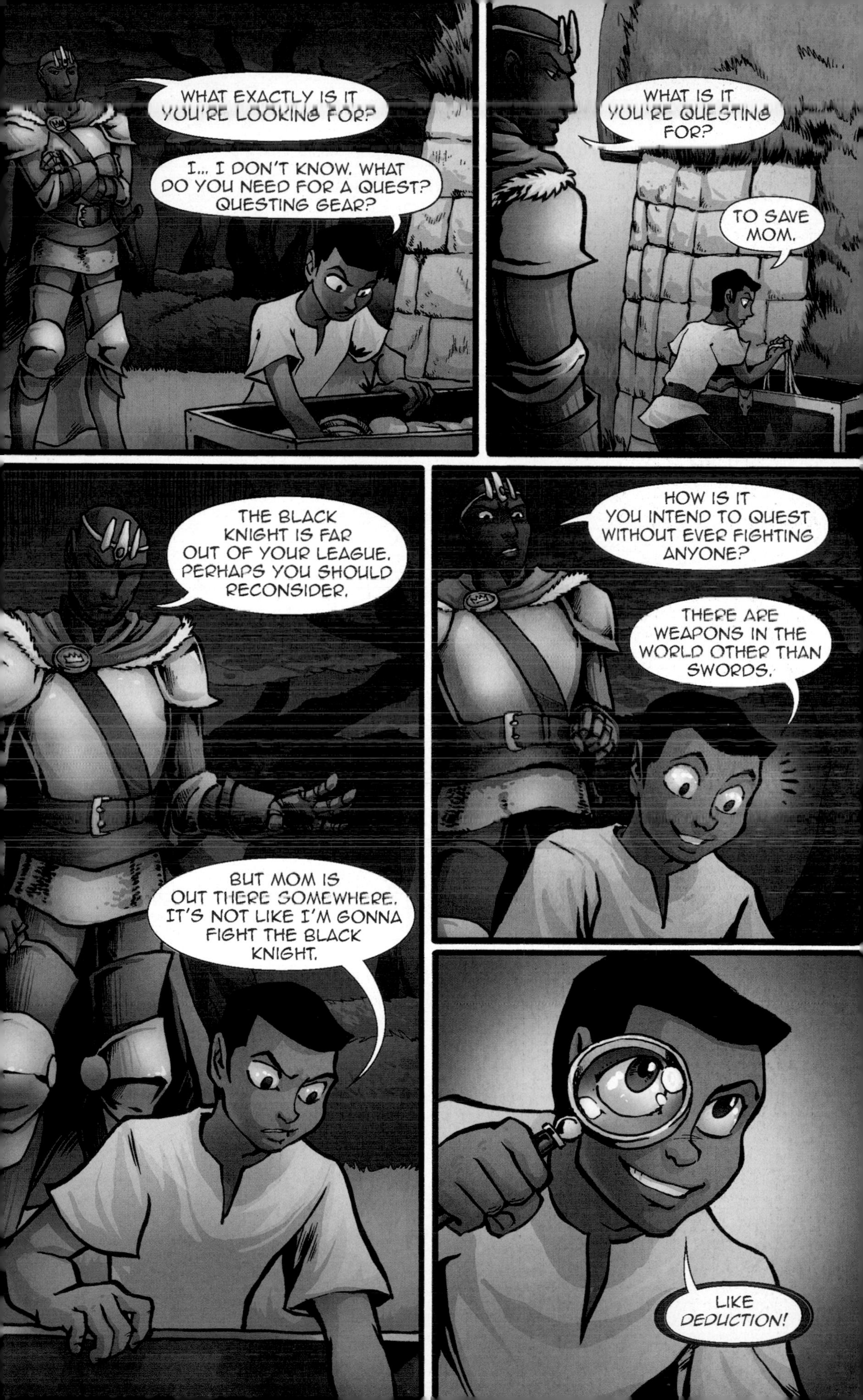
WHAT EXACTLY IS IT YOU'RE LOOKING FOR?
I... I DON'T KNOW. WHAT DO YOU NEED FOR A QUEST? QUESTING GEAR?
WHAT IS IT YOU'RE QUESTING FOR?
TO SAVE MOM.
THE BLACK KNIGHT IS FAR OUT OF YOUR LEAGUE. PERHAPS YOU SHOULD RECONSIDER.
BUT MOM IS OUT THERE SOMEWHERE. IT'S NOT LIKE I'M GONNA FIGHT THE BLACK KNIGHT.
HOW IS IT YOU INTEND TO QUEST WITHOUT EVER FIGHTING ANYONE?
THERE ARE WEAPONS IN THE WORLD OTHER THAN SWORDS.
LIKE DEDUCTION!

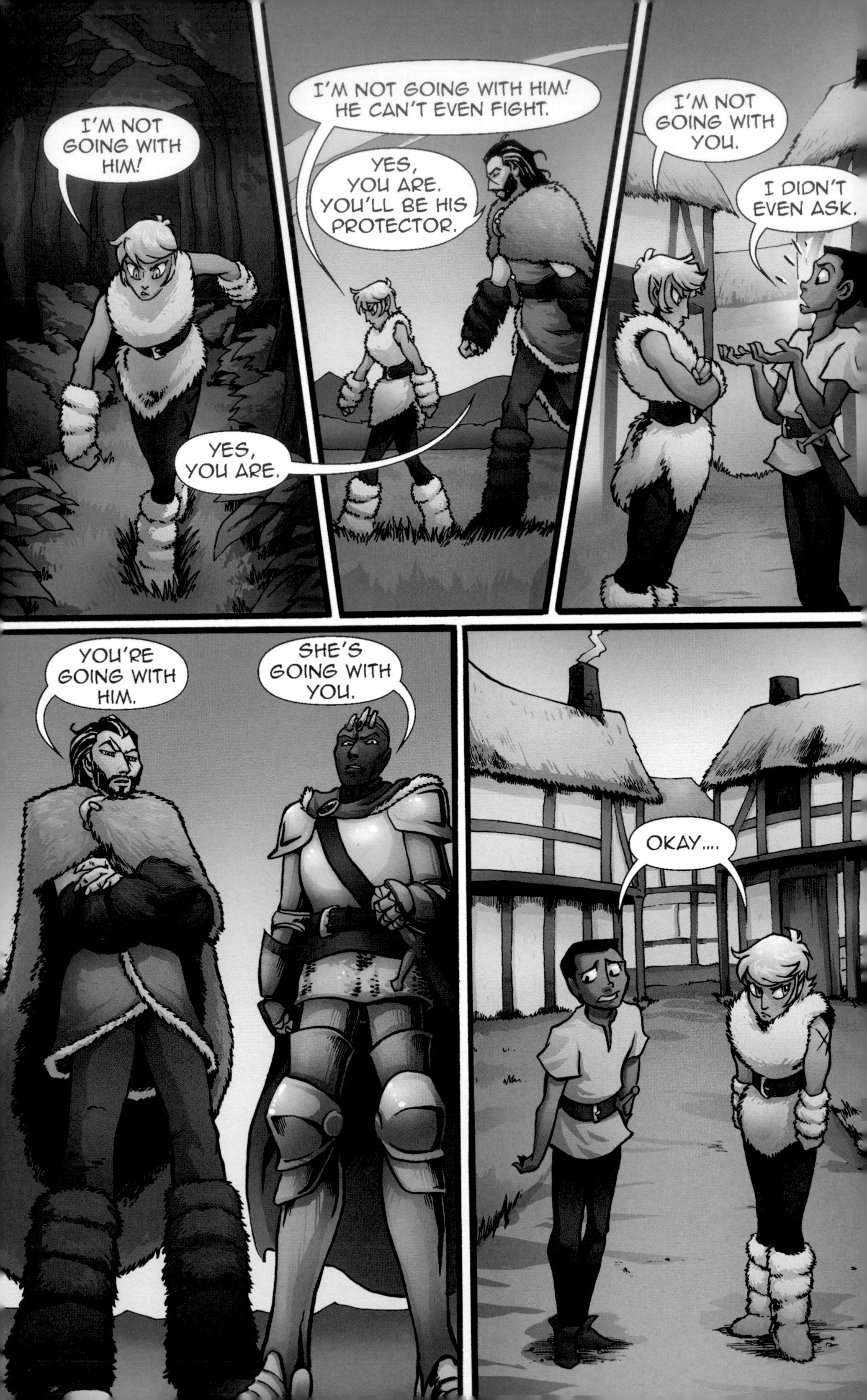
I'M NOT GOING WITH HIM!
YES, YOU ARE.
I'M NOT GOING WITH HIM! HE CAN'T EVEN FIGHT.
YES, YOU ARE. YOU'LL BE HIS PROTECTOR.
I'M NOT GOING WITH YOU.
I DIDN'T EVEN ASK.
YOU'RE GOING WITH HIM.
SHE'S GOING WITH YOU.
OKAY....

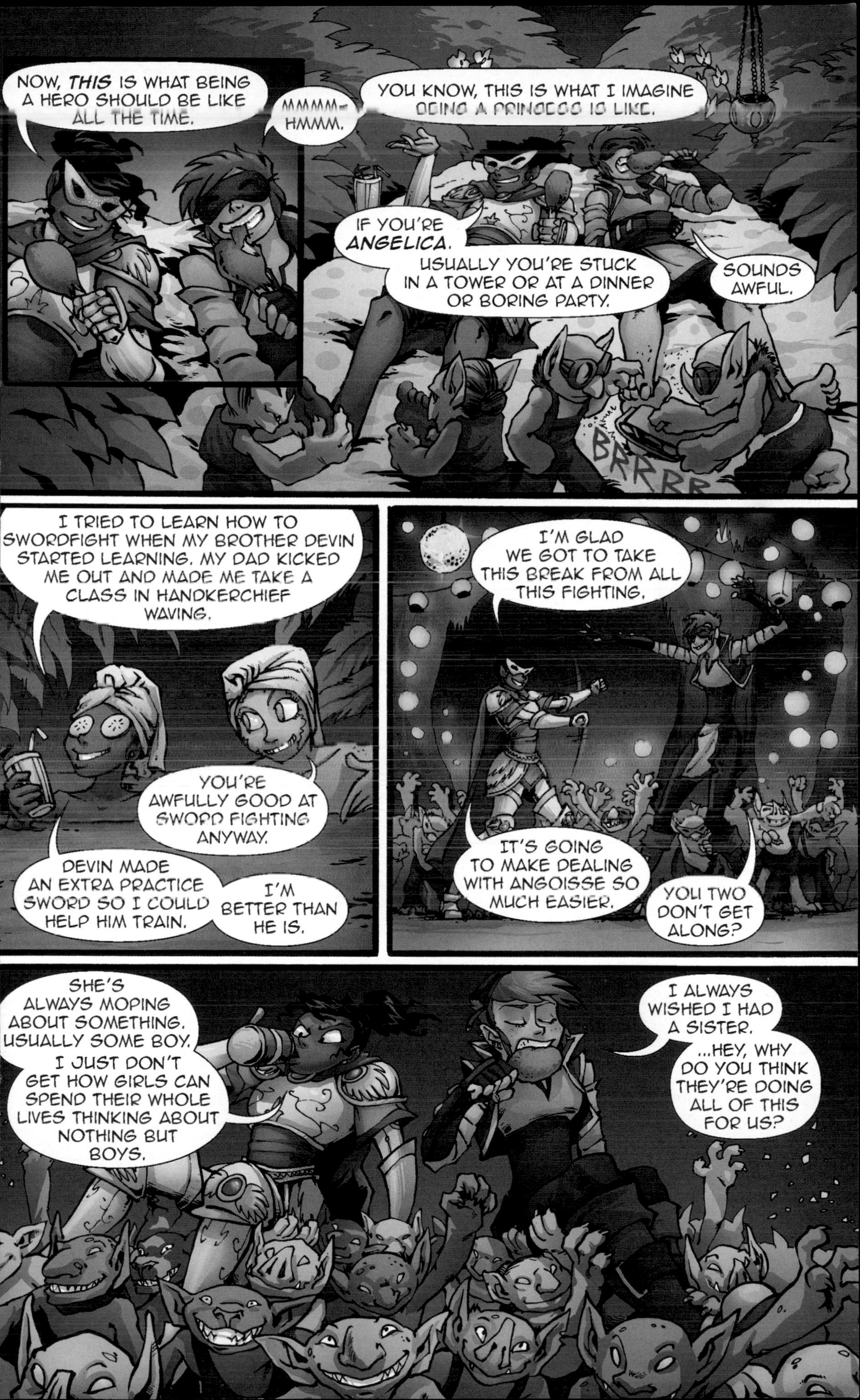
NOW, *THIS* IS WHAT BEING A HERO SHOULD BE LIKE ALL THE TIME.
MMMMM-HMMM.
YOU KNOW, THIS IS WHAT I IMAGINE BEING A PRINCESS IS LIKE.
IF YOU'RE *ANGELICA*.
USUALLY YOU'RE STUCK IN A TOWER OR AT A DINNER OR BORING PARTY.
SOUNDS AWFUL.
BRRRRR
I TRIED TO LEARN HOW TO SWORDFIGHT WHEN MY BROTHER DEVIN STARTED LEARNING. MY DAD KICKED ME OUT AND MADE ME TAKE A CLASS IN HANDKERCHIEF WAVING.
YOU'RE AWFULLY GOOD AT SWORD FIGHTING ANYWAY.
DEVIN MADE AN EXTRA PRACTICE SWORD SO I COULD HELP HIM TRAIN.
I'M BETTER THAN HE IS.
I'M GLAD WE GOT TO TAKE THIS BREAK FROM ALL THIS FIGHTING.
IT'S GOING TO MAKE DEALING WITH ANGOISSE SO MUCH EASIER.
YOU TWO DON'T GET ALONG?
SHE'S ALWAYS MOPING ABOUT SOMETHING. USUALLY SOME BOY.
I JUST DON'T GET HOW GIRLS CAN SPEND THEIR WHOLE LIVES THINKING ABOUT NOTHING BUT BOYS.
I ALWAYS WISHED I HAD A SISTER.
...HEY, WHY DO YOU THINK THEY'RE DOING ALL OF THIS FOR US?

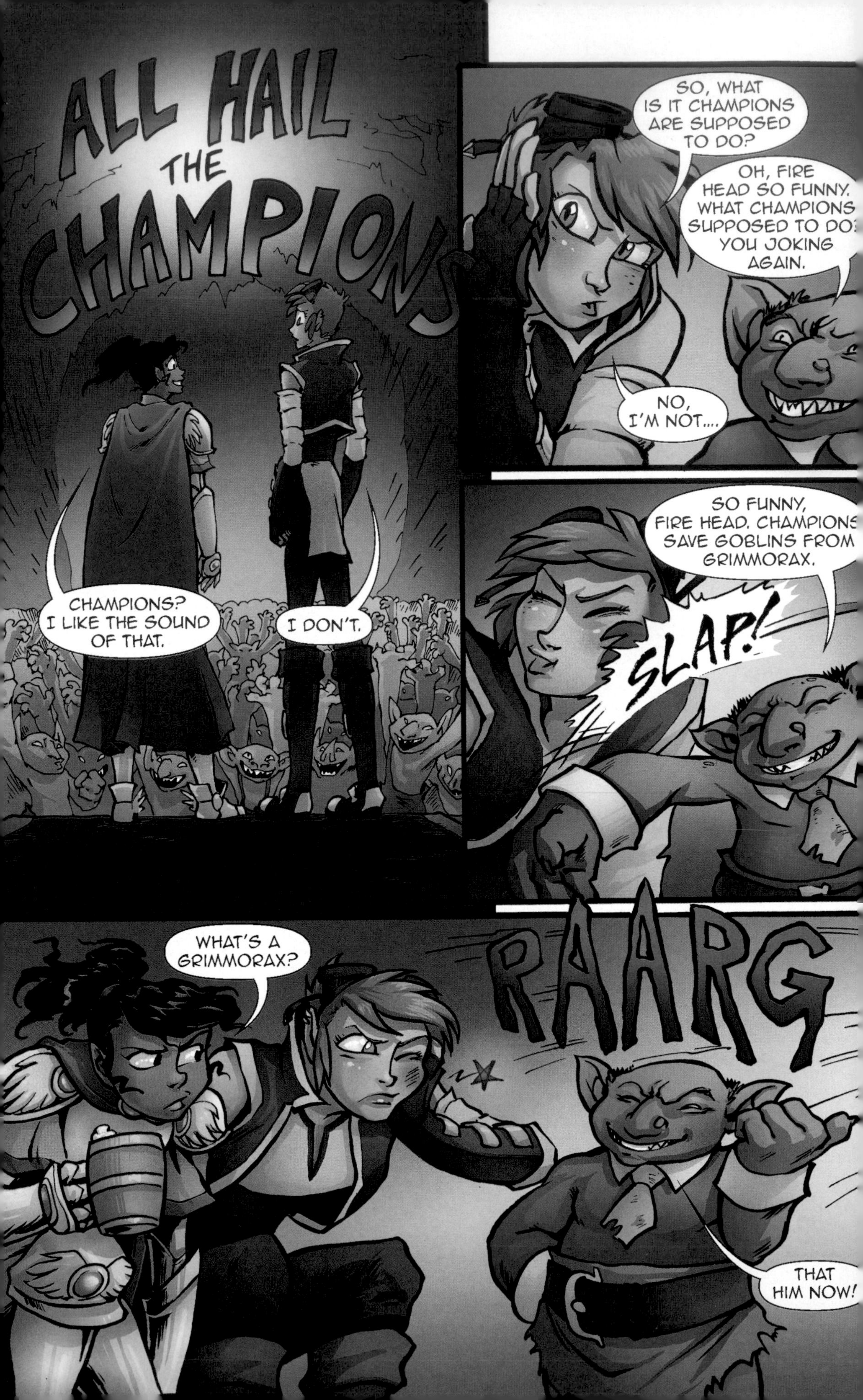
ALL HAIL THE CHAMPIONS
CHAMPIONS? I LIKE THE SOUND OF THAT.
I DON'T.
SO, WHAT IS IT CHAMPIONS ARE SUPPOSED TO DO?
OH, FIRE HEAD SO FUNNY. WHAT CHAMPIONS SUPPOSED TO DO? YOU JOKING AGAIN.
NO, I'M NOT....
SO FUNNY, FIRE HEAD. CHAMPIONS SAVE GOBLINS FROM GRIMMORAX.
SLAP!
WHAT'S A GRIMMORAX?
RAARG
THAT HIM NOW!

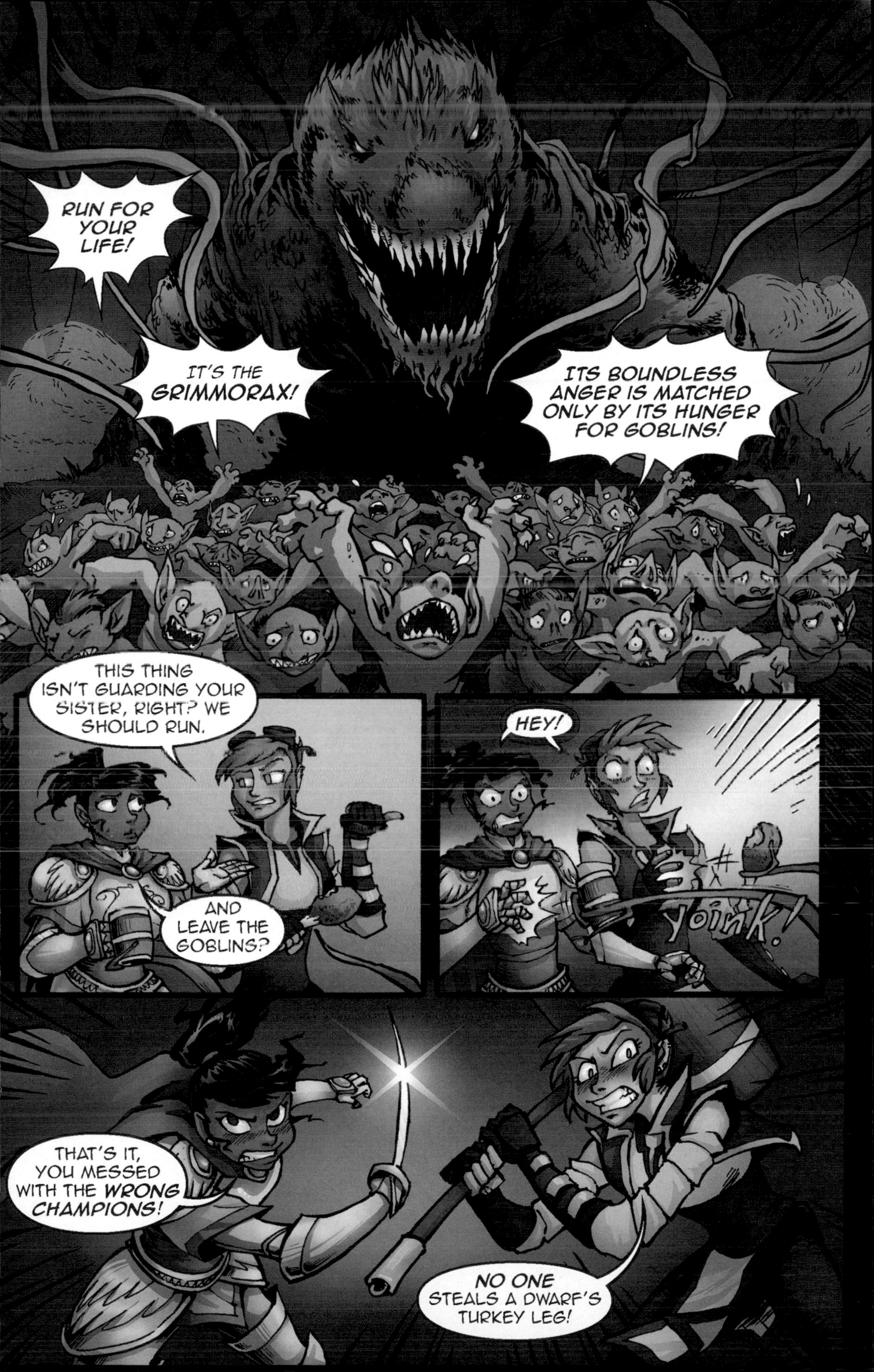
RUN FOR YOUR LIFE!
IT'S THE GRIMMORAX!
ITS BOUNDLESS ANGER IS MATCHED ONLY BY ITS HUNGER FOR GOBLINS!
THIS THING ISN'T GUARDING YOUR SISTER, RIGHT? WE SHOULD RUN.
AND LEAVE THE GOBLINS?
HEY!
yoink!
THAT'S IT, YOU MESSED WITH THE WRONG CHAMPIONS!
NO ONE STEALS A DWARF'S TURKEY LEG!

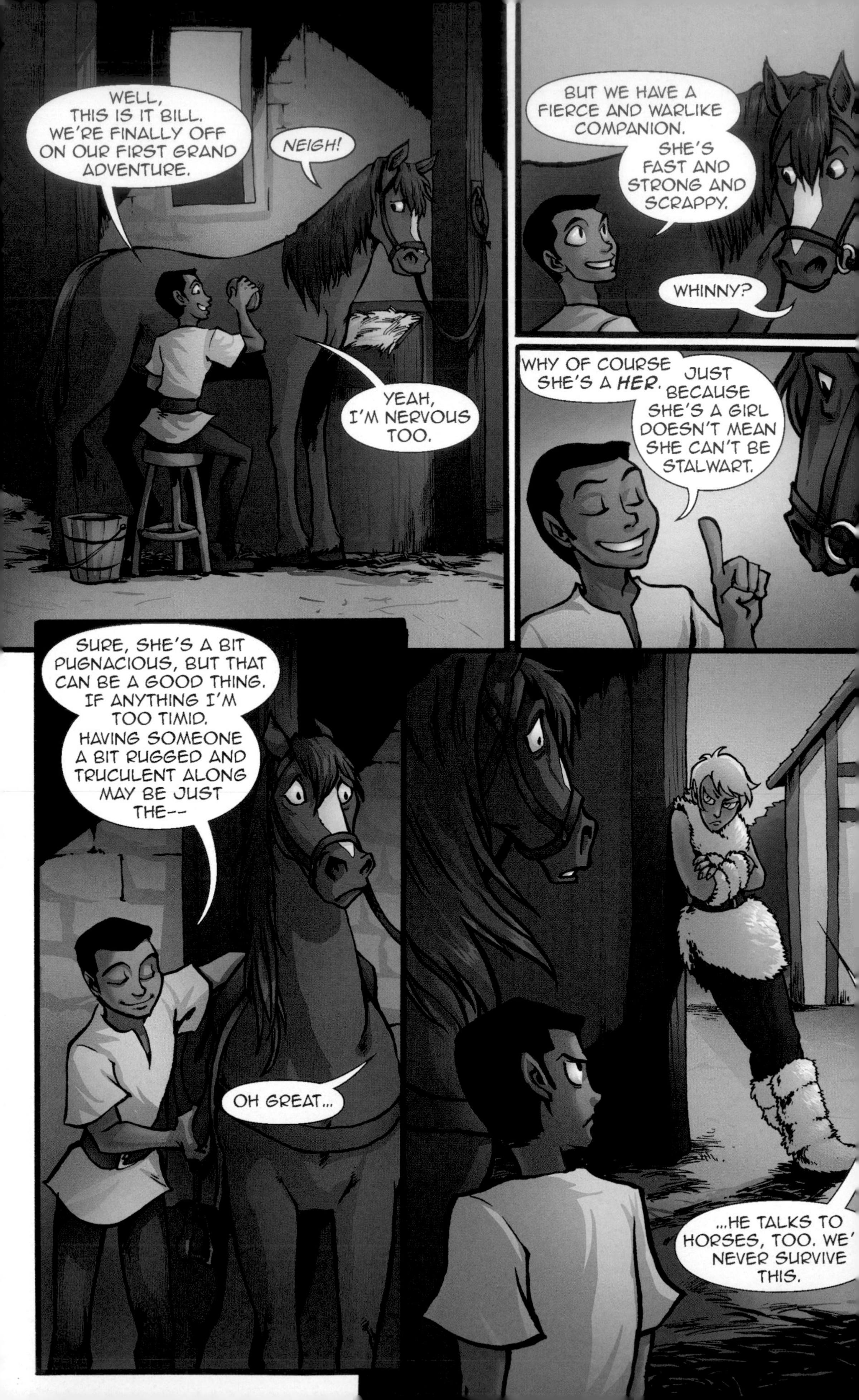
WELL, THIS IS IT BILL. WE'RE FINALLY OFF ON OUR FIRST GRAND ADVENTURE.
NEIGH!
YEAH, I'M NERVOUS TOO.
BUT WE HAVE A FIERCE AND WARLIKE COMPANION.
SHE'S FAST AND STRONG AND SCRAPPY.
WHINNY?
WHY OF COURSE SHE'S A *HER*.
JUST BECAUSE SHE'S A GIRL DOESN'T MEAN SHE CAN'T BE STALWART.
SURE, SHE'S A BIT PUGNACIOUS, BUT THAT CAN BE A GOOD THING. IF ANYTHING I'M TOO TIMID. HAVING SOMEONE A BIT RUGGED AND TRUCULENT ALONG MAY BE JUST THE--
OH GREAT...
...HE TALKS TO HORSES, TOO. WE' NEVER SURVIVE THIS.

WHINNY!

WOAH, BILL! THAT'S KIRA, SHE'S A GOOD GUY. SHE'S THE ONE COMING WITH US.

YOU NAMED YOUR HORSE BILL?

WELL, I HAD ALWAYS WANTED TO HAVE A PONY NAMED BILL, BUT MY FATHER WOULD NEVER LET ME.

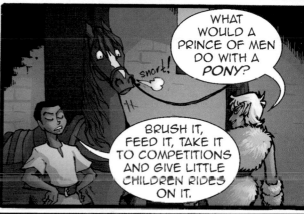

snort!

Pat Pat

WHAT WOULD A PRINCE OF MEN DO WITH A PONY?

BRUSH IT, FEED IT, TAKE IT TO COMPETITIONS AND GIVE LITTLE CHILDREN RIDES ON IT.

A PRINCE'S HORSE SHOULD BE AN ANIMAL OF WAR. WITH HOOVES OF IRON AND CLOCKWORK LIMBS!

BILL'S A FEARLESS STEED!

REALLY?

WHINNY!

AAHH!

RAARRL!

'FEARLESS STEED' INDEED.

YEAH, WELL WHERE'S YOUR HORSE?

I DON'T RIDE HORSES. HORSES ARE FOR THE WEAK AND SLOW.

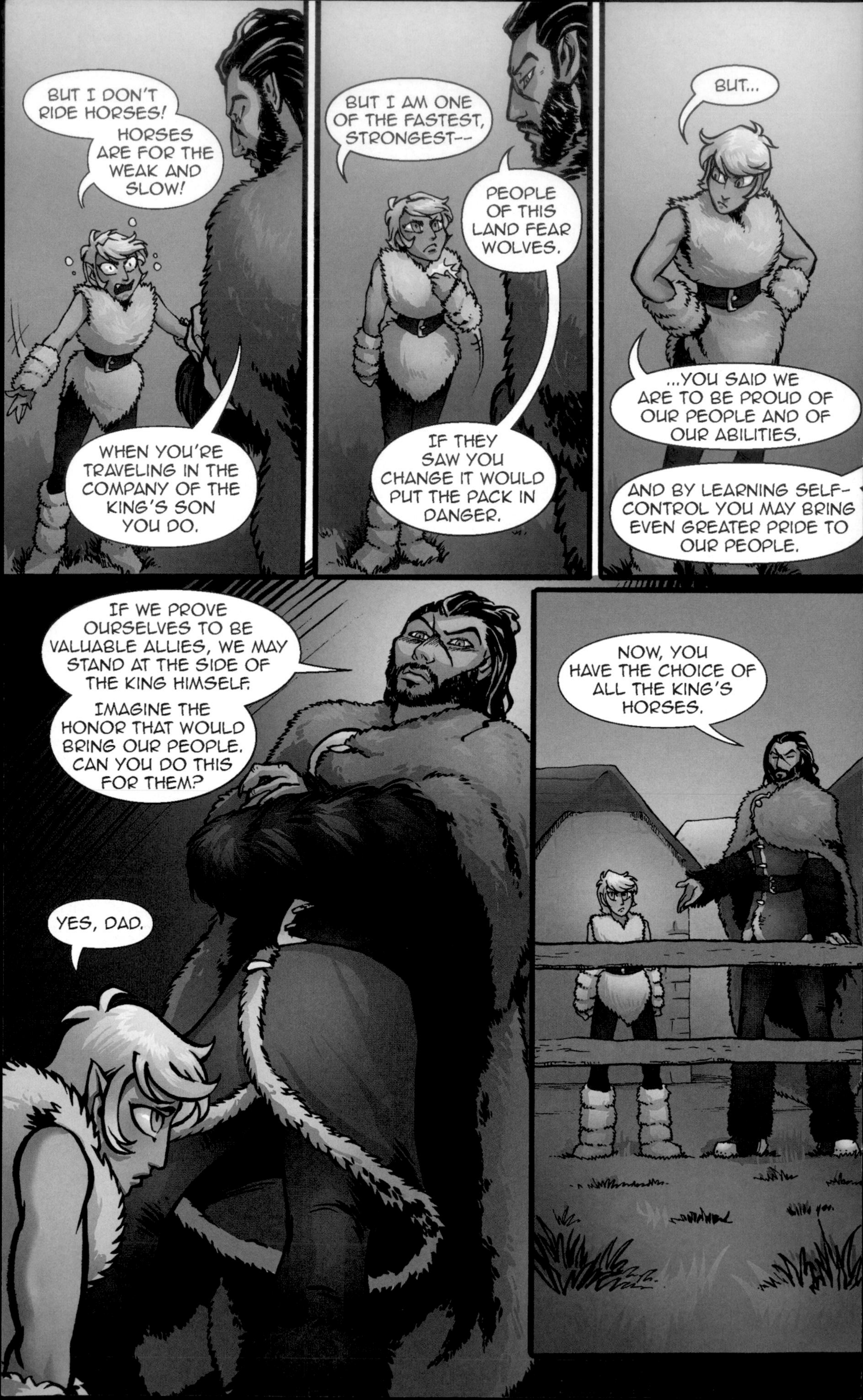
BUT I DON'T RIDE HORSES!
HORSES ARE FOR THE WEAK AND SLOW!
WHEN YOU'RE TRAVELING IN THE COMPANY OF THE KING'S SON YOU DO.
BUT I AM ONE OF THE FASTEST, STRONGEST--
PEOPLE OF THIS LAND FEAR WOLVES.
IF THEY SAW YOU CHANGE IT WOULD PUT THE PACK IN DANGER.
BUT...
...YOU SAID WE ARE TO BE PROUD OF OUR PEOPLE AND OF OUR ABILITIES.
AND BY LEARNING SELF-CONTROL YOU MAY BRING EVEN GREATER PRIDE TO OUR PEOPLE.
IF WE PROVE OURSELVES TO BE VALUABLE ALLIES, WE MAY STAND AT THE SIDE OF THE KING HIMSELF.
IMAGINE THE HONOR THAT WOULD BRING OUR PEOPLE. CAN YOU DO THIS FOR THEM?
YES, DAD.
NOW, YOU HAVE THE CHOICE OF ALL THE KING'S HORSES.

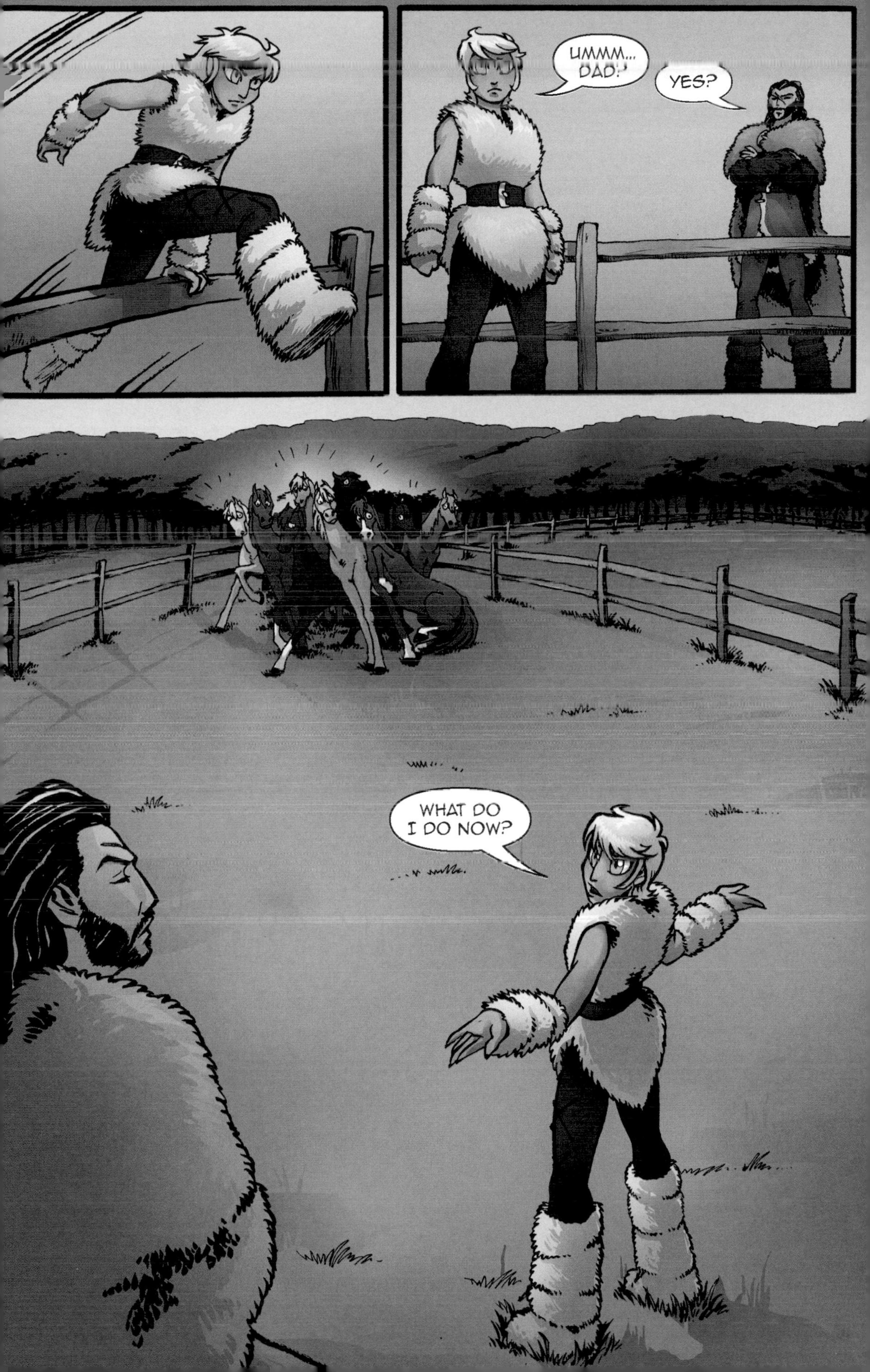
UMMM... DAD?
YES?
WHAT DO I DO NOW?

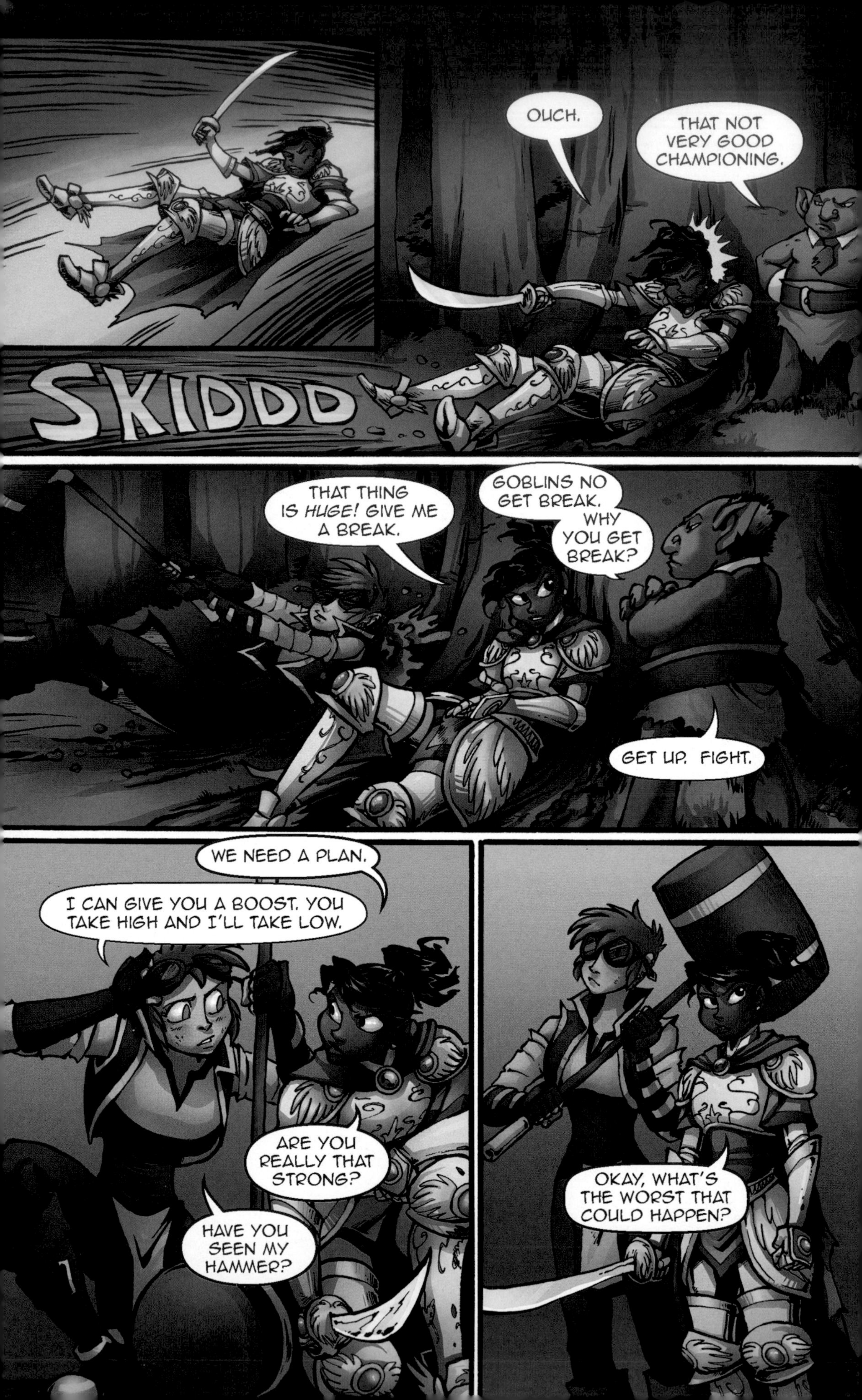
OUCH.
THAT NOT VERY GOOD CHAMPIONING.
SKIDDD
THAT THING IS *HUGE!* GIVE ME A BREAK.
GOBLINS NO GET BREAK.
WHY YOU GET BREAK?
GET UP. FIGHT.
WE NEED A PLAN.
I CAN GIVE YOU A BOOST. YOU TAKE HIGH AND I'LL TAKE LOW.
ARE YOU REALLY THAT STRONG?
HAVE YOU SEEN MY HAMMER?
OKAY, WHAT'S THE WORST THAT COULD HAPPEN?

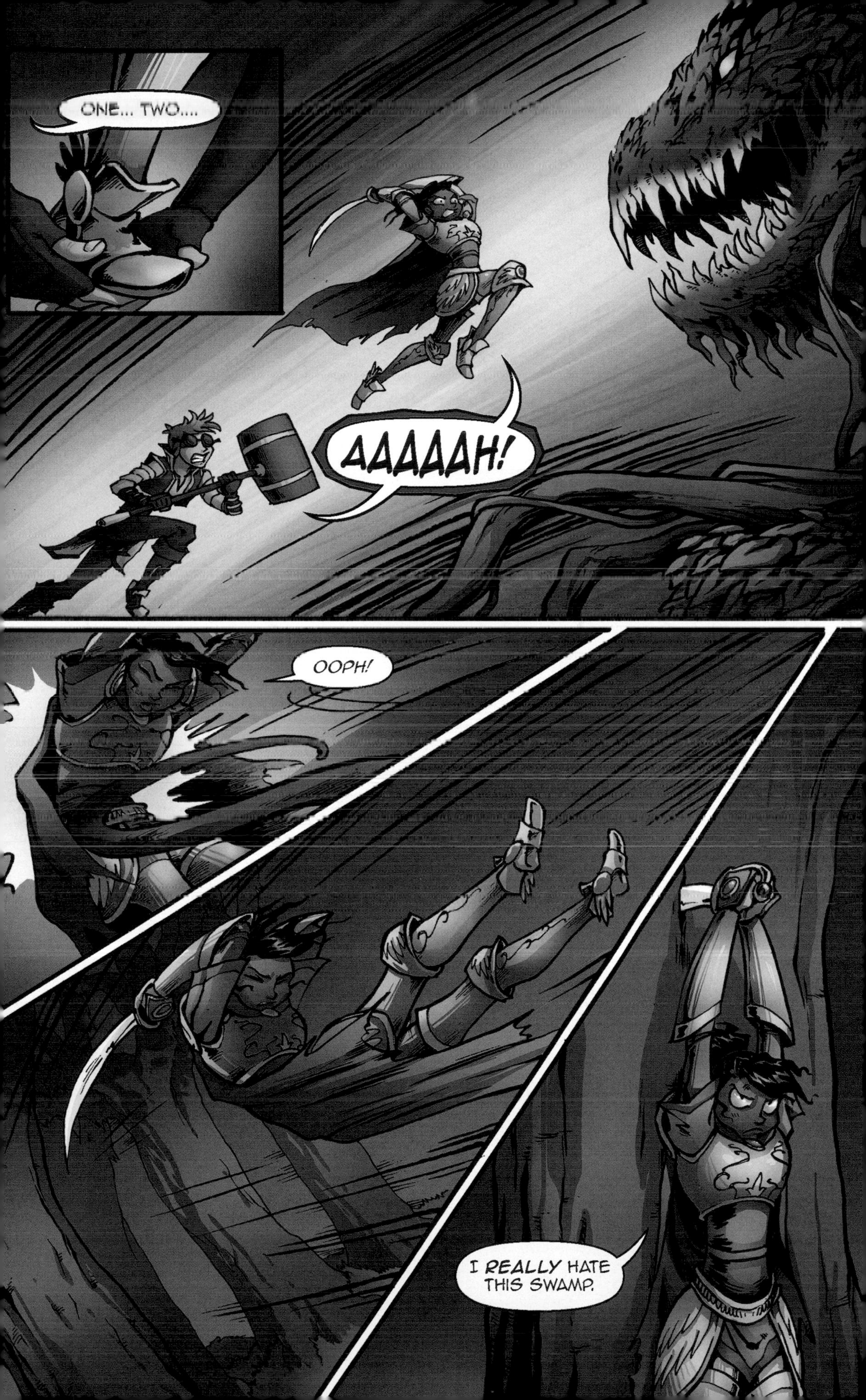
ONE... TWO....
AAAAAH!
OOPH!
I REALLY HATE THIS SWAMP.

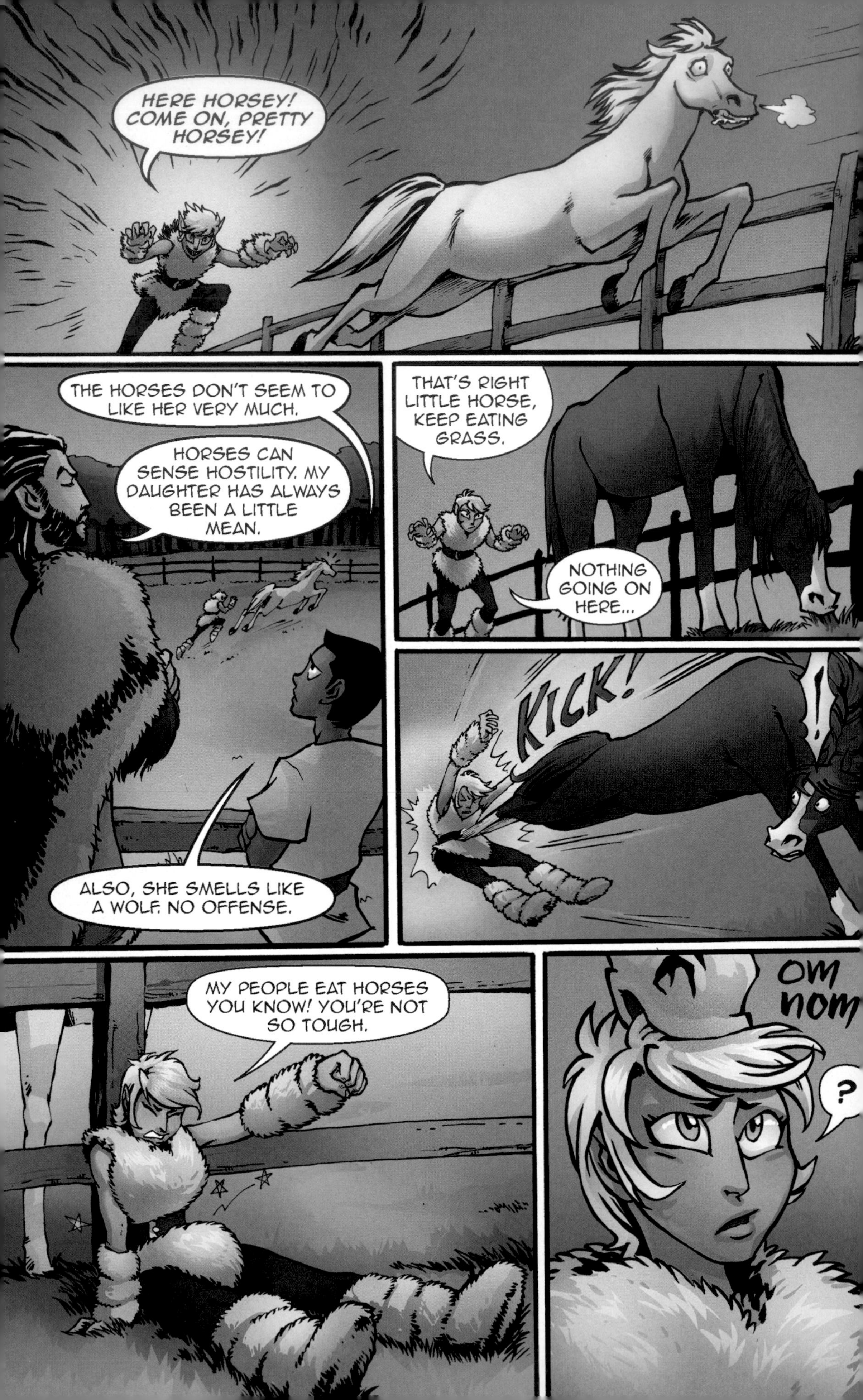
HERE HORSEY! COME ON, PRETTY HORSEY!
THE HORSES DON'T SEEM TO LIKE HER VERY MUCH.
HORSES CAN SENSE HOSTILITY. MY DAUGHTER HAS ALWAYS BEEN A LITTLE MEAN.
ALSO, SHE SMELLS LIKE A WOLF. NO OFFENSE.
THAT'S RIGHT LITTLE HORSE, KEEP EATING GRASS.
NOTHING GOING ON HERE...
KICK!
!
MY PEOPLE EAT HORSES YOU KNOW! YOU'RE NOT SO TOUGH.
om nom
?

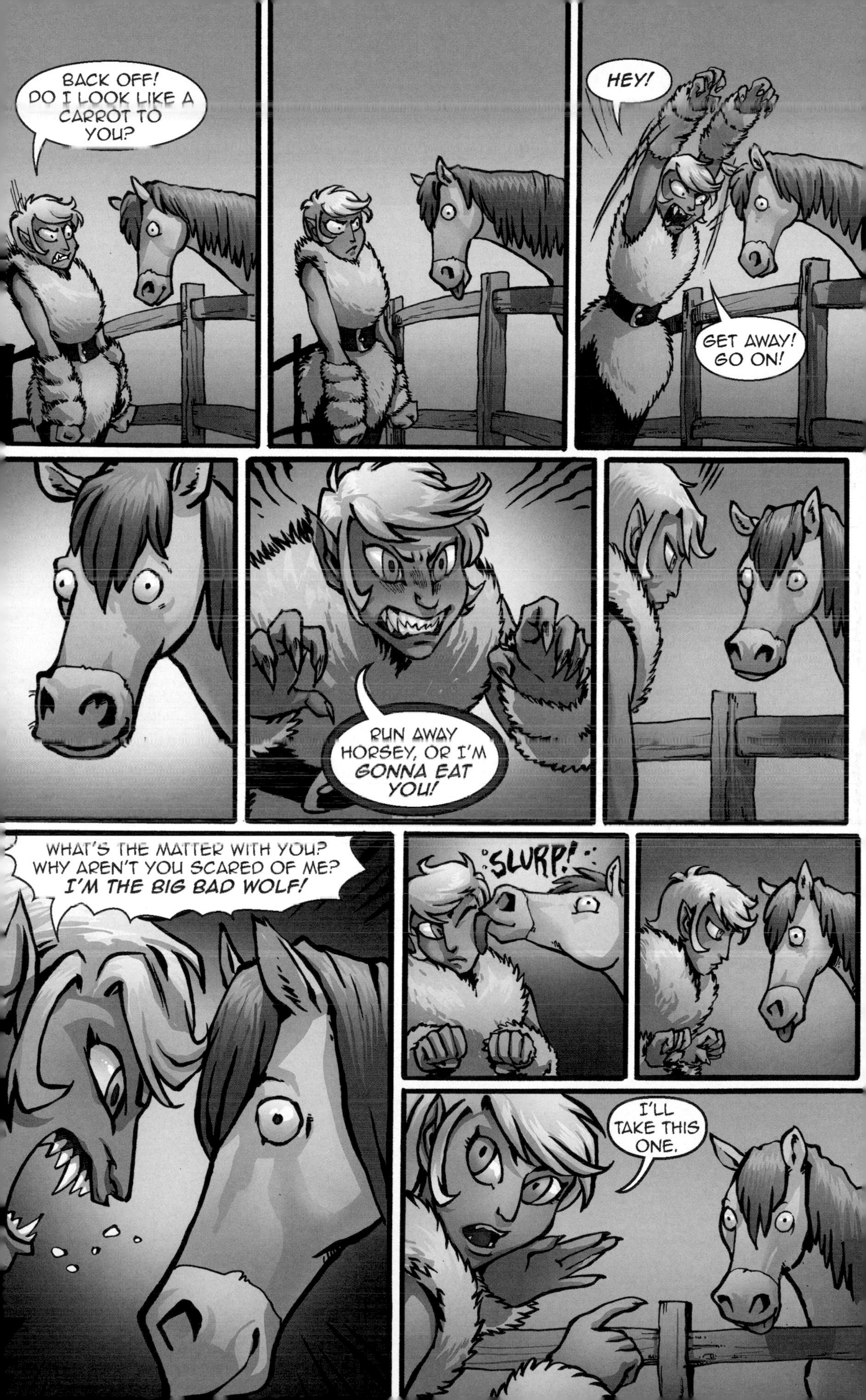
BACK OFF! DO I LOOK LIKE A CARROT TO YOU?
HEY!
GET AWAY! GO ON!
RUN AWAY HORSEY, OR I'M GONNA EAT YOU!
WHAT'S THE MATTER WITH YOU? WHY AREN'T YOU SCARED OF ME? I'M THE BIG BAD WOLF!
SLURP!
I'LL TAKE THIS ONE.

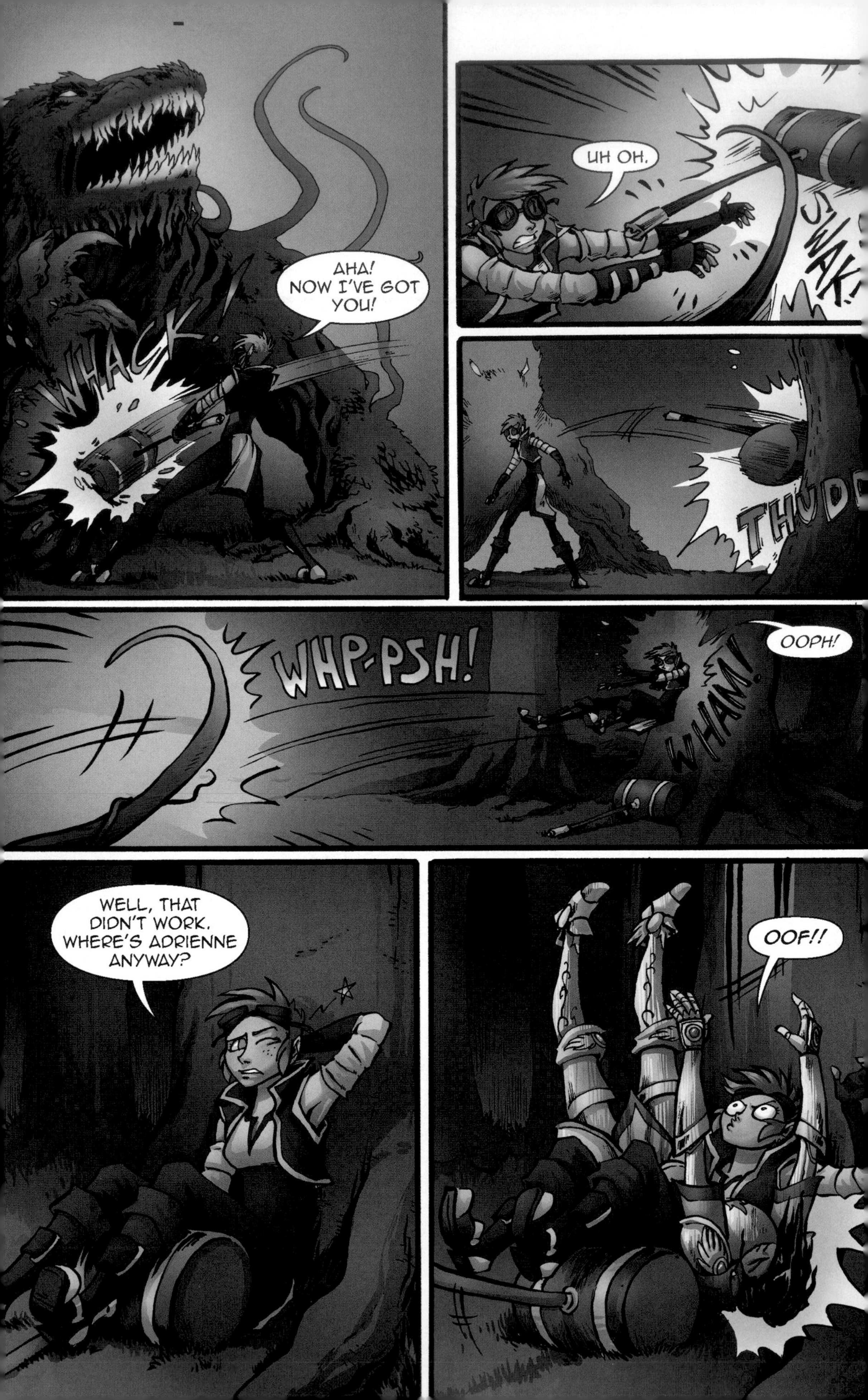
WHACK!
AHA! NOW I'VE GOT YOU!
UH OH.
SWAK!
THUD
WHP-PSH!
WHAM!
OOPH!
WELL, THAT DIDN'T WORK. WHERE'S ADRIENNE ANYWAY?
OOF!!

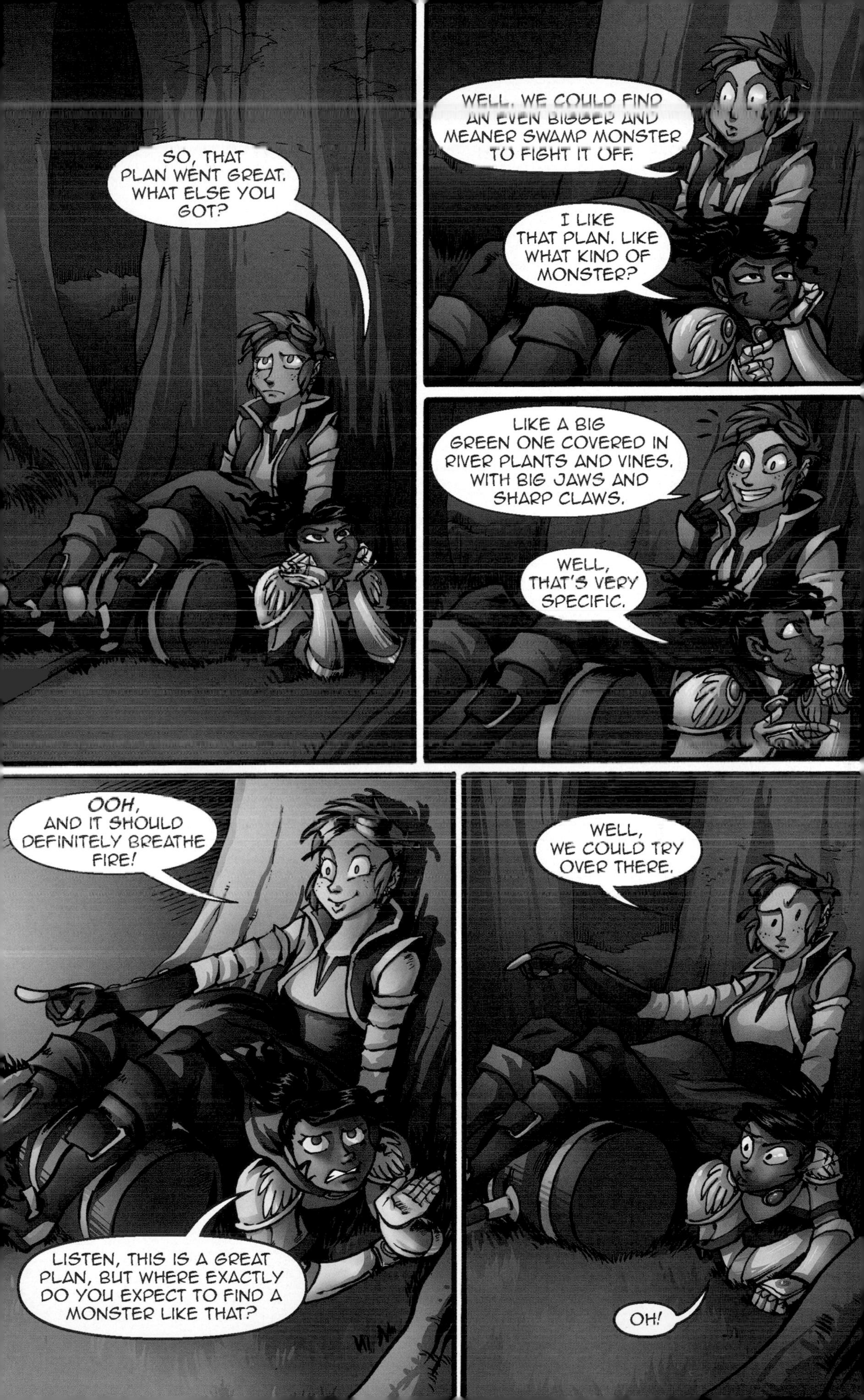
SO, THAT PLAN WENT GREAT. WHAT ELSE YOU GOT?
WELL, WE COULD FIND AN EVEN BIGGER AND MEANER SWAMP MONSTER TO FIGHT IT OFF.
I LIKE THAT PLAN. LIKE WHAT KIND OF MONSTER?
LIKE A BIG GREEN ONE COVERED IN RIVER PLANTS AND VINES. WITH BIG JAWS AND SHARP CLAWS.
WELL, THAT'S VERY SPECIFIC.
OOH, AND IT SHOULD DEFINITELY BREATHE FIRE!
LISTEN, THIS IS A GREAT PLAN, BUT WHERE EXACTLY DO YOU EXPECT TO FIND A MONSTER LIKE THAT?
WELL, WE COULD TRY OVER THERE.
OH!

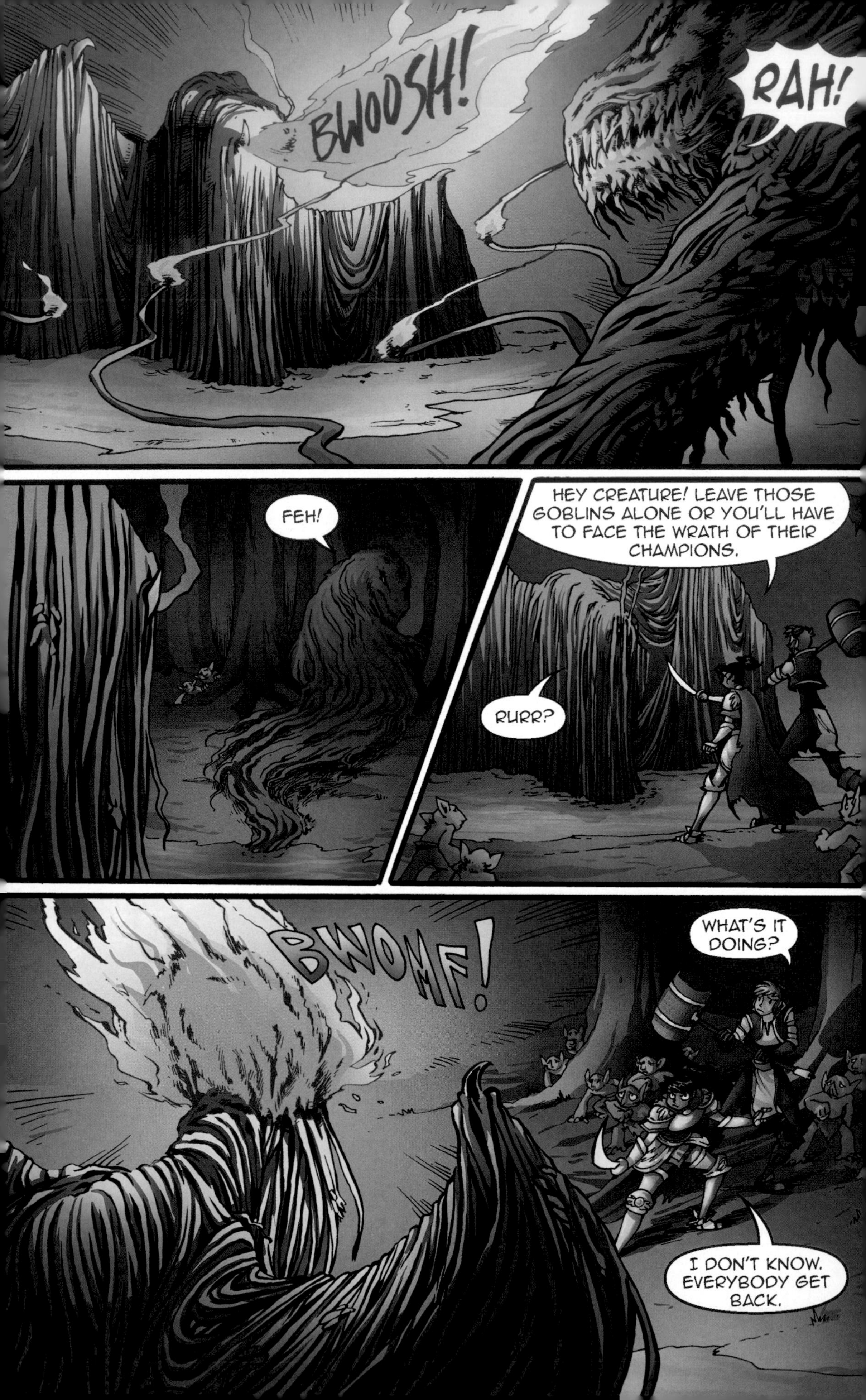
BWOOSH!
RAH!
FEH!
HEY CREATURE! LEAVE THOSE GOBLINS ALONE OR YOU'LL HAVE TO FACE THE WRATH OF THEIR CHAMPIONS.
RURR?
BWOMF!
WHAT'S IT DOING?
I DON'T KNOW. EVERYBODY GET BACK.

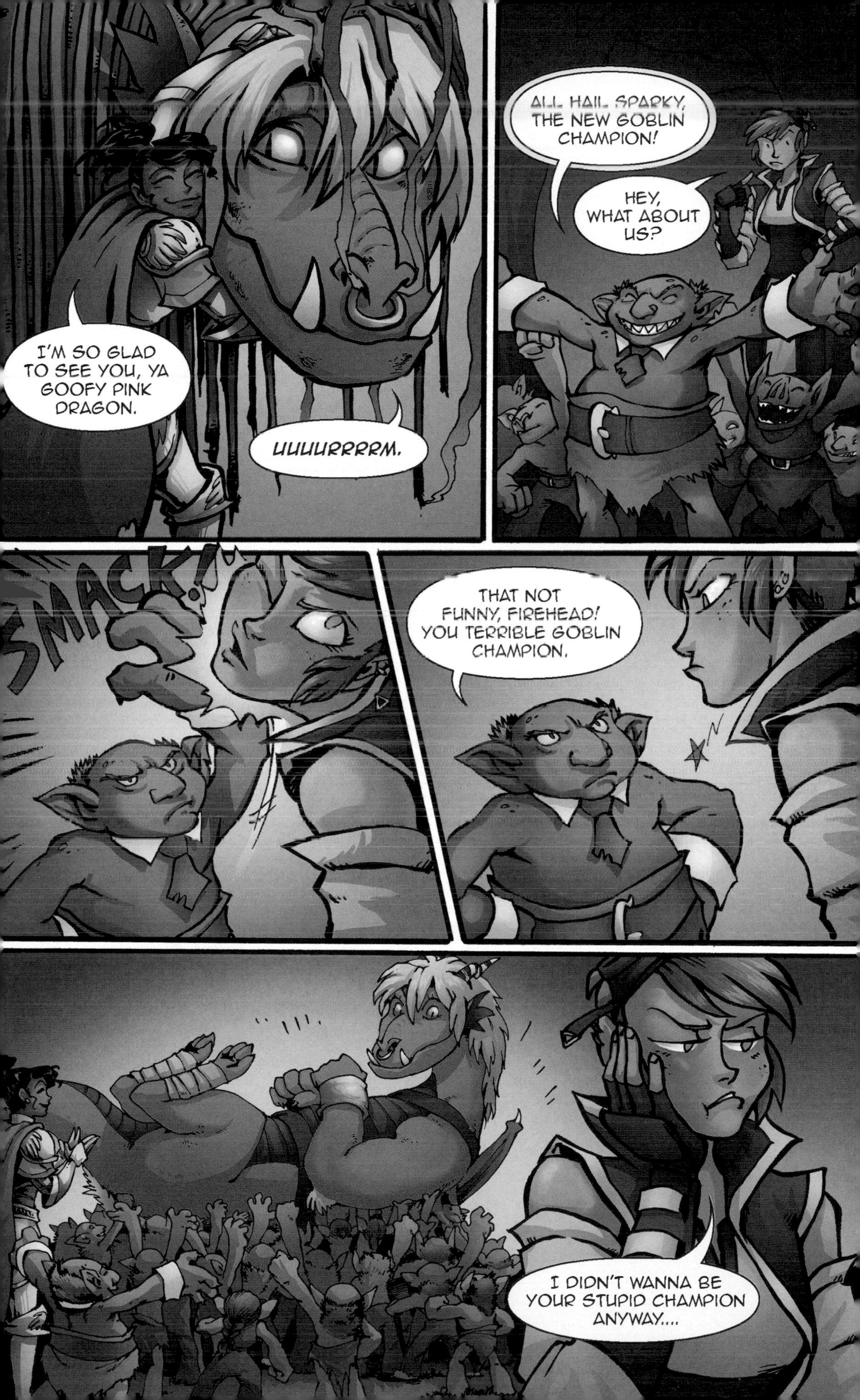

I'M SO GLAD TO SEE YOU, YA GOOFY PINK DRAGON.
UUUURRRRM.
ALL HAIL SPARKY, THE NEW GOBLIN CHAMPION!
HEY, WHAT ABOUT US?
SMACK!
THAT NOT FUNNY, FIREHEAD! YOU TERRIBLE GOBLIN CHAMPION.
I DIDN'T WANNA BE YOUR STUPID CHAMPION ANYWAY....

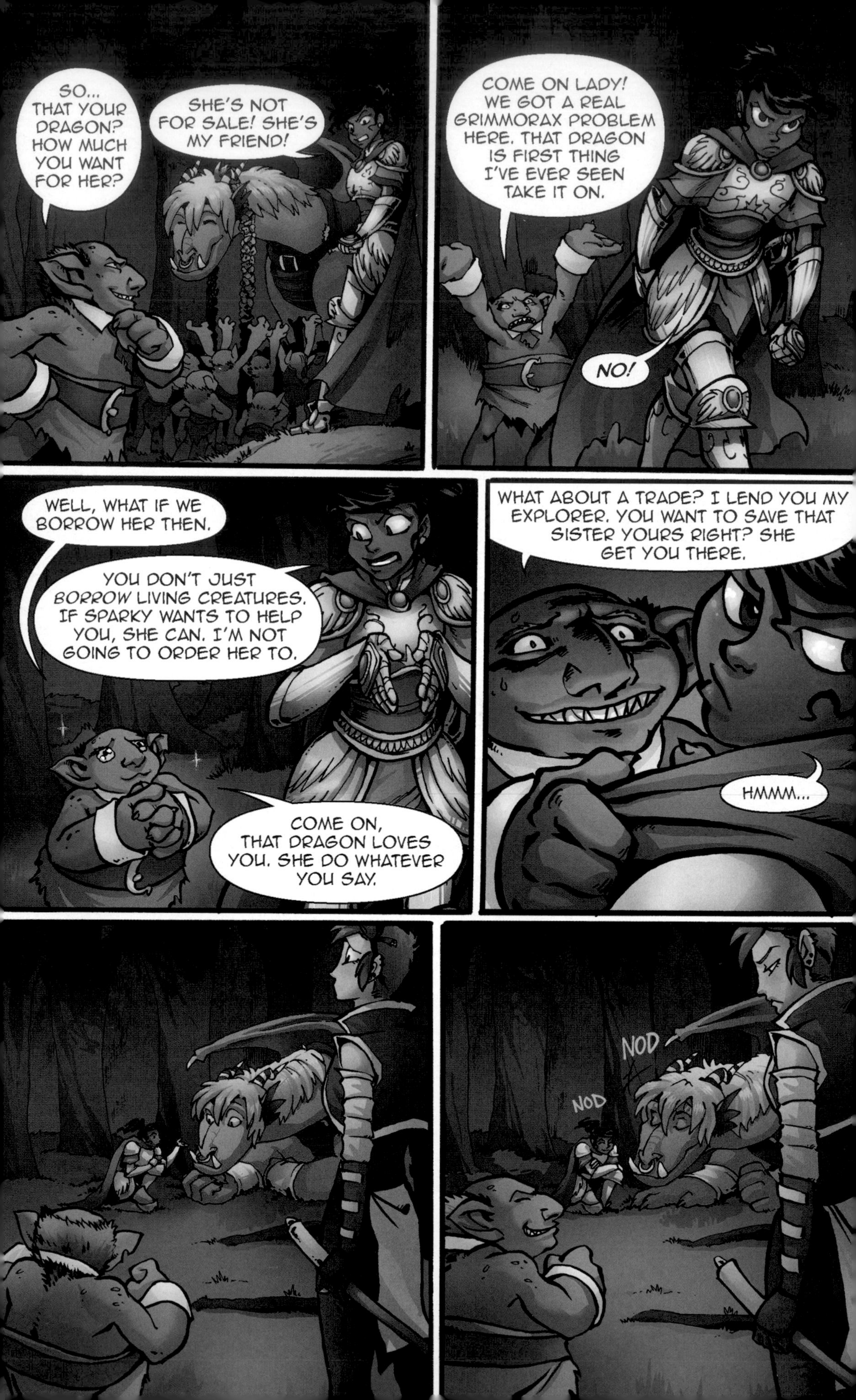

SO... THAT YOUR DRAGON? HOW MUCH YOU WANT FOR HER?
SHE'S NOT FOR SALE! SHE'S MY FRIEND!
COME ON LADY! WE GOT A REAL GRIMMORAX PROBLEM HERE. THAT DRAGON IS FIRST THING I'VE EVER SEEN TAKE IT ON.
NO!
WELL, WHAT IF WE BORROW HER THEN.
YOU DON'T JUST *BORROW* LIVING CREATURES. IF SPARKY WANTS TO HELP YOU, SHE CAN. I'M NOT GOING TO ORDER HER TO.
COME ON, THAT DRAGON LOVES YOU. SHE DO WHATEVER YOU SAY.
WHAT ABOUT A TRADE? I LEND YOU MY EXPLORER. YOU WANT TO SAVE THAT SISTER YOURS RIGHT? SHE GET YOU THERE.
HMMM...
NOD
NOD

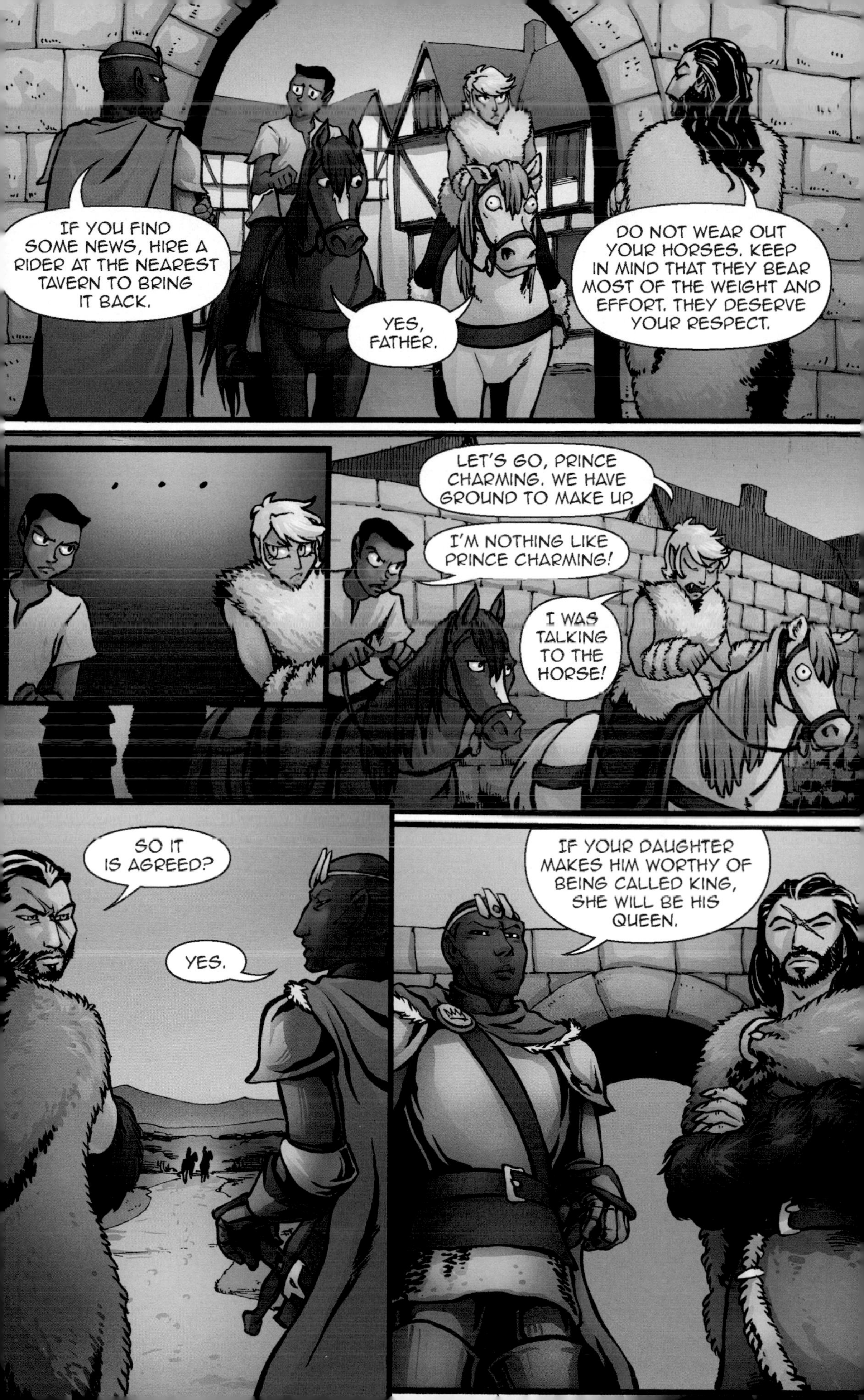
IF YOU FIND SOME NEWS, HIRE A RIDER AT THE NEAREST TAVERN TO BRING IT BACK.
YES, FATHER.
DO NOT WEAR OUT YOUR HORSES. KEEP IN MIND THAT THEY BEAR MOST OF THE WEIGHT AND EFFORT. THEY DESERVE YOUR RESPECT.
. . .
LET'S GO, PRINCE CHARMING. WE HAVE GROUND TO MAKE UP.
I'M NOTHING LIKE PRINCE CHARMING!
I WAS TALKING TO THE HORSE!
SO IT IS AGREED?
YES.
IF YOUR DAUGHTER MAKES HIM WORTHY OF BEING CALLED KING, SHE WILL BE HIS QUEEN.

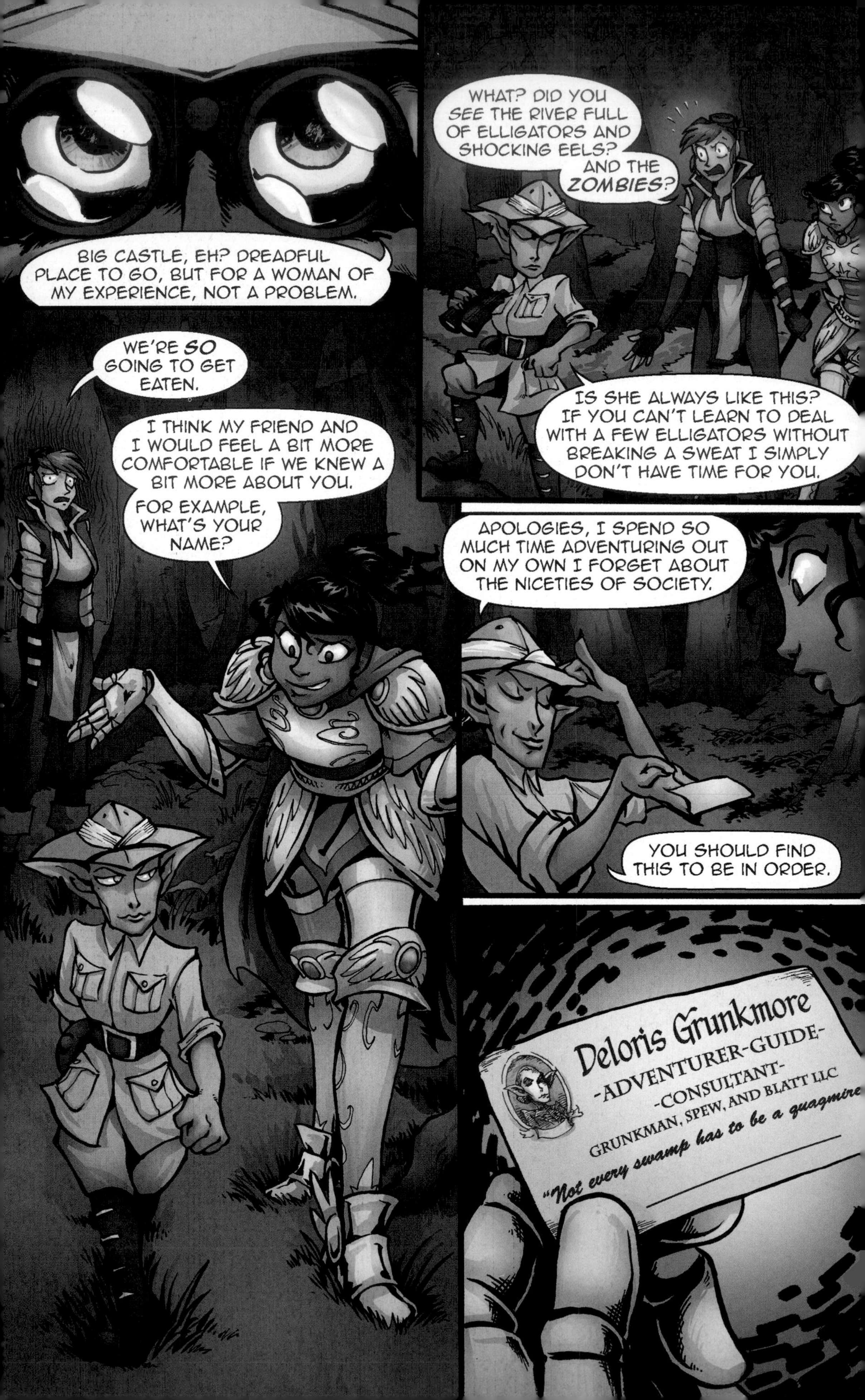
BIG CASTLE, EH? DREADFUL PLACE TO GO, BUT FOR A WOMAN OF MY EXPERIENCE, NOT A PROBLEM.
WE'RE SO GOING TO GET EATEN.
I THINK MY FRIEND AND I WOULD FEEL A BIT MORE COMFORTABLE IF WE KNEW A BIT MORE ABOUT YOU.
FOR EXAMPLE, WHAT'S YOUR NAME?
WHAT? DID YOU SEE THE RIVER FULL OF ELLIGATORS AND SHOCKING EELS?
AND THE ZOMBIES?
IS SHE ALWAYS LIKE THIS? IF YOU CAN'T LEARN TO DEAL WITH A FEW ELLIGATORS WITHOUT BREAKING A SWEAT I SIMPLY DON'T HAVE TIME FOR YOU.
APOLOGIES, I SPEND SO MUCH TIME ADVENTURING OUT ON MY OWN I FORGET ABOUT THE NICETIES OF SOCIETY.
YOU SHOULD FIND THIS TO BE IN ORDER.
Deloris Grunkmore
-ADVENTURER-GUIDE-
-CONSULTANT-
GRUNKMAN, SPEW, AND BLATT LLC
"Not every swamp has to be a quagmire

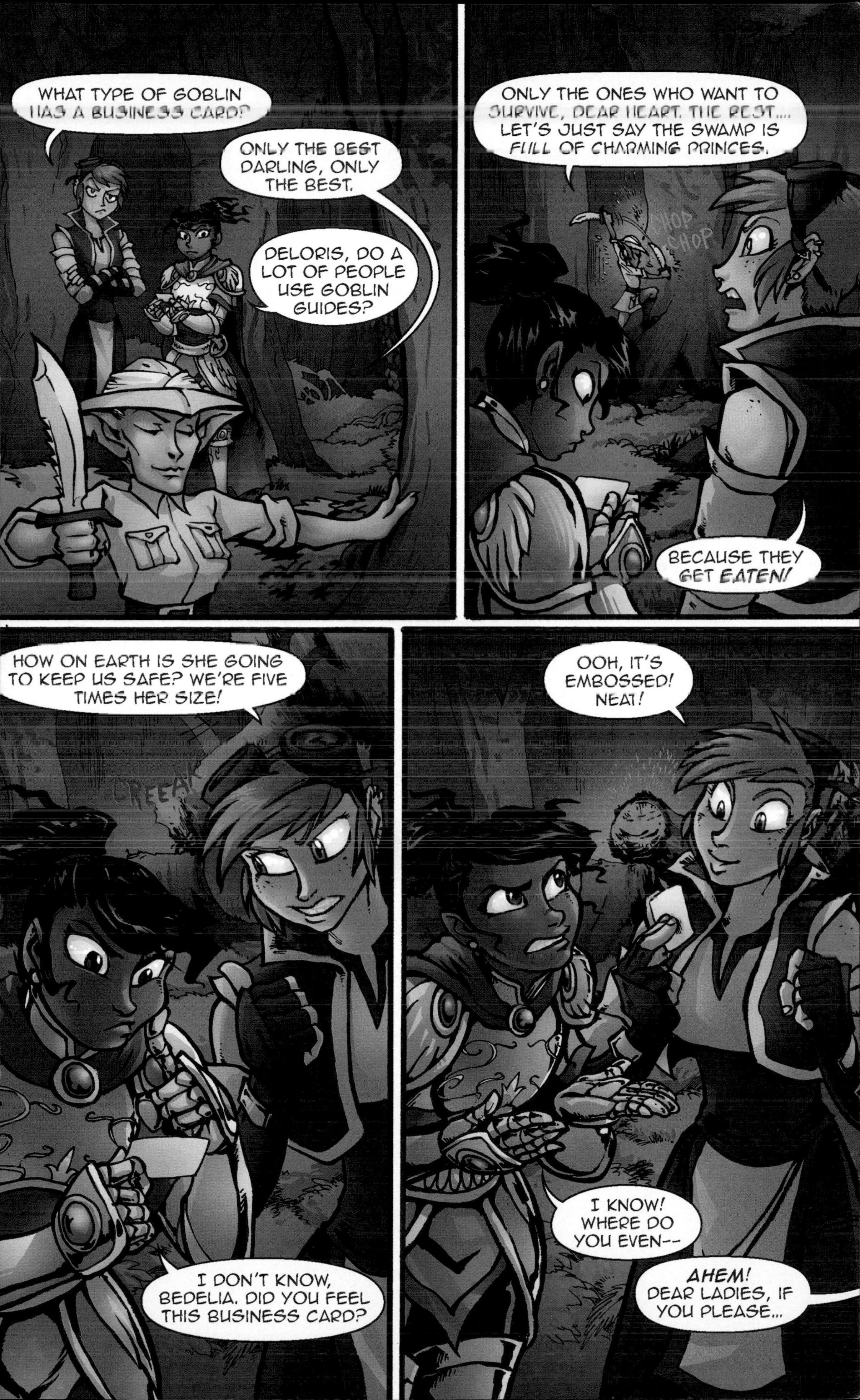

WHAT TYPE OF GOBLIN HAS A BUSINESS CARD?
ONLY THE BEST DARLING, ONLY THE BEST.
DELORIS, DO A LOT OF PEOPLE USE GOBLIN GUIDES?
ONLY THE ONES WHO WANT TO SURVIVE, DEAR HEART. THE REST.... LET'S JUST SAY THE SWAMP IS FULL OF CHARMING PRINCES.
CHOP CHOP
BECAUSE THEY GET EATEN!
HOW ON EARTH IS SHE GOING TO KEEP US SAFE? WE'RE FIVE TIMES HER SIZE!
CREEAK
I DON'T KNOW, BEDELIA. DID YOU FEEL THIS BUSINESS CARD?
OOH, IT'S EMBOSSED! NEAT!
I KNOW! WHERE DO YOU EVEN--
AHEM! DEAR LADIES, IF YOU PLEASE...

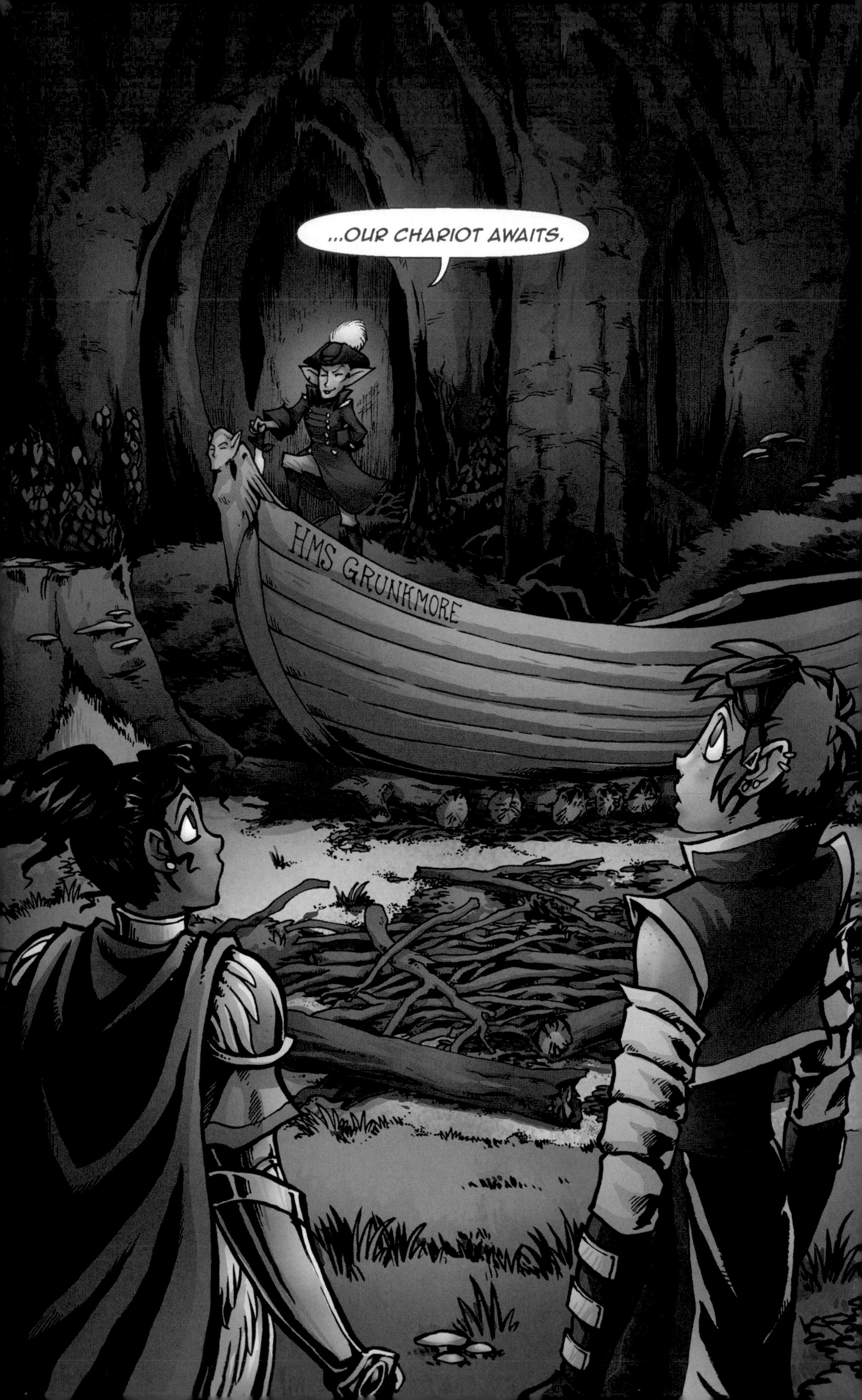
...OUR CHARIOT AWAITS.
HMS GRUNKMORE

3: Of Swamps and Quagmires

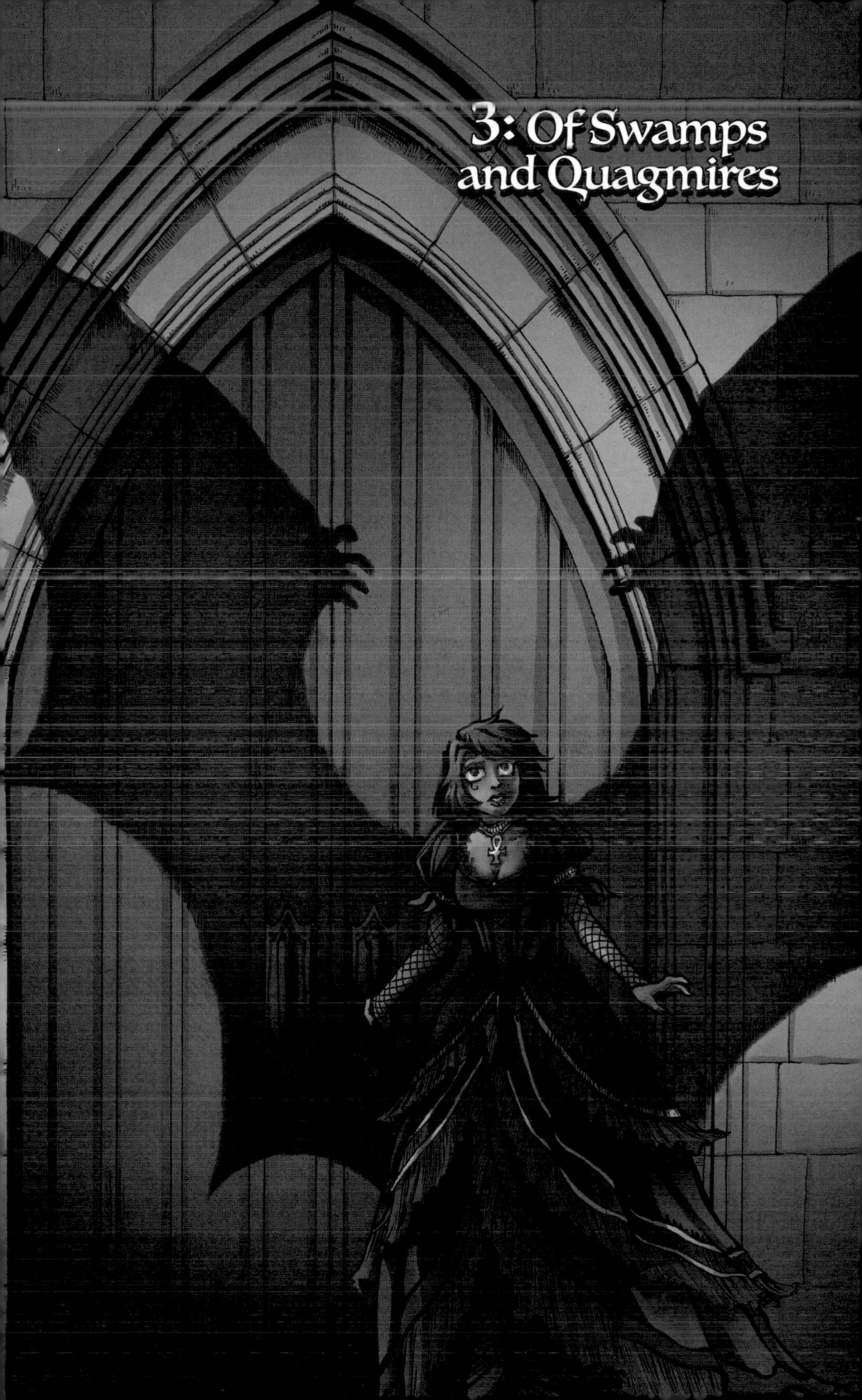

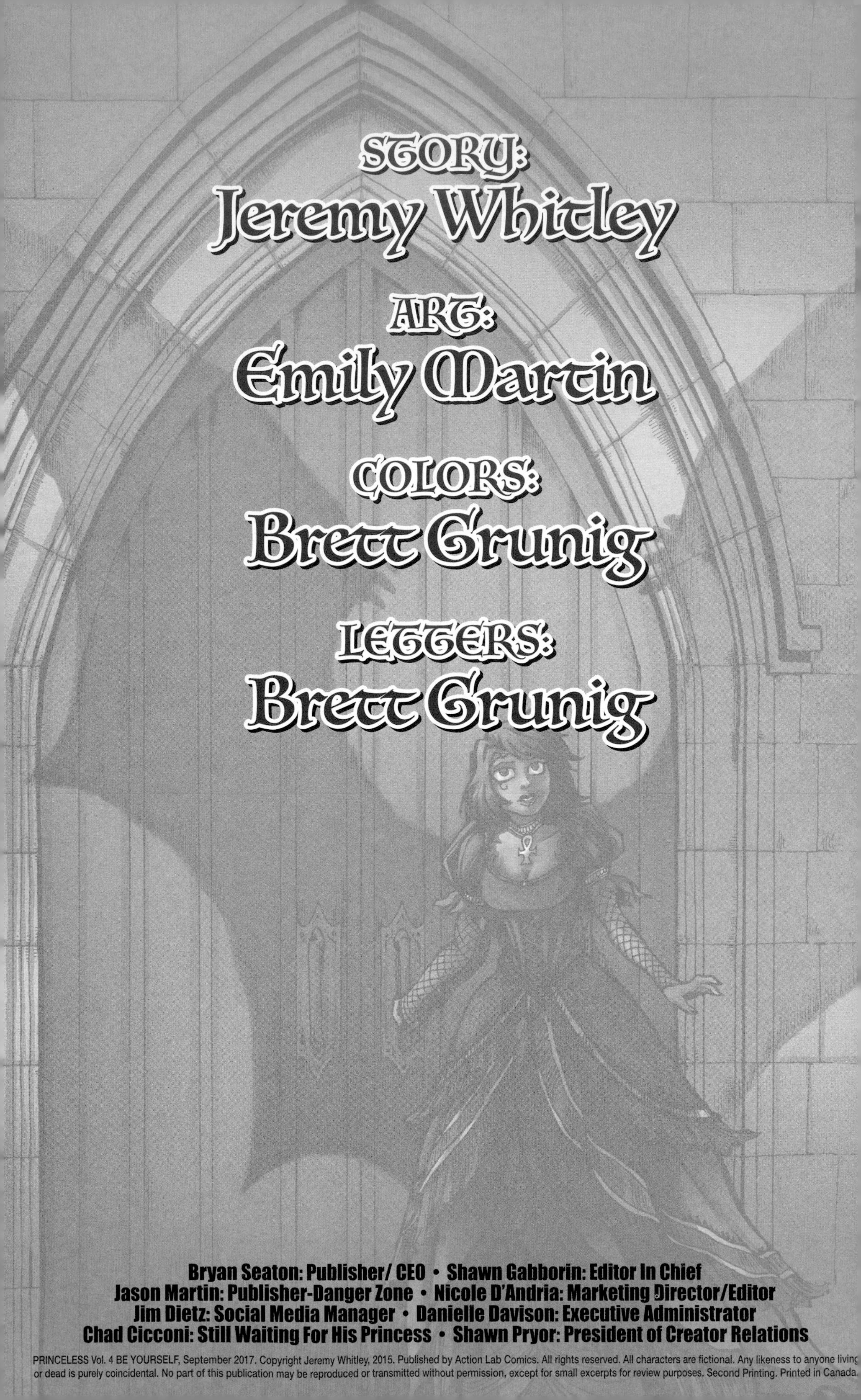

STORY:
Jeremy Whitley

ART:
Emily Martin

COLORS:
Brett Grunig

LETTERS:
Brett Grunig

Bryan Seaton: Publisher/ CEO • Shawn Gabborin: Editor In Chief
Jason Martin: Publisher-Danger Zone • Nicole D'Andria: Marketing Director/Editor
Jim Dietz: Social Media Manager • Danielle Davison: Executive Administrator
Chad Cicconi: Still Waiting For His Princess • Shawn Pryor: President of Creator Relations

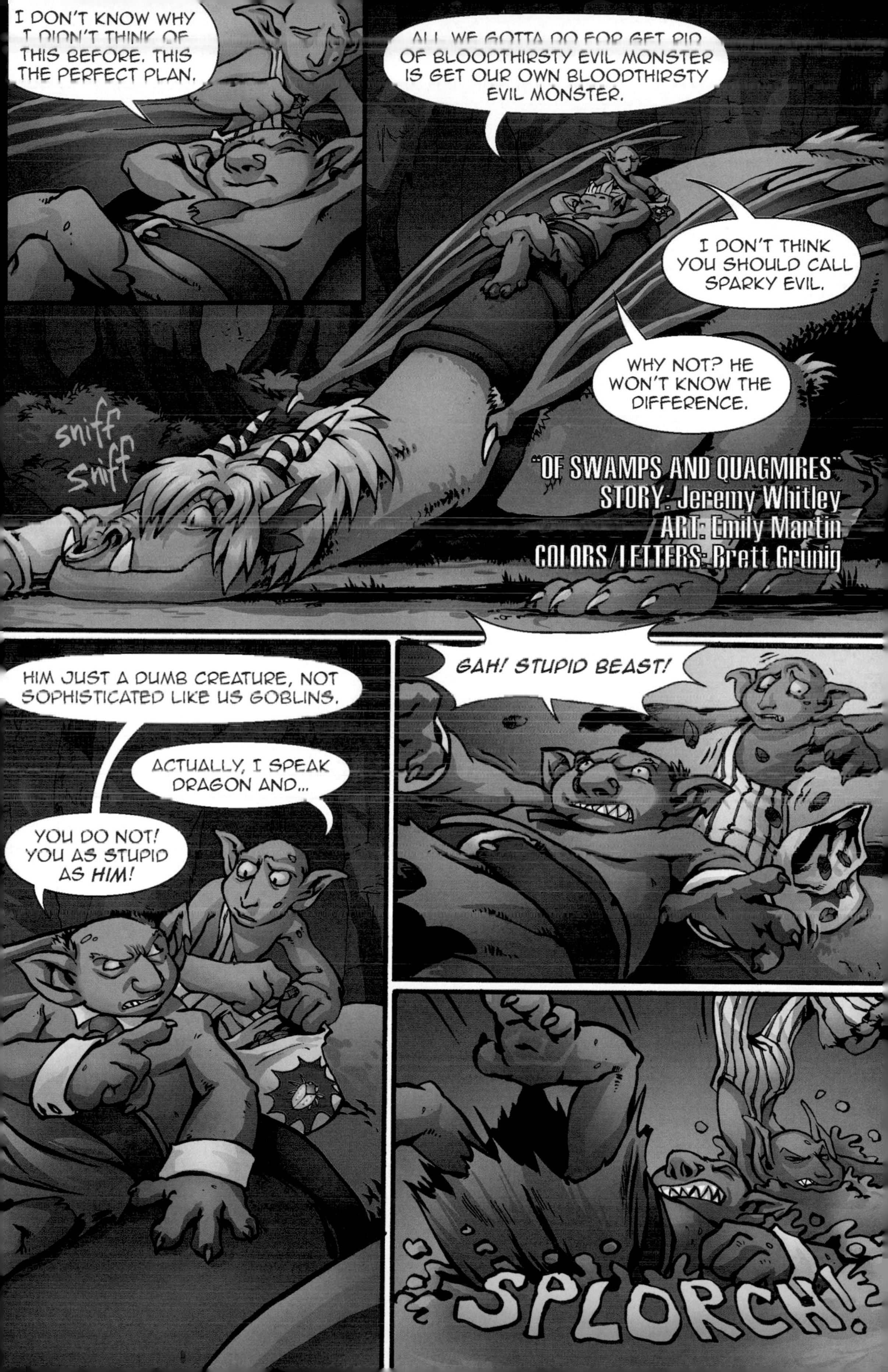
I DON'T KNOW WHY I DIDN'T THINK OF THIS BEFORE. THIS THE PERFECT PLAN.
ALL WE GOTTA DO FOR GET RID OF BLOODTHIRSTY EVIL MONSTER IS GET OUR OWN BLOODTHIRSTY EVIL MONSTER.
I DON'T THINK YOU SHOULD CALL SPARKY EVIL.
WHY NOT? HE WON'T KNOW THE DIFFERENCE.
sniff sniff
"OF SWAMPS AND QUAGMIRES"
STORY: Jeremy Whitley
ART: Emily Martin
COLORS/LETTERS: Brett Grunig
HIM JUST A DUMB CREATURE, NOT SOPHISTICATED LIKE US GOBLINS.
ACTUALLY, I SPEAK DRAGON AND...
YOU DO NOT! YOU AS STUPID AS HIM!
GAH! STUPID BEAST!
SPLORCH!

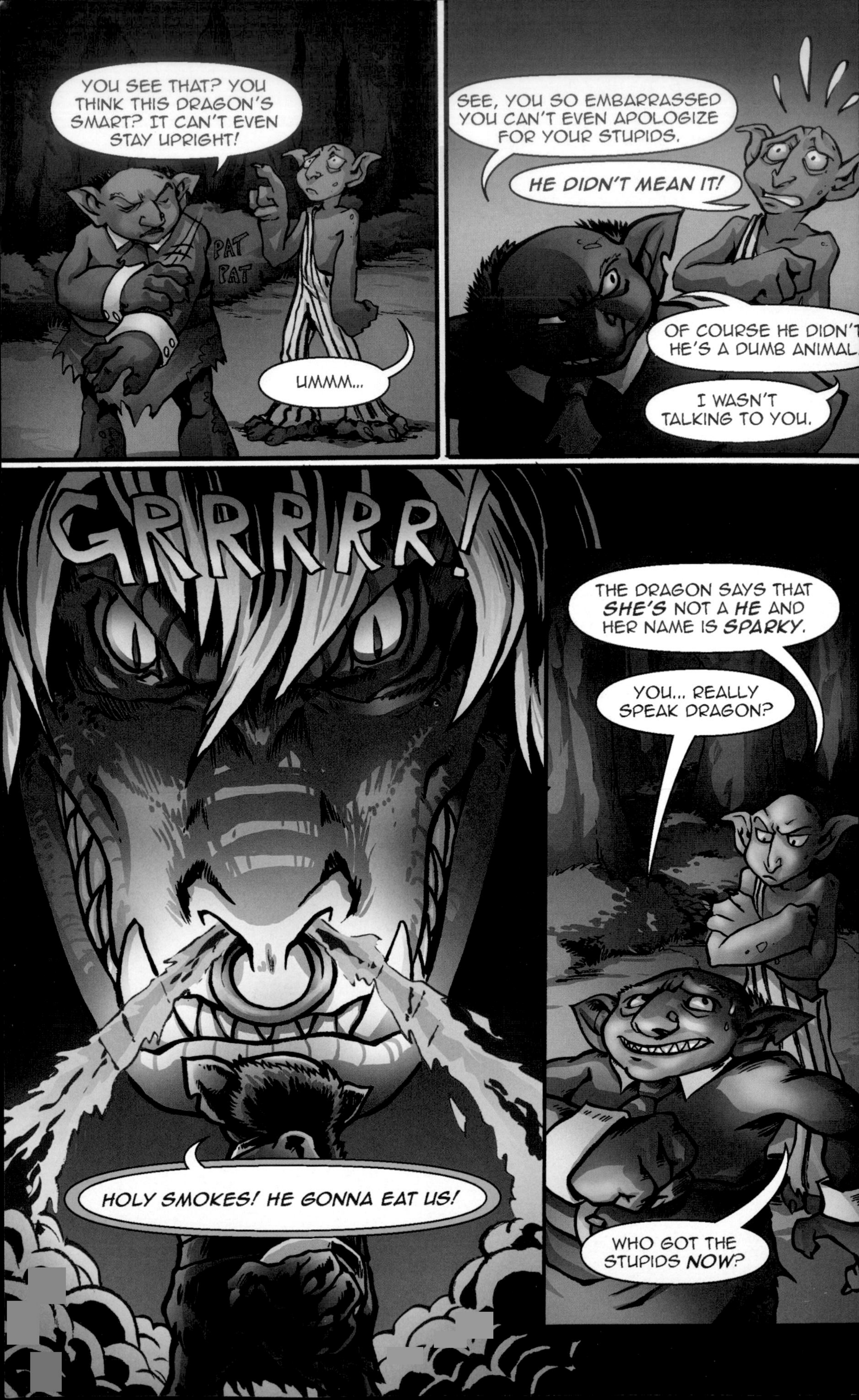
YOU SEE THAT? YOU THINK THIS DRAGON'S SMART? IT CAN'T EVEN STAY UPRIGHT!
PAT PAT
UMMM...
SEE, YOU SO EMBARRASSED YOU CAN'T EVEN APOLOGIZE FOR YOUR STUPIDS.
HE DIDN'T MEAN IT!
OF COURSE HE DIDN'T HE'S A DUMB ANIMAL.
I WASN'T TALKING TO YOU.
GRRRRR!
HOLY SMOKES! HE GONNA EAT US!
THE DRAGON SAYS THAT SHE'S NOT A HE AND HER NAME IS SPARKY.
YOU... REALLY SPEAK DRAGON?
WHO GOT THE STUPIDS NOW?

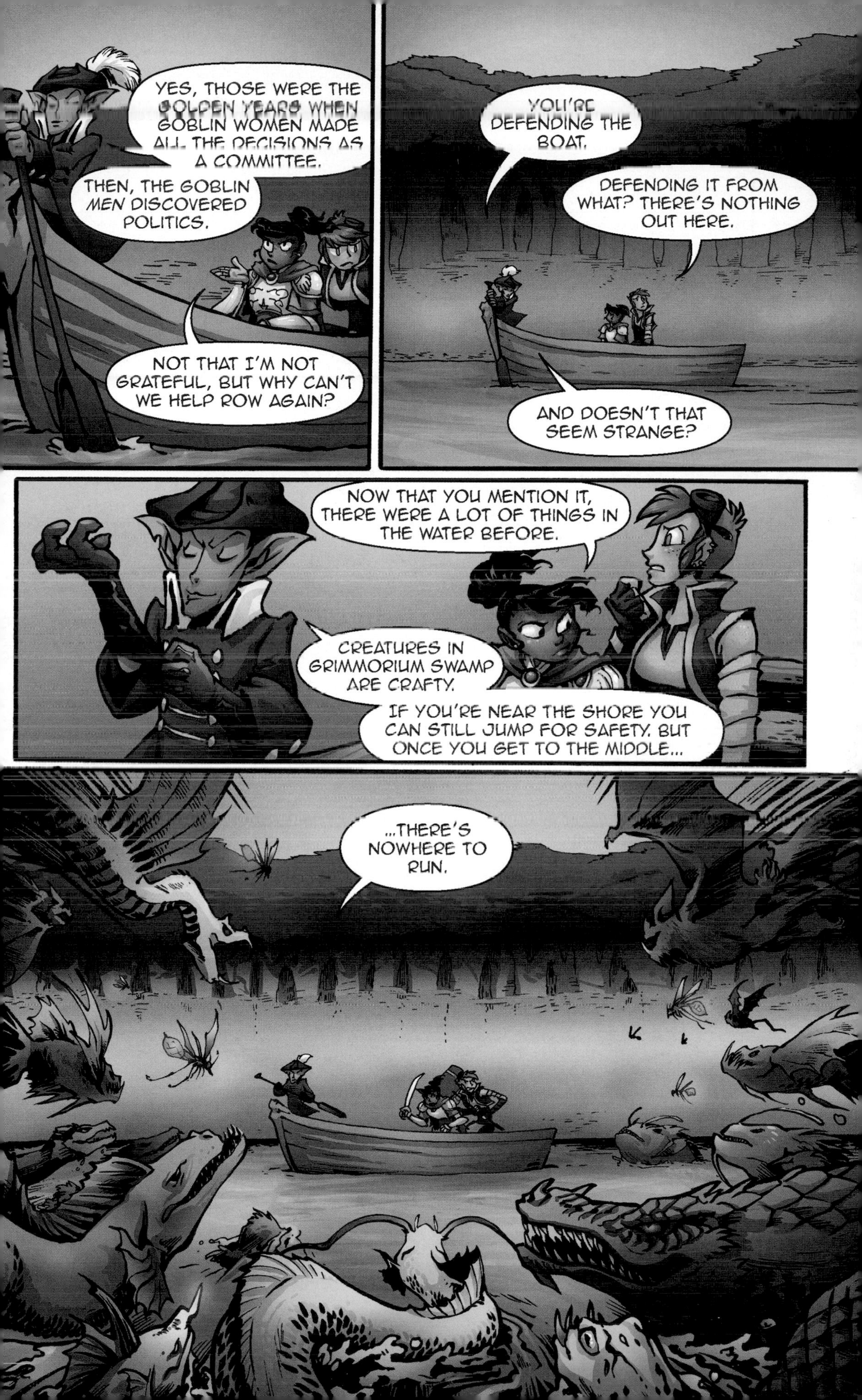
YES, THOSE WERE THE GOLDEN YEARS WHEN GOBLIN WOMEN MADE ALL THE DECISIONS AS A COMMITTEE.
THEN, THE GOBLIN MEN DISCOVERED POLITICS.
NOT THAT I'M NOT GRATEFUL, BUT WHY CAN'T WE HELP ROW AGAIN?
YOU'RE DEFENDING THE BOAT.
DEFENDING IT FROM WHAT? THERE'S NOTHING OUT HERE.
AND DOESN'T THAT SEEM STRANGE?
NOW THAT YOU MENTION IT, THERE WERE A LOT OF THINGS IN THE WATER BEFORE.
CREATURES IN GRIMMORIUM SWAMP ARE CRAFTY.
IF YOU'RE NEAR THE SHORE YOU CAN STILL JUMP FOR SAFETY. BUT ONCE YOU GET TO THE MIDDLE...
...THERE'S NOWHERE TO RUN.

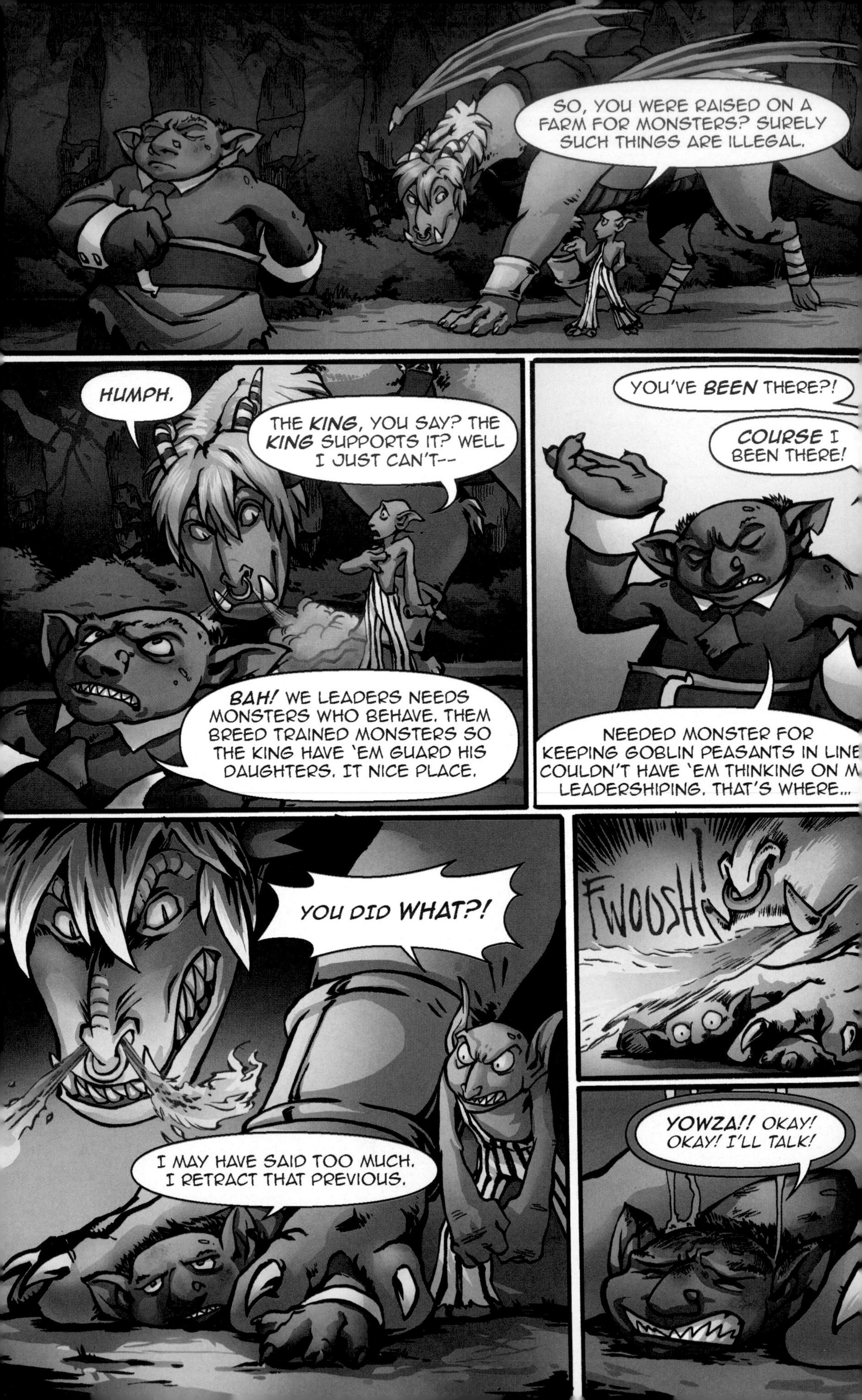
SO, YOU WERE RAISED ON A FARM FOR MONSTERS? SURELY SUCH THINGS ARE ILLEGAL.
HUMPH.
BAH! WE LEADERS NEEDS MONSTERS WHO BEHAVE. THEM BREED TRAINED MONSTERS SO THE KING HAVE 'EM GUARD HIS DAUGHTERS. IT NICE PLACE.
THE KING, YOU SAY? THE KING SUPPORTS IT? WELL I JUST CAN'T--
YOU'VE BEEN THERE?!
COURSE I BEEN THERE!
NEEDED MONSTER FOR KEEPING GOBLIN PEASANTS IN LINE COULDN'T HAVE 'EM THINKING ON M LEADERSHIPING. THAT'S WHERE...
YOU DID WHAT?!
I MAY HAVE SAID TOO MUCH. I RETRACT THAT PREVIOUS.
FWOOSH!
YOWZA!! OKAY! OKAY! I'LL TALK!

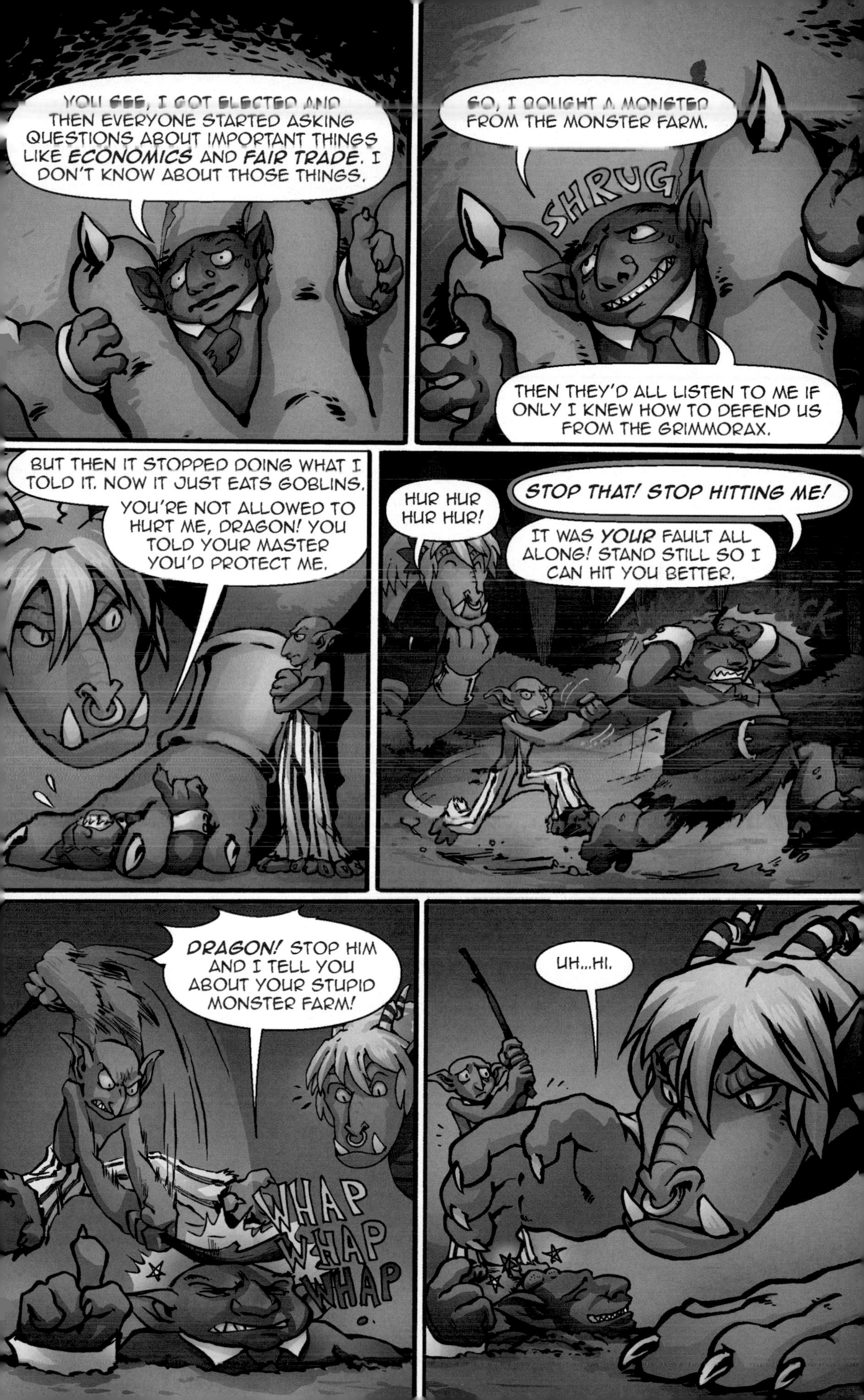
YOU SEE, I GOT ELECTED AND THEN EVERYONE STARTED ASKING QUESTIONS ABOUT IMPORTANT THINGS LIKE *ECONOMICS* AND *FAIR TRADE*. I DON'T KNOW ABOUT THOSE THINGS.
SO, I BOUGHT A MONSTER FROM THE MONSTER FARM.
SHRUG
THEN THEY'D ALL LISTEN TO ME IF ONLY I KNEW HOW TO DEFEND US FROM THE GRIMMORAX.
BUT THEN IT STOPPED DOING WHAT I TOLD IT. NOW IT JUST EATS GOBLINS.
YOU'RE NOT ALLOWED TO HURT ME, DRAGON! YOU TOLD YOUR MASTER YOU'D PROTECT ME.
HUR HUR HUR HUR!
STOP THAT! STOP HITTING ME!
IT WAS *YOUR* FAULT ALL ALONG! STAND STILL SO I CAN HIT YOU BETTER.
DRAGON! STOP HIM AND I TELL YOU ABOUT YOUR STUPID MONSTER FARM!
WHAP
WHAP
WHAP
UH...HI.

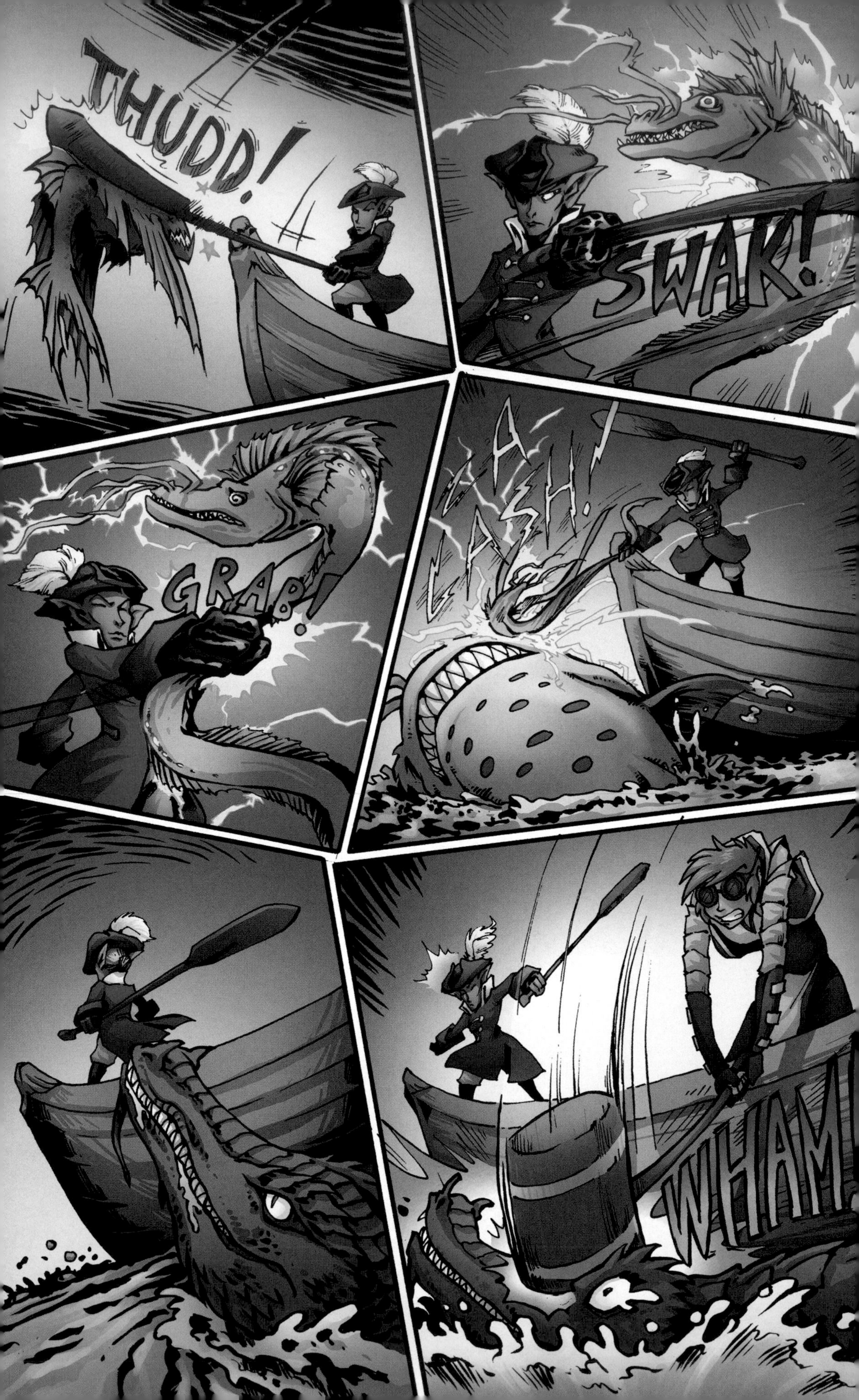
THUDD!
SWAK!
GRAB!
WHAM

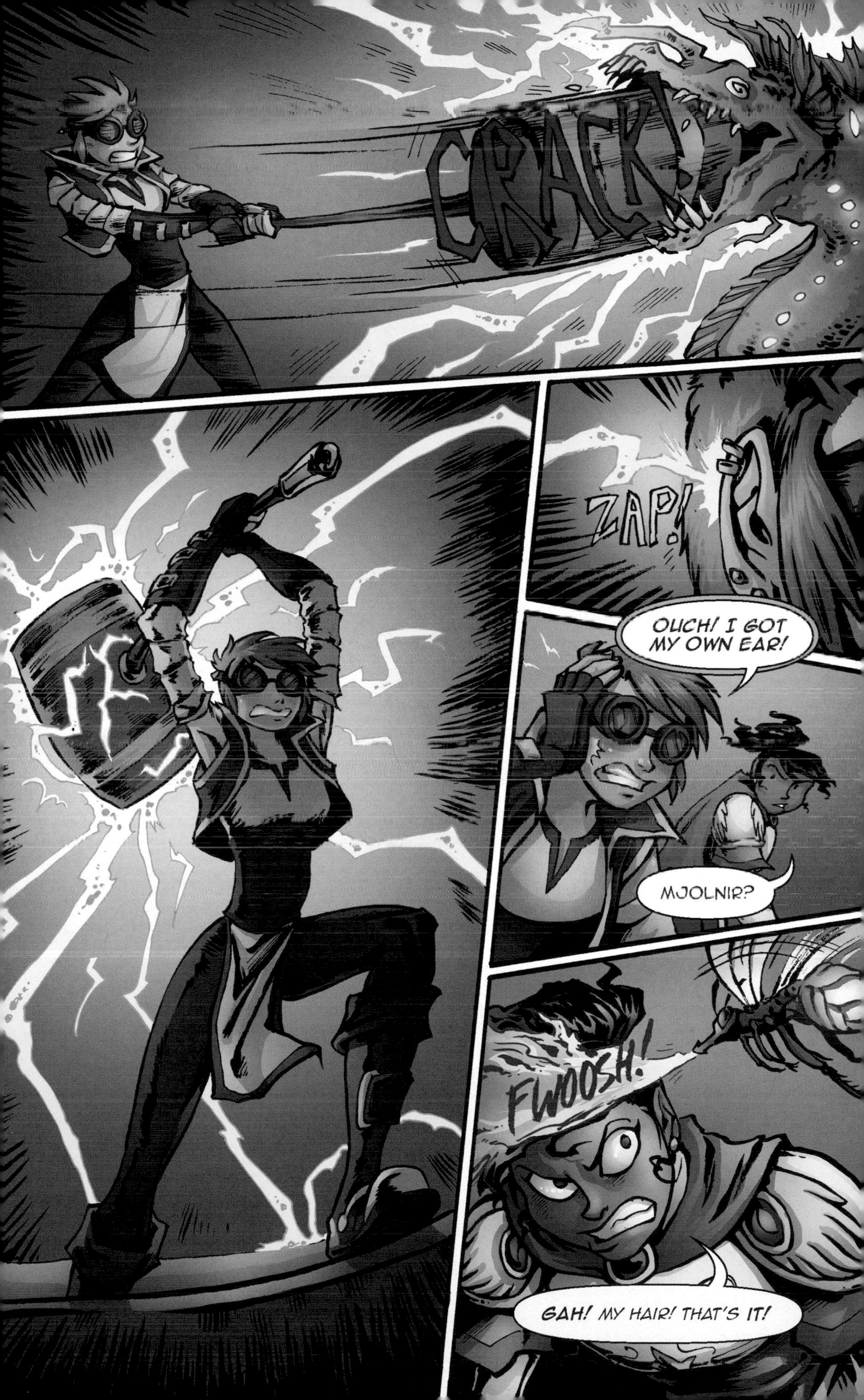
CRACK!
ZAP!
OUCH! I GOT MY OWN EAR!
MJOLNIR?
FWOOSH!
GAH! MY HAIR! THAT'S IT!

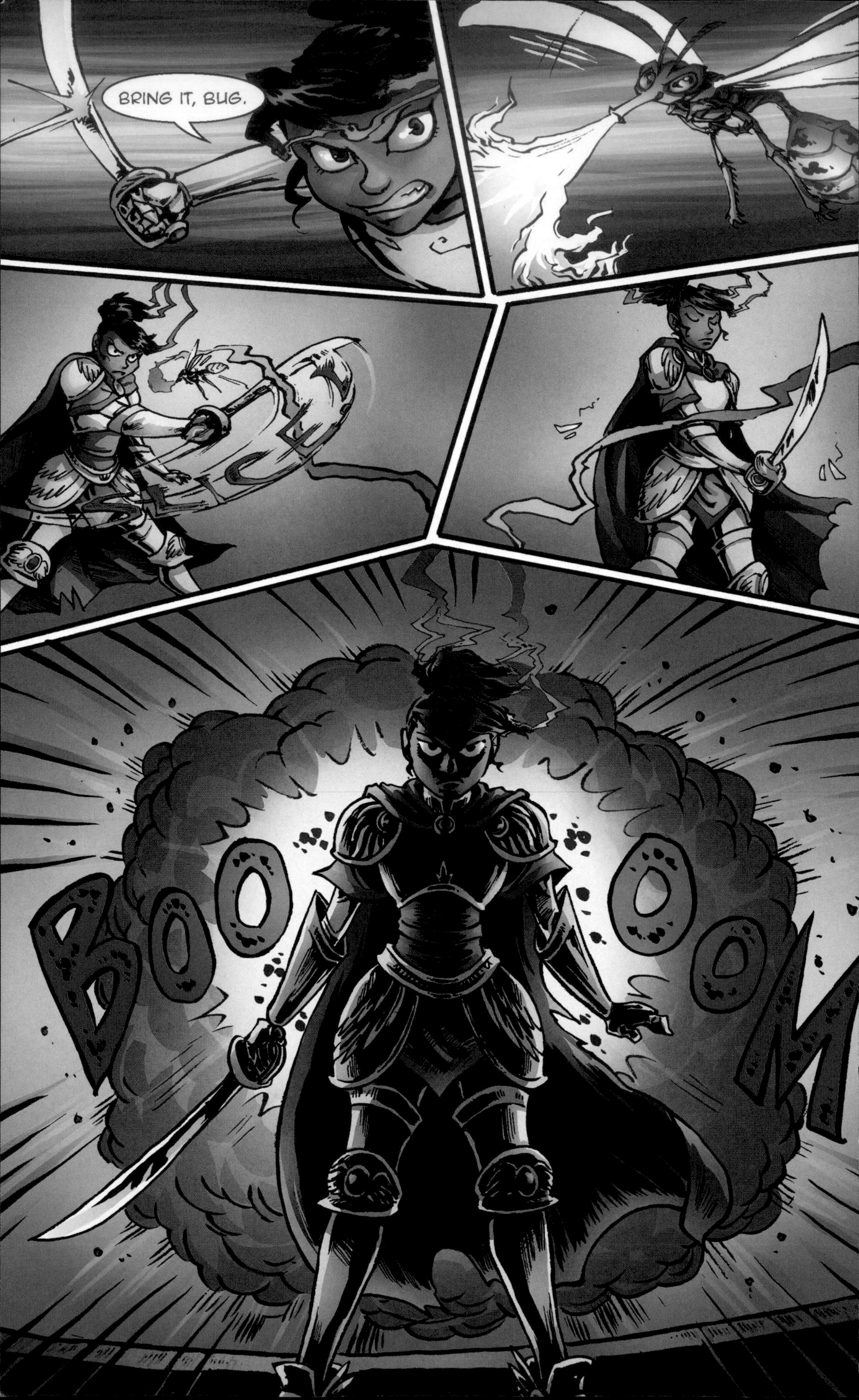
BRING IT, BUG.
BOOOOM

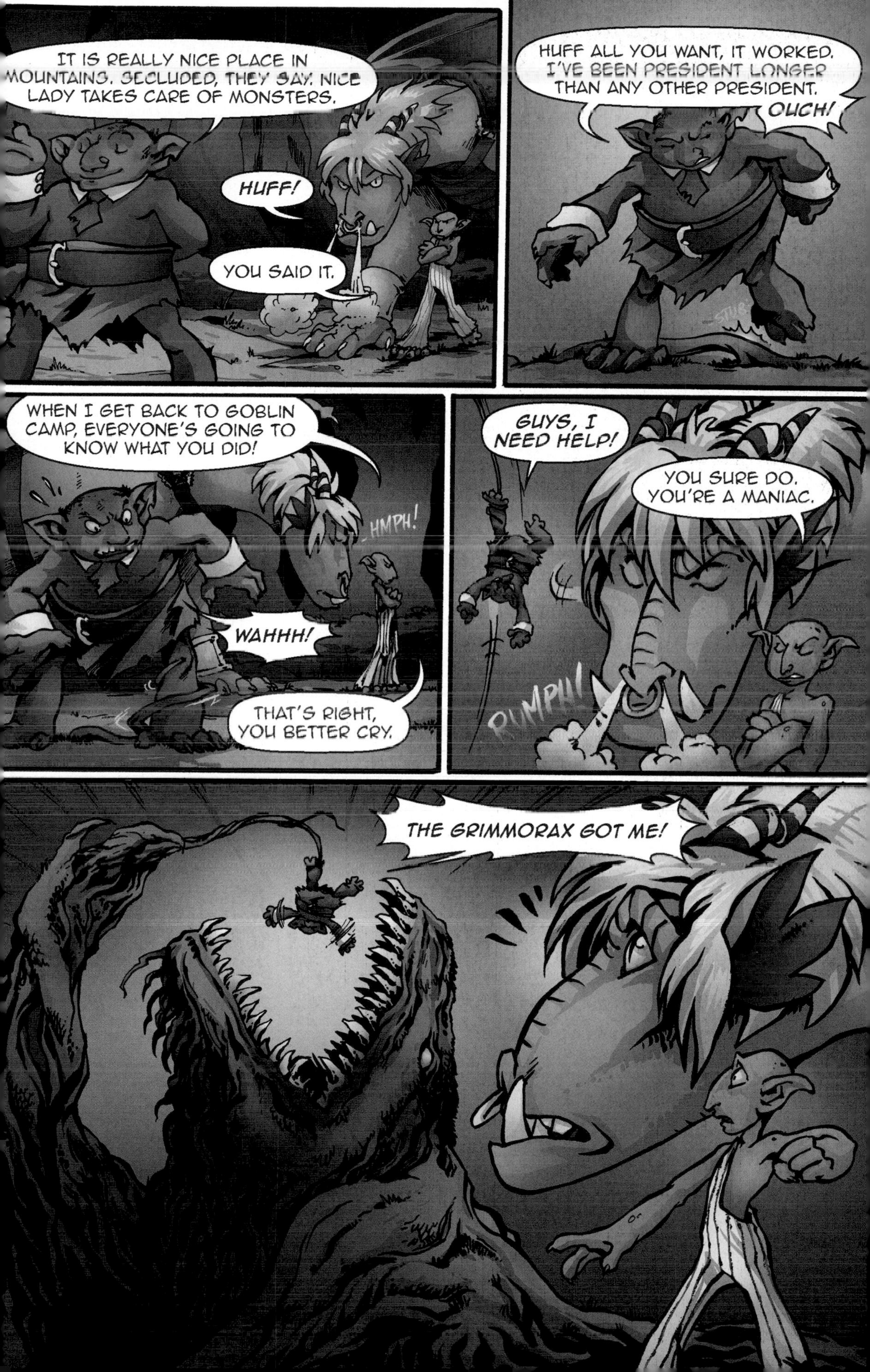
IT IS REALLY NICE PLACE IN MOUNTAINS. SECLUDED, THEY SAY. NICE LADY TAKES CARE OF MONSTERS.
HUFF!
YOU SAID IT.
HUFF ALL YOU WANT, IT WORKED. I'VE BEEN PRESIDENT LONGER THAN ANY OTHER PRESIDENT.
OUCH!
WHEN I GET BACK TO GOBLIN CAMP, EVERYONE'S GOING TO KNOW WHAT YOU DID!
HMPH!
WAHHH!
THAT'S RIGHT, YOU BETTER CRY.
GUYS, I NEED HELP!
YOU SURE DO. YOU'RE A MANIAC.
RUMPH!
THE GRIMMORAX GOT ME!

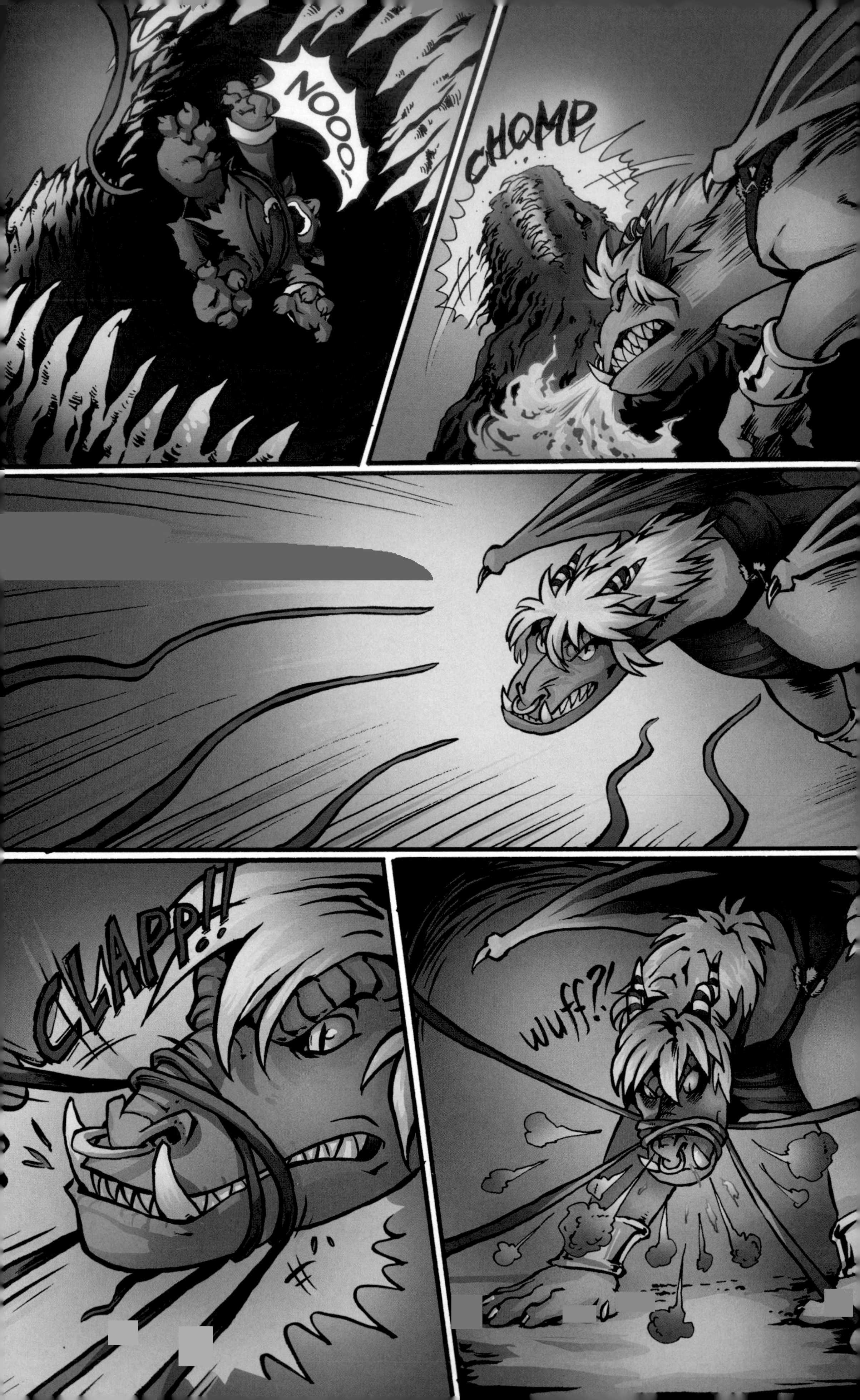
NOOO!
CHOMP
CLAPP!!
wuff?!

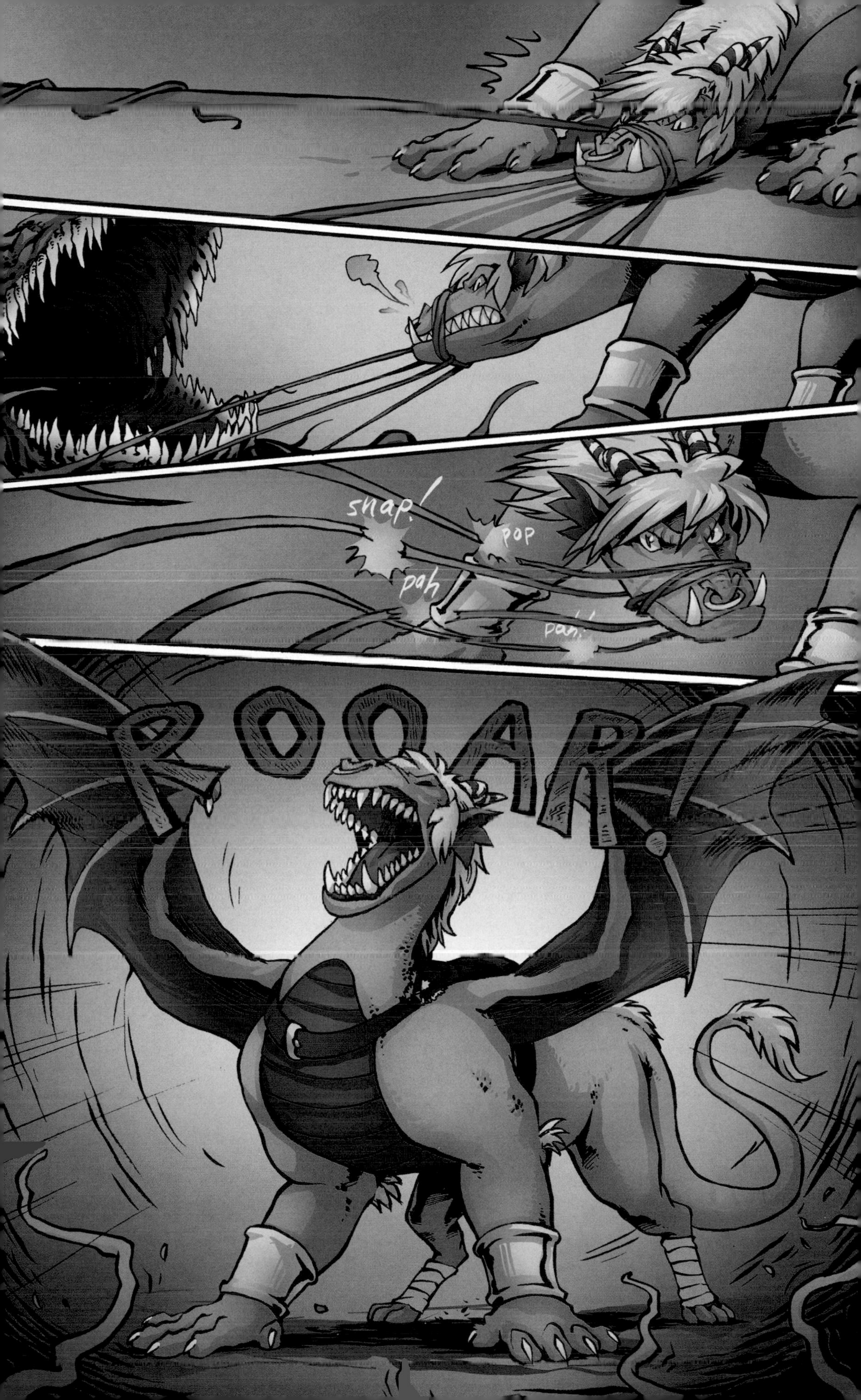
snap!
pop
pah
pah!
ROOAR!

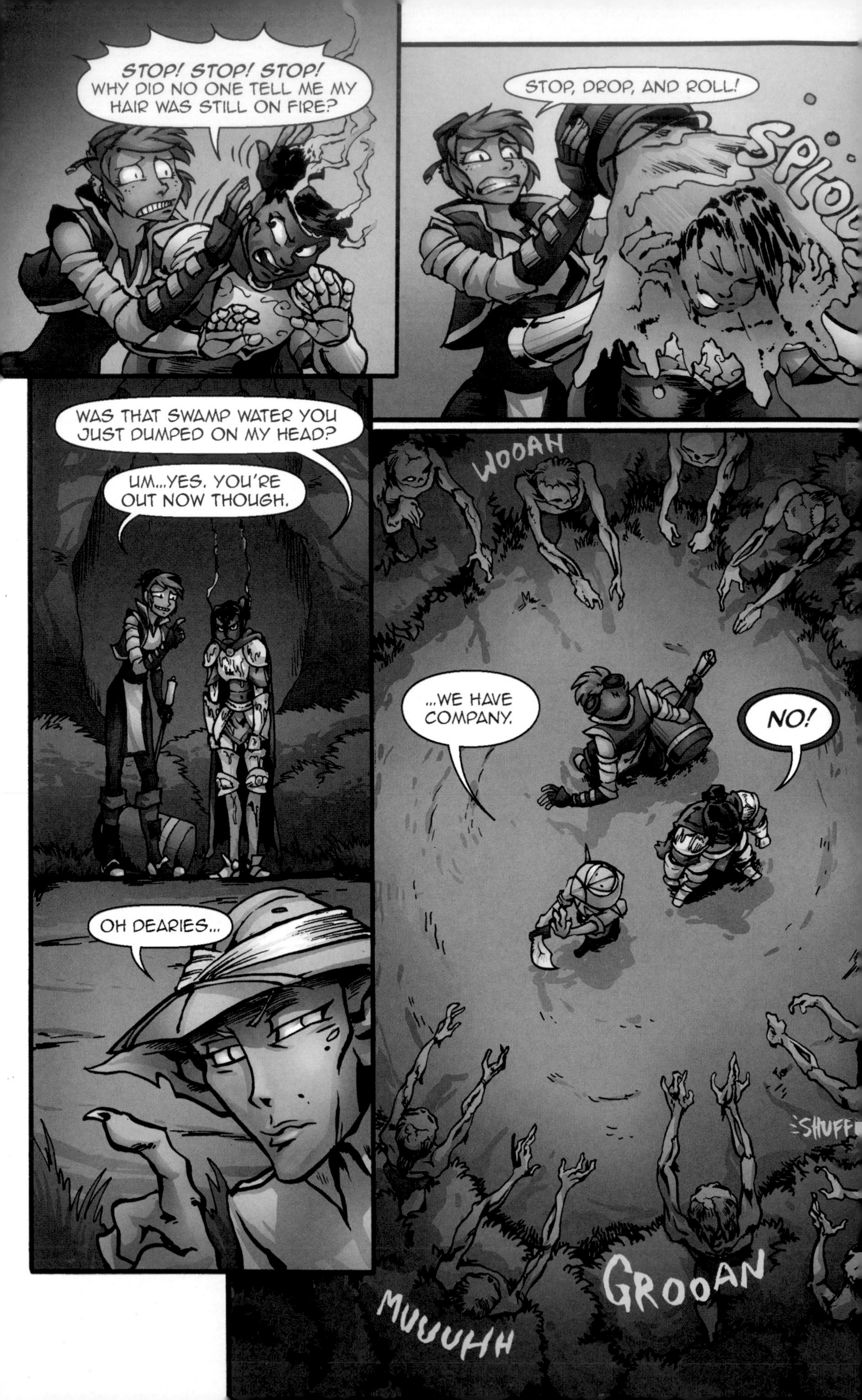
STOP! STOP! STOP! WHY DID NO ONE TELL ME MY HAIR WAS STILL ON FIRE?
STOP, DROP, AND ROLL!
SPLOO
WAS THAT SWAMP WATER YOU JUST DUMPED ON MY HEAD?
UM...YES. YOU'RE OUT NOW THOUGH.
OH DEARIES...
WOOAH
...WE HAVE COMPANY.
NO!
SHUFF
GROOAN
MUUUHH

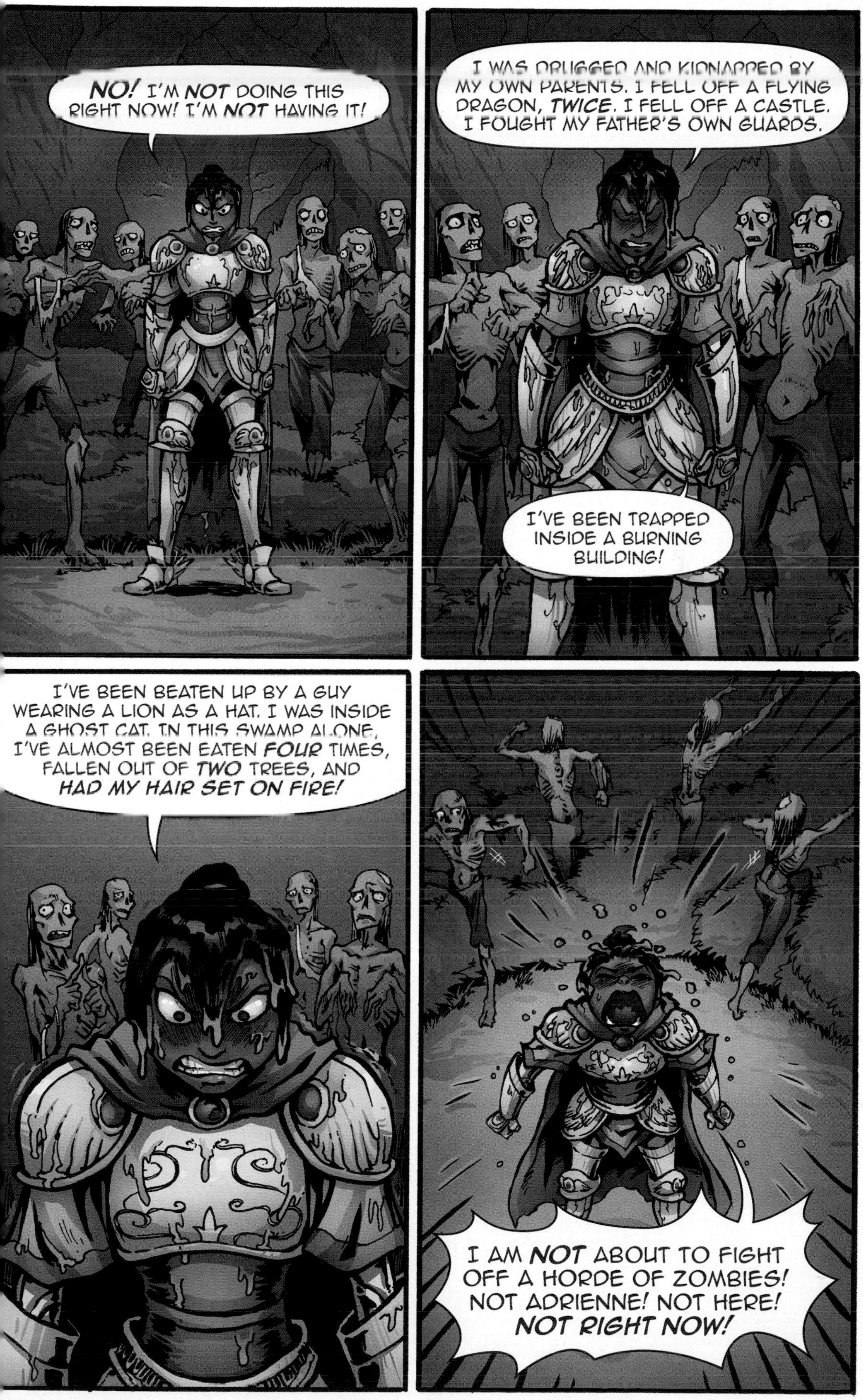
NO! I'M NOT DOING THIS RIGHT NOW! I'M NOT HAVING IT!
I WAS DRUGGED AND KIDNAPPED BY MY OWN PARENTS. I FELL OFF A FLYING DRAGON, TWICE. I FELL OFF A CASTLE. I FOUGHT MY FATHER'S OWN GUARDS.
I'VE BEEN TRAPPED INSIDE A BURNING BUILDING!
I'VE BEEN BEATEN UP BY A GUY WEARING A LION AS A HAT. I WAS INSIDE A GHOST CAT. IN THIS SWAMP ALONE, I'VE ALMOST BEEN EATEN FOUR TIMES, FALLEN OUT OF TWO TREES, AND HAD MY HAIR SET ON FIRE!
I AM NOT ABOUT TO FIGHT OFF A HORDE OF ZOMBIES! NOT ADRIENNE! NOT HERE! NOT RIGHT NOW!

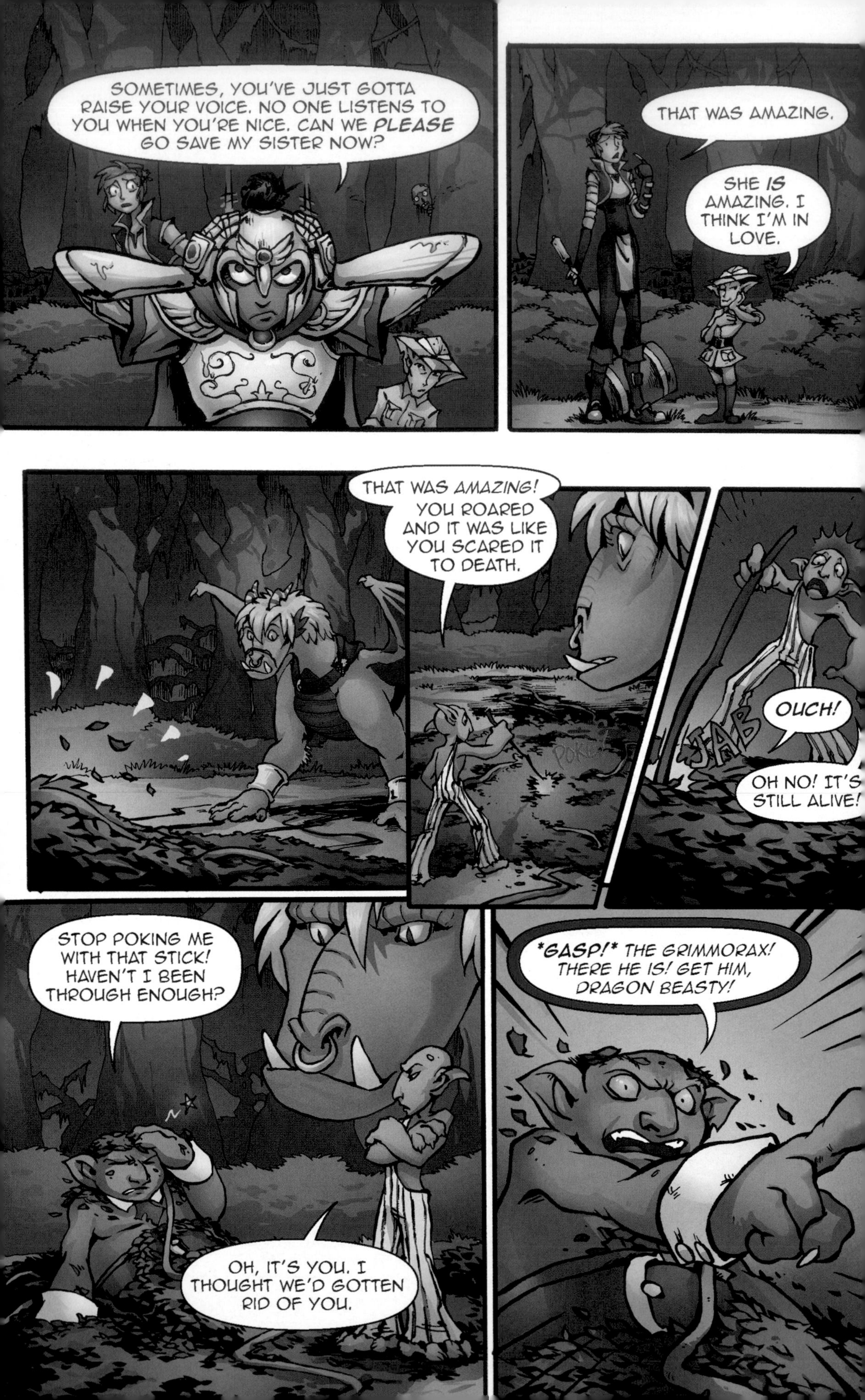
SOMETIMES, YOU'VE JUST GOTTA RAISE YOUR VOICE. NO ONE LISTENS TO YOU WHEN YOU'RE NICE. CAN WE *PLEASE* GO SAVE MY SISTER NOW?
THAT WAS AMAZING.
SHE *IS* AMAZING. I THINK I'M IN LOVE.
THAT WAS *AMAZING!* YOU ROARED AND IT WAS LIKE YOU SCARED IT TO DEATH.
POKE
JAB
OUCH!
OH NO! IT'S STILL ALIVE!
STOP POKING ME WITH THAT STICK! HAVEN'T I BEEN THROUGH ENOUGH?
OH, IT'S YOU. I THOUGHT WE'D GOTTEN RID OF YOU.
GASP! THE GRIMMORAX! THERE HE IS! GET HIM, DRAGON BEASTY!

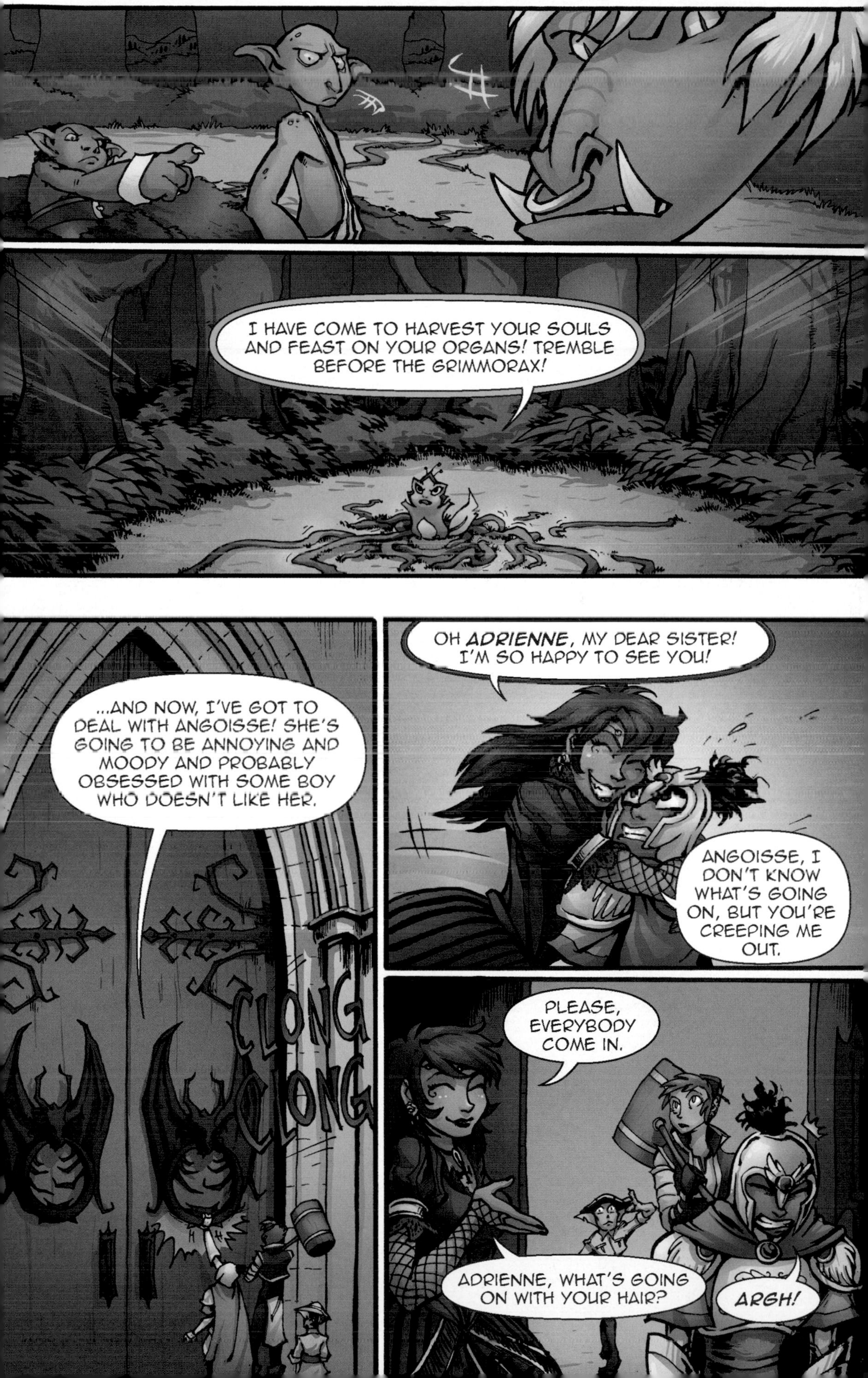
I HAVE COME TO HARVEST YOUR SOULS AND FEAST ON YOUR ORGANS! TREMBLE BEFORE THE GRIMMORAX!
...AND NOW, I'VE GOT TO DEAL WITH ANGOISSE! SHE'S GOING TO BE ANNOYING AND MOODY AND PROBABLY OBSESSED WITH SOME BOY WHO DOESN'T LIKE HER.
CLONG
CLONG
OH *ADRIENNE*, MY DEAR SISTER! I'M SO HAPPY TO SEE YOU!
ANGOISSE, I DON'T KNOW WHAT'S GOING ON, BUT YOU'RE CREEPING ME OUT.
PLEASE, EVERYBODY COME IN.
ADRIENNE, WHAT'S GOING ON WITH YOUR HAIR?
ARGH!

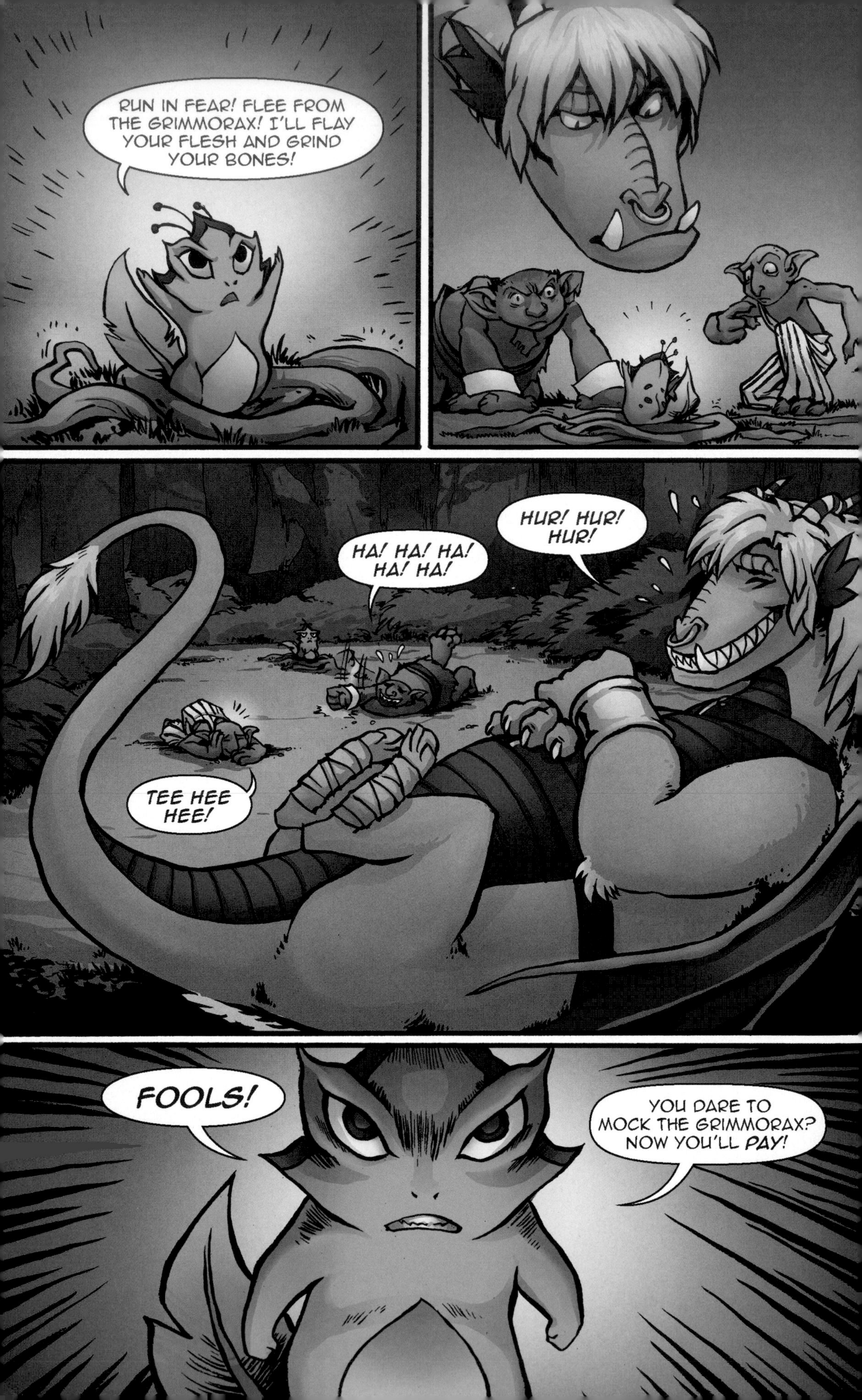
RUN IN FEAR! FLEE FROM THE GRIMMORAX! I'LL FLAY YOUR FLESH AND GRIND YOUR BONES!
HA! HA! HA! HA! HA!
HUR! HUR! HUR!
TEE HEE HEE!
FOOLS!
YOU DARE TO MOCK THE GRIMMORAX? NOW YOU'LL *PAY*!

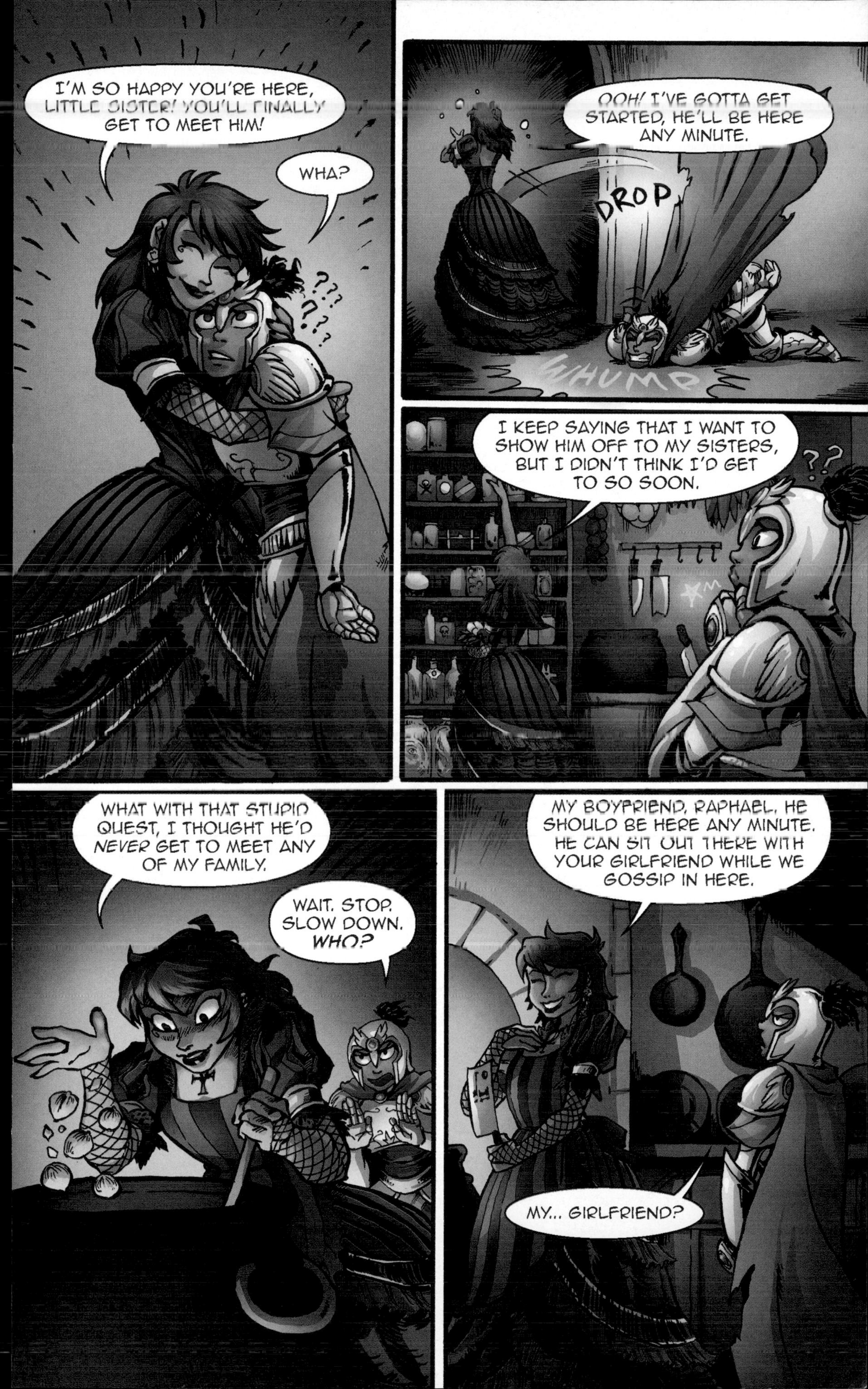
I'M SO HAPPY YOU'RE HERE, LITTLE SISTER! YOU'LL FINALLY GET TO MEET HIM!
WHA?
???
OOH! I'VE GOTTA GET STARTED, HE'LL BE HERE ANY MINUTE.
DROP
WHUMP
I KEEP SAYING THAT I WANT TO SHOW HIM OFF TO MY SISTERS, BUT I DIDN'T THINK I'D GET TO SO SOON.
??
WHAT WITH THAT STUPID QUEST, I THOUGHT HE'D NEVER GET TO MEET ANY OF MY FAMILY.
WAIT. STOP. SLOW DOWN. WHO?
MY BOYFRIEND, RAPHAEL. HE SHOULD BE HERE ANY MINUTE. HE CAN SIT OUT THERE WITH YOUR GIRLFRIEND WHILE WE GOSSIP IN HERE.
MY... GIRLFRIEND?

NOPE, NOTHING CREEPY ABOUT THIS PLACE... BIG SCARY CASTLE FULL OF CANDLES AND CURTAINS. BUNCH OF ZOMBIES HANGING AROUND...

CREEAK

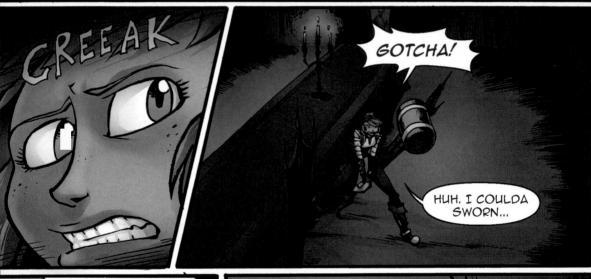

GOTCHA!

HUH, I COULDA SWORN...

PULL IT TOGETHER, BEDELIA. NO ONE'S--

EXCUSE ME--

ZOMBIE!!

WHAM!

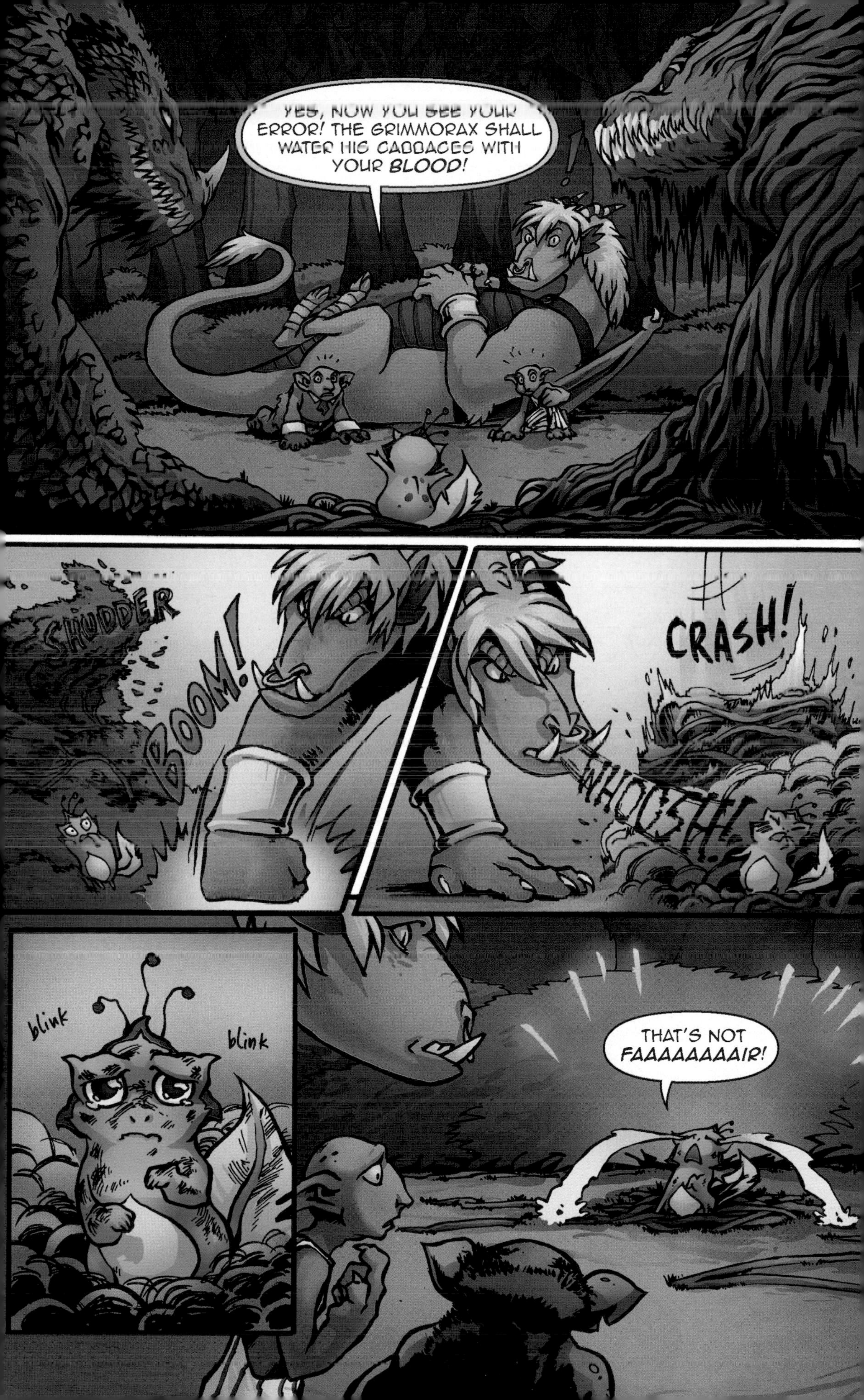
YES, NOW YOU SEE YOUR ERROR! THE GRIMMORAX SHALL WATER HIS CABBAGES WITH YOUR *BLOOD*!
!
SHUDDER
BOOM!
CRASH!
WHOOSH!
blink
blink
THAT'S NOT *FAAAAAAAAAIR*!

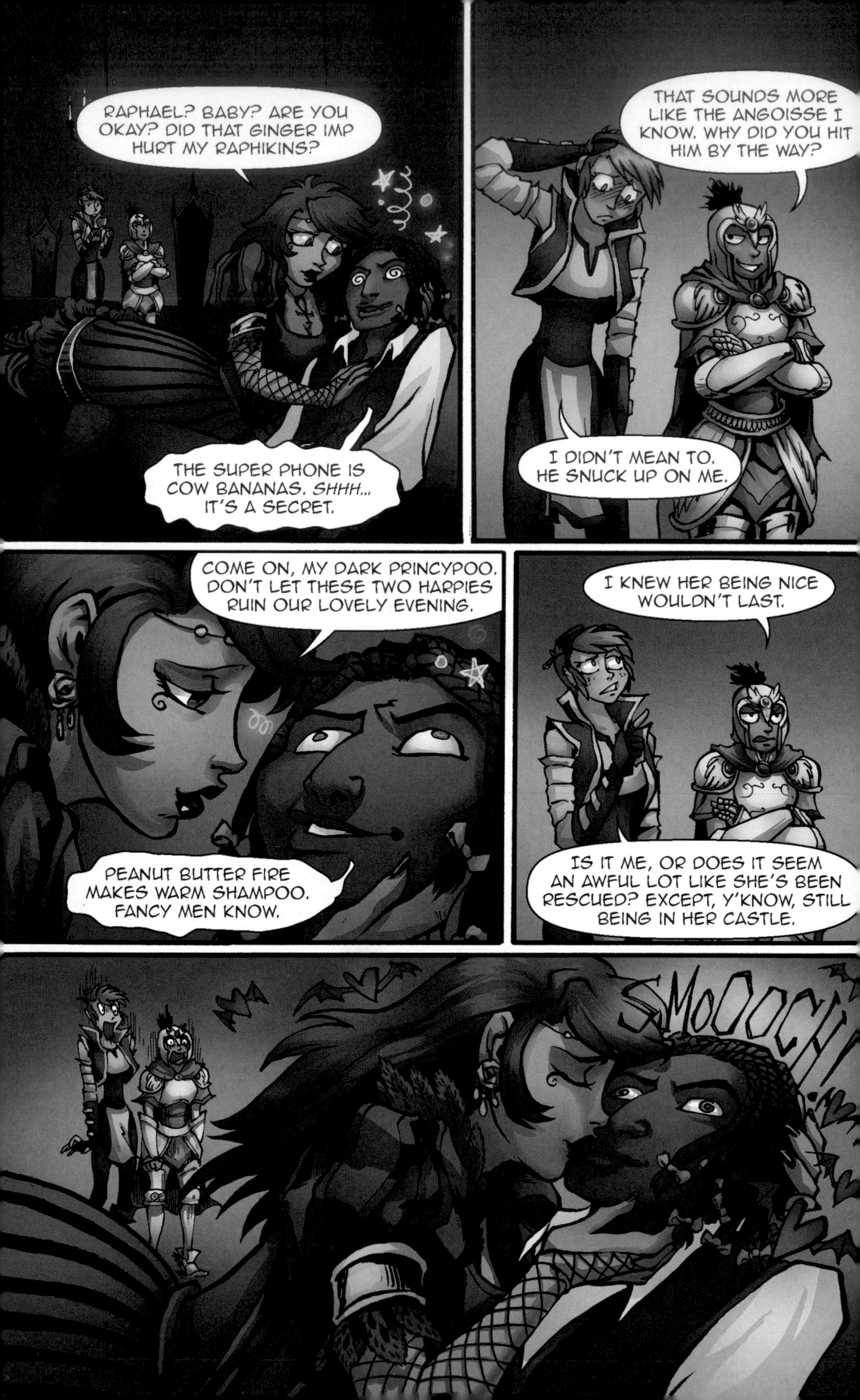
RAPHAEL? BABY? ARE YOU OKAY? DID THAT GINGER IMP HURT MY RAPHIKINS?
THE SUPER PHONE IS COW BANANAS. SHHH... IT'S A SECRET.
THAT SOUNDS MORE LIKE THE ANGOISSE I KNOW. WHY DID YOU HIT HIM BY THE WAY?
I DIDN'T MEAN TO. HE SNUCK UP ON ME.
COME ON, MY DARK PRINCYPOO. DON'T LET THESE TWO HARPIES RUIN OUR LOVELY EVENING.
PEANUT BUTTER FIRE MAKES WARM SHAMPOO. FANCY MEN KNOW.
I KNEW HER BEING NICE WOULDN'T LAST.
IS IT ME, OR DOES IT SEEM AN AWFUL LOT LIKE SHE'S BEEN RESCUED? EXCEPT, Y'KNOW, STILL BEING IN HER CASTLE.
SMOOOCH!

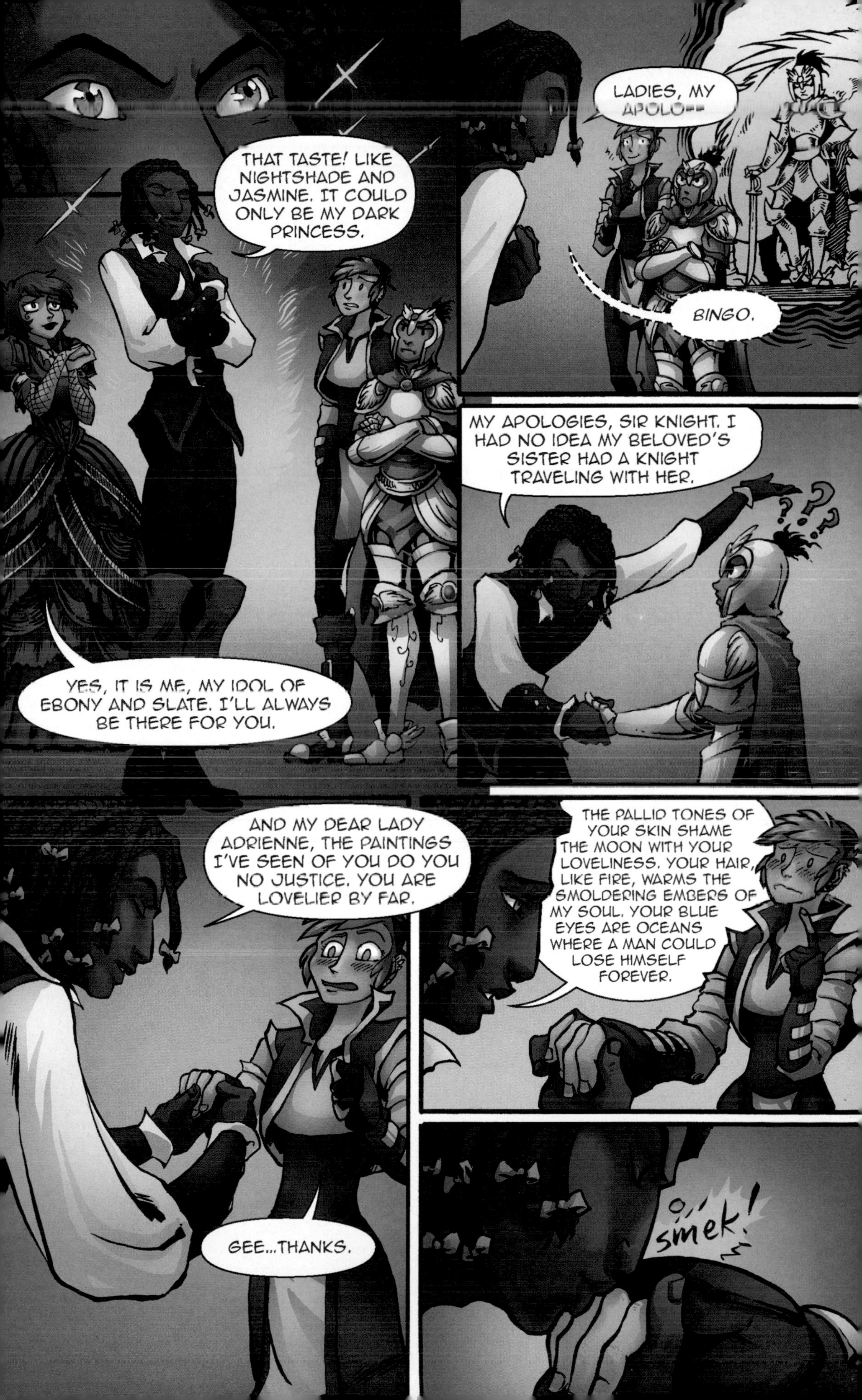

THAT TASTE! LIKE NIGHTSHADE AND JASMINE. IT COULD ONLY BE MY DARK PRINCESS.
YES, IT IS ME, MY IDOL OF EBONY AND SLATE. I'LL ALWAYS BE THERE FOR YOU.
LADIES, MY APOLO--
BINGO.
MY APOLOGIES, SIR KNIGHT. I HAD NO IDEA MY BELOVED'S SISTER HAD A KNIGHT TRAVELING WITH HER.
?? ?
AND MY DEAR LADY ADRIENNE, THE PAINTINGS I'VE SEEN OF YOU DO YOU NO JUSTICE. YOU ARE LOVELIER BY FAR.
GEE...THANKS.
THE PALLID TONES OF YOUR SKIN SHAME THE MOON WITH YOUR LOVELINESS. YOUR HAIR, LIKE FIRE, WARMS THE SMOLDERING EMBERS OF MY SOUL. YOUR BLUE EYES ARE OCEANS WHERE A MAN COULD LOSE HIMSELF FOREVER.
smek!

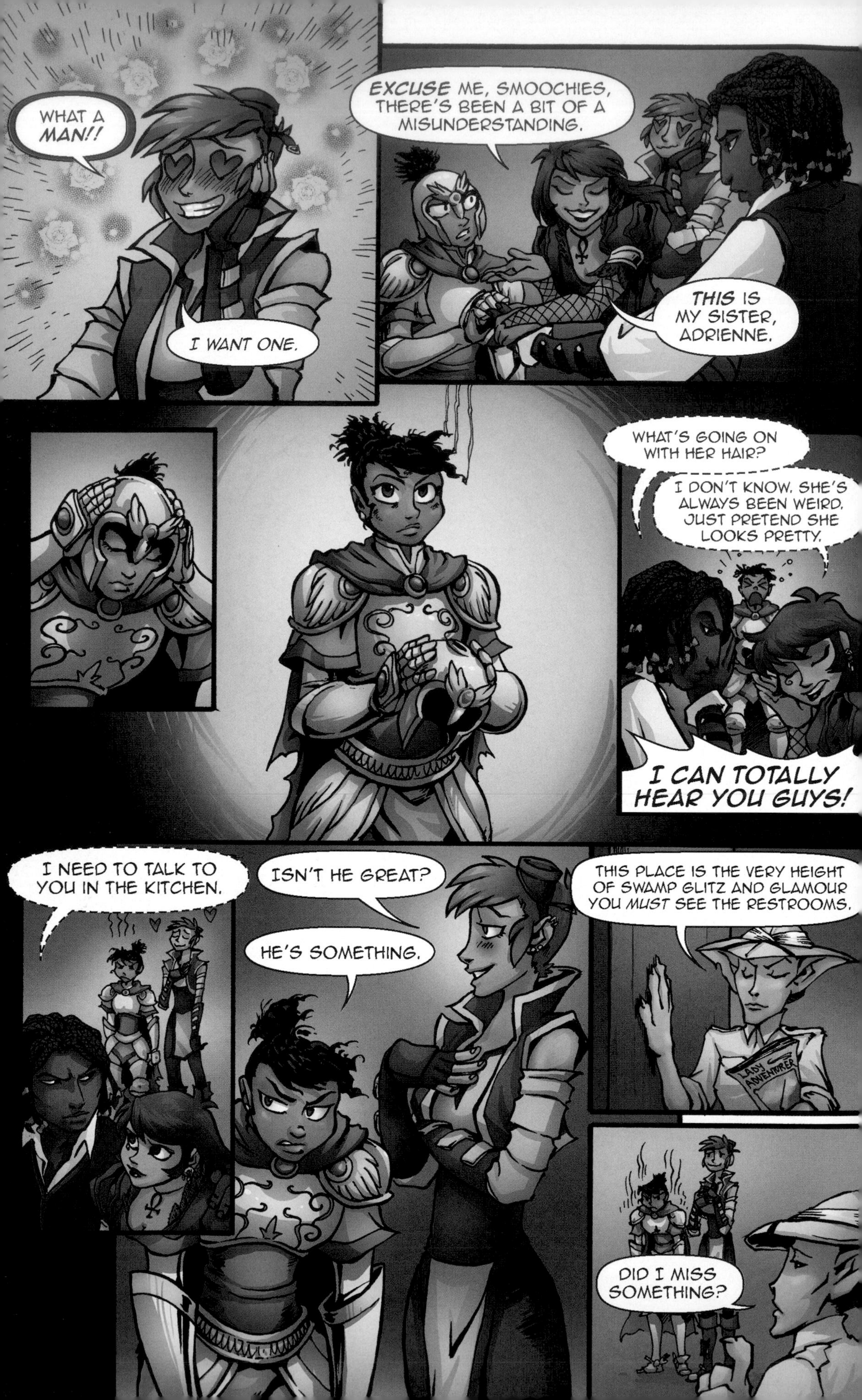
WHAT A MAN!!
I WANT ONE.
EXCUSE ME, SMOOCHIES, THERE'S BEEN A BIT OF A MISUNDERSTANDING.
THIS IS MY SISTER, ADRIENNE.
WHAT'S GOING ON WITH HER HAIR?
I DON'T KNOW. SHE'S ALWAYS BEEN WEIRD. JUST PRETEND SHE LOOKS PRETTY.
I CAN TOTALLY HEAR YOU GUYS!
I NEED TO TALK TO YOU IN THE KITCHEN.
ISN'T HE GREAT?
HE'S SOMETHING.
THIS PLACE IS THE VERY HEIGHT OF SWAMP GLITZ AND GLAMOUR YOU MUST SEE THE RESTROOMS.
LADY ADVENTURER
DID I MISS SOMETHING?

AND WE WERE ALL SUCH GREAT FRIENDS. THE HANDLER LADY WAS LIKE MY MOTHER. SHE HAD THIS BEAUTIFUL GOLD HAIR LIKE WARM SUNLIGHT.

IT MUST HAVE BEEN HARD FOR YOU TO LEAVE.

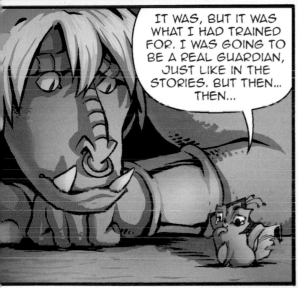

IT WAS, BUT IT WAS WHAT I HAD TRAINED FOR. I WAS GOING TO BE A REAL GUARDIAN, JUST LIKE IN THE STORIES. BUT THEN... THEN...

...IT TURNED OUT EVEN *THAT* WASN'T TRUUUUUUE!

HOW COULD YOU MAKE HIM STAY OUT HERE ALONE AND TERRORIZE OTHER GOBLINS? YOU'RE A BAD PERSON!

PBBT! SOME TIME LEADERS GOTTA MAKE THEM TOUGH DECISIONS.

BULLYING OTHERS IS NEVER A GOOD DECISION.

PURRRR

NUZZLE NUZZLE

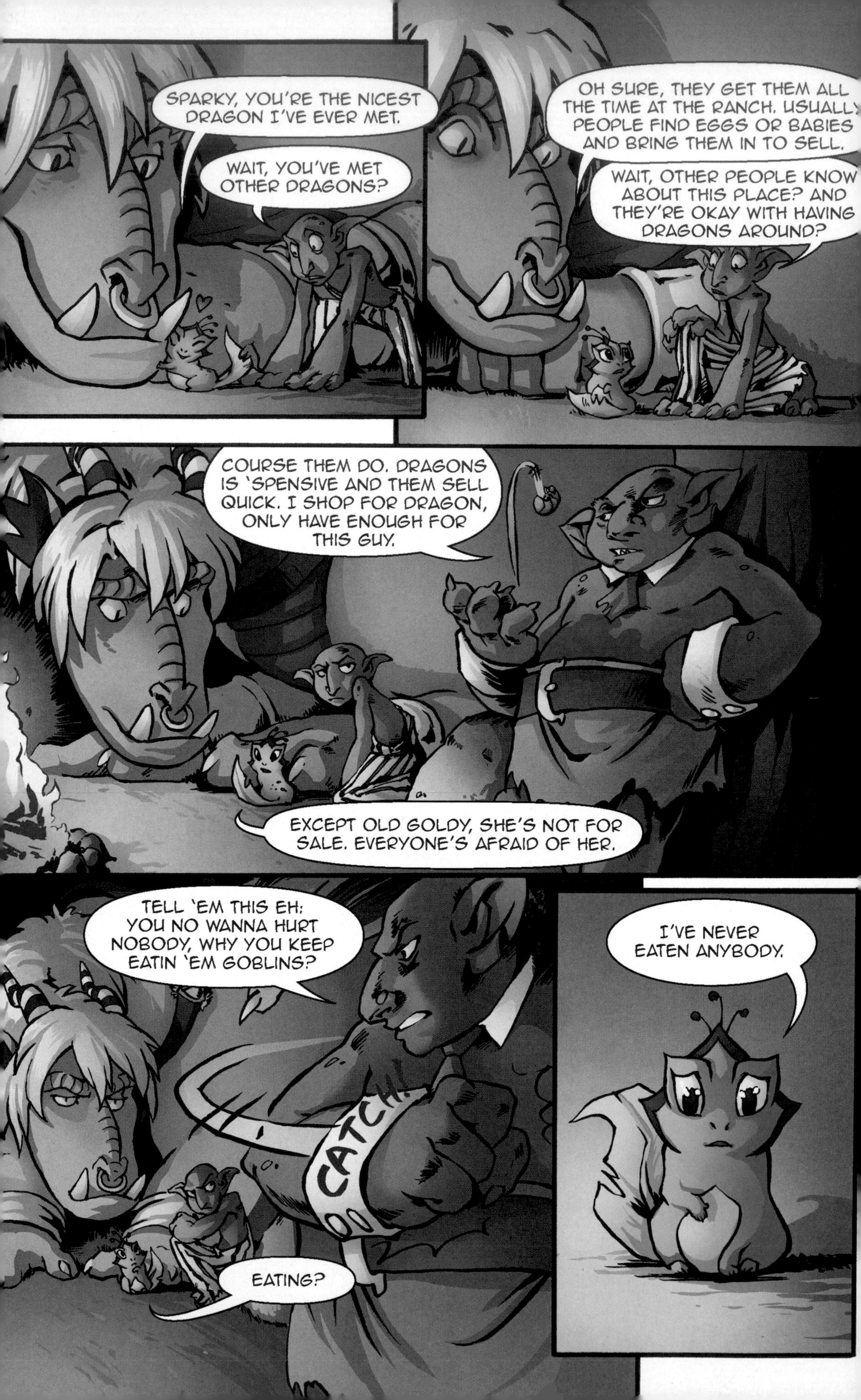
SPARKY, YOU'RE THE NICEST DRAGON I'VE EVER MET.
WAIT, YOU'VE MET OTHER DRAGONS?
OH SURE, THEY GET THEM ALL THE TIME AT THE RANCH. USUALLY PEOPLE FIND EGGS OR BABIES AND BRING THEM IN TO SELL.
WAIT, OTHER PEOPLE KNOW ABOUT THIS PLACE? AND THEY'RE OKAY WITH HAVING DRAGONS AROUND?
COURSE THEM DO. DRAGONS IS 'SPENSIVE AND THEM SELL QUICK. I SHOP FOR DRAGON, ONLY HAVE ENOUGH FOR THIS GUY.
EXCEPT OLD GOLDY, SHE'S NOT FOR SALE. EVERYONE'S AFRAID OF HER.
TELL 'EM THIS EH: YOU NO WANNA HURT NOBODY, WHY YOU KEEP EATIN 'EM GOBLINS?
CATCH.
EATING?
I'VE NEVER EATEN ANYBODY.

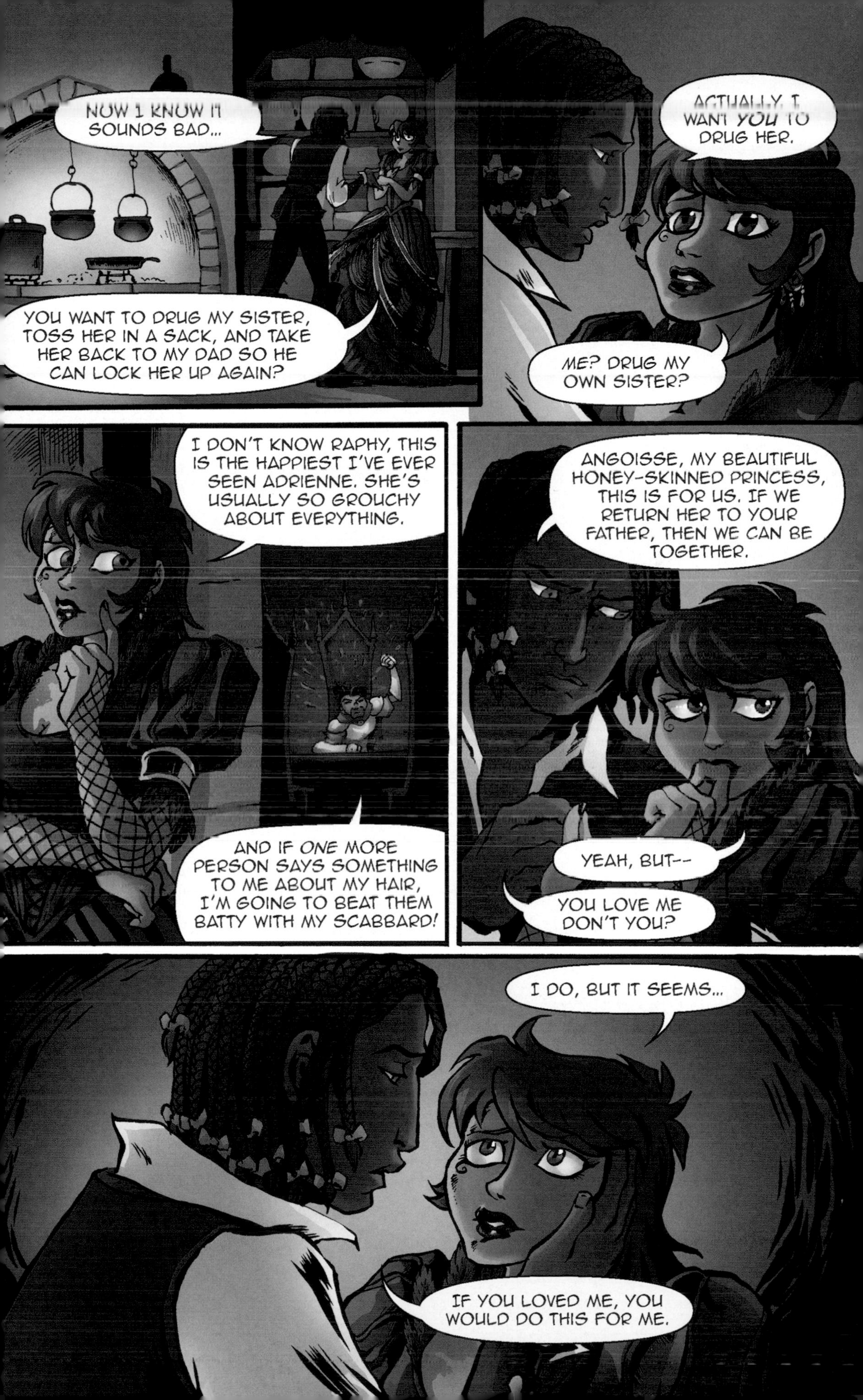
NOW I KNOW IT SOUNDS BAD...
YOU WANT TO DRUG MY SISTER, TOSS HER IN A SACK, AND TAKE HER BACK TO MY DAD SO HE CAN LOCK HER UP AGAIN?
ACTUALLY, I WANT YOU TO DRUG HER.
ME? DRUG MY OWN SISTER?
I DON'T KNOW RAPHY, THIS IS THE HAPPIEST I'VE EVER SEEN ADRIENNE. SHE'S USUALLY SO GROUCHY ABOUT EVERYTHING.
AND IF ONE MORE PERSON SAYS SOMETHING TO ME ABOUT MY HAIR, I'M GOING TO BEAT THEM BATTY WITH MY SCABBARD!
ANGOISSE, MY BEAUTIFUL HONEY-SKINNED PRINCESS, THIS IS FOR US. IF WE RETURN HER TO YOUR FATHER, THEN WE CAN BE TOGETHER.
YEAH, BUT--
YOU LOVE ME DON'T YOU?
I DO, BUT IT SEEMS...
IF YOU LOVED ME, YOU WOULD DO THIS FOR ME.

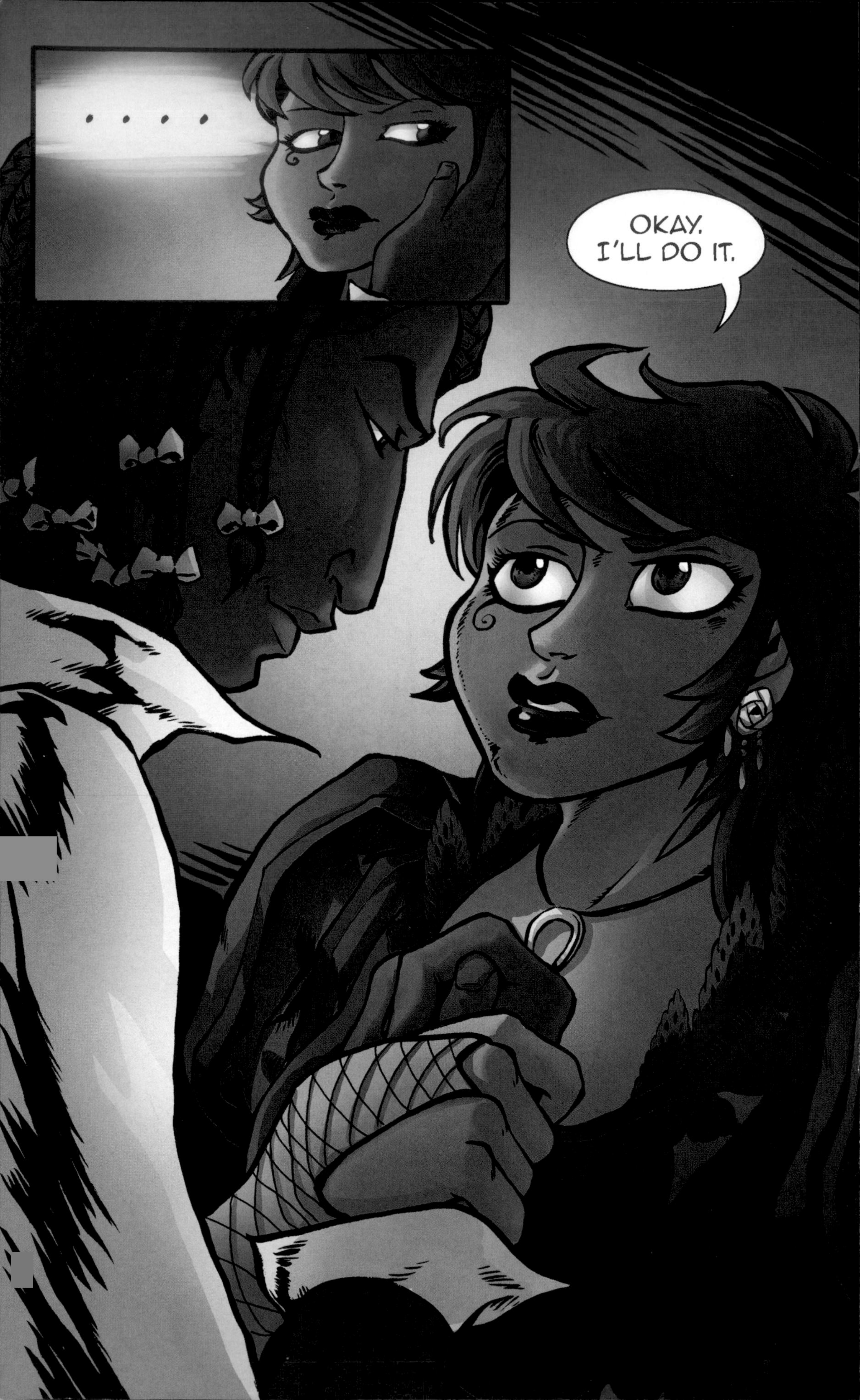
. . . .
OKAY. I'LL DO IT.

4: The Middlest Sister of All

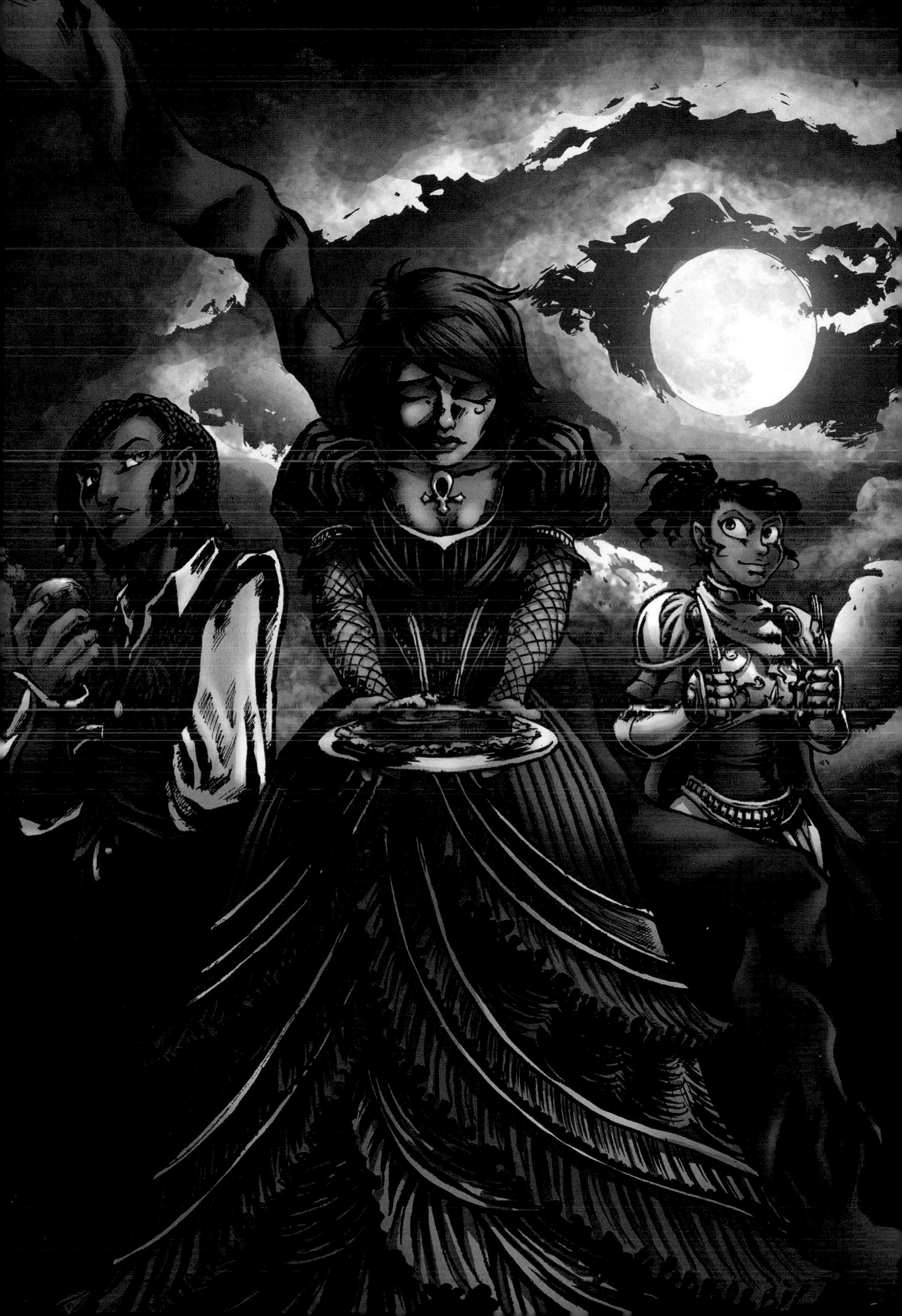

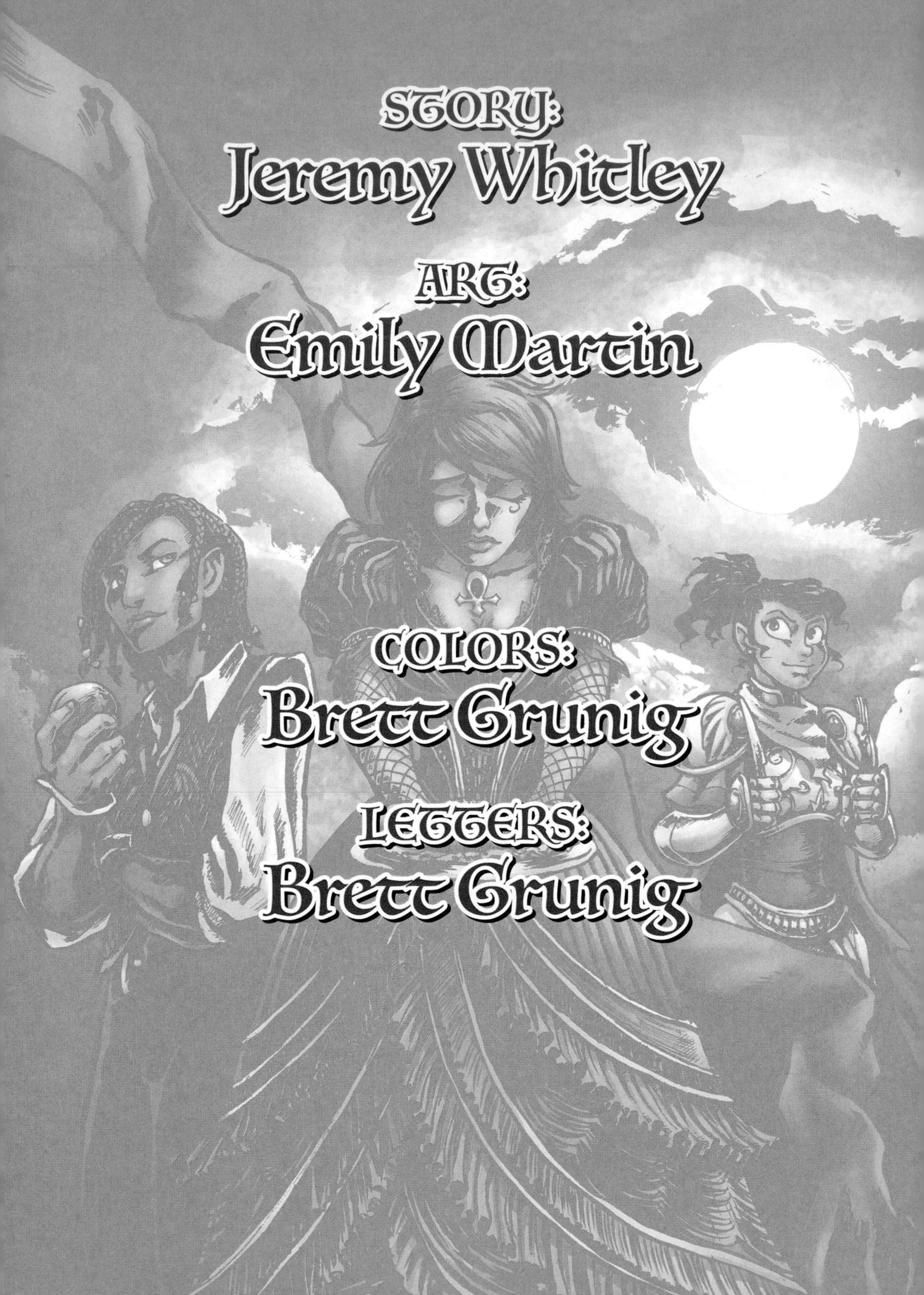

STORY:
Jeremy Whitley

ART:
Emily Martin

COLORS:
Brett Grunig

LETTERS:
Brett Grunig

Bryan Seaton: Publisher/ CEO • Shawn Gabborin: Editor In Chief
Jason Martin: Publisher-Danger Zone • Nicole D'Andria: Marketing Director/Editor
Jim Dietz: Social Media Manager • Danielle Davison: Executive Administrator
Chad Cicconi: Still Waiting For His Princess • Shawn Pryor: President of Creator Relations

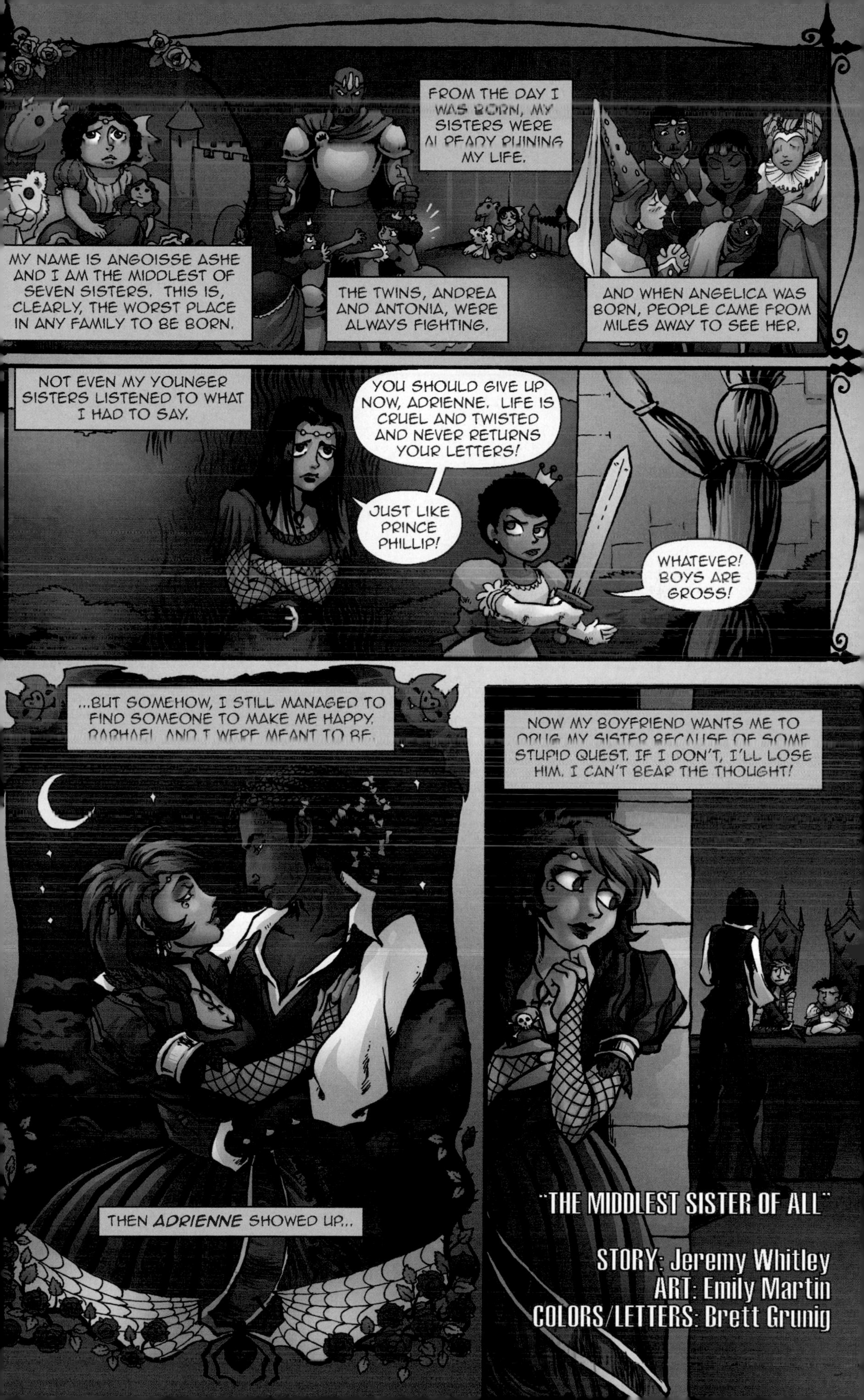
MY NAME IS ANGOISSE ASHE AND I AM THE MIDDLEST OF SEVEN SISTERS. THIS IS, CLEARLY, THE WORST PLACE IN ANY FAMILY TO BE BORN.
FROM THE DAY I WAS BORN, MY SISTERS WERE ALREADY RUINING MY LIFE.
THE TWINS, ANDREA AND ANTONIA, WERE ALWAYS FIGHTING.
AND WHEN ANGELICA WAS BORN, PEOPLE CAME FROM MILES AWAY TO SEE HER.
NOT EVEN MY YOUNGER SISTERS LISTENED TO WHAT I HAD TO SAY.
YOU SHOULD GIVE UP NOW, ADRIENNE. LIFE IS CRUEL AND TWISTED AND NEVER RETURNS YOUR LETTERS!
JUST LIKE PRINCE PHILLIP!
WHATEVER! BOYS ARE GROSS!
...BUT SOMEHOW, I STILL MANAGED TO FIND SOMEONE TO MAKE ME HAPPY. RAPHAEL AND I WERE MEANT TO BE.
THEN *ADRIENNE* SHOWED UP...
NOW MY BOYFRIEND WANTS ME TO DRUG MY SISTER BECAUSE OF SOME STUPID QUEST. IF I DON'T, I'LL LOSE HIM. I CAN'T BEAR THE THOUGHT!
"THE MIDDLEST SISTER OF ALL"
STORY: Jeremy Whitley
ART: Emily Martin
COLORS/LETTERS: Brett Grunig

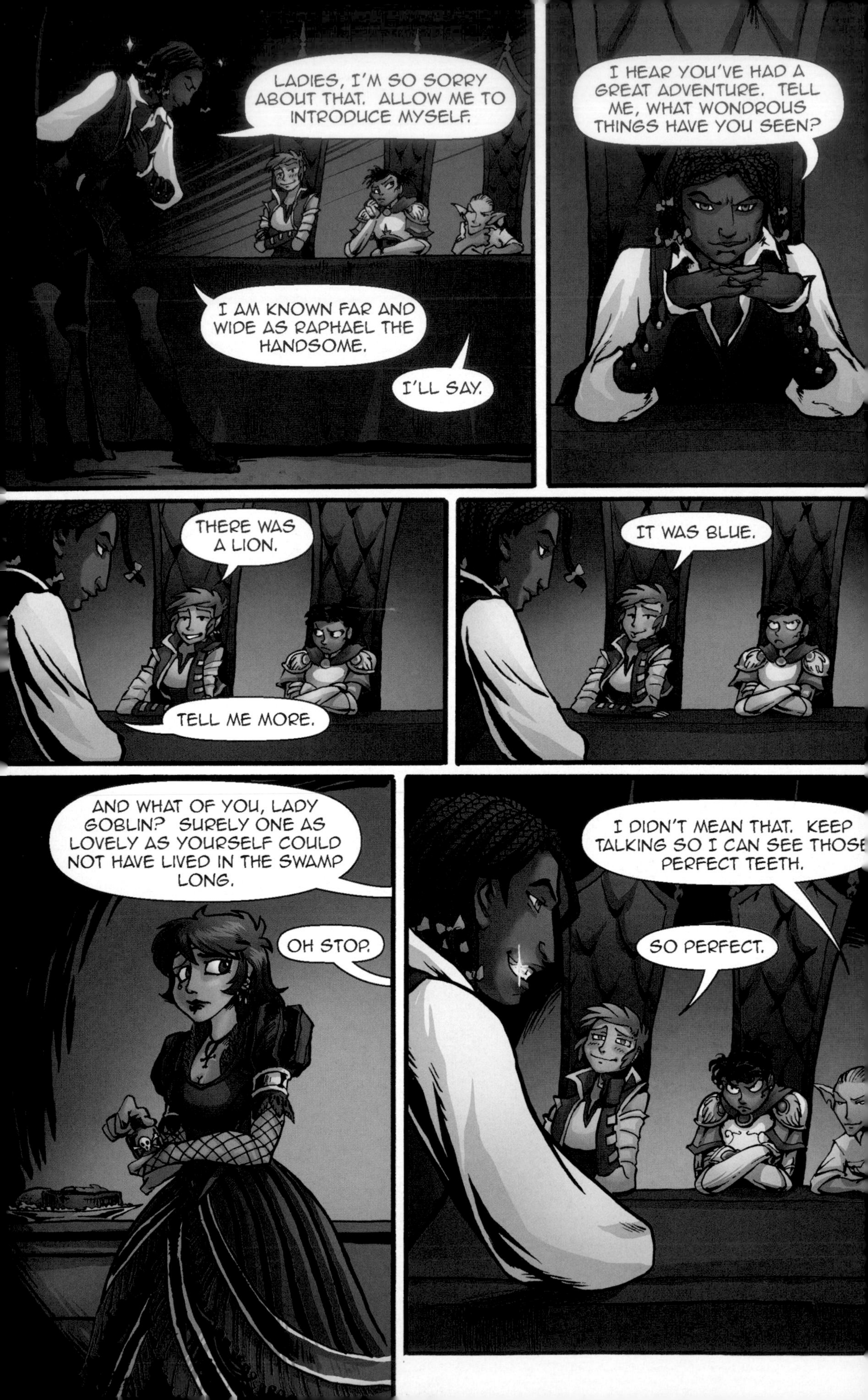
LADIES, I'M SO SORRY ABOUT THAT. ALLOW ME TO INTRODUCE MYSELF.
I AM KNOWN FAR AND WIDE AS RAPHAEL THE HANDSOME.
I'LL SAY.
I HEAR YOU'VE HAD A GREAT ADVENTURE. TELL ME, WHAT WONDROUS THINGS HAVE YOU SEEN?
THERE WAS A LION.
TELL ME MORE.
IT WAS BLUE.
AND WHAT OF YOU, LADY GOBLIN? SURELY ONE AS LOVELY AS YOURSELF COULD NOT HAVE LIVED IN THE SWAMP LONG.
OH STOP.
I DIDN'T MEAN THAT. KEEP TALKING SO I CAN SEE THOSE PERFECT TEETH.
SO PERFECT.

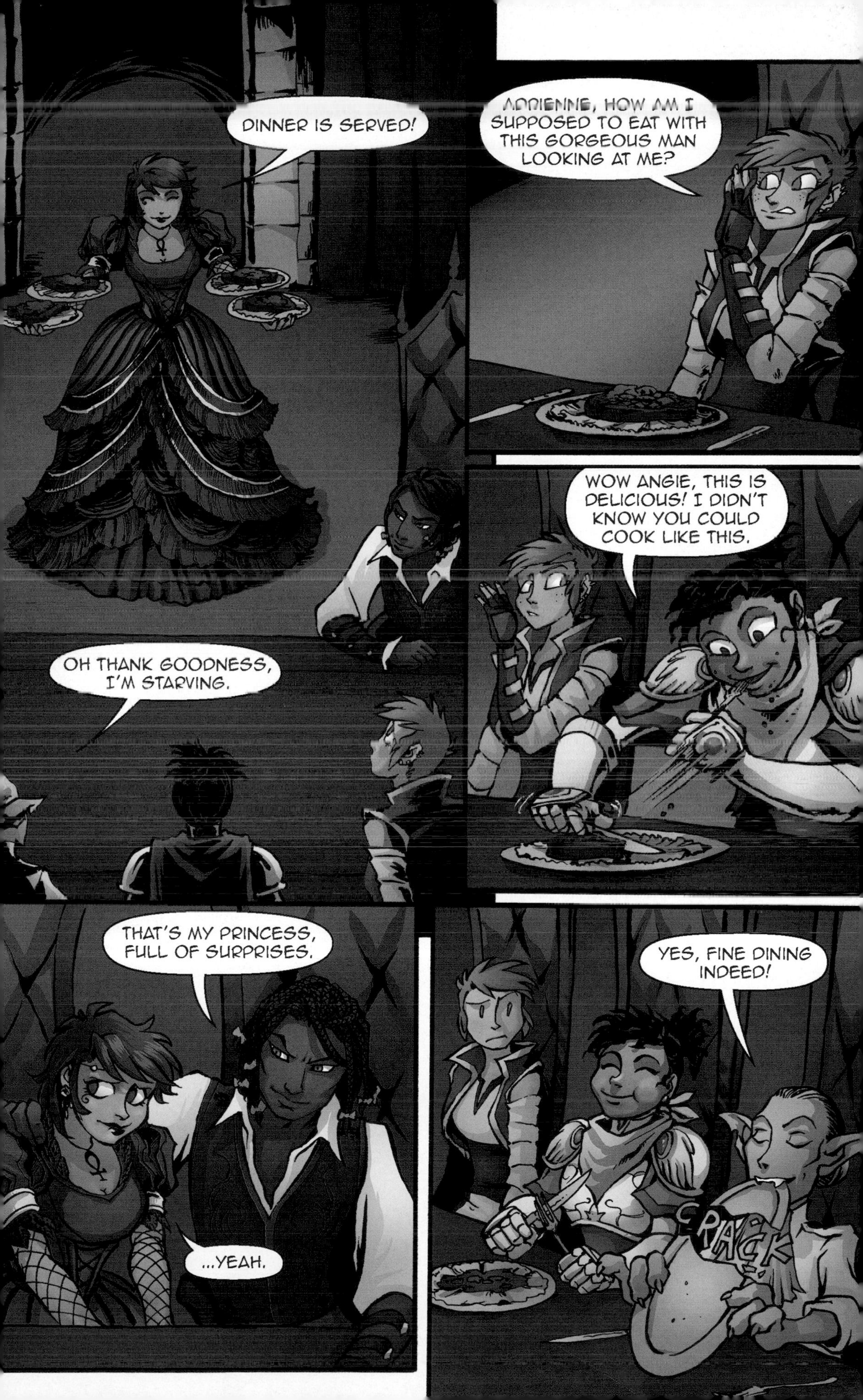
DINNER IS SERVED!
ADRIENNE, HOW AM I SUPPOSED TO EAT WITH THIS GORGEOUS MAN LOOKING AT ME?
OH THANK GOODNESS, I'M STARVING.
WOW ANGIE, THIS IS DELICIOUS! I DIDN'T KNOW YOU COULD COOK LIKE THIS.
THAT'S MY PRINCESS, FULL OF SURPRISES.
...YEAH.
YES, FINE DINING INDEED!
CRACK

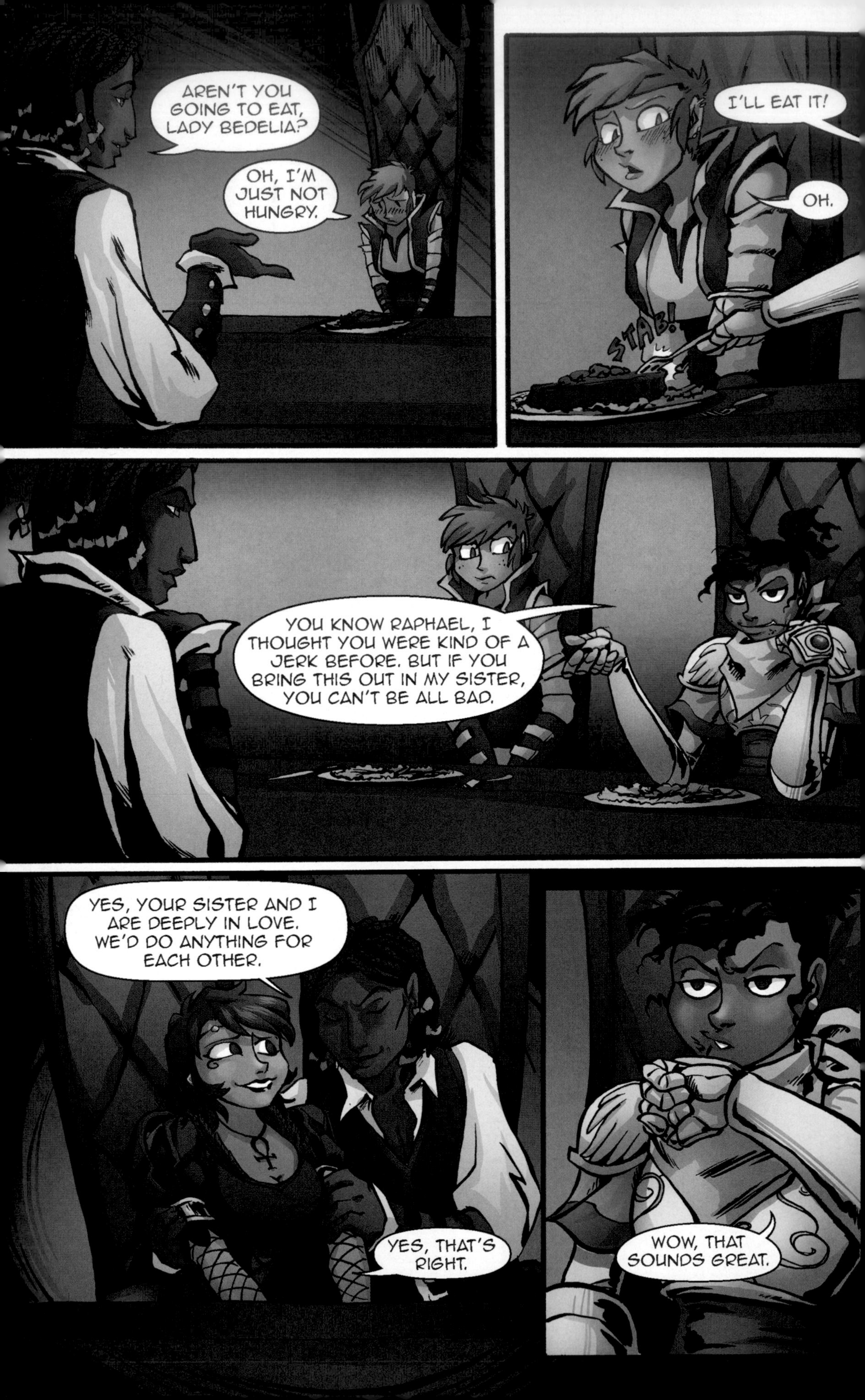
AREN'T YOU GOING TO EAT, LADY BEDELIA?
OH, I'M JUST NOT HUNGRY.
I'LL EAT IT!
OH.
STAB!
YOU KNOW RAPHAEL, I THOUGHT YOU WERE KIND OF A JERK BEFORE. BUT IF YOU BRING THIS OUT IN MY SISTER, YOU CAN'T BE ALL BAD.
YES, YOUR SISTER AND I ARE DEEPLY IN LOVE. WE'D DO ANYTHING FOR EACH OTHER.
YES, THAT'S RIGHT.
WOW, THAT SOUNDS GREAT.

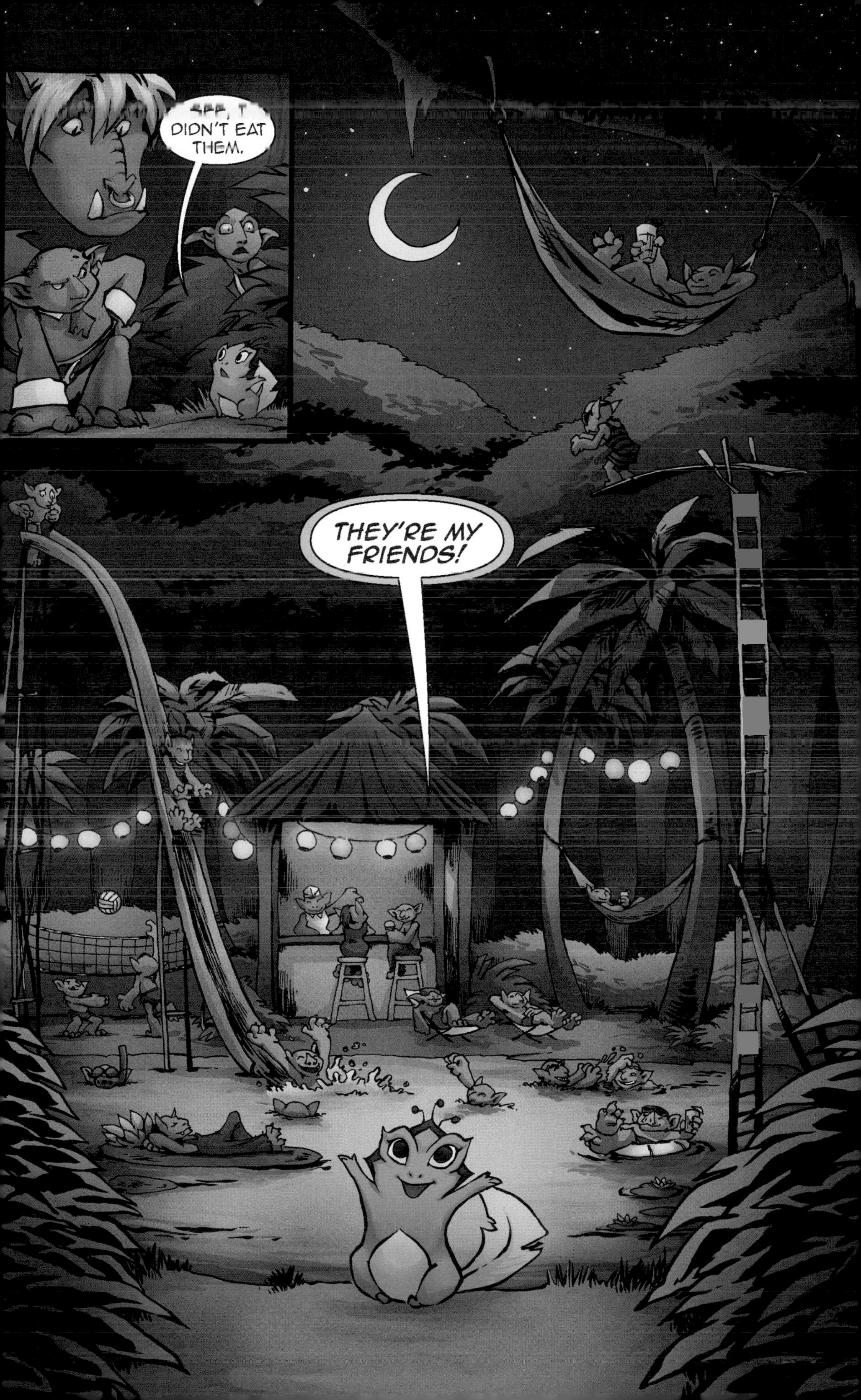
DIDN'T EAT THEM.
THEY'RE MY FRIENDS!

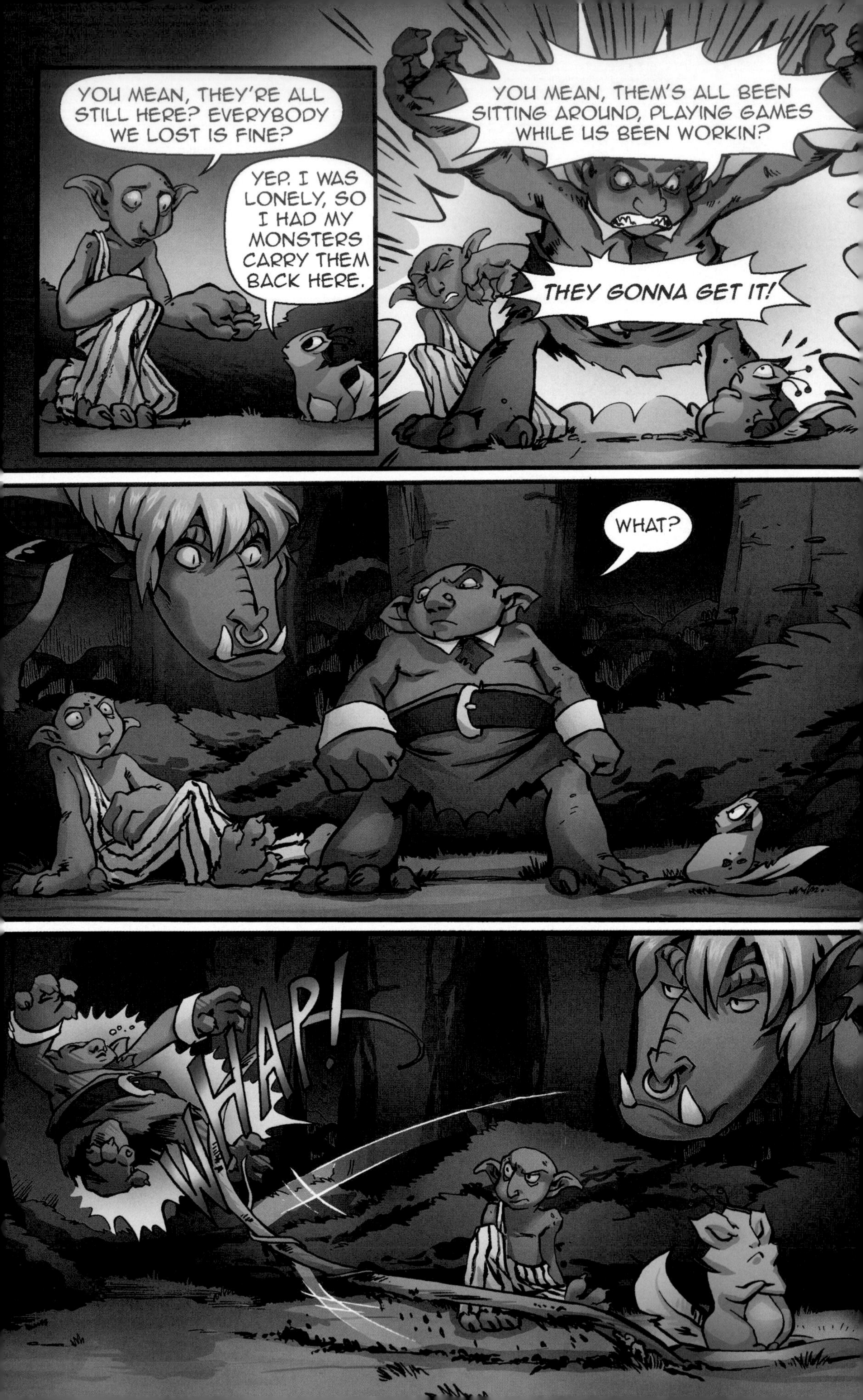
YOU MEAN, THEY'RE ALL STILL HERE? EVERYBODY WE LOST IS FINE?
YEP. I WAS LONELY, SO I HAD MY MONSTERS CARRY THEM BACK HERE.
YOU MEAN, THEM'S ALL BEEN SITTING AROUND, PLAYING GAMES WHILE US BEEN WORKIN?
THEY GONNA GET IT!
WHAT?
WHAP!

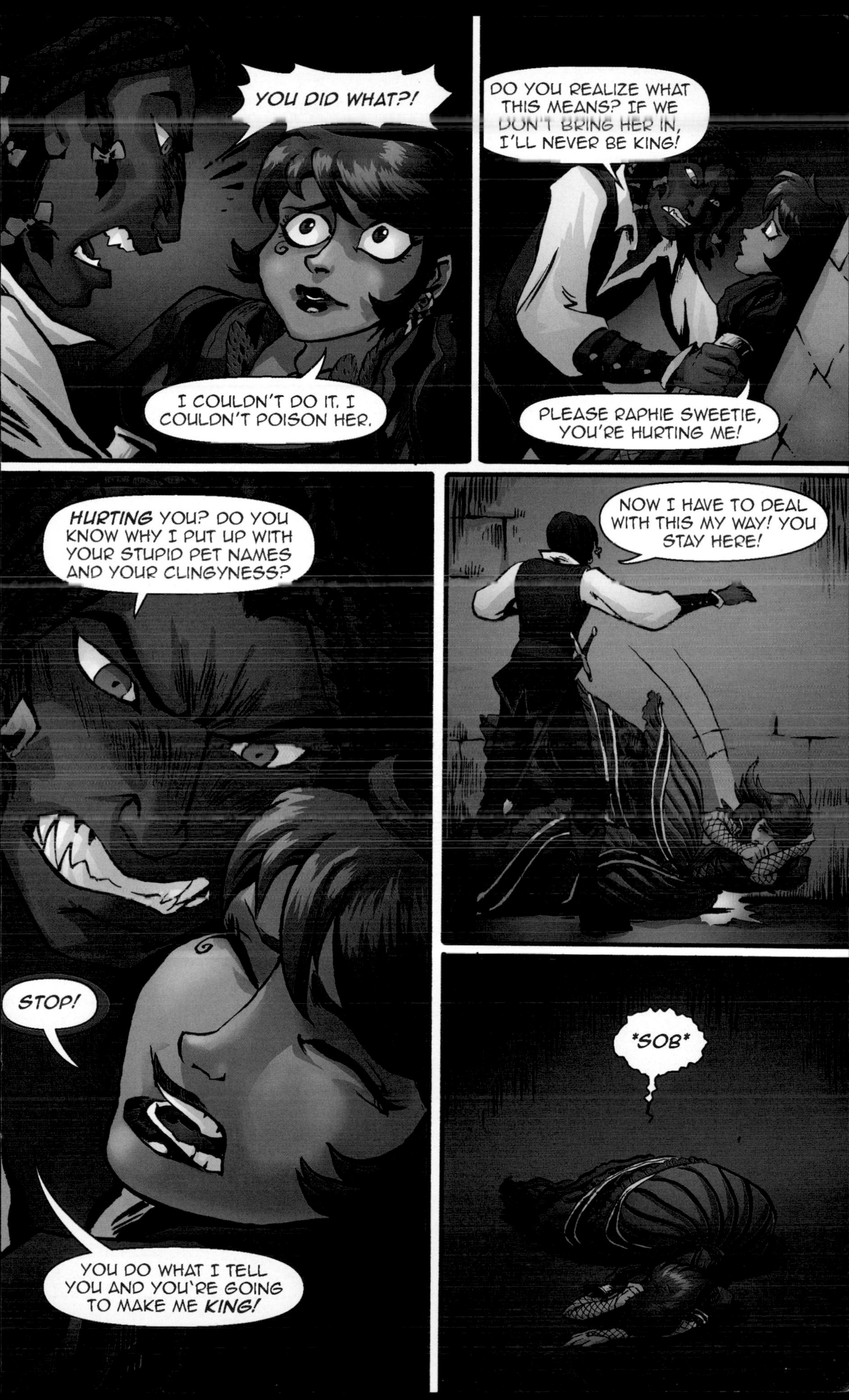
YOU DID WHAT?!
I COULDN'T DO IT. I COULDN'T POISON HER.
DO YOU REALIZE WHAT THIS MEANS? IF WE DON'T BRING HER IN, I'LL NEVER BE KING!
PLEASE RAPHIE SWEETIE, YOU'RE HURTING ME!
HURTING YOU? DO YOU KNOW WHY I PUT UP WITH YOUR STUPID PET NAMES AND YOUR CLINGYNESS?
STOP!
YOU DO WHAT I TELL YOU AND YOU'RE GOING TO MAKE ME KING!
NOW I HAVE TO DEAL WITH THIS MY WAY! YOU STAY HERE!
SOB

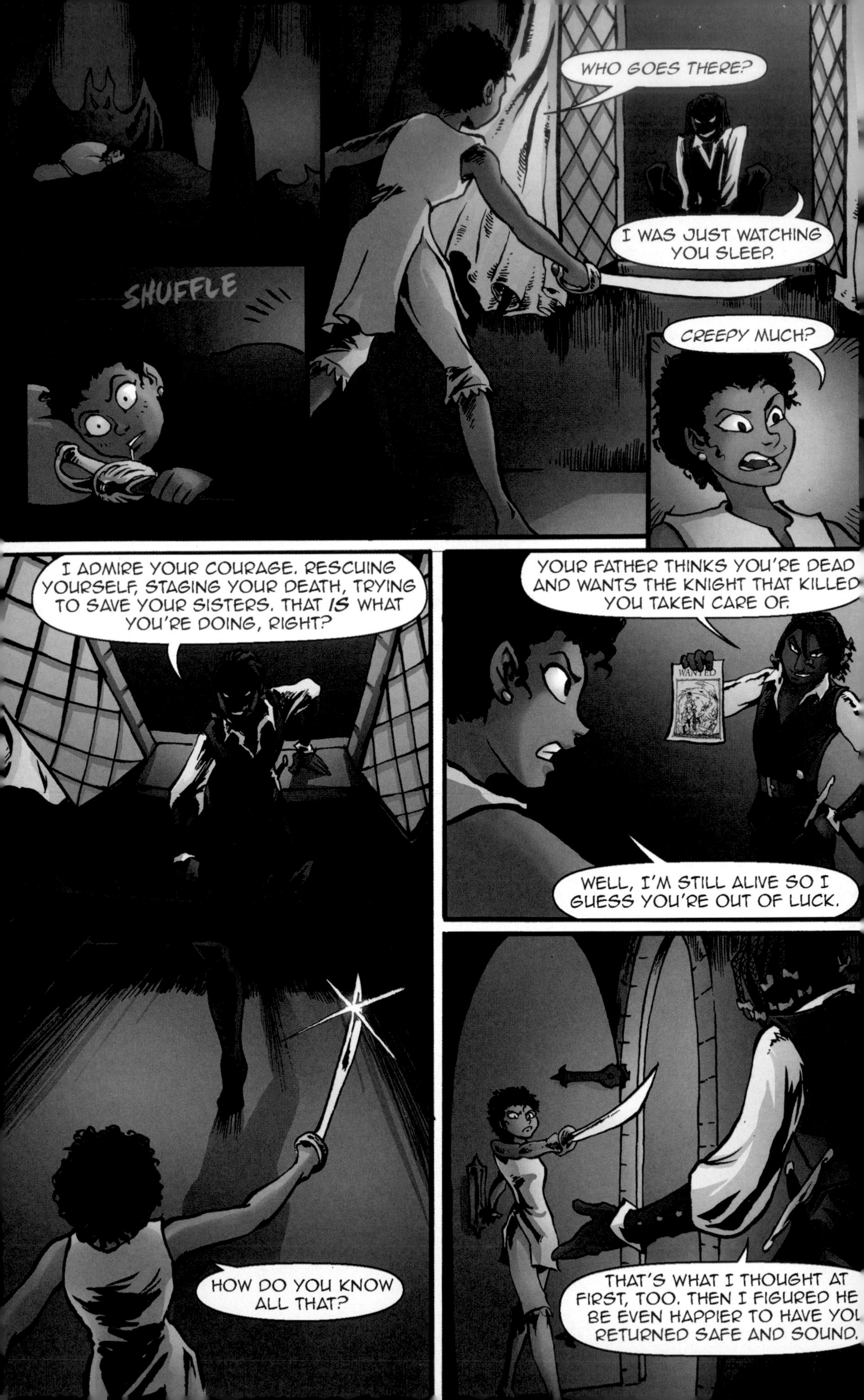
SHUFFLE
WHO GOES THERE?
I WAS JUST WATCHING YOU SLEEP.
CREEPY MUCH?
I ADMIRE YOUR COURAGE. RESCUING YOURSELF, STAGING YOUR DEATH, TRYING TO SAVE YOUR SISTERS. THAT *IS* WHAT YOU'RE DOING, RIGHT?
HOW DO YOU KNOW ALL THAT?
YOUR FATHER THINKS YOU'RE DEAD AND WANTS THE KNIGHT THAT KILLED YOU TAKEN CARE OF.
WANTED
WELL, I'M STILL ALIVE SO I GUESS YOU'RE OUT OF LUCK.
THAT'S WHAT I THOUGHT AT FIRST, TOO. THEN I FIGURED HE BE EVEN HAPPIER TO HAVE YOU RETURNED SAFE AND SOUND.

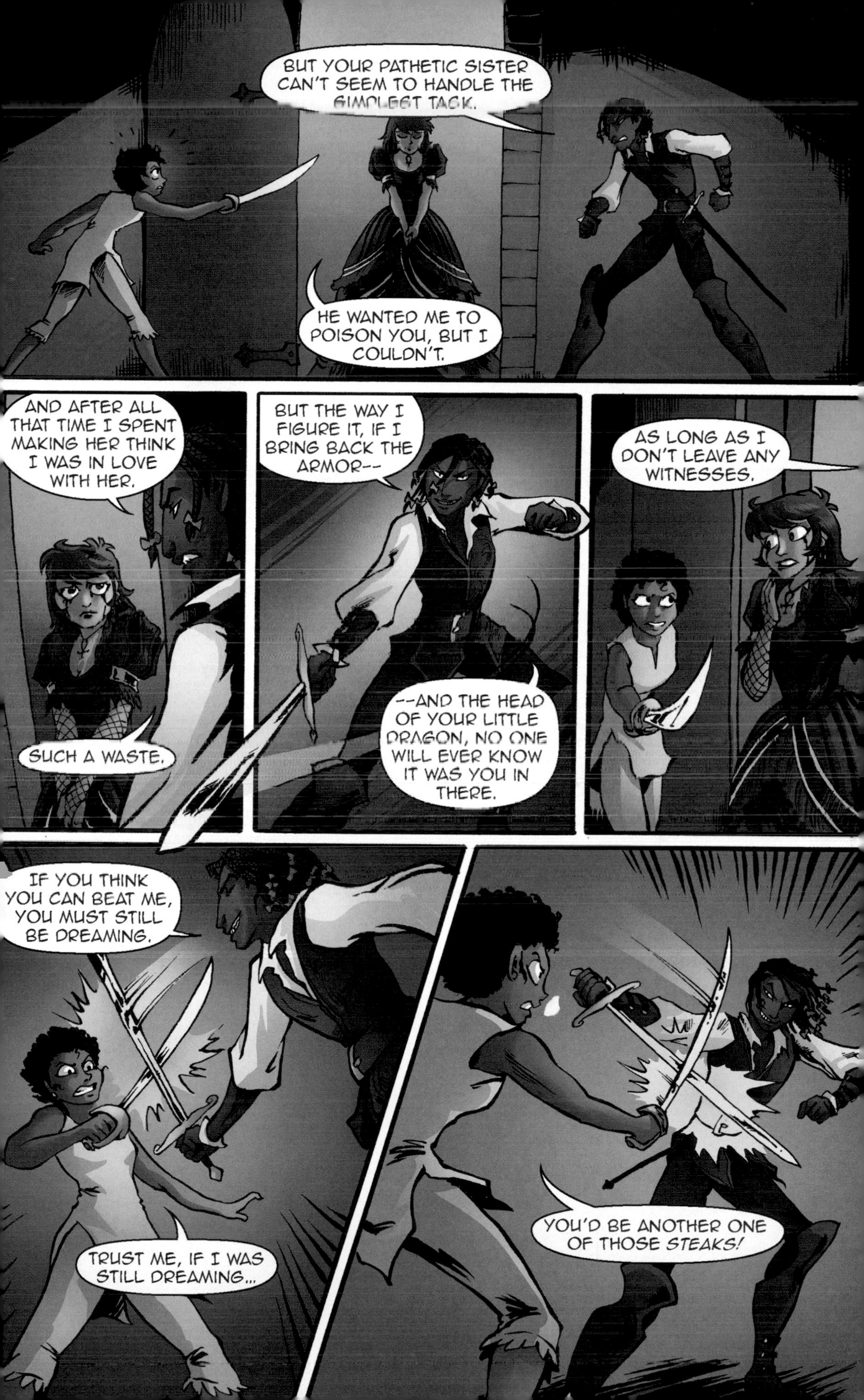
BUT YOUR PATHETIC SISTER CAN'T SEEM TO HANDLE THE SIMPLEST TASK.
HE WANTED ME TO POISON YOU, BUT I COULDN'T.
AND AFTER ALL THAT TIME I SPENT MAKING HER THINK I WAS IN LOVE WITH HER.
SUCH A WASTE.
BUT THE WAY I FIGURE IT, IF I BRING BACK THE ARMOR--
--AND THE HEAD OF YOUR LITTLE DRAGON, NO ONE WILL EVER KNOW IT WAS YOU IN THERE.
AS LONG AS I DON'T LEAVE ANY WITNESSES.
IF YOU THINK YOU CAN BEAT ME, YOU MUST STILL BE DREAMING.
TRUST ME, IF I WAS STILL DREAMING...
YOU'D BE ANOTHER ONE OF THOSE *STEAKS!*

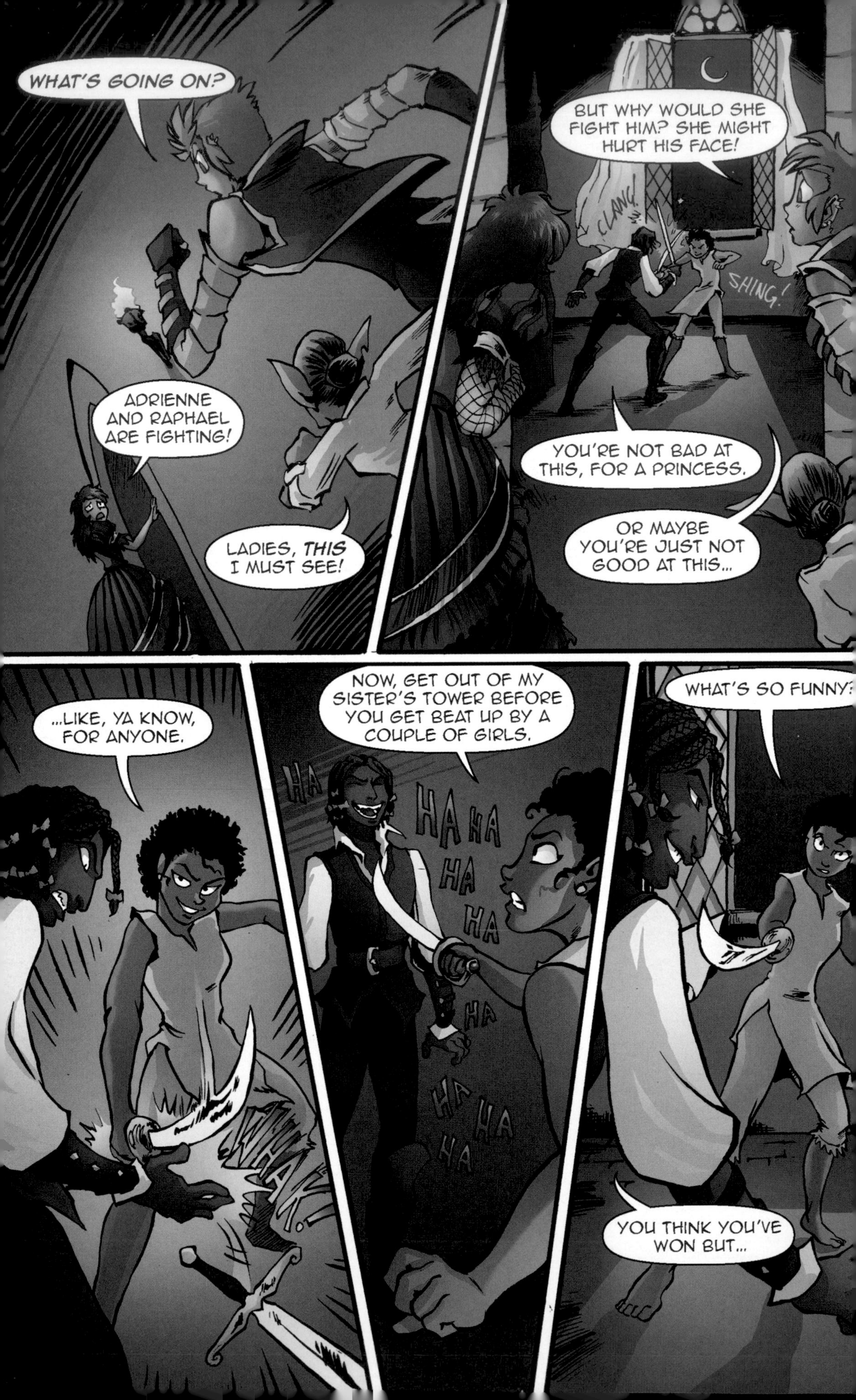
WHAT'S GOING ON?
ADRIENNE AND RAPHAEL ARE FIGHTING!
LADIES, THIS I MUST SEE!
BUT WHY WOULD SHE FIGHT HIM? SHE MIGHT HURT HIS FACE!
CLANG!
SHING!
YOU'RE NOT BAD AT THIS, FOR A PRINCESS.
OR MAYBE YOU'RE JUST NOT GOOD AT THIS...
...LIKE, YA KNOW, FOR ANYONE.
NOW, GET OUT OF MY SISTER'S TOWER BEFORE YOU GET BEAT UP BY A COUPLE OF GIRLS.
HA HA HA HA HA HA HA HA HA HA
WHAT'S SO FUNNY?
YOU THINK YOU'VE WON BUT...

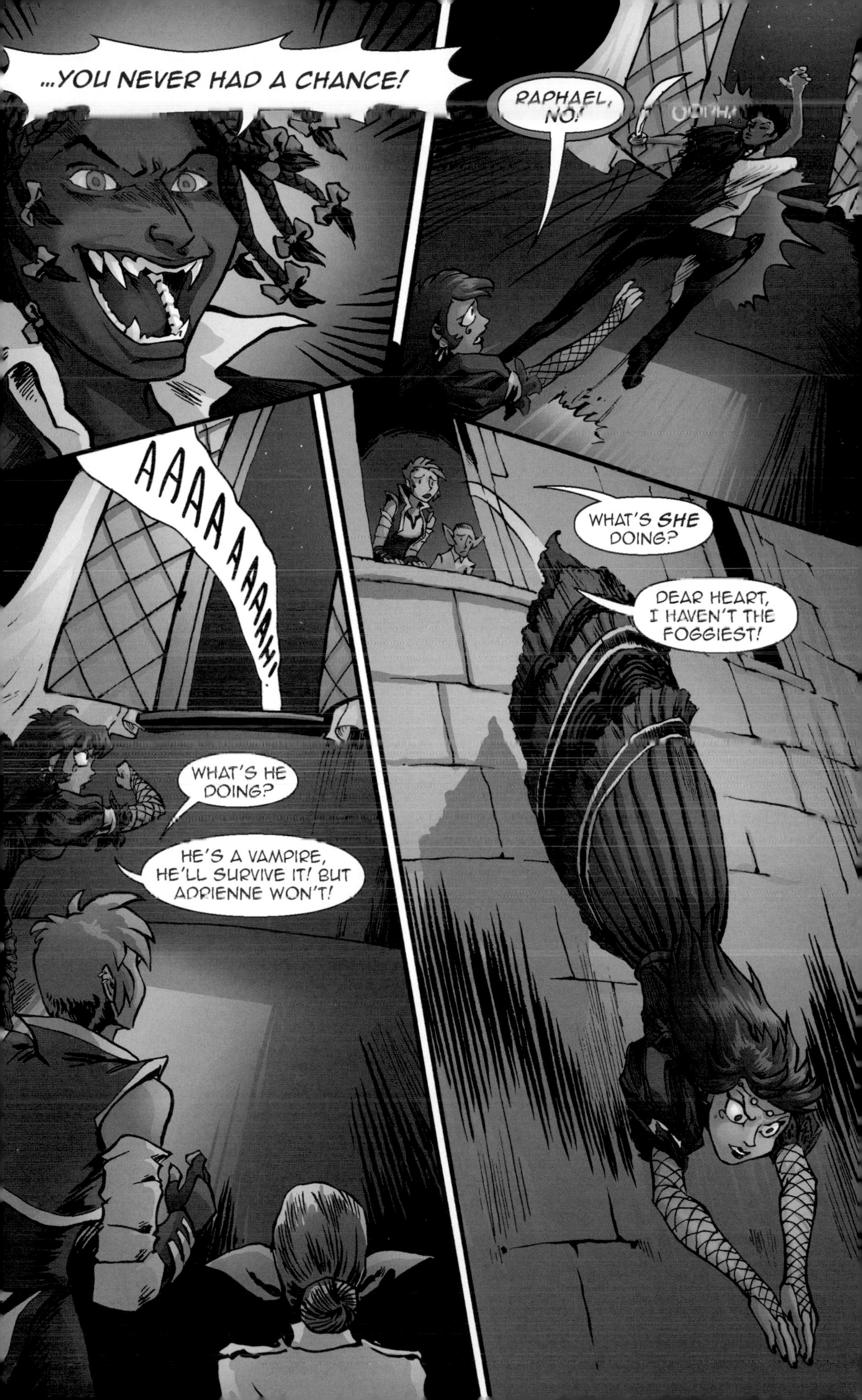
...YOU NEVER HAD A CHANCE!
RAPHAEL, NO!
AAAAAAAAAAH!
WHAT'S HE DOING?
HE'S A VAMPIRE, HE'LL SURVIVE IT! BUT ADRIENNE WON'T!
WHAT'S SHE DOING?
DEAR HEART, I HAVEN'T THE FOGGIEST!

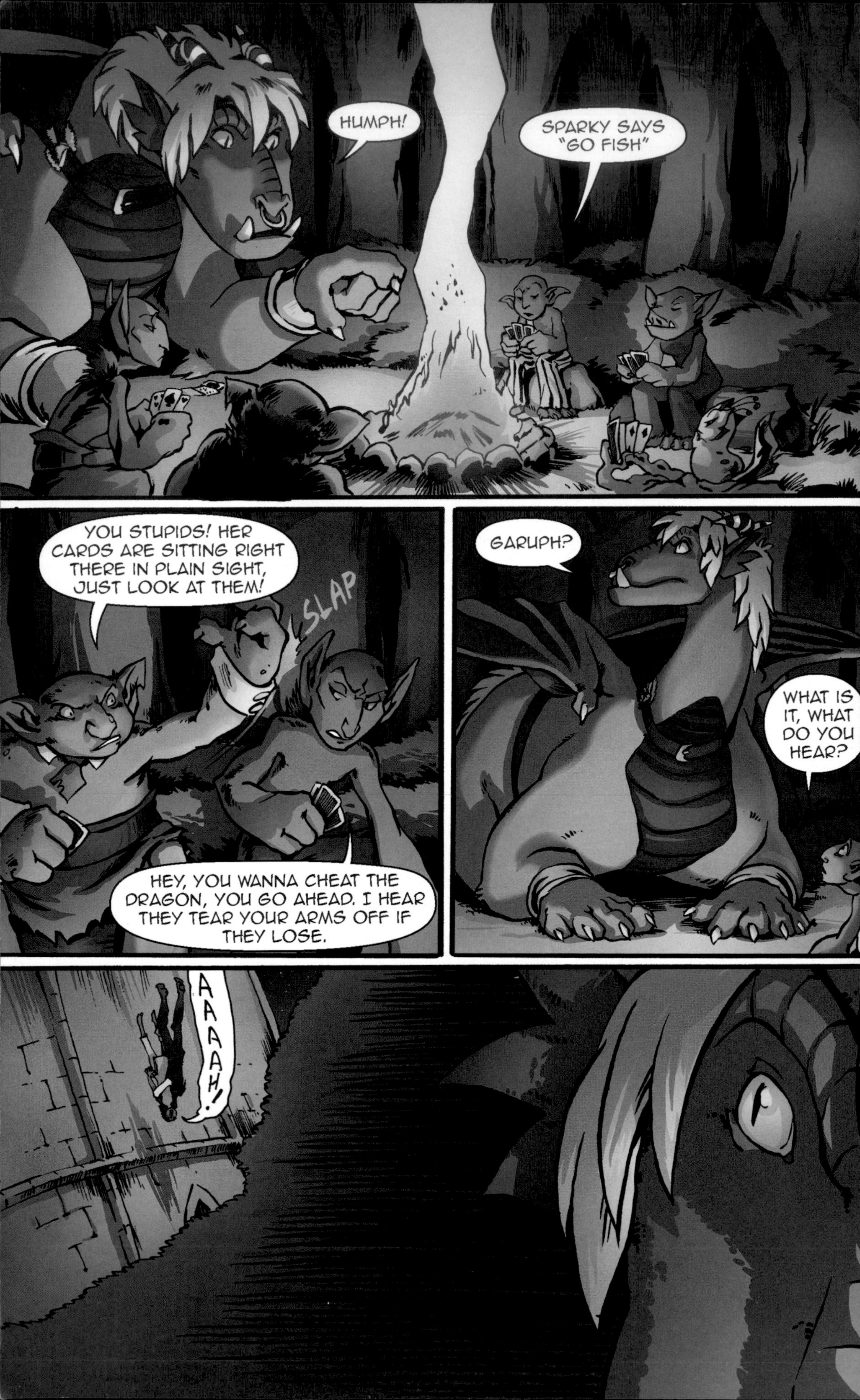
HUMPH!
SPARKY SAYS "GO FISH"
YOU STUPIDS! HER CARDS ARE SITTING RIGHT THERE IN PLAIN SIGHT, JUST LOOK AT THEM!
SLAP
HEY, YOU WANNA CHEAT THE DRAGON, YOU GO AHEAD. I HEAR THEY TEAR YOUR ARMS OFF IF THEY LOSE.
GARUPH?
WHAT IS IT, WHAT DO YOU HEAR?
AAAAAH!

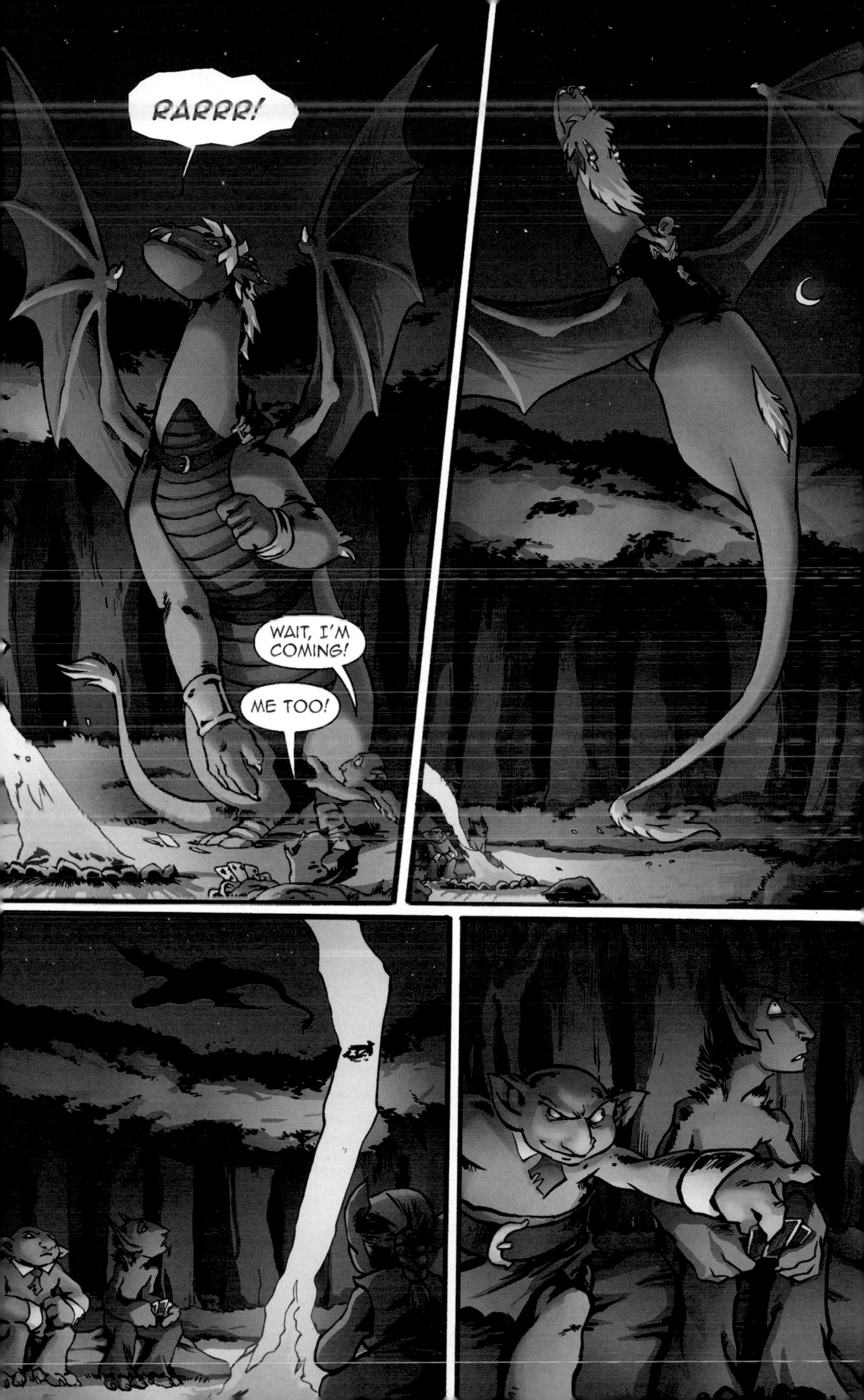
RARRR!
WAIT, I'M COMING!
ME TOO!

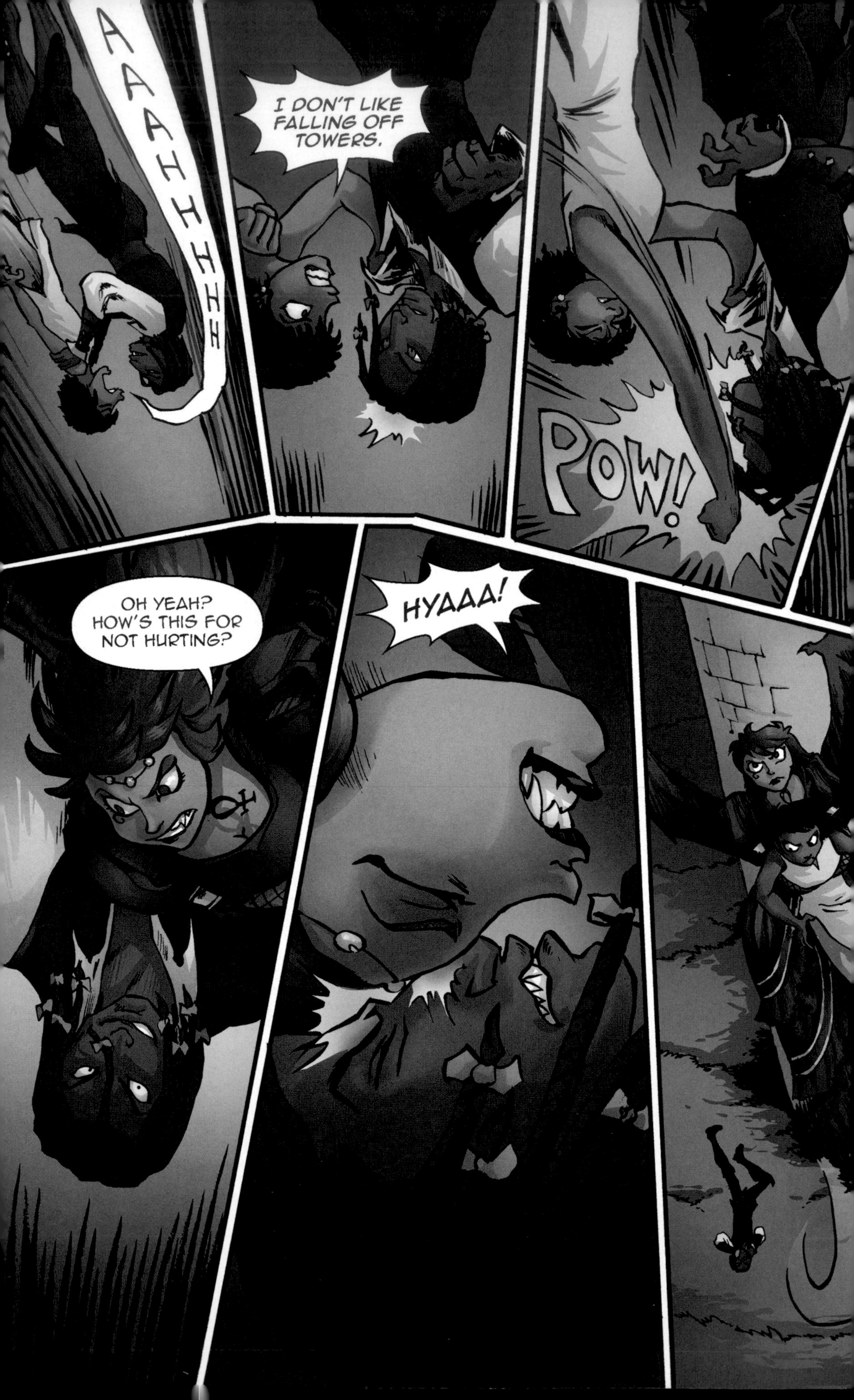
AAAHHHHH
I DON'T LIKE FALLING OFF TOWERS.
POW!
OH YEAH? HOW'S THIS FOR NOT HURTING?
HYAAA!

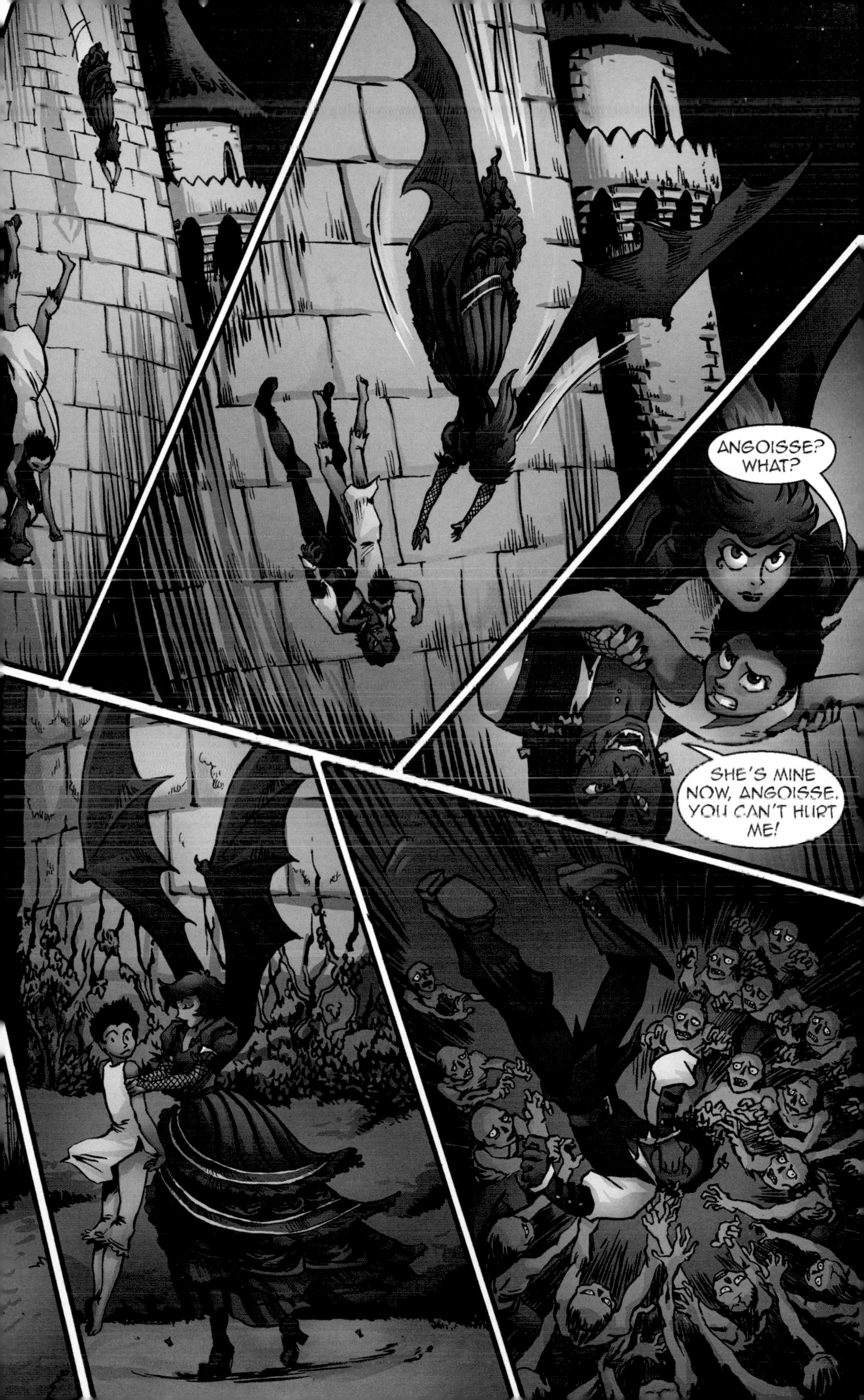
ANGOISSE? WHAT?
SHE'S MINE NOW, ANGOISSE. YOU CAN'T HURT ME!

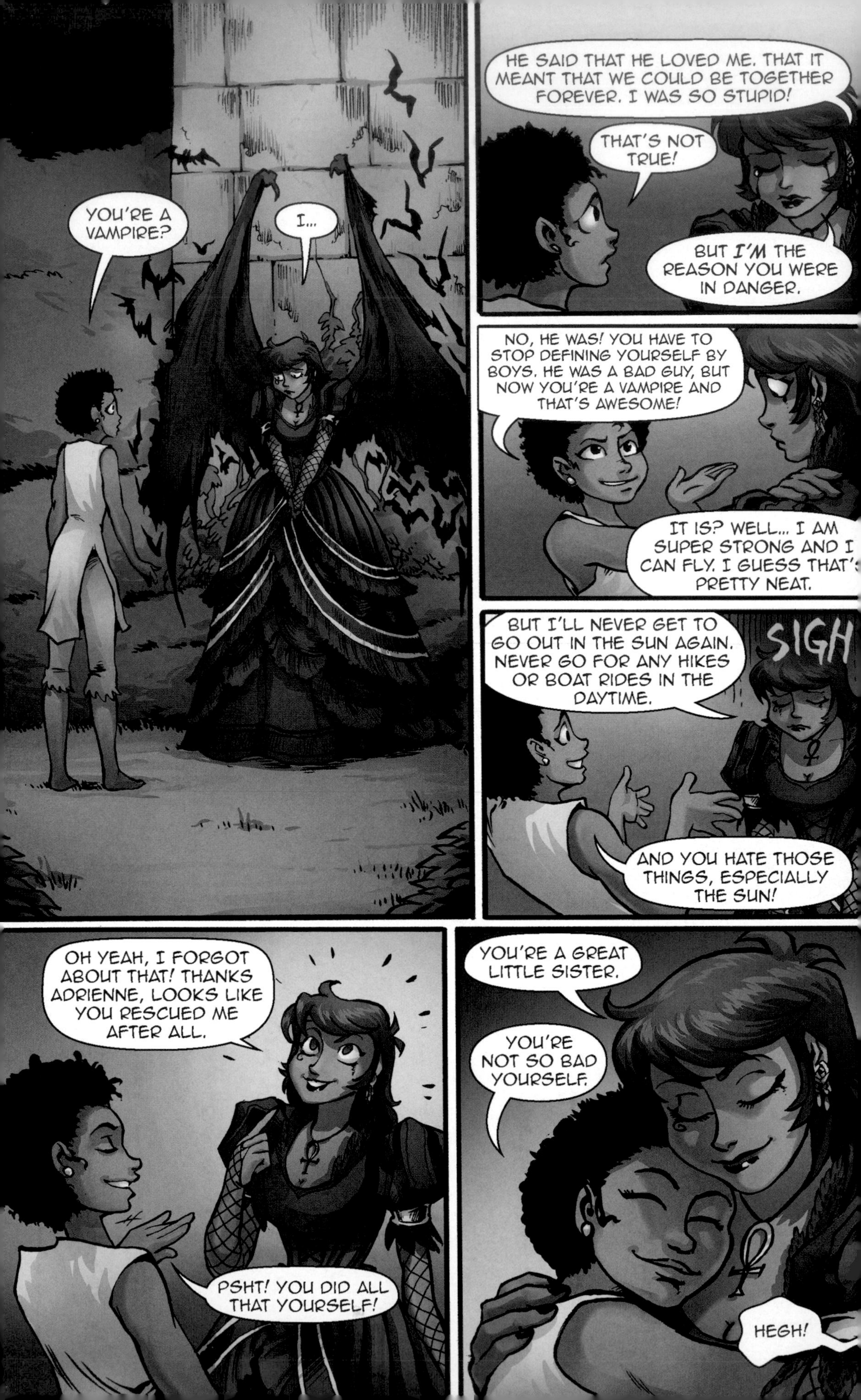
YOU'RE A VAMPIRE?
I...
HE SAID THAT HE LOVED ME. THAT IT MEANT THAT WE COULD BE TOGETHER FOREVER. I WAS SO STUPID!
THAT'S NOT TRUE!
BUT I'M THE REASON YOU WERE IN DANGER.
NO, HE WAS! YOU HAVE TO STOP DEFINING YOURSELF BY BOYS. HE WAS A BAD GUY, BUT NOW YOU'RE A VAMPIRE AND THAT'S AWESOME!
IT IS? WELL... I AM SUPER STRONG AND I CAN FLY. I GUESS THAT'S PRETTY NEAT.
BUT I'LL NEVER GET TO GO OUT IN THE SUN AGAIN. NEVER GO FOR ANY HIKES OR BOAT RIDES IN THE DAYTIME.
SIGH
AND YOU HATE THOSE THINGS, ESPECIALLY THE SUN!
OH YEAH, I FORGOT ABOUT THAT! THANKS ADRIENNE, LOOKS LIKE YOU RESCUED ME AFTER ALL.
PSHT! YOU DID ALL THAT YOURSELF!
YOU'RE A GREAT LITTLE SISTER.
YOU'RE NOT SO BAD YOURSELF.
HEGH!

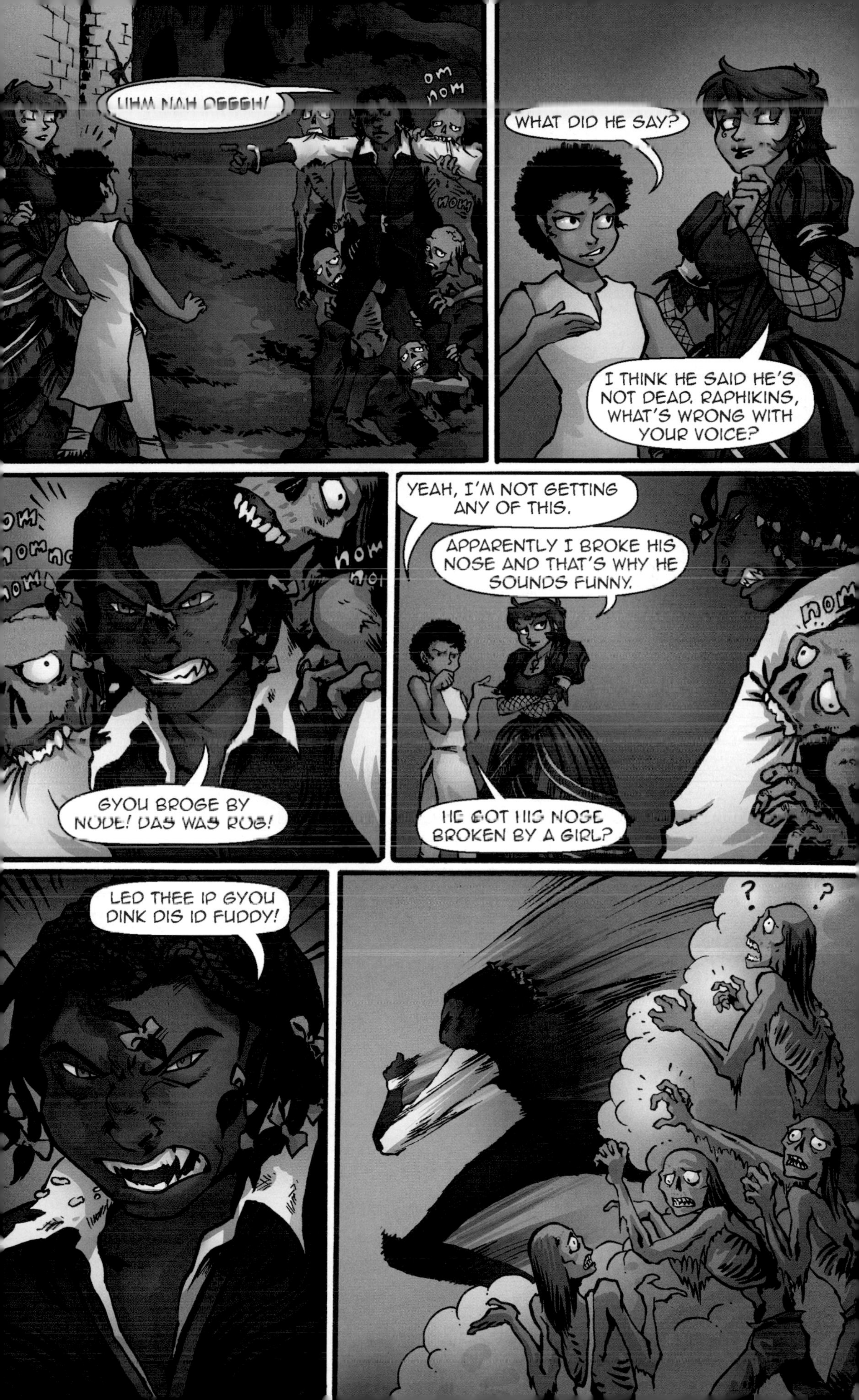
UHM NAH DEEEH!
OM NOM
NOM
NOM
WHAT DID HE SAY?
I THINK HE SAID HE'S NOT DEAD. RAPHIKINS, WHAT'S WRONG WITH YOUR VOICE?
NOM NOM NOM
NOM
GYOU BROGE BY NODE! DAS WAS RUG!
YEAH, I'M NOT GETTING ANY OF THIS.
APPARENTLY I BROKE HIS NOSE AND THAT'S WHY HE SOUNDS FUNNY.
NOM
HE GOT HIS NOSE BROKEN BY A GIRL?
LED THEE IP GYOU DINK DIS ID FUDDY!
? ?

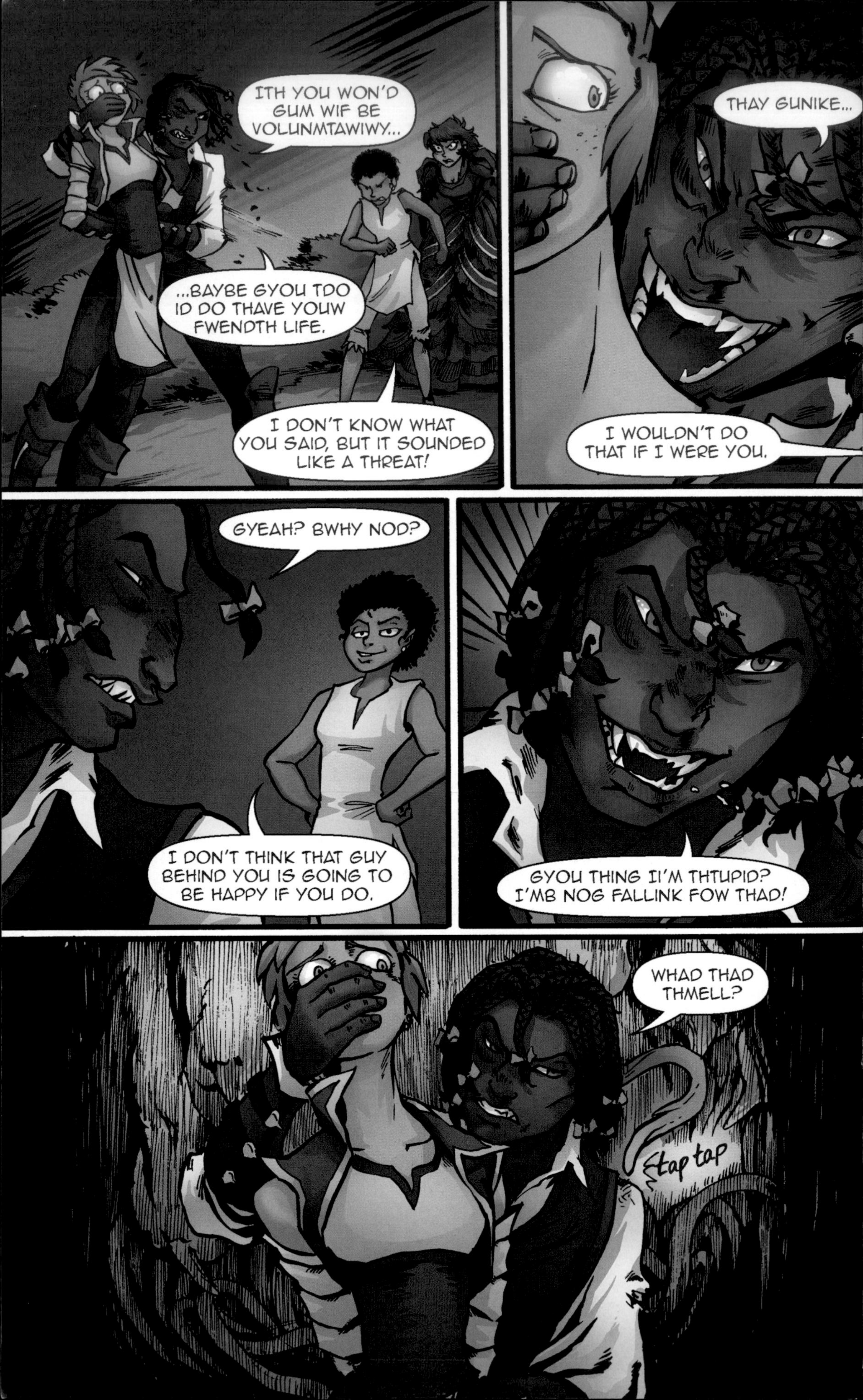
ITH YOU WON'D GUM WIF BE VOLUNMTAWIWY...
...BAYBE GYOU TDO ID DO THAVE YOUW FWENDTH LIFE.
I DON'T KNOW WHAT YOU SAID, BUT IT SOUNDED LIKE A THREAT!
THAY GUNIKE...
I WOULDN'T DO THAT IF I WERE YOU.
GYEAH? BWHY NOD?
I DON'T THINK THAT GUY BEHIND YOU IS GOING TO BE HAPPY IF YOU DO.
GYOU THING II'M THTUPID? I'MB NOG FALLINK FOW THAD!
WHAD THAD THMELL?
tap tap

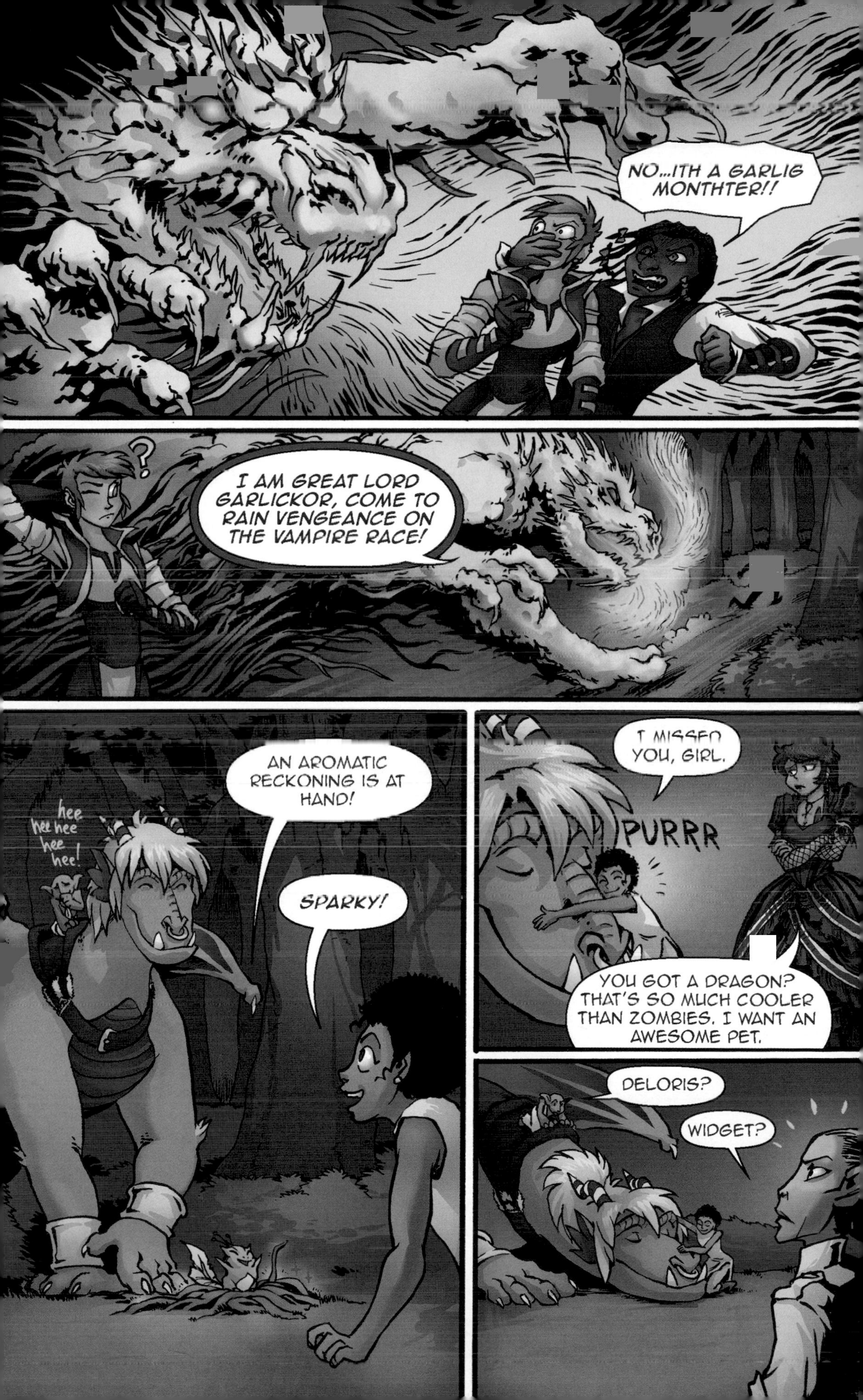
NO...ITH A GARLIG MONTHTER!!
I AM GREAT LORD GARLICKOR, COME TO RAIN VENGEANCE ON THE VAMPIRE RACE!
hee hee hee hee hee!
AN AROMATIC RECKONING IS AT HAND!
SPARKY!
I MISSED YOU, GIRL.
PURRR
YOU GOT A DRAGON? THAT'S SO MUCH COOLER THAN ZOMBIES. I WANT AN AWESOME PET.
DELORIS?
WIDGET?

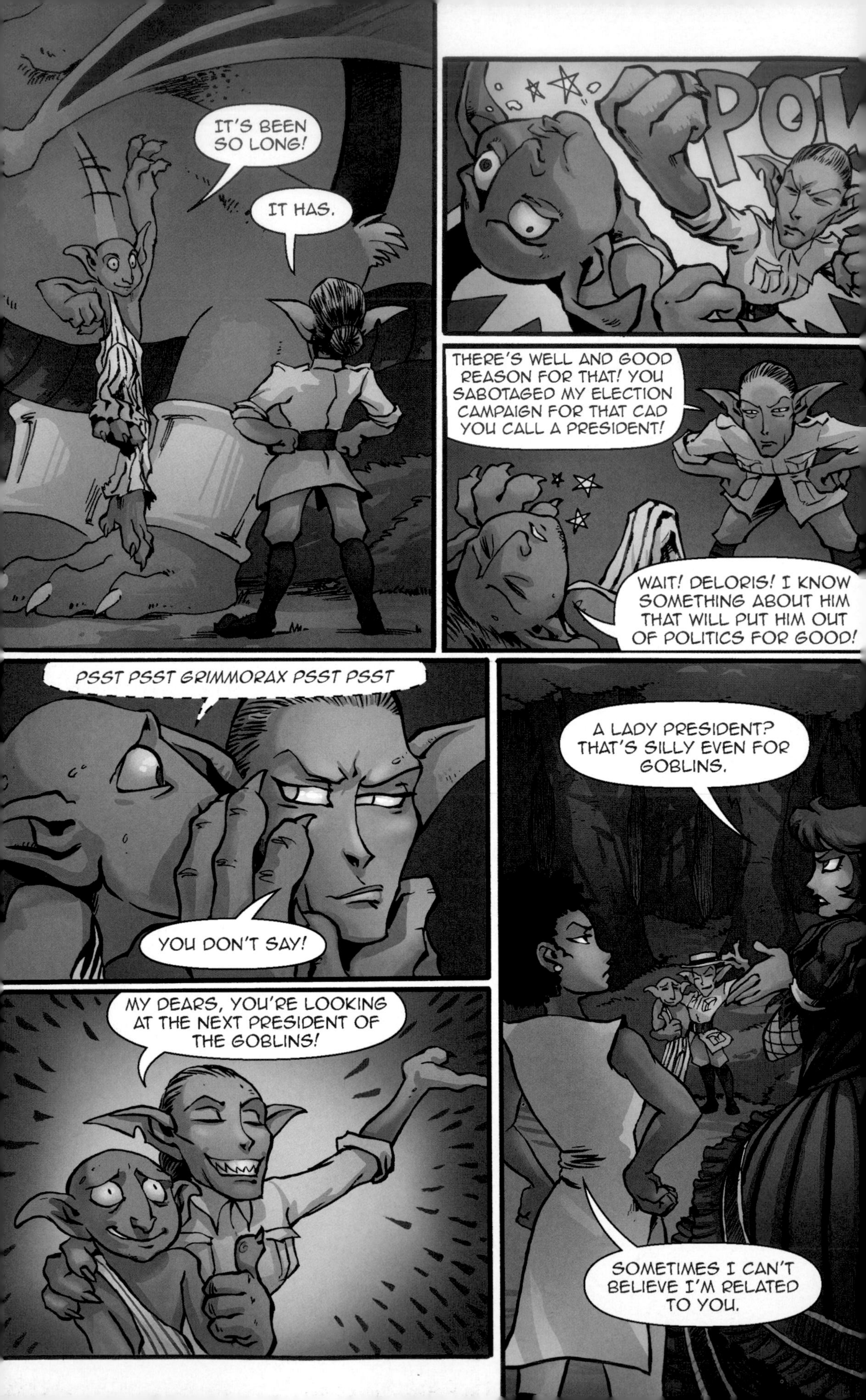
IT'S BEEN SO LONG!
IT HAS.
POW
THERE'S WELL AND GOOD REASON FOR THAT! YOU SABOTAGED MY ELECTION CAMPAIGN FOR THAT CAD YOU CALL A PRESIDENT!
WAIT! DELORIS! I KNOW SOMETHING ABOUT HIM THAT WILL PUT HIM OUT OF POLITICS FOR GOOD!
PSST PSST GRIMMORAX PSST PSST
YOU DON'T SAY!
MY DEARS, YOU'RE LOOKING AT THE NEXT PRESIDENT OF THE GOBLINS!
A LADY PRESIDENT? THAT'S SILLY EVEN FOR GOBLINS.
SOMETIMES I CAN'T BELIEVE I'M RELATED TO YOU.

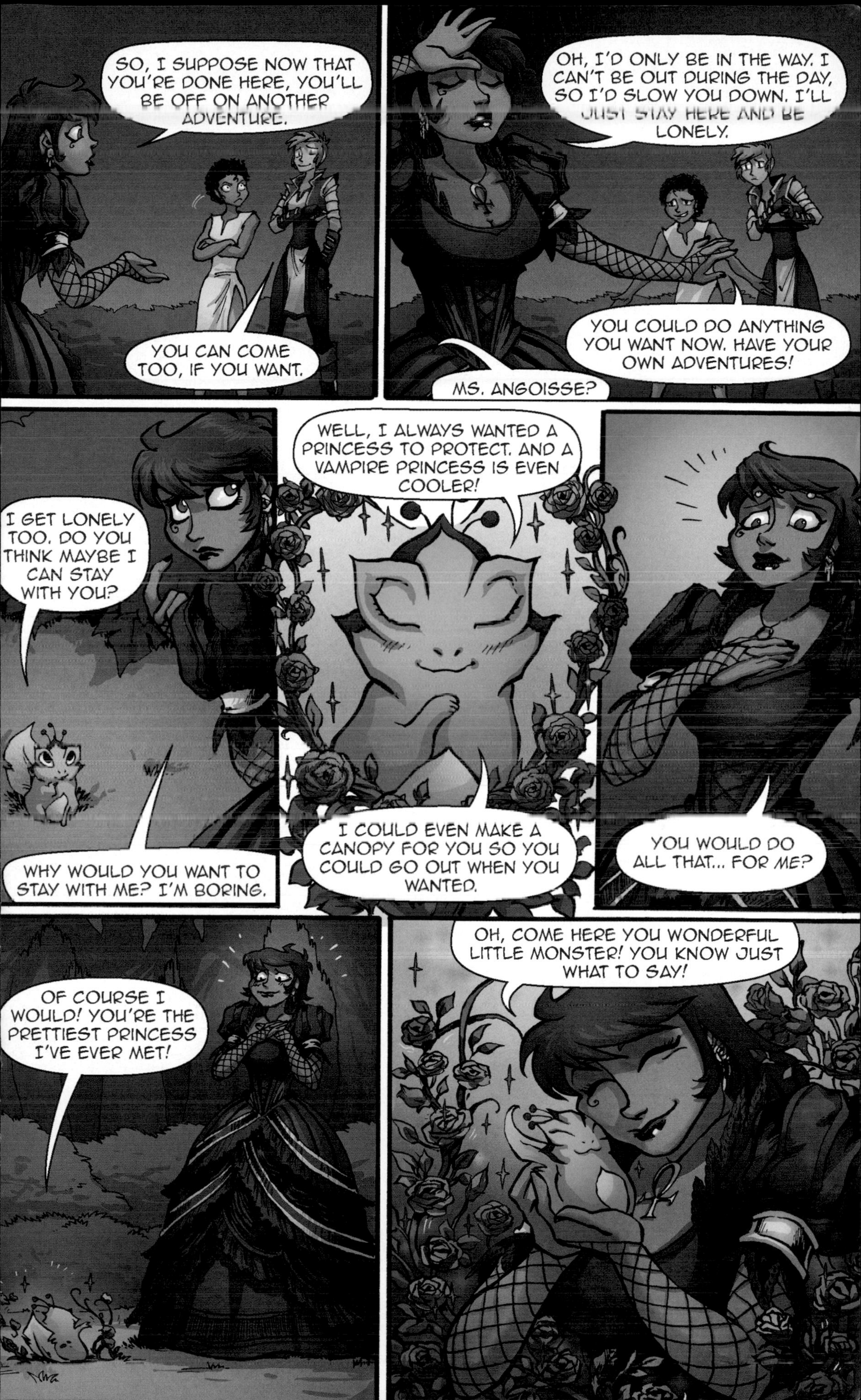
SO, I SUPPOSE NOW THAT YOU'RE DONE HERE, YOU'LL BE OFF ON ANOTHER ADVENTURE.
YOU CAN COME TOO, IF YOU WANT.
OH, I'D ONLY BE IN THE WAY. I CAN'T BE OUT DURING THE DAY, SO I'D SLOW YOU DOWN. I'LL JUST STAY HERE AND BE LONELY.
YOU COULD DO ANYTHING YOU WANT NOW. HAVE YOUR OWN ADVENTURES!
MS. ANGOISSE?
I GET LONELY TOO. DO YOU THINK MAYBE I CAN STAY WITH YOU?
WHY WOULD YOU WANT TO STAY WITH ME? I'M BORING.
WELL, I ALWAYS WANTED A PRINCESS TO PROTECT. AND A VAMPIRE PRINCESS IS EVEN COOLER!
I COULD EVEN MAKE A CANOPY FOR YOU SO YOU COULD GO OUT WHEN YOU WANTED.
YOU WOULD DO ALL THAT... FOR ME?
OF COURSE I WOULD! YOU'RE THE PRETTIEST PRINCESS I'VE EVER MET!
OH, COME HERE YOU WONDERFUL LITTLE MONSTER! YOU KNOW JUST WHAT TO SAY!

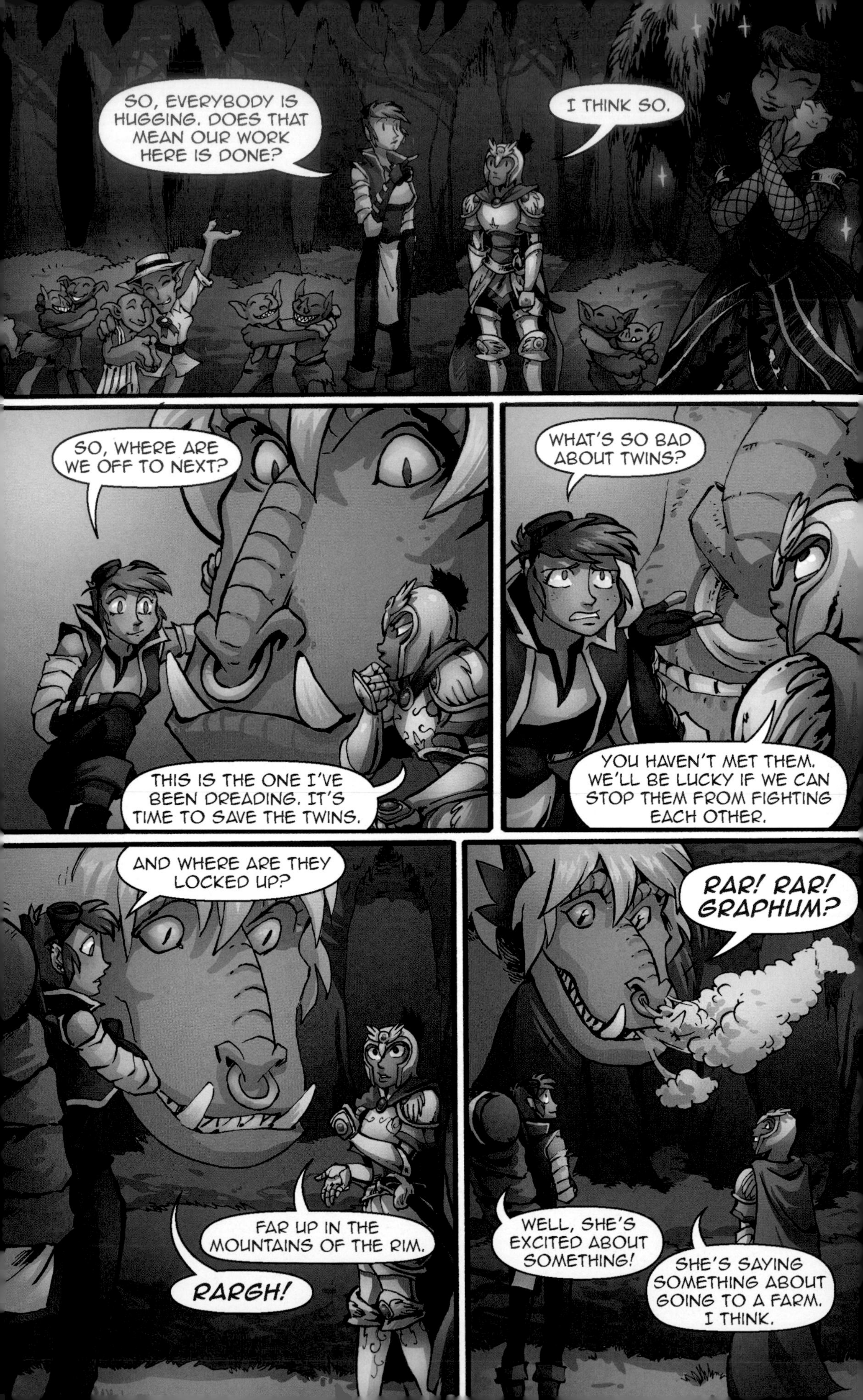
SO, EVERYBODY IS HUGGING. DOES THAT MEAN OUR WORK HERE IS DONE?
I THINK SO.
SO, WHERE ARE WE OFF TO NEXT?
THIS IS THE ONE I'VE BEEN DREADING. IT'S TIME TO SAVE THE TWINS.
WHAT'S SO BAD ABOUT TWINS?
YOU HAVEN'T MET THEM. WE'LL BE LUCKY IF WE CAN STOP THEM FROM FIGHTING EACH OTHER.
AND WHERE ARE THEY LOCKED UP?
FAR UP IN THE MOUNTAINS OF THE RIM.
RARGH!
RAR! RAR! GRAPHUM?
WELL, SHE'S EXCITED ABOUT SOMETHING!
SHE'S SAYING SOMETHING ABOUT GOING TO A FARM. I THINK.

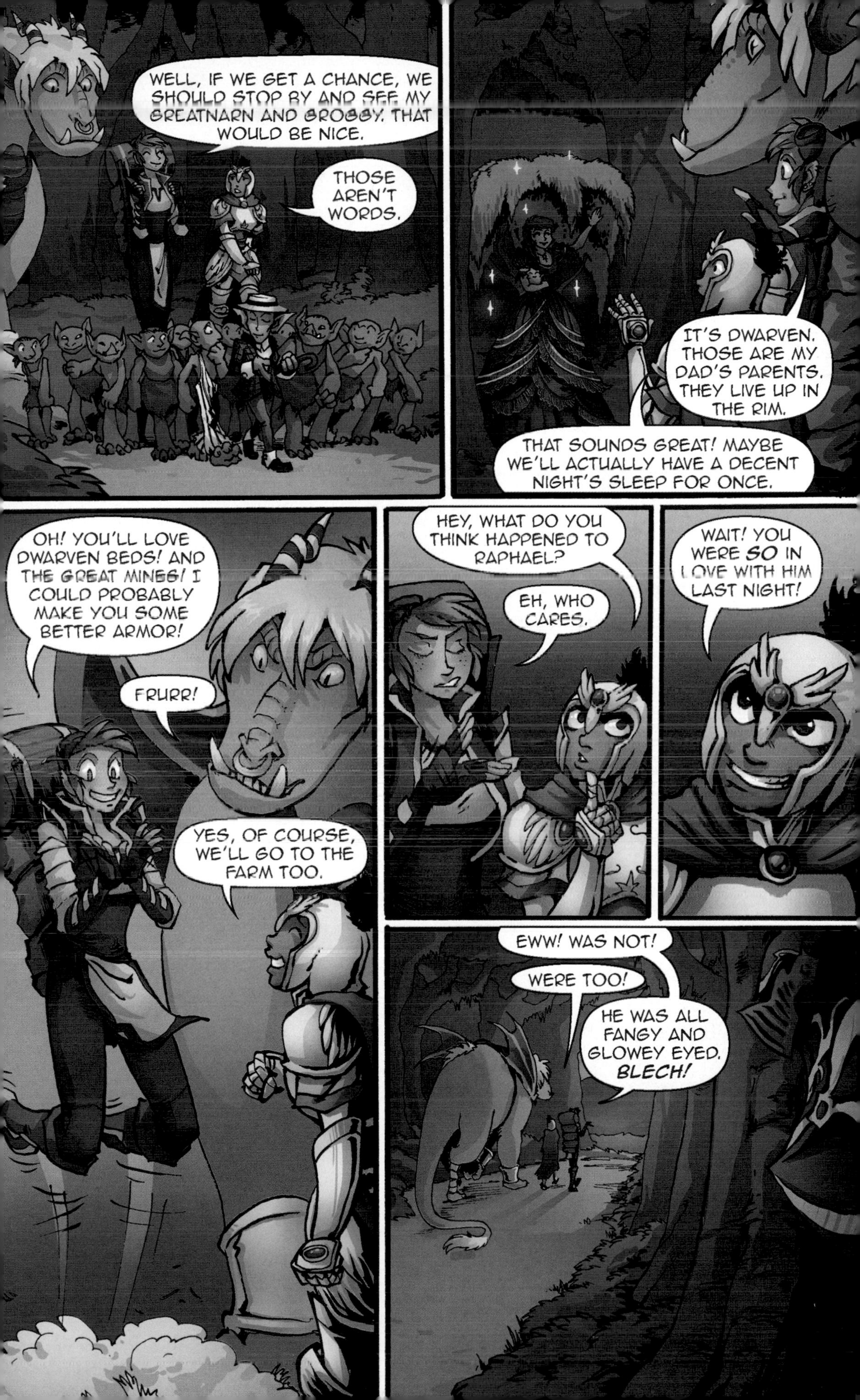

WELL, IF WE GET A CHANCE, WE SHOULD STOP BY AND SEE MY GREATNARN AND GROBBY. THAT WOULD BE NICE.
THOSE AREN'T WORDS.
IT'S DWARVEN. THOSE ARE MY DAD'S PARENTS. THEY LIVE UP IN THE RIM.
THAT SOUNDS GREAT! MAYBE WE'LL ACTUALLY HAVE A DECENT NIGHT'S SLEEP FOR ONCE.
OH! YOU'LL LOVE DWARVEN BEDS! AND THE GREAT MINES! I COULD PROBABLY MAKE YOU SOME BETTER ARMOR!
FRURR!
YES, OF COURSE, WE'LL GO TO THE FARM TOO.
HEY, WHAT DO YOU THINK HAPPENED TO RAPHAEL?
EH, WHO CARES.
WAIT! YOU WERE *SO* IN LOVE WITH HIM LAST NIGHT!
EWW! WAS NOT!
WERE TOO!
HE WAS ALL FANGY AND GLOWEY EYED. *BLECH!*

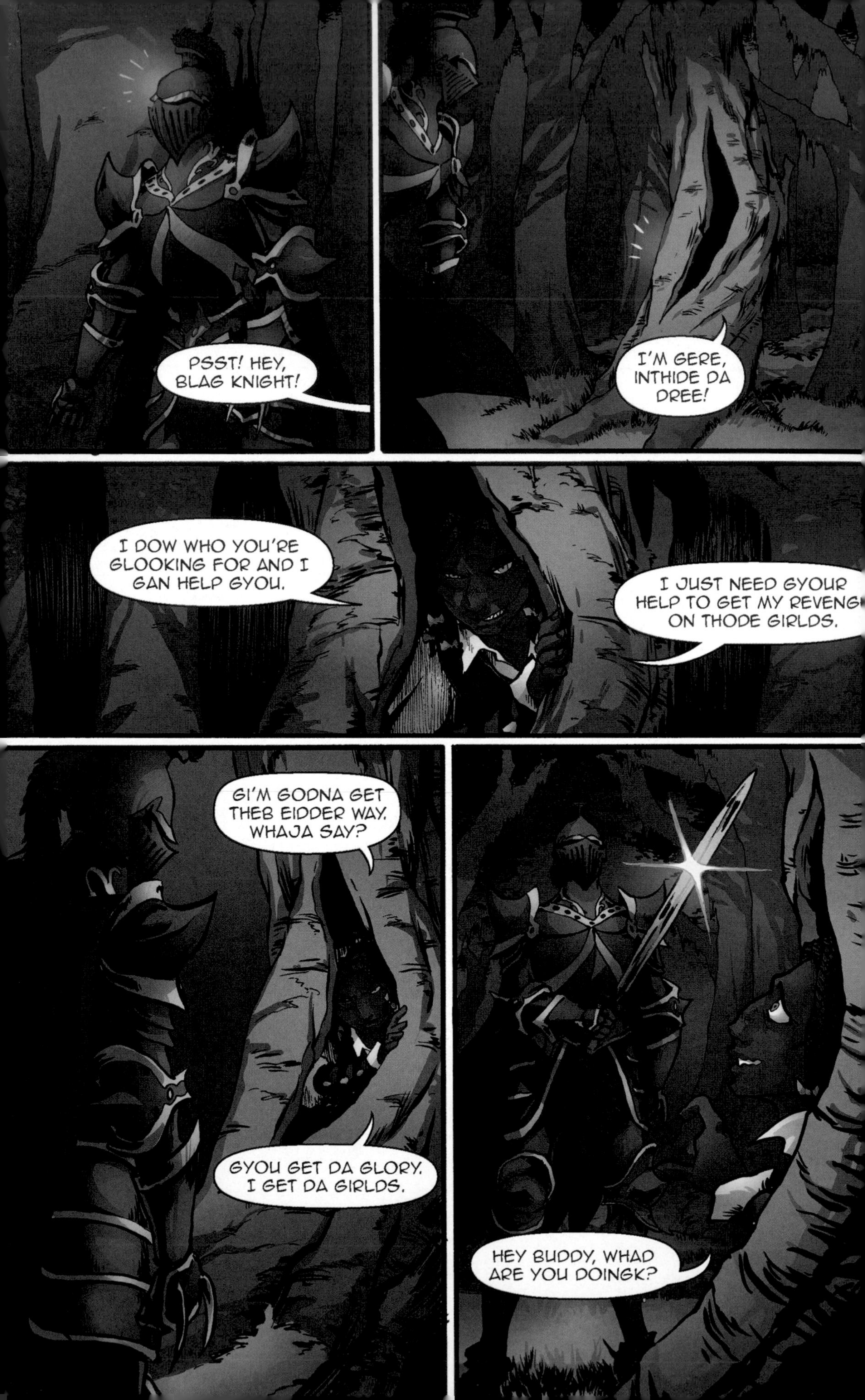
PSST! HEY, BLAG KNIGHT!
I'M GERE, INTHIDE DA DREE!
I DOW WHO YOU'RE GLOOKING FOR AND I GAN HELP GYOU.
I JUST NEED GYOUR HELP TO GET MY REVENG ON THODE GIRLDS.
GI'M GODNA GET THEB EIDDER WAY. WHAJA SAY?
GYOU GET DA GLORY. I GET DA GIRLDS.
HEY BUDDY, WHAD ARE YOU DOINGK?

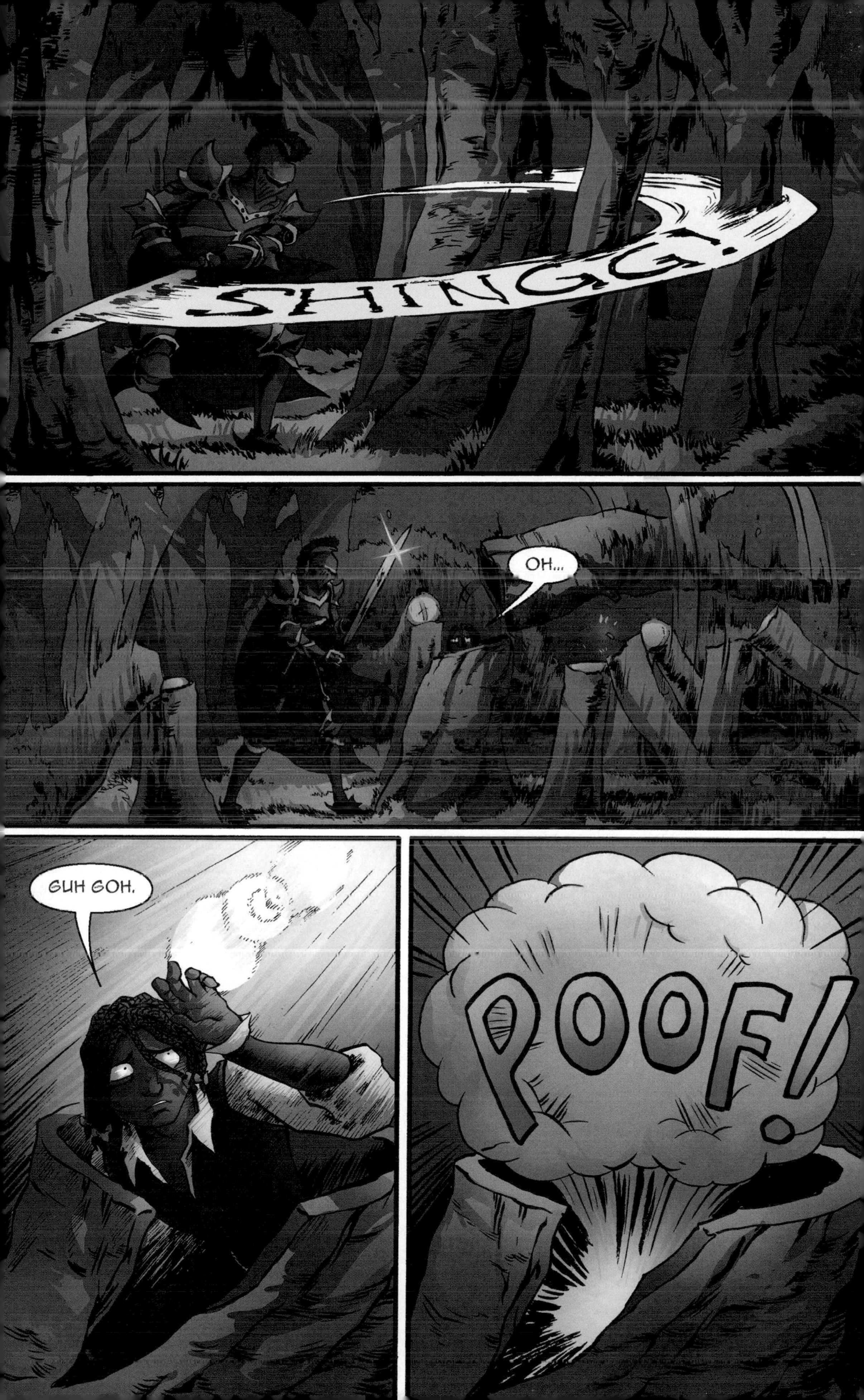
SHINGG!
OH...
GUH GOH.
POOF!

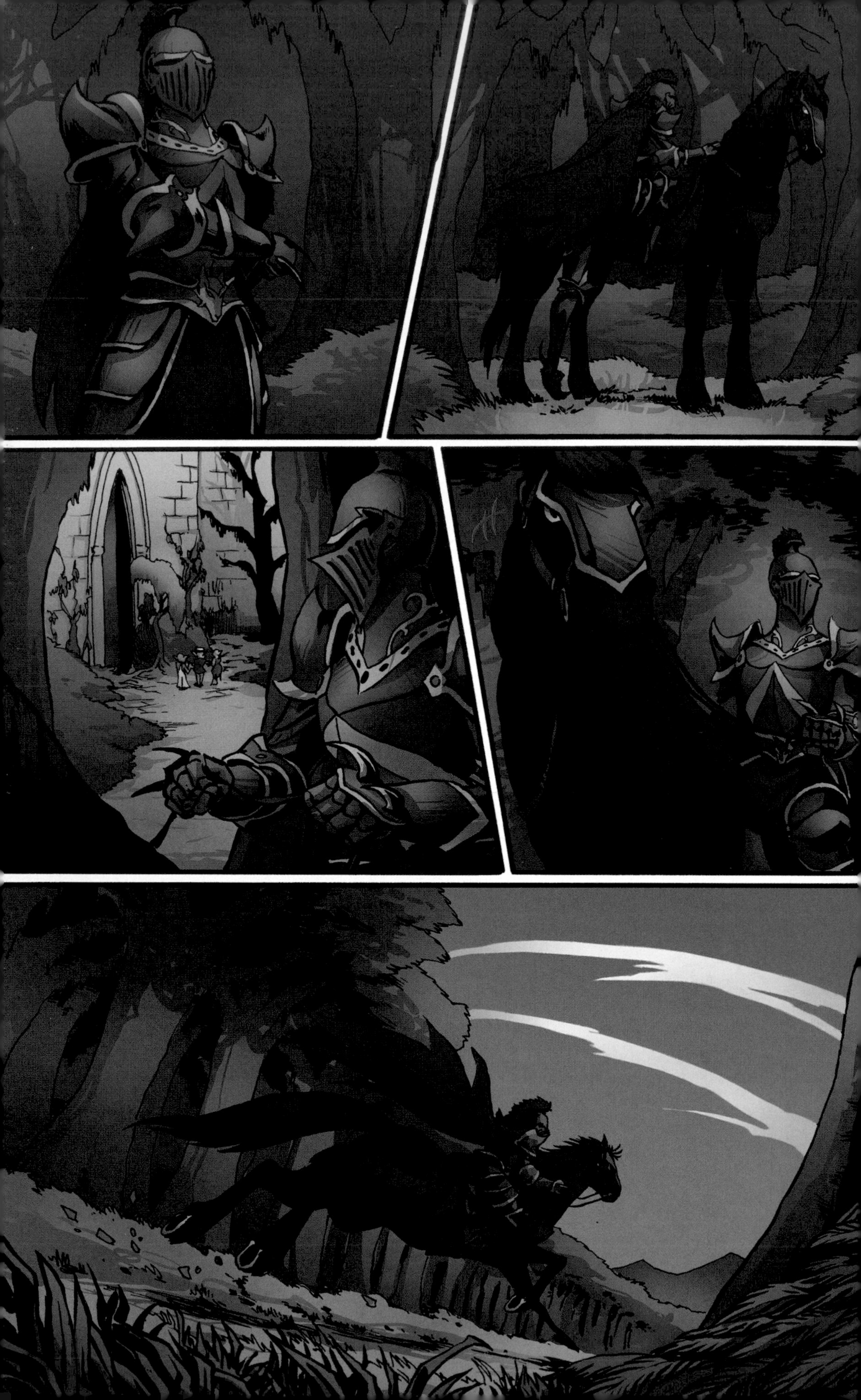

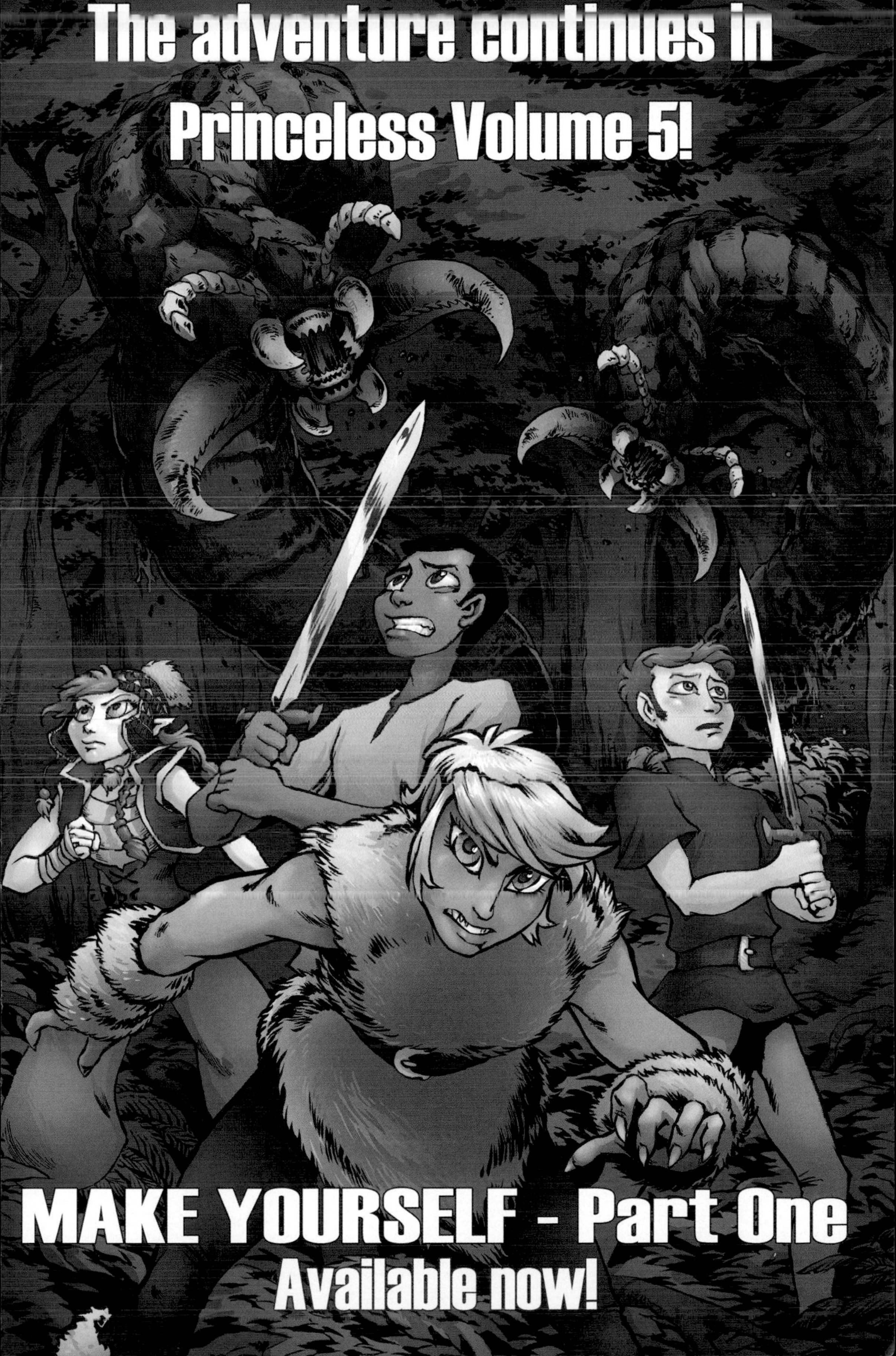
The adventure continues in
Princeless Volume 5!
MAKE YOURSELF - Part One
Available now!

Princeless

Volume 4: Be Yourself
Design and Process

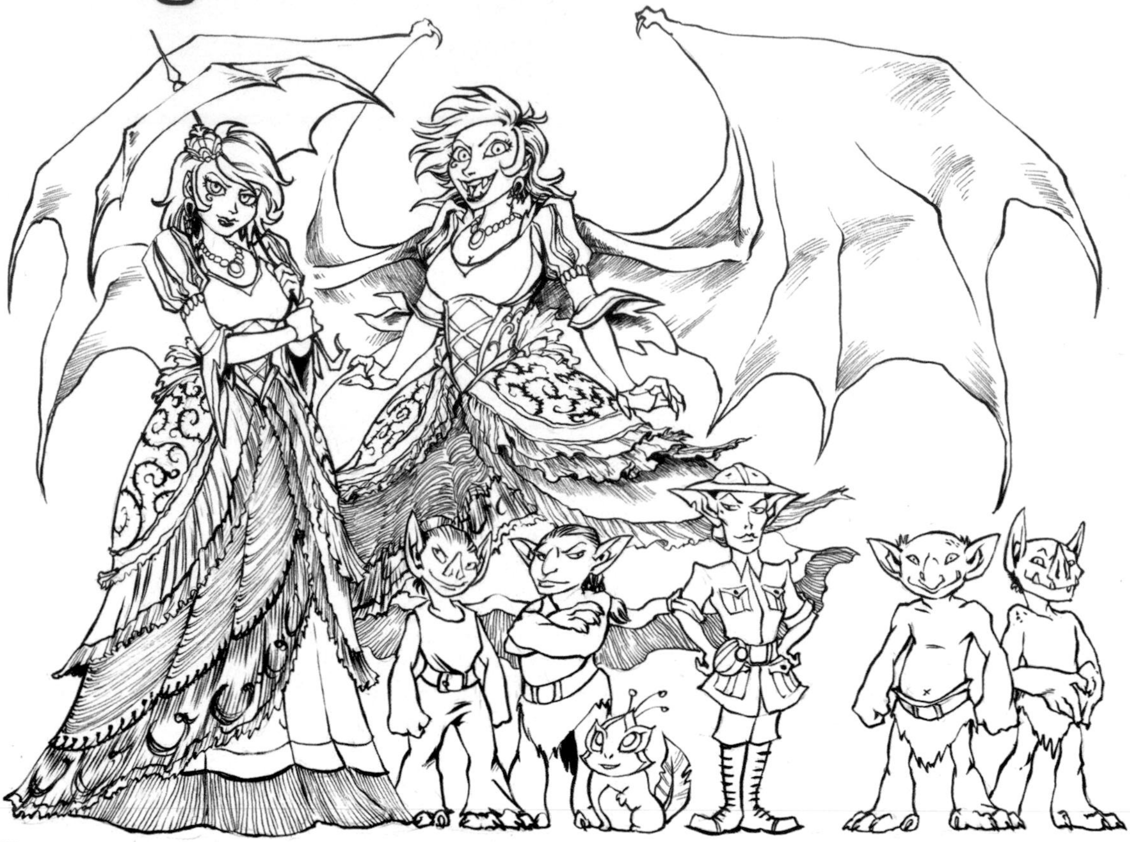

OUR GOAL WITH VOLUME 4 WAS TO HIT ON ALL THE ELEMENTS OF FANTASY HORROR, OBVIOUSLY WITHOUT MAKING IT TOO SCARY. WE WANTED TO DO THAT CLASSIC D&D SETTING OF "THE SWAMP" WHERE EVERYTHING IS WILD AND WANTS TO KILL YOU. IT'S FULL OF UNSEEN DANGERS, DERANGED CREATURES, AND THE NORMAL RULES YOU USE TO NAVIGATE DON'T APPLY. SQUIRRELS ARE EVIL AND GOBLINS, IT TURNS OUT, ARE MOSTLY FINE.

MAYBE EVEN MORE IMPORTANT THOUGH IS THAT WE PULL IN THE FANTASY HORROR WORLD THAT A LOT OF YOUNGER READERS MIGHT BE FAMILIAR WITH: THE ONE WITH SPARKLY VAMPIRES AND QUESTIONABLY MENACING ROMANCE. WE WANTED TO GIVE EVERYTHING A FEELING OF A GOTHIC ROMANCE WITH BIG DRESSES AND AN OBNOXIOUSLY HANDSOME SUITOR.

AND THEN OF COURSE THERE'S GRIMMORAX, THE MIGHTY BEAST THAT STALKS AND THREATENS EVERY INCH OF THE SWAMP...

TAKE A LOOK AND SEE SOME OF THE DESIGNS THAT SERIES ARTIST EMILY C. MARTIN CAME UP WITH FOR THE NEW CHARACTERS OF THIS CHAPTER.

-JEREMY

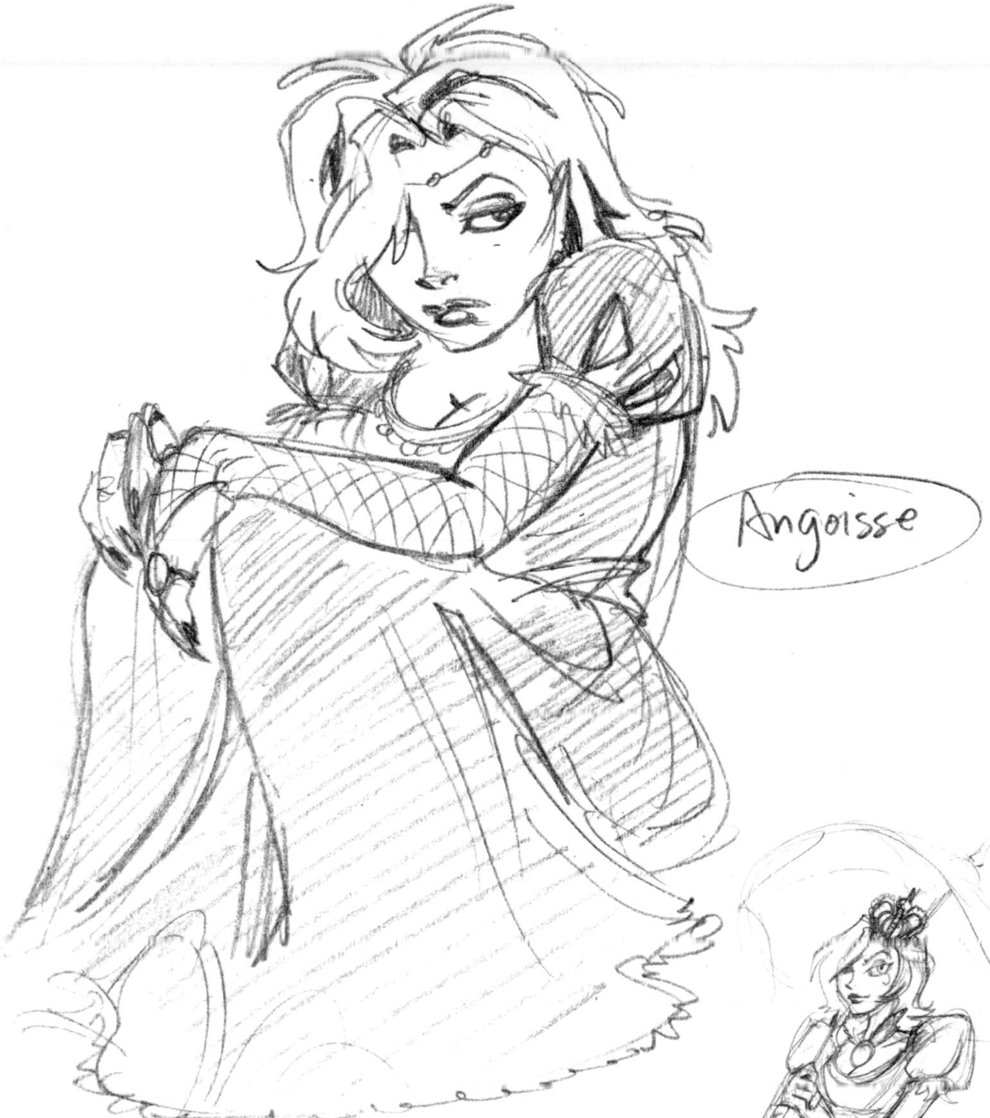
Angoisse

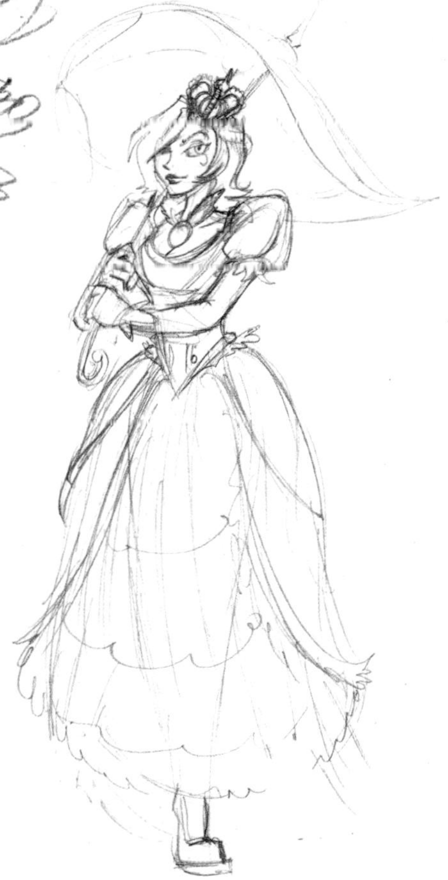

SOME EARLY SKETCHES OF ANGOISSE. I DREW FROM MY LONG-PAST PERSONAL EXPERIENCE FOR HER EARLY "MOPEY GOTH" DESIGN. LATER ON I MADE HER A BIT MORE ORNATE GOTH—A LOT MORE FUN TO DRAW!

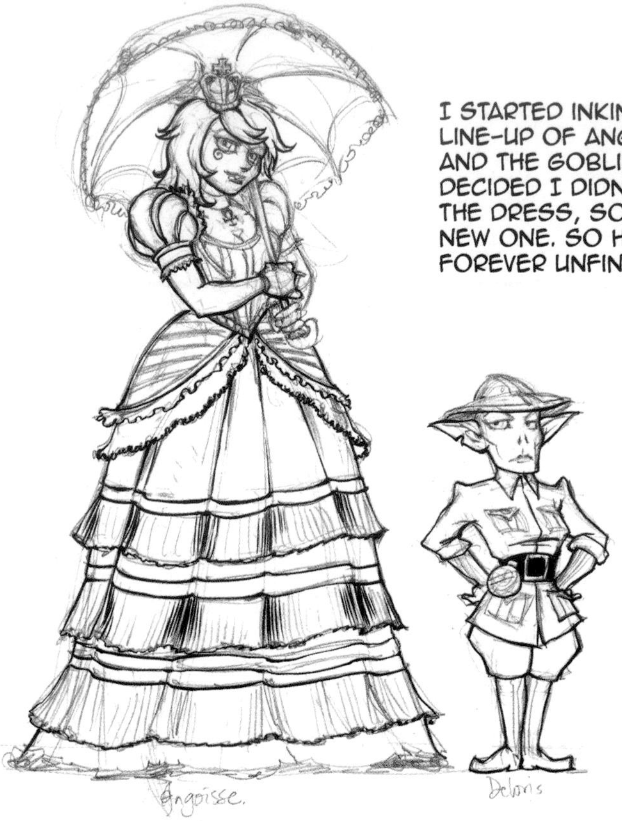
Angoisse.
Deloris

I STARTED INKING THIS LINE-UP OF ANGOISSE AND THE GOBLINS, UNTIL DECIDED I DIDN'T LIKE THE DRESS, SO I DID A NEW ONE. SO HERE IT IS, FOREVER UNFINISHED...

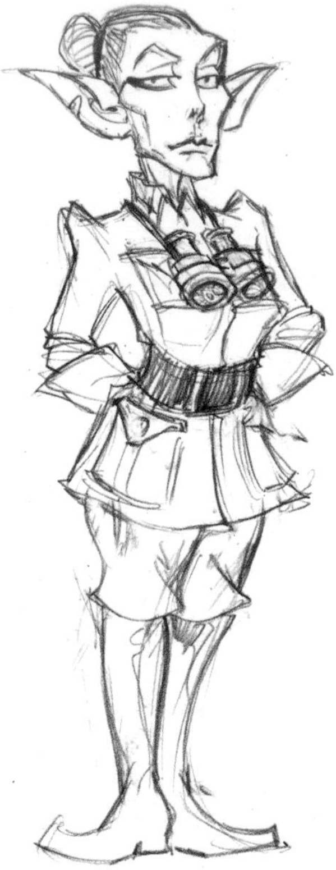

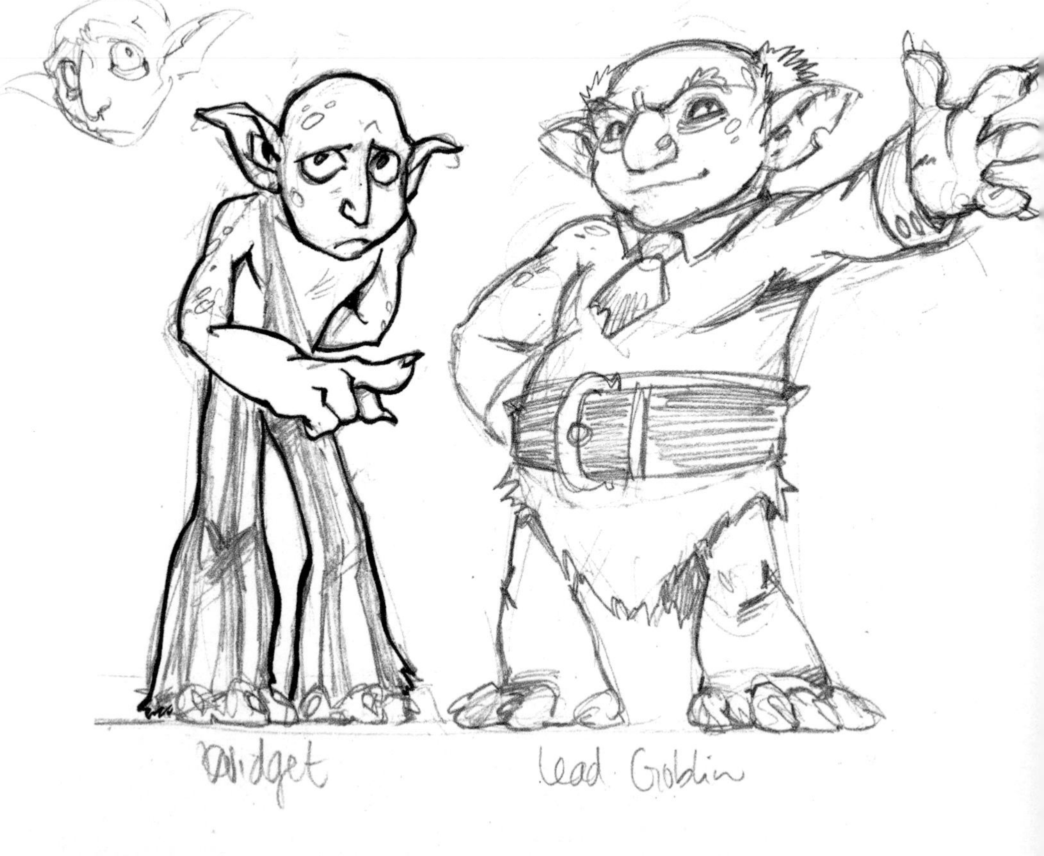
Widget
Lead Goblin

BEHOLD! THE EARLIEST OF GOBLINS. THE LEAD GOBLIN STARTED OUT PRETTY GROSS! WELL, HE WAS ALWAYS GROSS, BUT I WAS MUCH MORE SATISFIED WITH HIS FINAL DESIGN.

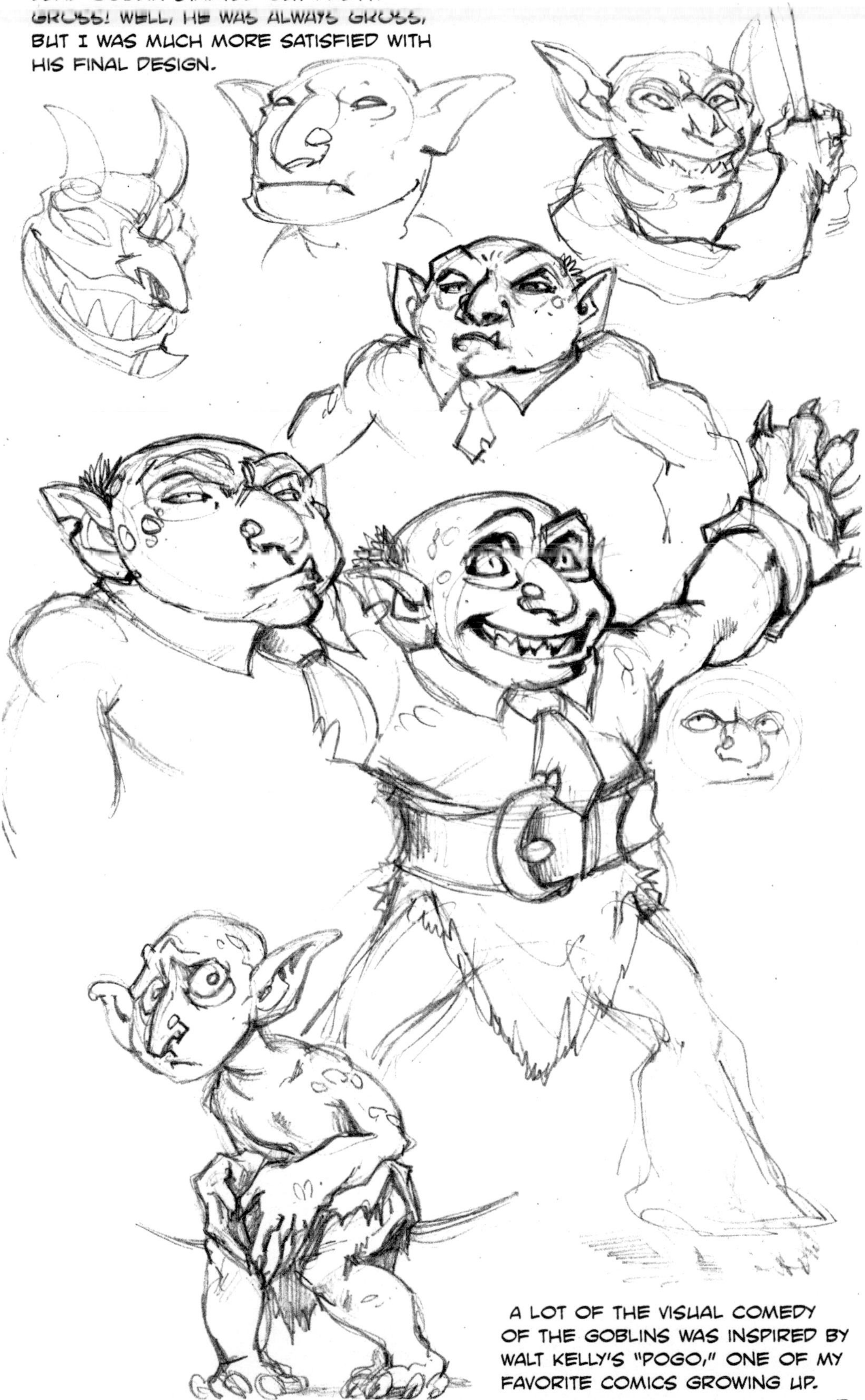

A LOT OF THE VISUAL COMEDY OF THE GOBLINS WAS INSPIRED BY WALT KELLY'S "POGO," ONE OF MY FAVORITE COMICS GROWING UP.

-E

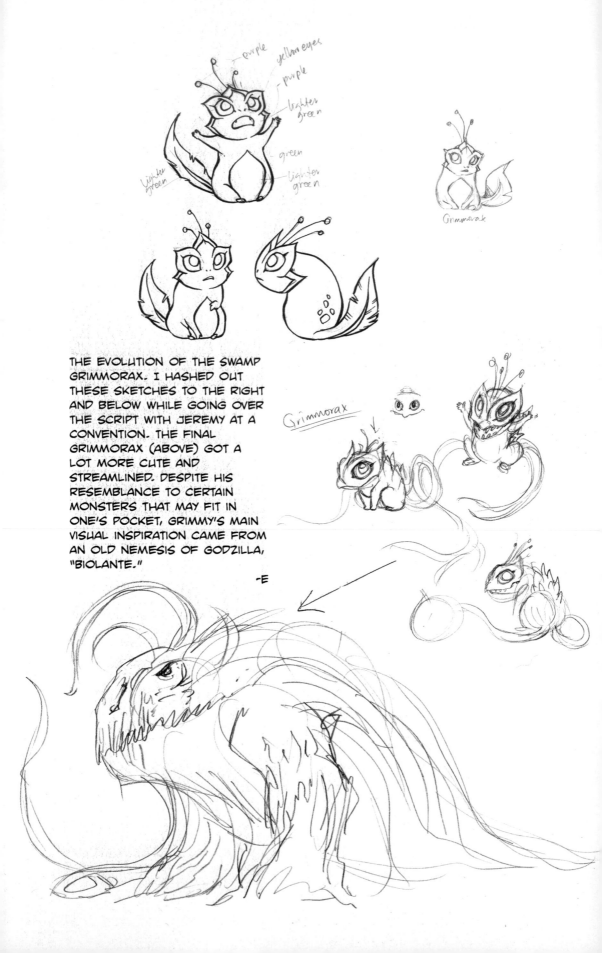

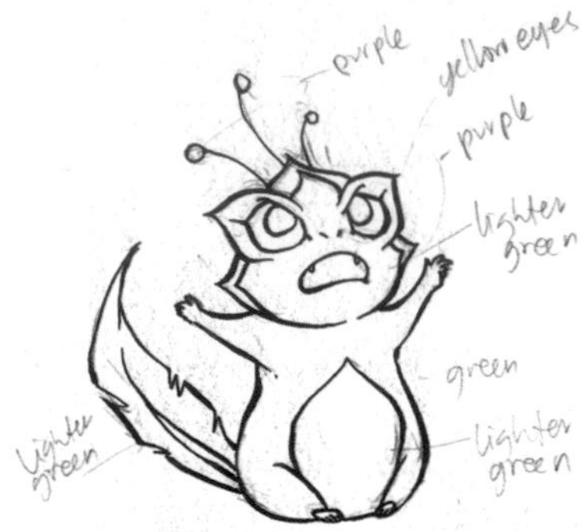
purple
yellow eyes
purple
lighter green
green
lighter green
lighter green

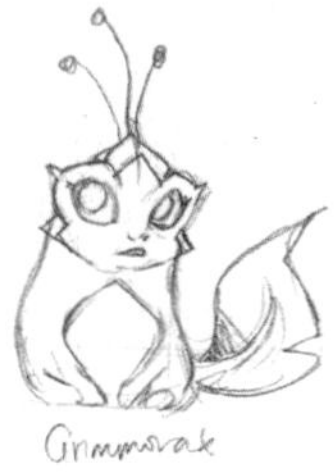
Grimmorax

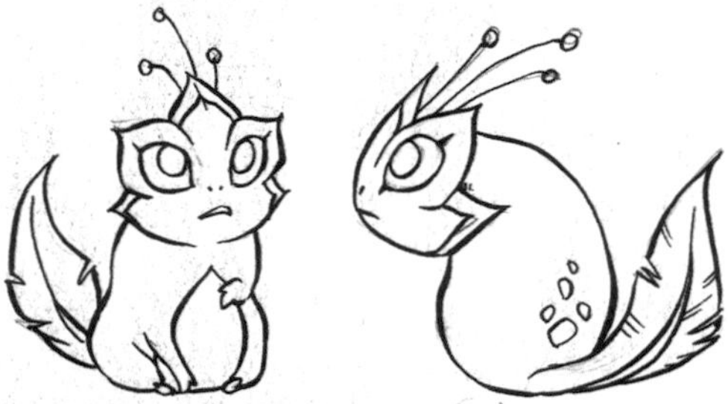

THE EVOLUTION OF THE SWAMP GRIMMORAX. I HASHED OUT THESE SKETCHES TO THE RIGHT AND BELOW WHILE GOING OVER THE SCRIPT WITH JEREMY AT A CONVENTION. THE FINAL GRIMMORAX (ABOVE) GOT A LOT MORE CUTE AND STREAMLINED. DESPITE HIS RESEMBLANCE TO CERTAIN MONSTERS THAT MAY FIT IN ONE'S POCKET, GRIMMY'S MAIN VISUAL INSPIRATION CAME FROM AN OLD NEMESIS OF GODZILLA, "BIOLANTE."

-E

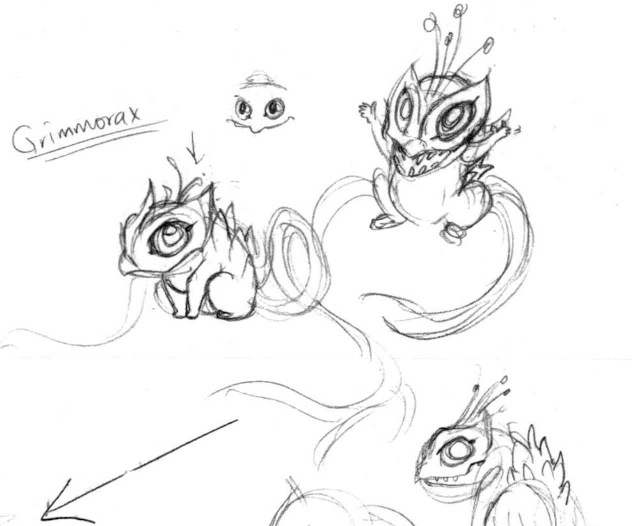
Grimmorax

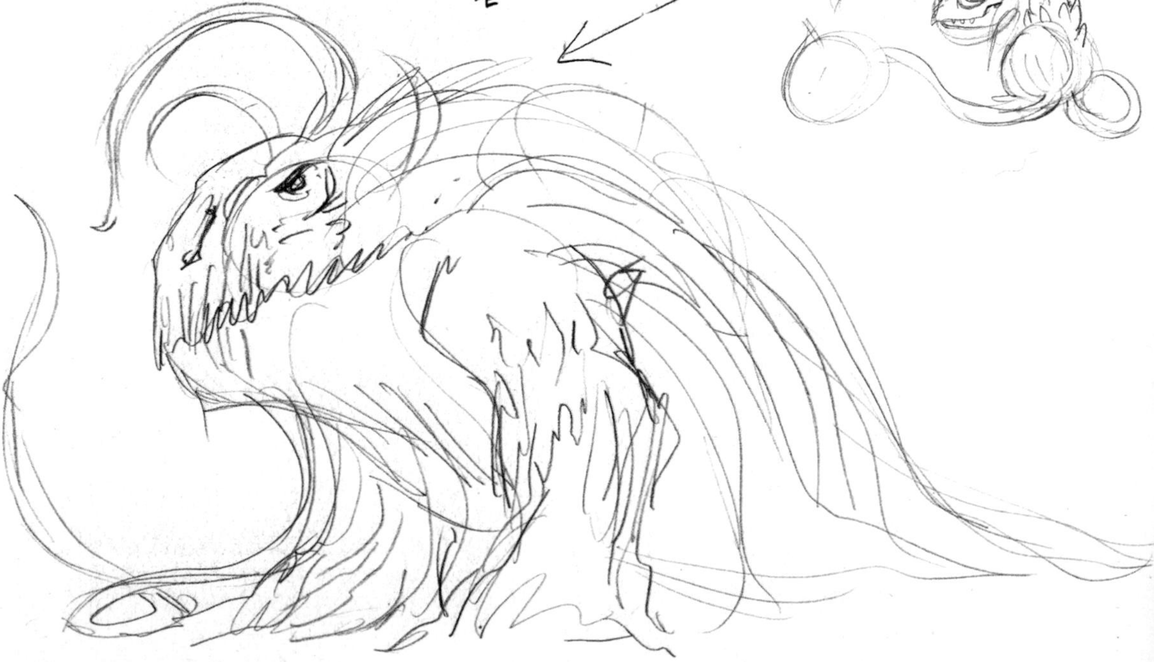

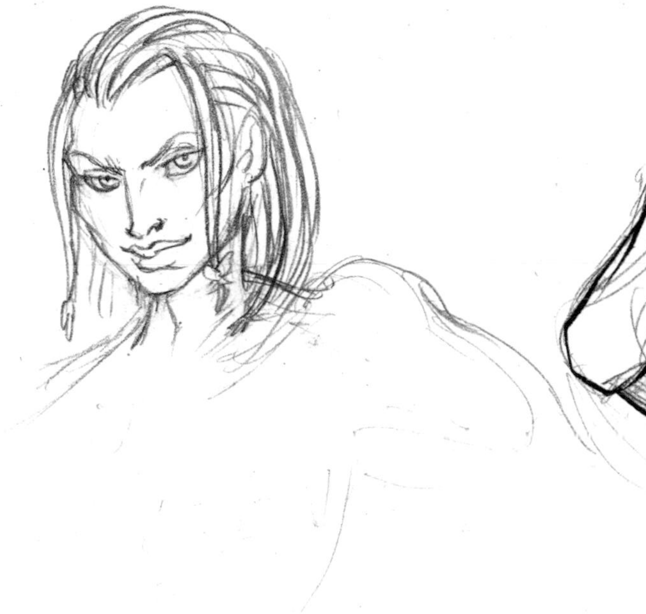

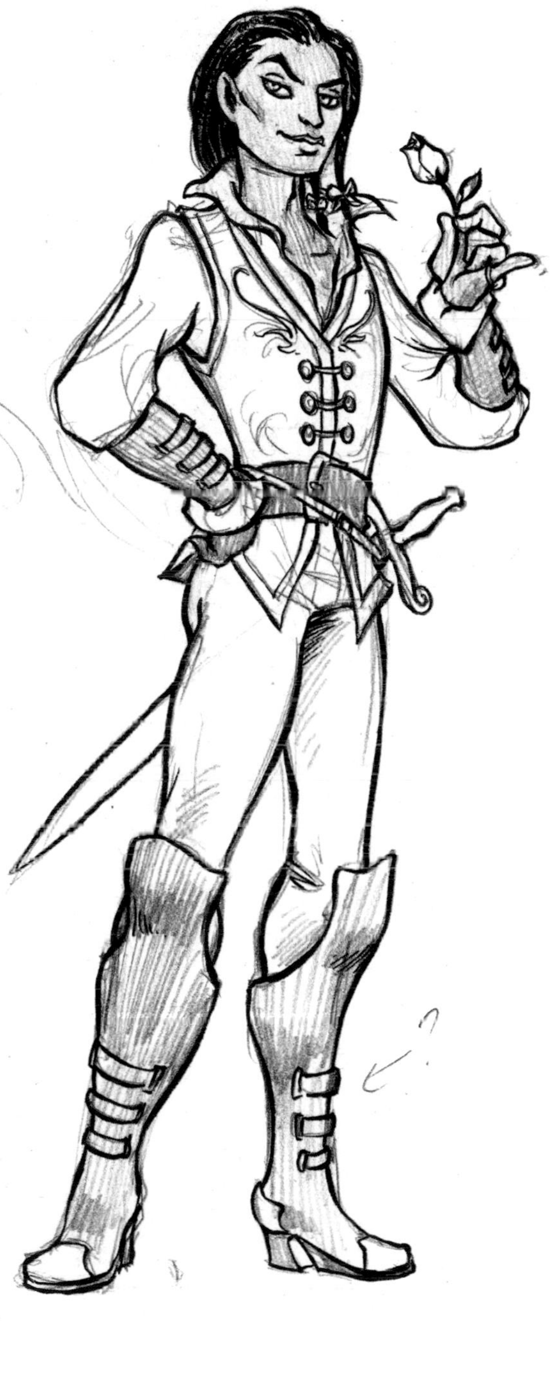

JEREMY HAD VERY SPECIFIC DETAILS FOR INTRODUCING RAPHAEL BACK IN VOLUME 2. IT WAS THEN THAT I WAS TOLD THAT HE WAS A VAMPIRE, AND HIS LOOK CAME TO ME PRETTY NATURALLY. I'VE ENCOUNTERED MORE THAN A FEW SELF-INVOLVED VAMPIRES IN MY TIME...

-E

Page 5: (4 panels)

Panel 1: Adrienne and Bedelia are wearing masquerade masks and reclining next to each other. Each one has a turkey drumstick. We can only see the top halves of their bodies.

ADRIENNE
Now, this is what being a hero should be like all the time.

BEDELIA
Mmmm-hmmm.

Panel 2: Goblins are rubbing their feet. Adrienne has one goblin per foot as. Bedelia has one working a sander and one directing him. They both wear safety goggles.

BEDELIA
You know, this is what I imagine being a Princess is like.

ADRIENNE
Maybe, if you're Angelica. Usually you're stuck in a tower or dinner or a boring party.

BEDELIA
Sounds AWFUL.

Panel 3: Adrienne and Bedelia are in a mud bath. Both of them have their hair up in a towel. Bedelia has mud on her face and Adrienne has cucumbers on her eyes.

ADRIENNE
I tried to learn how to swordfight when my brother Devin started learning. My dad kicked me out and made me take a class in handkerchief waving.

BEDELIA
You're awfully good at sword fighting anyway.

ADRIENNE
Devin made an extra practice sword so I could help him train. I'm better than he is.

Panel 4: Adrienne and Bedelia are dancing with the goblins in a makeshift swamp club.

ADRIENNE
I'm glad we got to take this break from all this fighting. It's going to make dealing with Angoisse so much easier.

BEDELIA
You two don't get along?

Panel 5: Adrienne and Bedelia are held aloft by goblins. Bedelia has another turkey leg. Adrienne is trying to drink something from a cup.

ADRIENNE
She's always moping about something. Usually some boy. I just don't get how girls can spend their whole lives thinking about nothing but boys.

BEDELIA
I always wished I had a sister. Hey, why do you think they're doing all of this for us?

PROCESS! WHEN JEREMY FINISHES A SCRIPT, I GENERALLY PRINT IT OUT AND SKETCH IDEAS FOR PANEL LAYOUTS DIRECTLY ON THE PAGES. THESE ARE PRETTY SIMPLE—JUST ENOUGH DETAIL TO GET CHARACTER PLACEMENT, WORD BUBBLE PLACEMENT AND EXPRESSIONS FOR THE NEXT DRAFT.

-E

Page 6: (4 panels)

Panel 1: Adrienne and Bedelia stand at the head of a group of kneeling goblins. The goblins are all bowing to them.

ALL HAIL
RARG

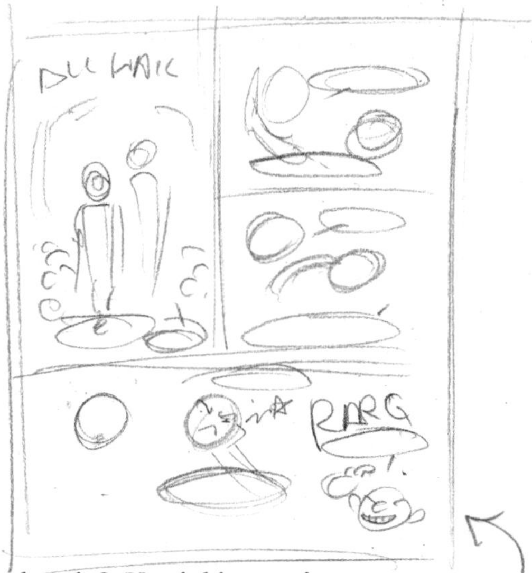

GOBLINS
All hail the goblin champions!

ADRIENNE
Champions? I like the sound of that.

BEDELIA
I don't.

Panel 2: Bedelia talks to the lead goblin.

BEDELIA
So, what is it champions are supposed to do?

LEAD GOBLIN
Oh, fire head so funny. What champions supposed to do? You joking again.

ALL HAIL
ALL HAIL

BEDELIA
No, I'm not…

Panel 3: The goblin slaps her again.

LEAD GOBLIN
So funny, fire head. Champions save goblins from Grimmorax.

Panel 4: Bedelia is rubbing her cheek.

BEDELIA
What's a Grimmorax?

OFF PANEL
Raaargh!

LEAD GOBLIN → smiling?
That him now!

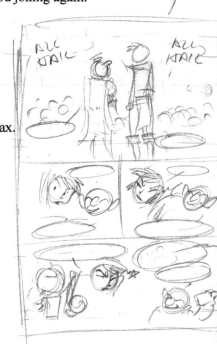

Page 7: (4 panel)

Panel 1: The Grimmorax, a large swamp creature with sweeping tentacles comes bursting forth into the camp. Goblins scatter. Near the bottom of the panel we see the heads of screaming goblins running off panel in the manner of a horror movie poster. The other panels are inset and smaller.

GOBLIN 1
Run for your life! It's the Grimmorax!

GOBLIN 2
It's boundless anger is matched only by its hunger for goblins!

Panel 2: Adrienne and Bedelia watch the carnage. Vines wrap around their food.

BEDELIA
This thing isn't guarding your sister, right? We should run.

ADRIENNE
And leave the goblins?

Panel 3: The drink and turkey leg are ripped away by the Grimmorax's tentacles.

ADRIENNE and BEDELIA
Hey!

Panel 4: Anime action background as the two draw their weapons and prepare for battle.

ADRIENNE
That's it, you messed with the wrong champions!

BEDELIA
No one steals a dwarf's turkey leg!

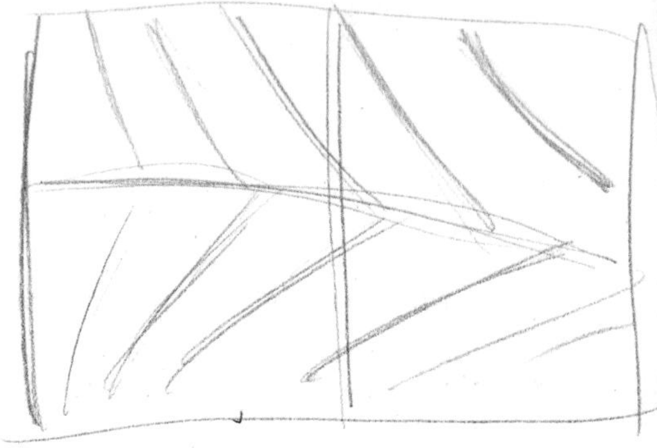

Page 14 & 15: (10 panels)

Panel 1: Adrienne and Raphael fall out the window.

ADRIENNE
Ahhhhh!

Panel 2: Adrienne grabs Raphael by the collar with one arm, pulling the other arm back.

ADRIENNE
I don't like falling off towers.

Panel 3: Adrienne hits Raphael across the face. The momentum starts them changing places.

Panel 4: Adrienne is now on top of Raphael. Above them, Angoisse is diving out of the window.

Panel 5: Angoisse grabs Adrienne under the arms. It begins to level them off.

ADRIENNE
Angoisse? What?

RAPHAEL
She's mine now, Angoisse. You can't hurt me!

Panel 6: Angoisse, up close.

ANGOISSE
Oh yeah? How's this for not hurting?

Panel 7: Angoisse head butts Raphael in the nose, breaking his nose.

ANGOISSE
Hi-ya!

RAPHAEL
Gah!

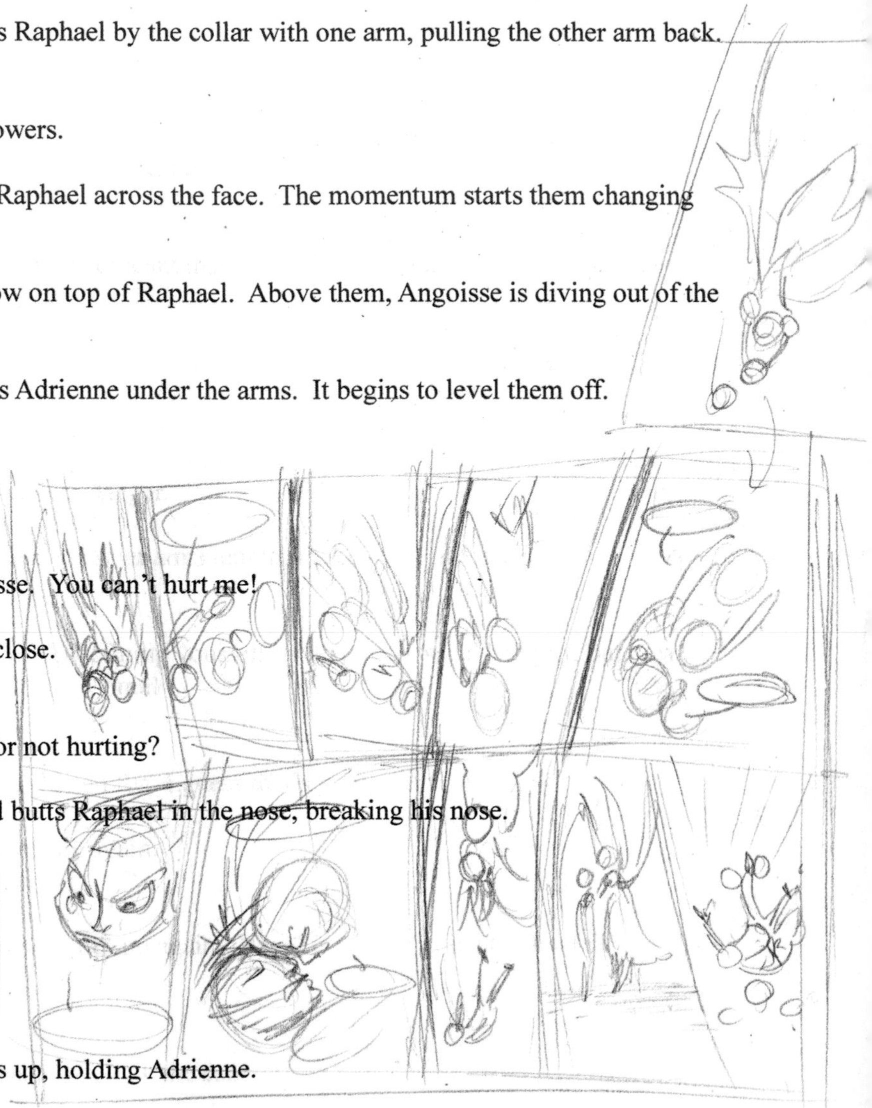

Panel 8: Angoisse pulls up, holding Adrienne.

Panel 9: Angoisse lands gracefully with Adrienne.

Panel 10: Raphael goes crashing through a crowd of zombies

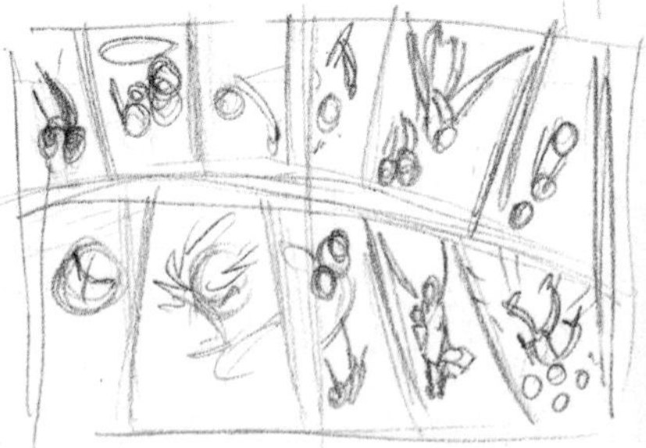

TWO-PAGE SPREADS ARE ALWAYS TRICKY. THIS ONE HAD A LOT OF ACTION, AND FLYING, AND ZOMBIES, SO IT WAS ACTUALLY PRETTY FUN. I LIKE TO USE A LOT OF ANGLED PANELS FOR ACTION SCENES, SO I WENT WITH THIS "HERRING-BONE" TYPE PATTERN FOR PANEL BORDERS.

-E

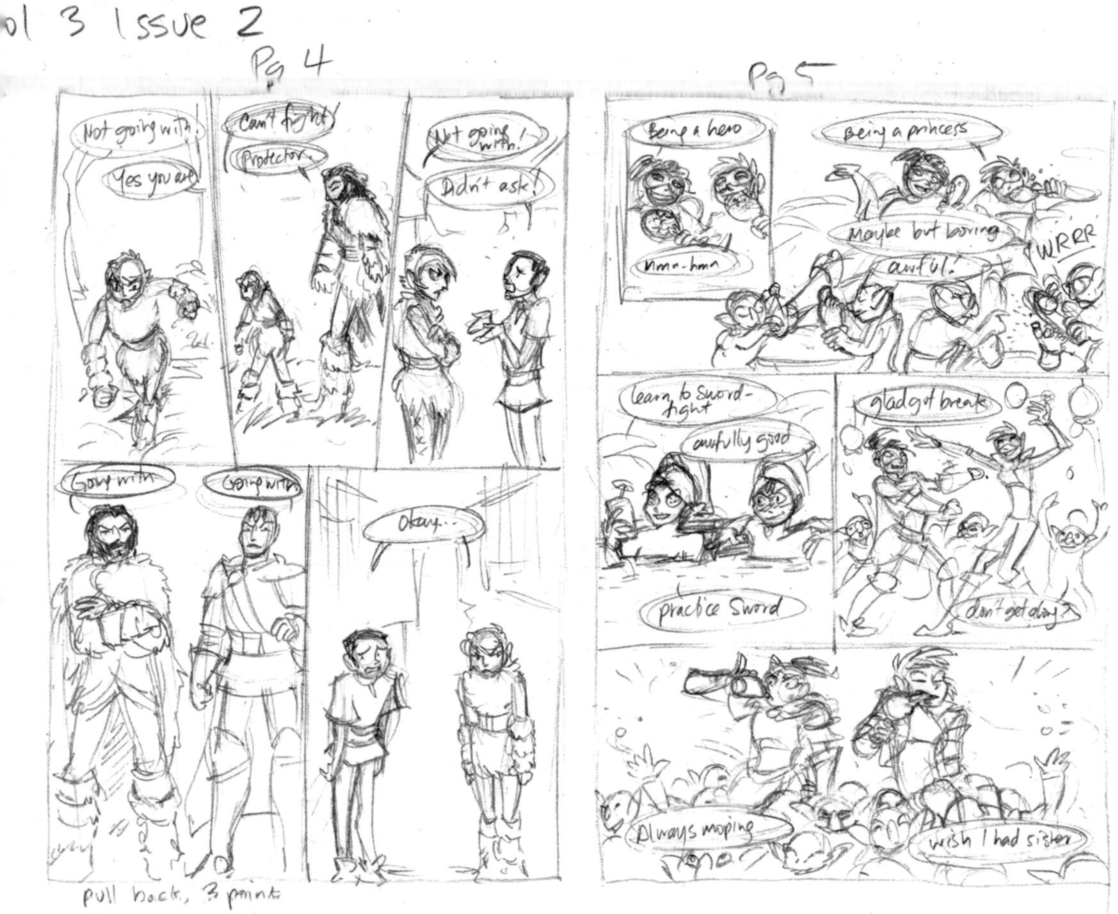
ol 3 Issue 2
Pg 4
Pg 5
Not going with!
Yes you are!
Can't fight!
Protector.
Not going with!
Didn't ask!
Going with
Going with
Okay...
pull back, 3 point
Being a hero
Mm-hmm
Being a princess
Maybe but boring
awful!
WRRR
learn to sword-fight
awfully good
practice Sword
glad got break
don't get along
Always moping
wish I had sister

AFTER I DECIDE ON A FINAL LOOK FOR MY FIRST, SUPER-MESSY THUMBNAILS ON THE SCRIPT, I MAKE A SECOND SET WHICH IS MUCH CLEANER. THIS IS TO SHOW TO JEREMY SO HE HAS AN IDEA OF HOW THE PAGES WILL LOOK BEFORE I START ON THE FINAL DRAFT. IT ALSO HELPS ME MAKE THE FINAL DRAFT MORE QUICKLY, SINCE IT IS A BETTER REFERENCE.

-E

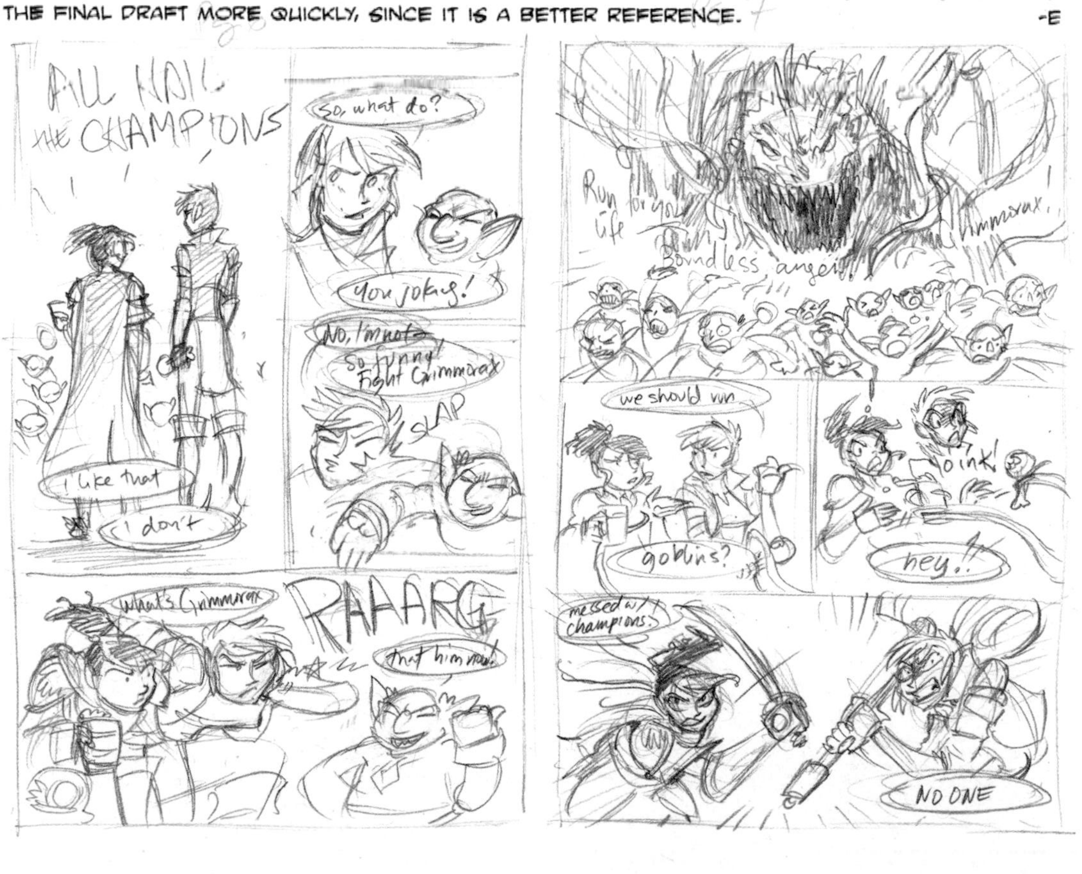
ALL HAIL THE CHAMPIONS
I like that
I don't
So, what do?
You joking!
No, I'm not so funny! Fight Grimmorax
SLAP
What's Grimmorax
RAAARG
That him roar
Run for your life
Boundless anger
Grimmorax!
we should run
goblins?
oink!
hey!!
messed w/ champions?
NO ONE

FINAL DRAFT PAGES IN THE FLESH. MY DUTIFUL ASSISTANT, COLORIST, AND HUSBAND, BRETT GRUNIG, HELPS ME PRINT OUT MARGINS IN BLUE ON THE FINAL DRAFT PAGES, WHICH IN THIS CASE ARE 11X14" BRISTOL PAPER.

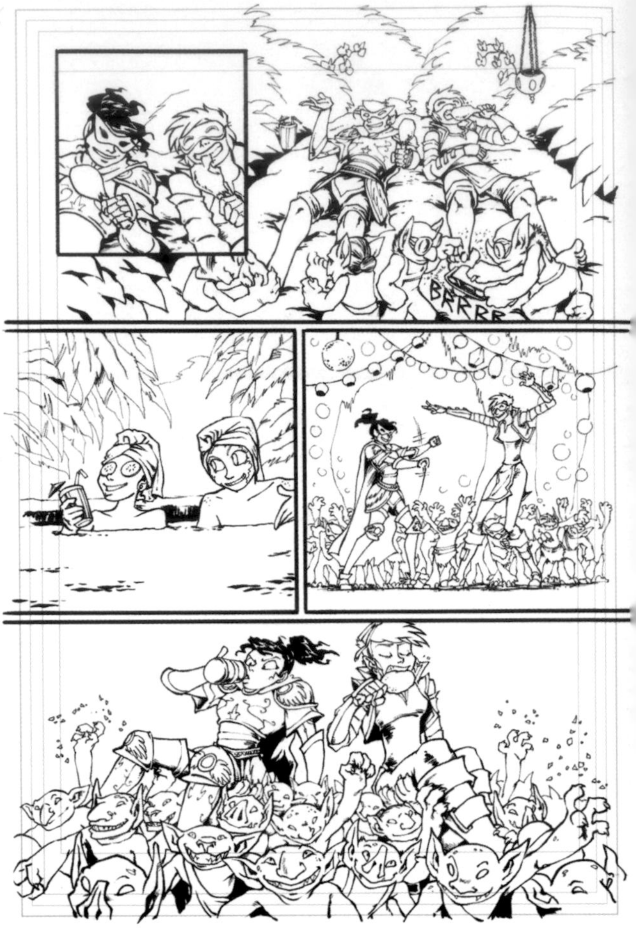
BRRRR

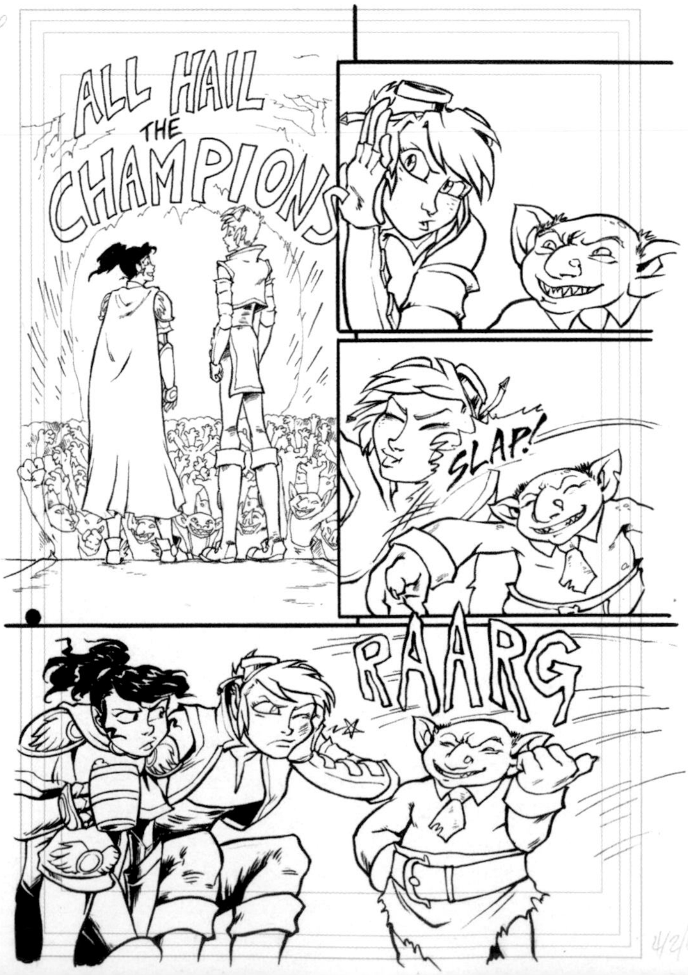
ALL HAIL THE CHAMPIONS
SLAP!
RAARG

WHY MARGINS? TO REPRESENT A "MARGIN OF ERROR" FOR ARTISTS TO KNOW WHERE THE EDGE OF THE FINAL PRINTED PAGE IS, SO THEY MAKE SURE NOT TO CUT OFF ANY IMPORTANT PART OF THE IMAGE. WHY BLUE? IT'S REALLY EASY TO REMOVE ON THE COMPUTER.

-E

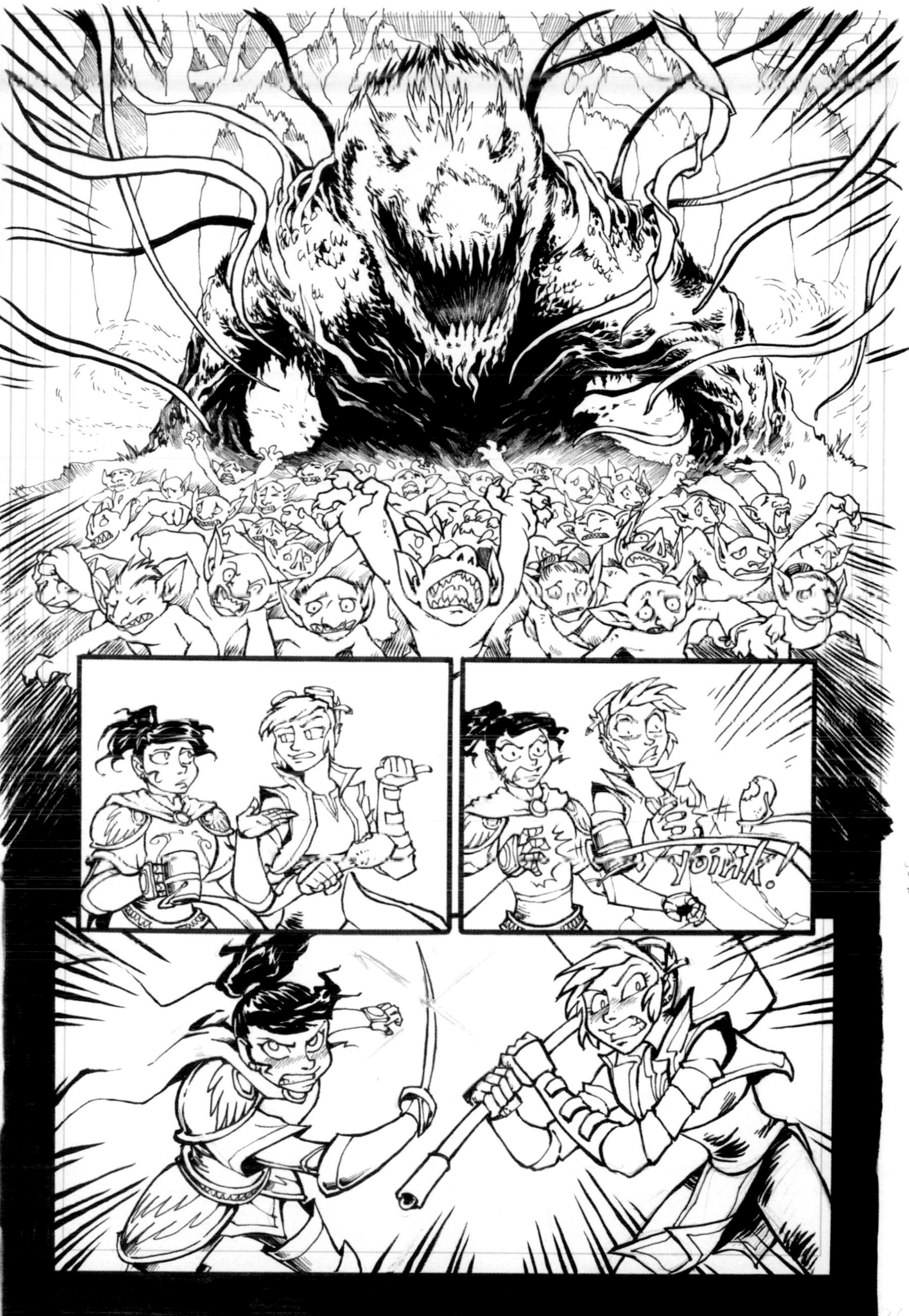
yoink!

ONCE THE MARGINS ARE PRINTED OUT, I SKETCH OUT A ROUGH DRAFT TO BE INKED. THESE DAYS, I HAVE A ROUGH DRAFT STAGE IN BLUE PENCIL (SAME EASY-TO-REMOVE BLUE), THEN I DRAW IN REGULAR PENCIL ON TOP, TO MAKE THINGS CLEAR. THEN I INK WITH GOOD-OLD-FASHIONED PENS.

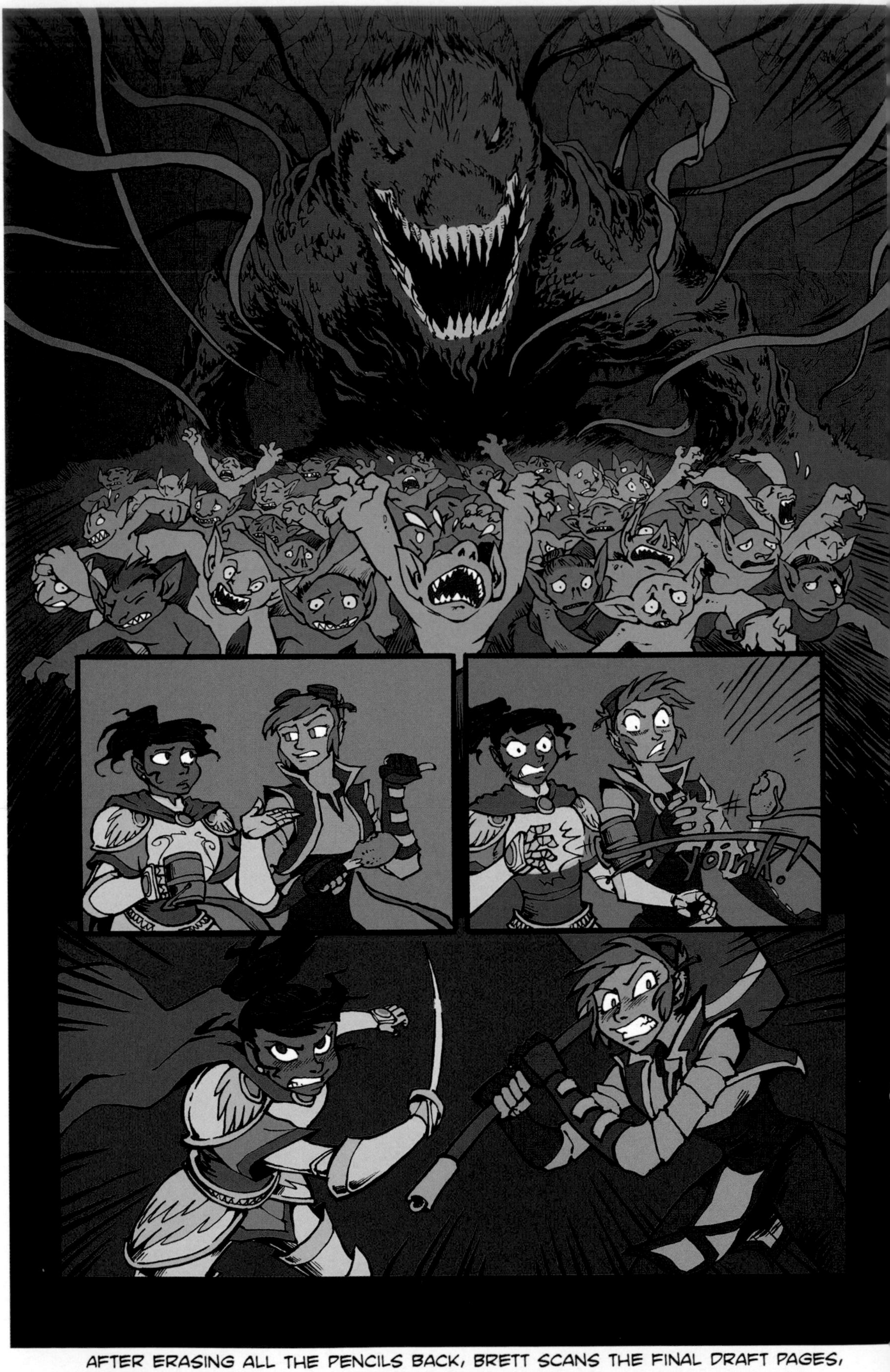
yoink!

AFTER ERASING ALL THE PENCILS BACK, BRETT SCANS THE FINAL DRAFT PAGES, EDITS THE IMAGE TO MAKE THINGS CLEAR, AND STARTS COLORING WITH THE COMPUTER. THIS HAPPENS IN STAGES- FIRST THE FLATS...

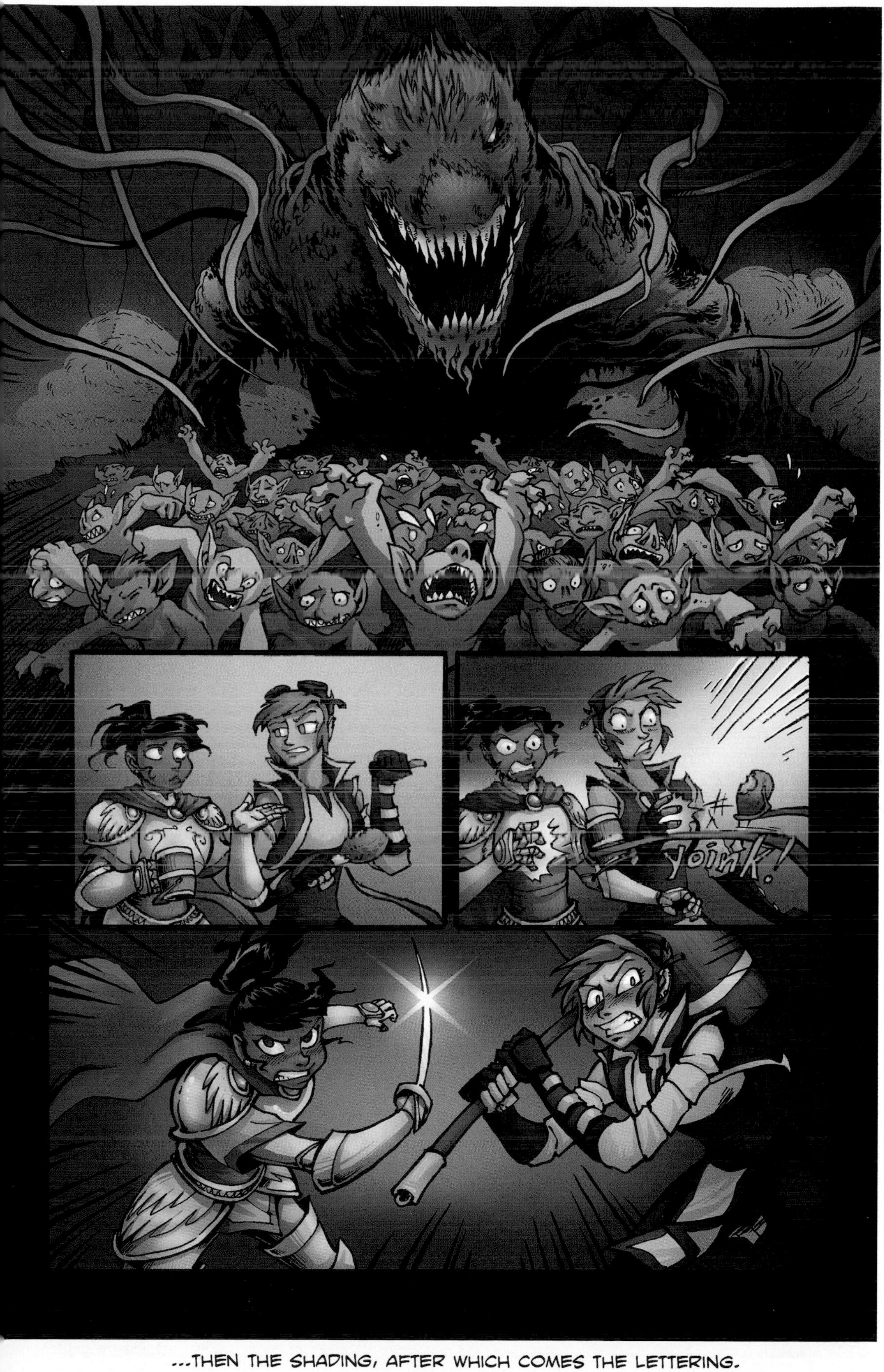
#
yoink!

...THEN THE SHADING, AFTER WHICH COMES THE LETTERING.
-E

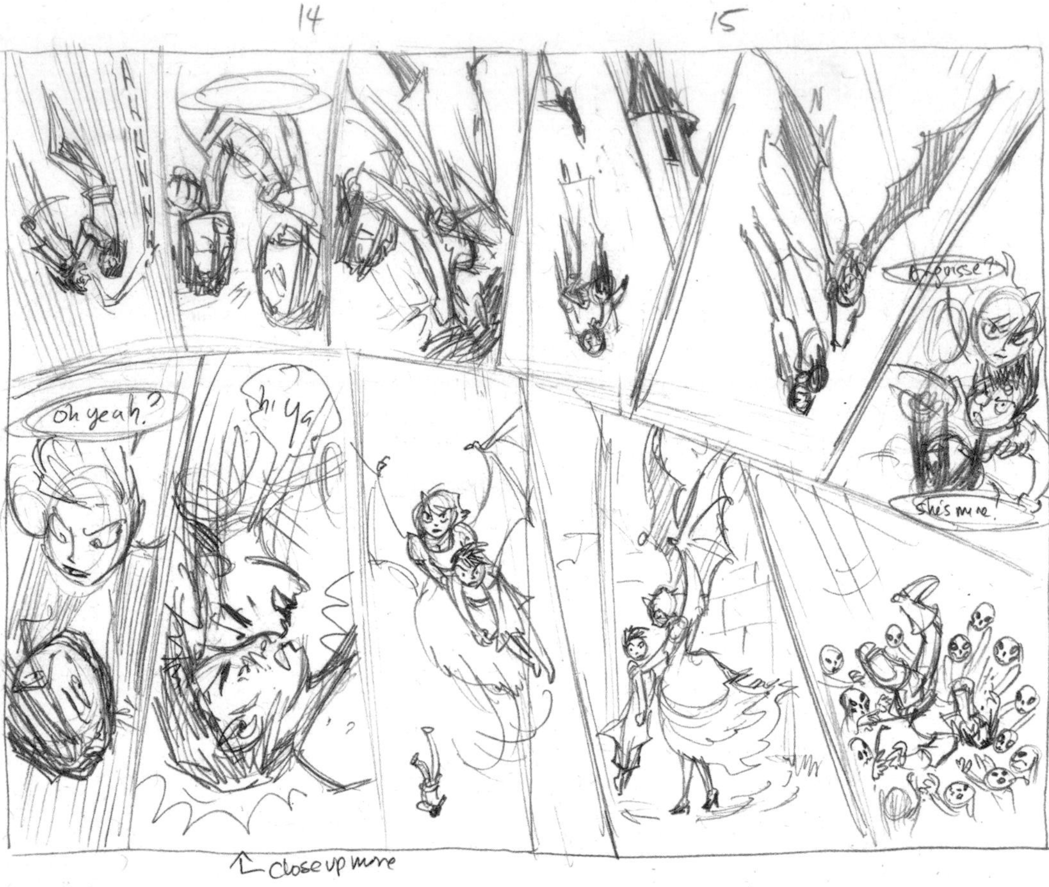
14
15
oh yeah?
hi ya
she's mine!
close up more

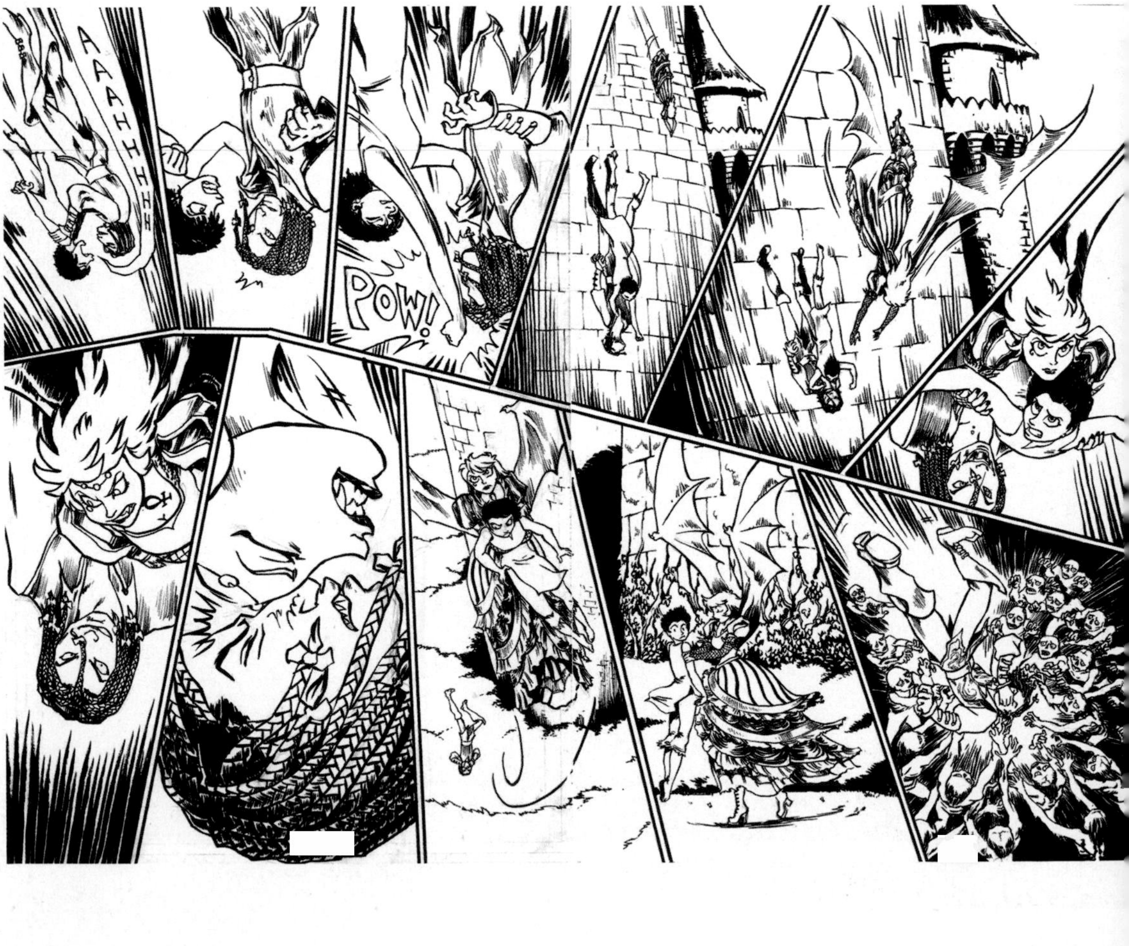
AAAHHHHH
POW!

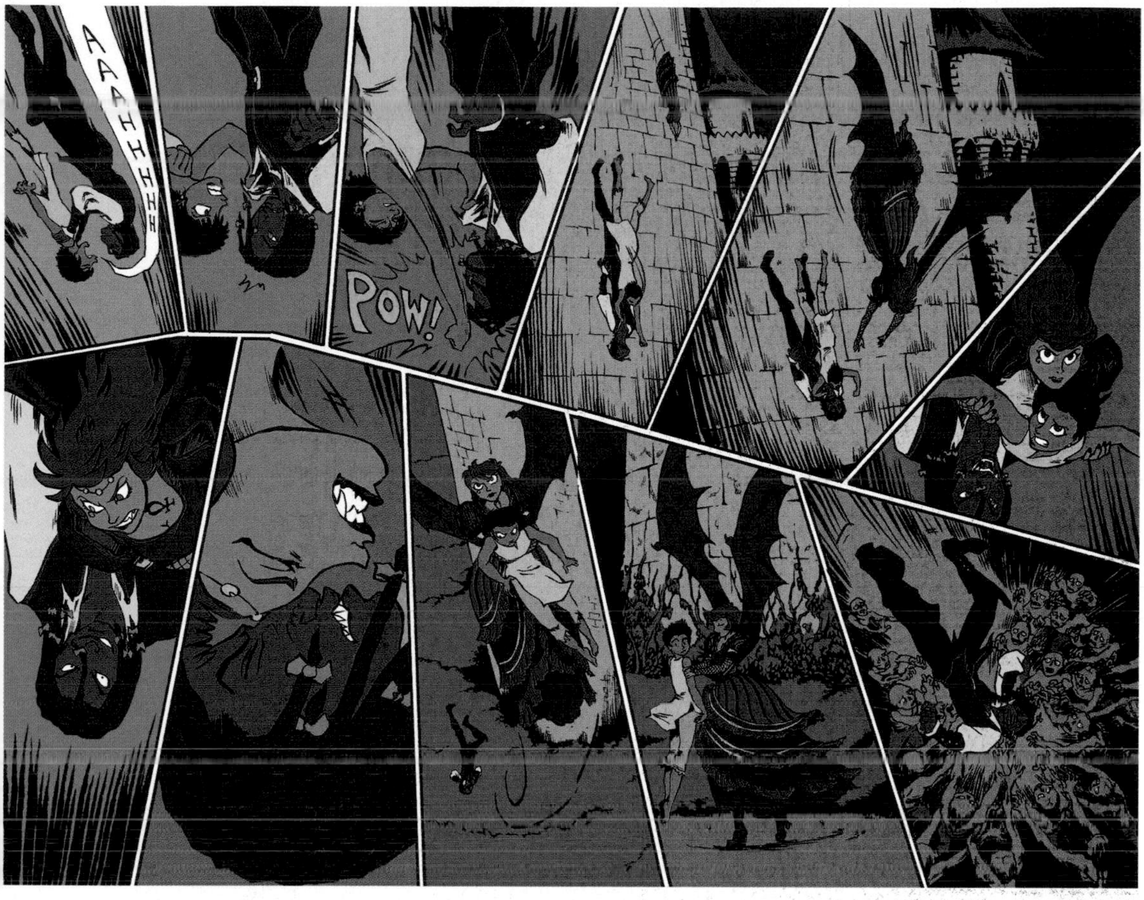
AAAHHHHHH
POW!

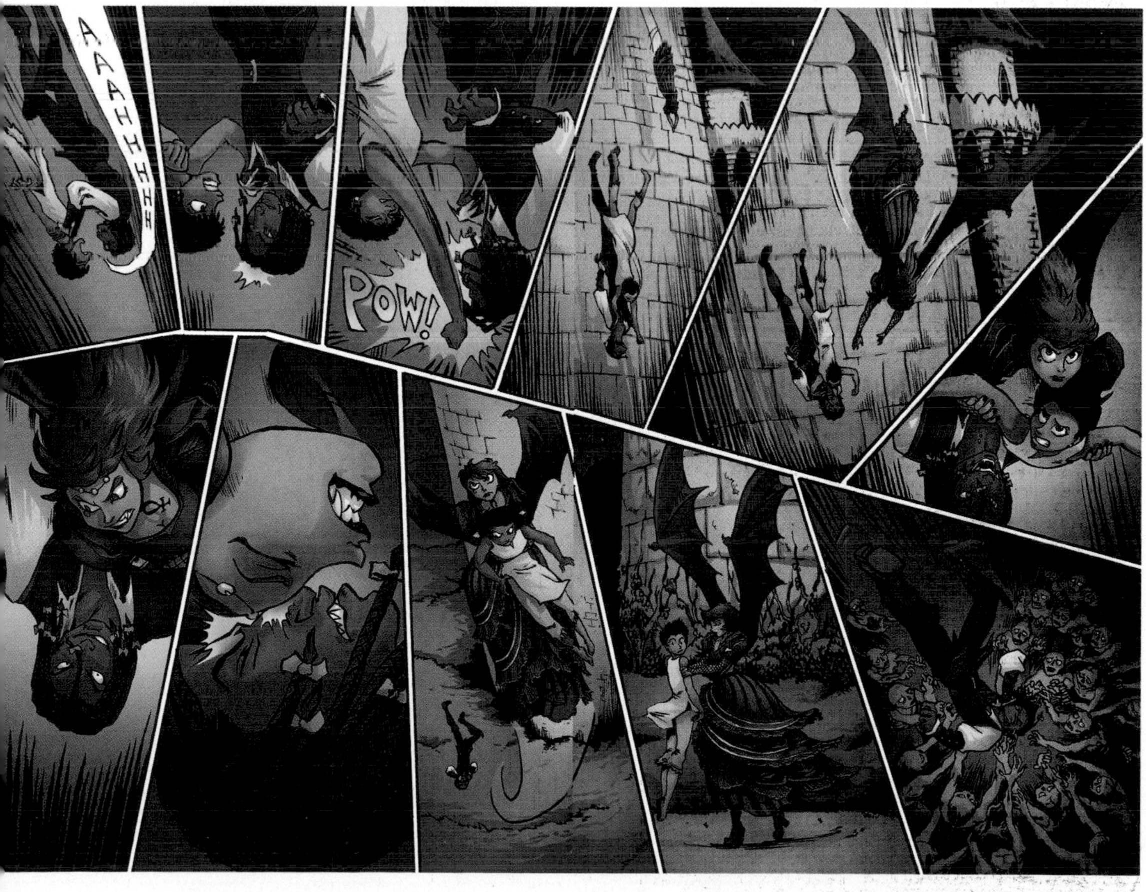
AAAHHHHHH
POW!

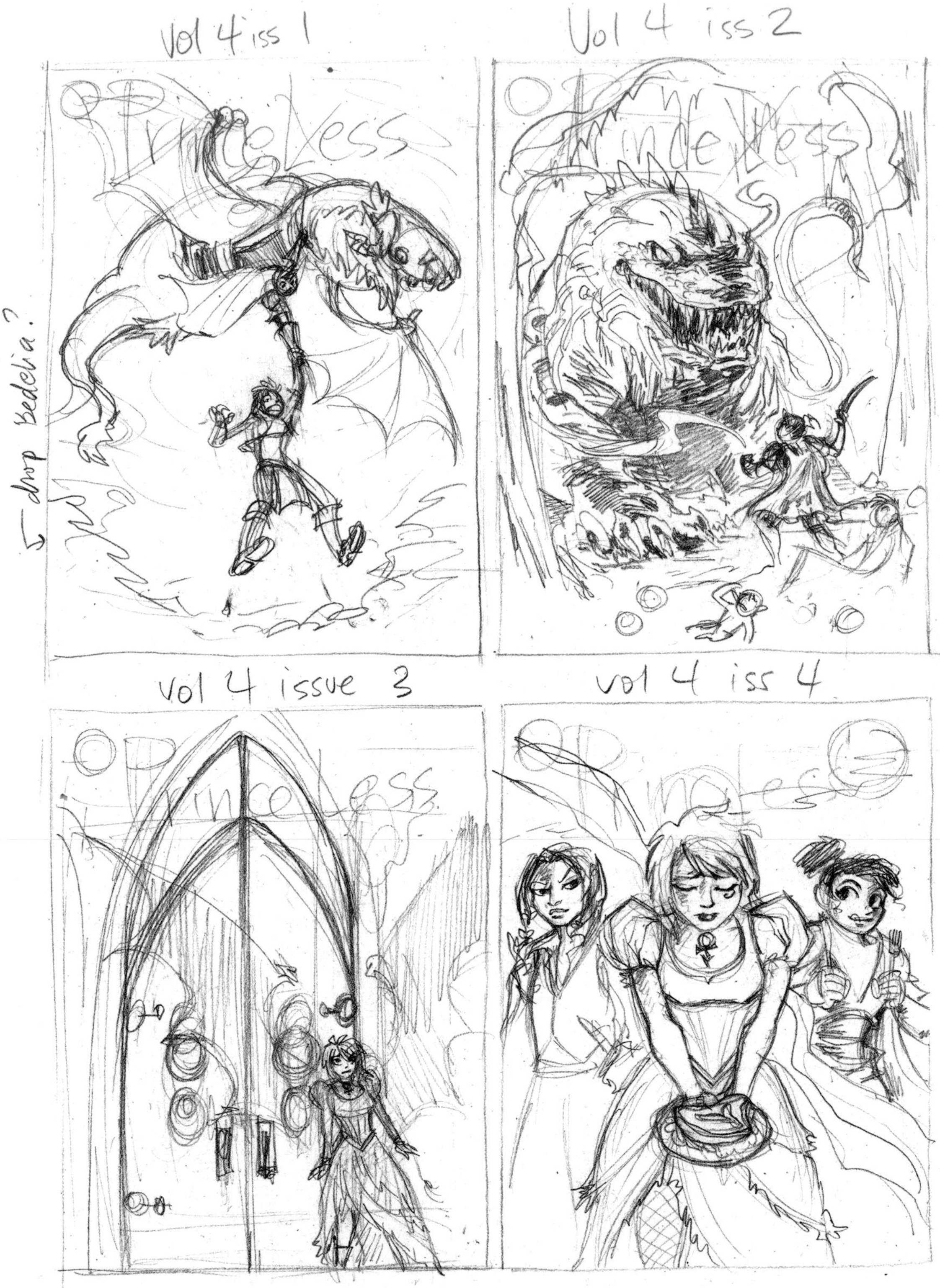
Vol 4 iss 1
Vol 4 iss 2
vol 4 issue 3
vol 4 iss 4
I drop Bedelia?

ROUGH DRAFTS OF COVERS! JEREMY PROVIDED MOST OF THE IDEAS FOR THESE, BUT ISSUE 3 WAS MY HOMMAGE TO THE MOST "GOTH" THING I COULD THINK OF–A STILL FROM AN OLD SILENT FILM WHICH FEATURES ON THE COVER OF BAUHAUS' SINGLE, "BELA LUGOSI'S DEAD."

-E